W9-AYR-355

WEYCOMBE

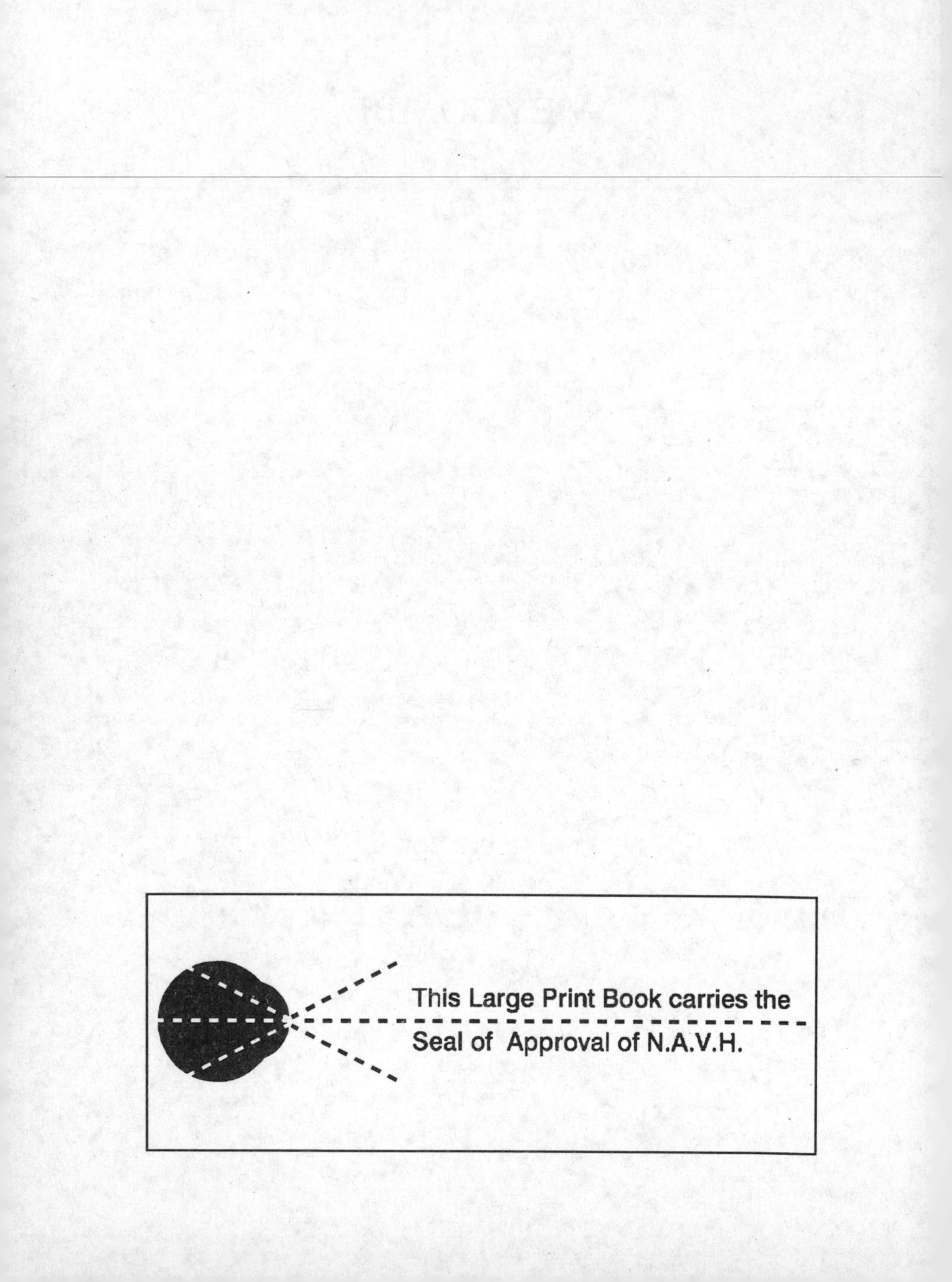
This Large Print Book carries the
Seal of Approval of N.A.V.H.

Weycombe

A Novel of Suspense

G. M. Malliet

THORNDIKE PRESS
A part of Gale, a Cengage Company

Farmington Hills, Mich • San Francisco • New York • Waterville, Maine
Meriden, Conn • Mason, Ohio • Chicago

Thorndike Press, a part of Gale, a Cengage Company.

Thorndike Press® Large Print Mystery.
The text of this Large Print edition is unabridged.
Other aspects of the book may vary from the original edition.
Set in 16 pt. Plantin.

**LIBRARY OF CONGRESS CIP DATA ON FILE.
CATALOGUING IN PUBLICATION FOR THIS BOOK
IS AVAILABLE FROM THE LIBRARY OF CONGRESS**

ISBN-13: 978-1-4328-4560-5 (hardcover)
ISBN-10: 1-4328-4560-8 (hardcover)

Published in 2018 by arrangement with Midnight Ink, an imprint of Llewellyn Publications, Woodbury, MN 55125-2989 USA

Printed in the United States of America
1 2 3 4 5 6 7 22 21 20 19 18

For my dear and greatly missed friend
Rebecca.
And as always, for Bob.

ACKNOWLEDGMENTS

My thanks to Bill Krause, Terri Bischoff, Katie Mickschl, and Sandy Sullivan for the warm welcome. Apparently, you *can* go home again. And special thanks to Lisa Black and Dale Steventon for their guidance on forensics. All mistakes are my own.

Prologue

I remember Anna clearly. Not Anna as I wish she had been. Anna as she really was.

We tend to deify the dead. It's simpler to build a temple to them and seal them inside than to keep tearing open the old wounds, replaying their transgressions until our blood is stirred by a familiar anger. And so we resist the memories of bad times. We forget the many failings, although if we're smart and we've learned our lesson, we do not forgive.

I won't paper over Anna's defects as I write the story of her fall: her selfishness, her indifference to anyone's suffering but her own, her off handed willingness to betray, her lies — most of all, the glibness of her lies. Who could forgive? Well, perhaps her husband, a man who excused her deceits as the lapses of a woman so special she could be allowed to bend every rule. I guess you could say gentle Alfie made Anna what she was.

I can call to mind every detail of her appearance, too. I made a video of her, to promote her business, but I don't need it to remember her by. She made a token offer to pay me for my trouble, but I didn't really mind. The equipment mostly sat unused in my closet otherwise.

So I spent the better part of a day trailing Anna, getting her to talk naturally, making a study of the few physical flaws she possessed. She was Rubenesque, with a lush build and that lit-from-within coloring, if thirty pounds lighter than Ruben's women, those women who always seemed to be dancing naked or having someone beheaded.

When you look at a person through a lens, it is the one time you are allowed to stare, when politeness does not dictate that you avert your eyes. Anna, looking the way she did, must have been used to stares. That white complexion — not just pale or ivory, but a pure and pore-less alabaster white. The perfect canvas for the black hair, the green eyes, the red lips. The camera loved her, obediently creating shadows and clefts that molded her face and drew attention to those shining emerald eyes, and I barely had to adjust for shadow and contrast. She sat preening and smiling, her teeth small and white against the fullness of her red lips, and almost in spite of myself, I could not get a bad image of her. It was on this occasion she talked to me about her background, and her worries about her stepson, in that plummy-posh voice she sometimes used to disguise her origins. To my American ear it sounded like music. I liked her then. She seemed so human.

When she died the village spiraled into deep mourning, not because of her big heart or her record of good deeds, but because someone so fair and so (relatively) young had been murdered. They could not get their heads around the fact that gorgeous Anna had been killed, had been done to death, and if someone like that could die in such a seemingly random fashion, so could they.

Of course, they didn't know Anna as well as I did.

Part 1

1

Weycombe: 2017

The reflectors on Anna's runners caught the eye, mirroring the sunlight, twinkling silver among sodden, fallen leaves. But the shoes were tied to feet that were motionless and oddly splayed, as if they'd snapped from the ankles. No one could not notice something was wrong. She looked posed, like a woman in a snuff film. Not that I would know what that looks like.

I rang 999 from my mobile, looking round and up and behind me before I punched in the numbers. You never knew who might be watching, and I felt exposed standing there on the river path. I resisted the ridiculous urge to clamber down the bank and tug at the legs of Anna's shorts where they ruched up around her hips, revealing the lace of her Fleur of England knickers. Her little wallet that presumably held her house key and some form of legal tender was still attached to her wrist, a wallet not large enough to hold a mobile or any form of self-defense, like pepper spray. The need for mace in broad daylight in the bubble-wrapped perfection of Weycombe was hard to fathom, anyway.

I stood in the path to block the view of anyone passing by, but there was only one helmeted cyclist going very fast and one woman who, with the sun in her eyes and a phone to her ear, didn't notice she was walking past a corpse. On a distant hill, a woman I thought I recognized walked two arthritic golden retrievers.

The first responder was a uniformed policeman. He strolled over from his small blue-and-yellow patrol car, taking his time and hitching up his trousers, looking for all the world like he was about to nail me for speeding. He told me he was Sergeant Milo and flashed his card. I told him I was Jillian White and pointed to the riverbed where Anna's body lay.

As if to humor me, he walked over for a look-see, peering down the steep bankside. He did a double take and stepped back quickly. Visibly shaken, he began barking into the mic on his shoulder. A woman's voice squawked back. I've never understood why they didn't just use mobile phones already but I suppose radios were more secure or something.

Keeping me in view, he began walking up the path and back, doing a visual search of the area. Soon we were swarmed by officialdom, all ranks and sizes and sexes in a group that grew large and loud as it became apparent what they were dealing with. This sort of thing does not happen in Weycombe, where the worst scofflaws go in more for antisocial behavior (a cozy British term covering a raft of sins from littering to vandalism) or the occasional shoplifting spree at Boots or Waitrose. Some of the guys in uniform were looking positively elated but trying to hide it.

Not Sergeant Milo. Solemnly, he indicated I should step aside and wait. He didn't seem to consider that I might just run away, although I did consider it. The assorted officials stood about arguing, pointing down the bank and gesturing downriver until finally it was decided the best way to reach the body — those eyes; no question it was a body — without destroying evidence was to get a skiff or two in the water; that way they could bring the examiners in as close as possible. It was probably going to be the only way to retrieve the body, too; it had landed at what was in effect the foot of a small cliff.

Where they got the skiffs from I don't know, as there were no official markings on them, but soon we were treated to the arrival of a forensics unit trying to look as dignified as Cleopatra being paddled upriver in her barge.

Some guy I took to be a police surgeon got out first, wading over to feel for a pulse and make sure she was dead. But anyone could see from the look of her there was no chance of revival and no call for heroics. Finally I looked away; that image of bulging eyes was too much. The surgeon studied his watch and although I couldn't hear what he said, it was clear he was making some official pronouncement to his colleagues; one of them checked his own watch and made a note. The surgeon was followed by two men in another boat, one of them wearing light blue disposable coveralls and something like a shower cap. He looked like a hazmat plague doctor. What I know of crime scene procedure I got from my former job and from watching *CSI* but that had to be a forensic pathologist or coroner. He carried with him a worn black leather bag, its edges scuffed gray. As he crawled out of the boat, wellies squelching in the shallow water, I was taken aback to realize he was someone I recognized. I guess it's true you get to know everyone in a village, but I had not known his profession when I'd seen him in the Bull the year before on the odd evening out with Will. Probably a good thing, since there is a huge *ick* factor attached to that job that doesn't allow for small talk. You can't ask them how their day was because you don't want to know.

He began murmuring into a small recorder and a few phrases drifted toward me on the breeze. Milo, engaged now with writing in his notebook, showed no sign of wanting me to leave or even of remembering my existence, so I openly eavesdropped. By now they'd begun putting up a cordon of sorts — they had to improvise with a tarp draped over the tree branches as the tent-like structure the occasion called for wouldn't hold on a riverbank. Words like "rigor" and "hemorrhages" floated back to me over the top of the screen, and finally "bring her in for an autopsy." That last word totally creeped me out. Dead was one thing, cut open like a tiger shark was another. Couldn't they just let it be?

Now a woman in an ill-fitting gray suit arrived; I guessed she was a plain-clothes detective from her gruff, knuckle-rubbing manner. Milo stepped away to have a word. At one point he gestured back with a nod to where I stood, no doubt pointing me out as the one who had found the body. She gave me a mistrustful once-over before returning her gaze to Milo. She hung on his words, her eyes never leaving his face, in a way that went beyond just getting information from him, even though he was a uniformed peon in their world of stripes and badges. Maybe she just thought he needed watching. Maybe she thought he was hot. I know I did.

Sergeant Milo, if he'd been wearing camo, might have jumped straight out of a Marine recruiting poster. Before the sight of Anna's body had wiped the smile off his face, I'd seen a flash of pearly teeth and brilliant blue eyes, and he'd revealed a bristly brown crewcut when he lifted his hat to smooth back his hair. Once he saw the body, that manly jaw had clamped shut, the searching gaze had narrowed to a glare, and the hat with its checkerboard band had settled low over his brow. The glare wasn't necessarily aimed at me, but seemed to be more a sort of free-floating distrust at the novelty of the situation. He began scanning the river as if expecting to see a pirate ship sail by. It was then I noticed that while his uniform might be crisp and his shoes shiny there were dark circles under his eyes. He looked haggard beneath the professional gloss. I thought he might have pulled some kind of all-nighter stakeout.

Eventually he ambled back over to where I waited at the sidelines. Uniforms were by now blocking the path at either end to passersby; I stood obediently behind a ribbon of crime scene tape. Milo sighed.

"She's in bad shape," he told me, pulling the notebook from the inner pocket of his jacket with a sigh.

"I know. Cellulite."

"I mean she's dead."

Realizing I might have sounded flippant — a habit when I'm nervous — I arranged my features into a suitable grimace of concern.

"You know her?" Almost as an afterthought, he added, "Ma'am?"

Ah. Well. As much as I was tempted to deny ever having met her, that wasn't an option, for Anna lived — had lived — in the terraced house right next to mine. Even in Surrey you can't pretend not to know that near a neighbor. Especially if she's in your book club. Correction: *had* been in your book club, before it dissolved in bitter tears and shouted accusations over Hilary Mantel's *Bring Up the Bodies.* The members of the Weycombe Court Book Club had stormed home, leaving behind their trays of canapés, carefully decorated with sprigs of parsley, but taking with them their half-empty bottles of good French wine.

"Sort of."

He crossed his arms. All the time in the world for me to explain, sort of. Every movement made him jangle and creak from all the stuff he had hanging from his belt. It reminded me I needed to call the plumber, the last guy I'd seen similarly accessorized.

"She liked *Eat Pray Love.* Thought it was life-changing. She sells houses. *Sold* houses. She sold us our house. Her husband is sort of an invalid — he caught some virus or other working for a development outfit in Africa. She has a son — stepson." (Insert a slight pause here, for Jason was a problem child, a bad and lingering odor in the staged perfection of the Monroe household.) "She used to do some sort of volunteer work helping a local MP get re-elected, but she quit. Said they were all liars, like she didn't know that going in."

"What's eat pray love? A restaurant?"

"It's a book," I told him. "We read it for book club." Unconsciously, I began speaking very slowly, using hand gestures to mime a person holding an open book and turning the pages, as if talking to someone with a less-than-perfect grasp of English. Then I reminded myself that *Eat Pray Love* was hardly Shakespearian. I started to summarize the plot for him but stopped at Italy as his eyes drifted impatiently over my shoulder in the direction of Anna's body. He'd just have to Netflix it.

I could hear the *whoop-whoop!* of sirens as more responders squeezed their way down Church Street and inched toward Cobbetts Hill, no doubt having to wait at this morning rush hour for eastbound drivers on their mobiles to get out of the way. Priorities get very skewed in the Stockbroker Belt as people claw to the top of their chosen anthill.

I sent up a small plea (*Do not let him ask about Jason right now — too soon*) and turned my attention back to Milo, warrant number 4992S8. He wore no shoulder identification and he'd barely flashed his card along with that gleaming smile but I have an eidetic memory that I have found useful for nothing much apart from passing exams and memorizing lines of plays.

"You say she has a stepson. Where is he?"

"I don't really know. She and I weren't that close."

So far, so true. Lately I'd only seen Anna to speak to as we stood by our respective recycling bins at seven a.m. on rubbish collection day, trying not to count the empty bottles of wine or comment on the number of yogurt containers. Until the book club went off like a bomb, she and I had had lunch with the same group of women every few weeks. We'd sailed together on the *Misty,* rented yearly by our homeowners' association in a forced show of goodwill that thus far had not resulted in any deaths by drowning, deliberate or otherwise. For Weycombe, this counted as an intensely close relationship but I didn't think Milo would understand the finely graded system used to judge these things. I'm not sure I understand it myself. I shook my head in frustration, for truly I wanted to help direct his inquiries in every way I could.

"She wasn't around a lot," I added. "Her job. You know."

"You're American?" he asked. Perhaps to him that was a logical springboard to the reasons Anna and I weren't close. Probably it was. After ten years in the UK I was used to people expecting me to chew gum and champion the war in Iraq.

I nodded. "She worked outside the home, you see, and I work inside the home."

Well, that right there was a stretch, and I was glad I wasn't hooked up to a polygraph just then. Okay, sure, I worked, if you can call it work "punching up" my CV and making the occasional fitful attempt to get a job after having been made redundant nine months before. That and reading blogs about stay-at-home moms, clearly far better people than I, who had established cottage industries at their kitchen tables and within weeks were cashing checks for millions of pounds by making documentary films or embroidering baby clothes to sell on Etsy or blogging about their trendy neighborhoods or inventing things they'd crowdsourced on Kickstarter. I also watched videos about, for example, how to make a hair dryer diffuser from chicken wire. In nine months I could have produced a baby, an irony not lost on me. Instead I'd produced nothing of interest but some disjointed notes for a novel I kept trying to write.

At one time I'd thought I might get into doing voiceovers — American accents were much in demand in London — and I had turned the guest bedroom closet into a soundproof recording studio with a professional-grade mic and editing software. If you call the American Museum in Britain or the American Air Museum after hours you might still hear my voice on their recordings. But apart from that, my voice-over career had not come to much.

"But the son lives nearby?" Clearly Milo was not going to let this go. I stifled the impulse to tell him to go ask Anna's husband if he was so interested. Anxiety broke in at the thought of Alfie. Who was going to tell him what had happened to his wife? How was he going to take the news? It wasn't as if he didn't have enough problems. His illness had reduced him pretty much to skin and bone, and to eating the only two foods he could keep down: low-fat yogurt and buckwheat. The Monroe recycle bin overflowed with sad little containers of Fage 2%. But Alfie's main regret about his illness was that it kept him from being of use helping others. That's how he thought. He was the Melanie Wilkes of Weycombe Court.

The news would probably bring son Jason home like a shot, just to add to Alfie's woes. Jason was a taker: that much I knew from everything Anna had told me, when she and I were still swapping confidences. No matter how she tried to gloss over it, Jason was very bad news.

"The last I heard, Jason lived in London, somewhere around Catford Bridge or Ladywell. But that was months ago — the last I heard." I shifted uneasily, placing all the activity around Anna's body more firmly out of my line of sight. The improvised screen had slipped and I could see they were putting little sock-puppet bags on her hands. The reality of all this was getting to me now and I doubted I'd sleep much that night, a doubt that held true for many nights to come. "May I please go now? I need to ring my husband and I really don't have anything to add. I was walking and I recognized her shoes, of all things. They were new, you see; she was wearing them the last time I saw her. I called it in. You know the rest. I haven't seen her since Monday, otherwise: rubbish collection day."

He asked for my address and phone number and asked me to remain available in case the investigators had further questions. I started to tell him sure, I'd cancel that flight to Belize, and then I thought better of it. Milo didn't look in the mood for jokes.

As he was turning to go I called him back. "Wait a minute. I just remembered — in all the excitement it went out of my head. I thought I saw someone walking away very fast — running, actually — toward the top of the hill. Just as I was approaching. Just before I found . . . her."

"A man? Woman?" He wrote something in his notebook with what looked like a golf pencil; it was nearly swallowed up in his large, hammy fist. He wrote like a child; I half expected to see his tongue protruding from one side of his mouth as he concentrated on forming his letters.

"A man, I'm pretty certain. Yes, it almost had to be, from the way he carried himself. That or a very large, rugged-individual type of woman. We have a few of those in the village." He smiled, a conspiratorial "don't I know it?" smile. "I didn't think too much about it because there are a lot of runners and walkers out this way. The thing is, he wasn't dressed for running or for any kind of sport, really. He or she looked sort of scruffy and he — or she — was wearing long pants."

"Coloring? Clothing?"

I shook my head. *Not sure.* "She lived next door," I added as he continued his scribbling. I figured I might as well come clean now, because even the dimmest detective was sure to figure it out soon. "Anna did. At number 24."

The dark eyebrows over the blue eyes shot upward. Somehow I just knew they would.

"Quite a coincidence," he said. "That you were both out taking your exercise on the river path today, and all."

"Not really," I said. I was annoyed by the

insinuation, but I kept my voice even. "I'm here nearly every day. Most days I walk all the way to Walton-on-Thames and back." I expected him to ask, who has time for that? It's a distance of seven and a half miles round trip. The answer was, in my case, the unemployed and the apparently unemployable. The bored and the lonely.

"Quite a coincidence," he repeated. The conspiratorial smile was gone.

2

Nothing is ever so perfect as it seems. Not even in Weycombe, where they've had centuries to get everything just right: the twee cottages with pitched thatch roofs and mullioned windows; the meandering cobblestone streets lined with tiny shops selling yarn and wine and stationery; the flower boxes stuffed with well-tended blooms; the ancient inn, still the beating heart of the place. It was said ghostlike ruins sat at the bottom of the duck pond on the village green and could still be glimpsed on a calm summer day.

There were a lot of "it was saids" in these retellings, many dubious tales preserved like insects in amber, but spookiest of all were the tales of the church with its ancient crypt and graveyard, its layers upon layers of the dead-and-buried faithful now turned to dust. It needed little effort as I walked down Church Street at twilight to imagine ghosts flitting just at the edge of my vision, or to fancy I could hear the sighs of lovers or the whispers of those plotting mischief. Back then there were so many chances to get it wrong if you mixed up your mushrooms or your magic potions, or you misjudged the constantly changing political and religious scene, or even if you simply drank water straight from the river. It was no wonder if ghosts did linger, fastened by their penitential chains to the earth.

Today's villagers live in luxury unimagined then, and a clean and sparkling river framed by willows runs beneath modern windows as it ripples eastward to London. My neighbors kept themselves to themselves, but from what I could tell their dreams were mundane: a new swimming pool and fresh wallpaper; a different hair color and adult braces; a new dress and nail tips for the annual charity ball at Branford-Sturgeon manor house. They were beautiful people, my neighbors. A lot of work went into being them.

Many in the UK dream of moving to America, but mainly those needing a fresh start. No one in Weycombe seemed to need that, at least not those living at my upscale postal code. If they had dreams of America, it was to wish for a winter house in Florida.

Their roots were firmly planted in Weycombe.

As Sergeant Milo noticed, I am from the US, that land of inventors and re-inventors, the people who brought you the Segway and Lady Gaga. It is a place of wide-open highways and land grant colleges and prairie schooners and buffaloes and homesteads on the Great Plains, but my leanings were always New England-small, and my yearnings had always been to live in a diamanté European city like Bruges or a walled medieval town in France.

Or a place like Weycombe, in all its pretty perfection.

I arrived in the village by way of Oxford and a graduate diploma in medieval studies. This qualified me, in ways I never entirely understood, to be a talent coordinator for the BBC in London, where my job was to interview and create videos of likely candidates for various re-enactment programs. The decision to hire me may have had something to do with my work in amateur theater at University. Before long, my efforts were centered almost exclusively on their true-crime show. This job in turn led me to meet and marry William White.

I rather quickly achieved what I had most wanted: a life lived in the land of my ancestors — who came to America to get away from it all.

I don't have words to tell you how shocking Anna's death was to the yuppie settlement of Weycombe. The level of fear it unleashed, once it was understood she hadn't just passed away from a dicky heart and overexertion. The shock was not in a "there but for the grace of God" or "never send to know for whom the bell tolls" sort of way, either. Because people like Anna just don't get themselves killed: they pay good money to live in gated communities where every chance of such a fate is reduced practically to zero. Weycombe Court had private security patrols; it had neighborhood watch; it had neurotic pedigreed dogs that barked at anything that moved. And without the gate, it had Sergeant Milo and Co.

"Security First" should have been the Weycombe motto, along with "Perfection at any Price." The council had people who came bi-monthly to mow the grass on the green in diagonal stripes *because it looked better that way.* The reasons behind this thinking should have been obvious to me, but I never learned all the rules. And when Anna died I was just beginning to understand that I never would learn them all.

■ ■ ■ ■

Weycombe is a character in and of itself in this story, no different from the creepy man with gooseberry eyes who ran the butcher shop on the High and always made me think of Sweeney Todd. I'd still advise anyone looking for murder suspects to start with him.

Ticking all the cozy boxes, Weycombe had — still has, I guess — a war memorial, a village hall, tea rooms, restaurants, that old inn, and a trendy wine bar. It boasted a second-tier celebrity commuter or two, and a Michelin-starred restaurant on the road to Walton-on-Thames. It had its own sports ground and clubhouse and a thriving cricket club. Nearby was a famous prep school; there was also a renowned private "hospital," actually a dry-out clinic for footballers and reality stars.

The village shop was a general store and off-license selling local produce and baked goods and packed with old-fashioned toiletries and patent medicines. There was a coffee shop on the High where I spent many of my waking hours. Writing, or trying to. The owner had a cat that would sun itself in the middle of the street, until some exasperated driver would finally climb out of his car and scoop it out of the way.

For culture, there was a bookshop, an antique shop or two, and a small art gallery owned by a woman with family money and appalling taste. Weycombe also had a theater for amateur dramatics; my husband took part in one production and was quite good, really. For years I kept the recording of his great booming baritone as he ran his lines.

Around harvest time, when Anna died, most of the village shops sported a straw mannequin dressed as, for example, Jack the Ripper or Margaret Thatcher. Halloween (or Hallowe'en) had become a bigger event each year. The pubs served local ciders and perries, and every street was a showcase of turning leaves.

I admit, I loved all this, at least at first. Weycombe looked like the setting for an episode of *Midsomer Murders,* which absolutely should have alerted me. As Agatha Christie wrote, "One does see so much evil in a village."

Will and I lived on a crescent at one end of the High in a gated estate of detached and terraced houses — thirty new-builds, each designed to complement the other without being too cookie-cutter. The entry gate was made of wrought iron with an arch that proclaimed you were entering Weycombe Court. Beyond our little bubble of privilege were individual cottages surrounded by tiny gardens, and beyond them, farms and woodland.

Weycombe Court — in case you thought North America has some monopoly on pretentious names for housing developments. At least the "Court" part of the name makes a certain sense. We held court; we were courted (some of us). We conducted ourselves in a courtly manner (some of us). And we judged each other nonstop.

At one time I got a certain thrill as we drove under that archway, Will and I. Thousands, millions, would never know the key code to that gate, and we did. Our back garden ran down to the shining River Wey. We also had a terrace and indoor and outdoor fireplaces. Perfect.

Few tourists realized the Court was there. The hidden location was one of the wiser decisions made by the developers; the least wise was to turn to some dicey pals and relatives to fund construction, which was further delayed by a bad winter. The developers couldn't wash their hands of the place fast enough so Will and I ended up paying about forty thousand pounds below market.

Our terrace house rose three stories above

ground and had an English basement with its own separate entrance. The basement was intended for an au pair, a mother-in-law, or live-in help. In some cases, grown children stayed there until forced to vacate. Ours became an office for Will. A man cave. As his career progressed and our marriage disintegrated, he spent more and more time holed up down there.

But that came later. For a while, it was all just flawless, Stepfordish in its perfection (*"but she won't take pictures and she won't be me!"*). Sometimes I looked at my neighbor Heather across the way and expected to see wire trailing from under the hem of her dress.

The first day we moved into Weycombe Court I looked across the crescent into one of the neighbor's bedrooms and watched a woman putting sheets on her king-size bed. As I watched this trim blonde dressed so impeccably to do her housework, I was overcome by a sense that finally, I had *arrived.* I now lived in this fairytale, ritzy postal code, and I was now one of the women who made their large beds (and lay in them) and somehow it was, I don't know, a reward, or a vindication. I was proud and happy. I was one of the chosen.

■ ■ ■ ■

Anna died on the northern stretch of the Weycombe path, a ribbon of paved asphalt that hugged the river where it ran below a precipice covered with small trees, bushes, and bramble. The path then passed several small villages on its way to Walton-on-Thames — hamlets where the cows outnumbered the people — curving around wherever the villages got in the way.

This well-maintained path was meant to be shared civilly by pedestrians and bicyclists, but in fact you walked or ran at your own risk, remaining ever alert to the soft whir of fast-approaching tires. Bike riders were the subject of many stroppy letters to the editor of the *Weycombe Chronicle,* letters the authors hoped might sway those who ruled with godlike indifference from the parish council.

What happened to Anna could so easily have been an accident. She could have been running flat out on her chubby legs, minding her own business, when some solicitor speeding by on his way to his office in Walton-on-Thames, anonymous in his ventilated helmet and ubiquitous black bike shorts, pushed her off the path, sending her rolling downhill and breaking her neck. That time of year, the path could be slick with wet fallen leaves. She might simply have slipped and fallen on her head.

That is certainly how it could have happened. Except that of course she was murdered, dead before her body came to rest at the edge of the river.

3

I returned home that day of discovery practically jumping out of my skin from all the adrenaline. I paced the living room in aimless circles in an effort to calm myself. Finally I began to load the dishwasher, my hands shaking, until I shattered a glass, dropping it on the floor. I searched out the broom and dustpan but soon gave up on finding the smallest shards. What did it matter?

I was doing what I always did, what I had been trained to do from childhood. Carry on, hang tough, for God's sake act normal. Make the fact the dishwasher hadn't been run for days and Will would hassle me about it more important than knowing Anna was dead.

She really was *dead,* my brain kept insisting; as in never coming back. I had done the same thing on 9/11 — finished composing an email to one of my professors about a late assignment, adding just the right amount of groveling to pretend regret at missing his class the week before. I hit send, then sat back and reread old emails in the queue, deciding whether to reply or delete. It's shock, of course. It's what people do — something dull and routine to make time stand still, to give the brain a chance to catch up to the horror of what's happened. I'd done much the same sort of thing when my brother died.

The broken glass had jolted me back to awareness. The clock was ticking — literally, the old grandfather clock Will had brought from his ancestral home when we married, over his mother's protests. The Demon Dowager had protested both the clock and the marriage. Little good it did her.

Will would be home any minute and I didn't think I could cope with his sniping about the state of the house. Not now. Dried egg on the breakfast plates would only distract us from the much larger subject at hand. I mean, *hello:* I was the one who called 999. I was the one who carried the memory of her dead, staring eyes. I had had to deal with Milo and all the rest of it. Surely today of all days we could call a truce.

Right then, I'd have done anything to avoid seeing that pissed-off look on his face when he walked in, not even bothering to say hello until he'd scanned the state of the house. That entrance would be followed by snarky inquiries as to how I passed my day, and pointed questions about the progress of my job search.

I'd told Milo I wanted to talk to my husband, but that was of course an excuse to get away, to collapse in private. I had no real idea how to break the news to Will. I really didn't want to see him until I'd looped the entire morning across my mind a few times. Will's compassion and awareness were sometimes, shall we say, lacking. The man had an edge. It's what I used to like about him. I mean, Lord Byron had an edge, too, and wouldn't you rather spend an hour in his company than a year in someone else's? But that gets old, all the "mad, bad, and dangerous to know" stuff. I never broached a subject with Will anymore without first rehearsing my opening lines, afraid of his reaction.

It was no way to live.

The house was actually in worse shape now than when I had worked full time. Something about time expanding to fill the allotted indifference. But now as I roughly slotted the dishes into the machine I thought about Milo, and about Anna, of course, and how the news of her death would ricochet about the neighborhood. What a total disruption it would mean to the Stepfordian status quo. The few murders that happened anywhere around Weycombe were confined to the chaotic council estates. Even there, I'd be hard-pressed to say if they had more than the occasional drug-related stabbing — the *Weycombe Chronicle* relegated such skirmishes to the inner pages, saving the front page for breaking news of the winner of the Women's Institute flower show.

The church clock was striking ten as Will finally got home that night. At a wild guess, he'd been at the Bull. It seemed as if most nights he only popped in to declare the house a disaster area. It was like I was an appointment scheduled into his day planner: "Complain to maid about untidy house. Terminate?"

His nagging had actually started a few years ago; it's just that memory plays with timelines. Hoovering is not one of my major talents and he knew this going in. I remember him coming home one night before I lost my job, saying, as he dropped his coat over a chair, "I tripped over a kayak in the garage again. I thought you were going to mount them on the ceiling."

Really? The way they do in *Better Homes and Gardens*? Yep. I was on it, honest I was.

Sometimes he'd start on the way I dressed. "Where are the pearls I gave you?"

His mother's pearls. Somehow he'd talked her out of them to give to me as a wedding present, carrying on a family tradition. The fact that handing them over nearly killed her was the only thing I liked about them. But he also gave me a beautiful diamond wristwatch that I always wore.

Once at large in Weycombe I rejoiced in dressing down: Jeans, jacket, booties, turtleneck. Hair loose at all angles, or in a pony, or in a twist pinned at my neck.

I used to wear the pearls just to please him sometimes, sometimes to bed with nothing else on, but when I wore them out to a party I kept hoping the clasp would break and they'd be stolen or lost. Drop like pebbles into the river so I'd never see them again.

As for my housekeeping? It was erratic because I didn't see the point. I'd get everything polished one day and the house would be falling apart the next. We used to have a maid come in every other week — Flora. Several of the neighbors, including

Anna, used her. Why his lordship didn't pitch in to help more often didn't seem to be a topic for his day planner. Once I was at home all day and no longer helping with expenses, the whole cleaning thing became my responsibility. I decided, waiting for Will that night, that Flora was coming back. Life is too short.

You could tell from his expression he'd been hoping I'd be in bed already — not waiting naked in some temptress pose, but sound asleep so he could avoid me. He spotted the bits of broken glass and started to say something. I cut him off.

"I'll get around to it," I said. "But I want to tell you what happened around here today. And, you know, talk. Like we used to." A shaky note had crept into my voice. I hated when that happened. I bit my lip to stop myself saying another word until I was under control.

He didn't seem to notice. Tiny shards of glass, yes; a distraught wife, no. He looked shaky himself — shaky and drunk as the proverbial lord, although that came as no surprise. Not drunk enough to be argumentative — he had passed that stage and gone into stupor mode — but too drunk to pick up on anything outside the storm roiling inside his own head.

From dealing with my father, I knew enough to leave a drunk alone until he'd slept it off. But this, I thought, was Will. This time things could be different — there was still a chance I could make them different.

I could learn. Will could learn.

I put aside my own glass of wine; the book I'd been trying to read sat abandoned on the table beside me. "You won't believe what hap—"

"I know what happened," he said. "Just . . . just leave me the fuck alone."

That did it: instantly, I was livid. At his words, at his tone. But I really was learning, because I snapped back the reply that would spin us out of control.

It took all I had simply to stand and walk out of the living room. Will could sleep it off on the couch in his office. Again.

PART 2

4

The day after Anna died the weather was perfect, the sky scrubbed blue, every blade of grass throwing off sunbeams. But winter was coming, you could smell it in the air, and you can't begin to appreciate how dreary a prospect that is until you've lived in England. I used to like winter, even in Maine, but England had the kind of damp cold that made you feel your bones might rot from the inside out. I came to understand why so many princesses from the Continent succumbed to disease after being shipped in to wed some chinless British royal.

The *Weycombe Chronicle,* a weekly, was late arriving. I guessed they had pulled an all-nighter putting together coverage of Anna's demise. But they hadn't called me for a quote, so maybe they hadn't heard of my role. They generally were the last to hear the news.

Everyone called it the *Chronic.* It was meant to be an adjunct to the broadsheets and tabloids of London, a cheaper alternative for local advertisers. Most recently the coverage had focused on a strip of riverfront being eyed by developers who were rumored to be in bed with our local MP, who was rumored to be in bed with nearly everyone.

Murder coverage was not the *Chronic*'s strong point, but on the occasion of Anna's death they put out a special edition. Their website was already full of the news, complete with typos and misspellings, so great was their haste to keep the village updated. Anna was one of their biggest advertisers, so the glowing tribute to her virtues as wife and mother might have been a stretch but the "heartfelt sadness" was not.

Reading the *Chronic* was always a Talmudic experience, given Garvin Barnes' penchant for digressions and explanations and footnotes. Garvin — owner, publisher, reporter, and editor — was a self-important little stoat who thought running a local paper made him a force to be reckoned with. He had reached retirement age in about 1985, a fact reflected in his rambling commentary on the rose-growing competition and the local school's A-level results. When he had extra space to fill he'd print one of his own poems, a rare treat, if not nearly rare enough. He seemed to rely heavily on spellcheck. That and scotch.

The coverage of the murder of Anna showed Garvin and the young intern he'd hired to do his website keeping well within their journalistic comfort zones. They had interviewed a few people to get quotes about their reactions on hearing the news. To a man and woman, they were "shocked." The hardest-hitting reportage went something like this comment from longtime Weycombe resident Jessup Bladeworthy: "It is usually such a quiet village. We are locking our doors now for the first time. And they shall stay locked until this vile monster is caught."

There were pages of this sort of stuff, with nearly every villager quoted, but that was understandable: the chances the police would confide anything like real news to someone like Garvin were zero to none, so he made do with outrage and hand-wringing.

There had never been a case like it in the village in recent memory. There had been the occasional dodgy overdose, but that was it. The place was as safe as the city fathers and mothers could make it. Anything else would discourage the tourist trade. (The actual residents were somehow less important — presumably we would not flee the village until someone was shot and left to die on our doorsteps.)

No, this story would be big — big enough to bring my former colleagues from the BBC to the scene. I wondered if, as the person to discover the body, I wouldn't be hearing from them at any moment. I debated for a bit and then unplugged the landline. I really didn't want to be quoted on anything just yet, and I knew too well how these people worked with out-of-context remarks.

I poured myself another cup of coffee and sat in the kitchen with the *Chronic* spread open before me, thinking. I noticed idly that Garvin had run one of the ads upside down.

I wasn't sure I wanted to be part of the investigation — if I didn't want my name kept out of it entirely. My grandmother swore by the old saying that your name should only appear in the newspaper when you were born, when you were married, and when you died. Every time I logged onto Twitter I saw the wisdom in that philosophy.

But an idea was beginning to form. I had contacts in the news world, contacts who would want access to the story. And I was at the center of things, in a manner of speaking, although I knew that didn't mean I would be kept in the loop by the police — far from it.

Still, I had something these BBC types wanted, and they had something I needed. I had inside information by virtue of being a first-on-the-scene witness, likely to be interviewed by investigators at least one more time. Perhaps I would be asked to testify at the inquest. On the other hand, the BBC would have access to the investigation in ways I would not be granted as a private citizen; unlike with Garvin, the police would not be so fast to brush them off.

Talk about networking. Will would be so proud.

It wouldn't hurt to get my name out there. To keep my options open.

All of these thoughts arrived in a muddle when what I needed to do was impose order. I dug out a new notebook from the stash in my office, along with a new disposable fountain pen. The notebook was purple with an engraved art deco design, and it had an elasticized band to hold the pages shut. It became my constant companion for a while — the repository of all my thoughts on the case of Anna Monroe.

I began by describing her, as objectively

as I could. Anna in life. And then, if I could bring myself to it, Anna in death.

She was a showstopper, despite the cellulite, with the showgirl looks of a bygone era. Not many people have skin of that true porcelain hue I've described — most of us, regardless of race, are shades of yellow and brown. But Anna's skin was Dresden-shepherdess porcelain, the purest of pure whites with not a tinge of yellow. In every group photo I have of her — on the *Misty* for the annual Weycombe Court Homeowners lovefest, at the occasional luncheon or party, boarding the train to London to see a play with the book club — she stands out like a white ghost among her dingy, sallow-skinned comrades. She seldom wore foundation — it was probably next to impossible to find that shade and anyway, why gild the lily? And despite her extra pounds, or because of them, she glowed with life and health, making me look particularly scrawny alongside her, my hair looking like I'd just swum ashore from a shipwreck. The eye was drawn to Anna, time and again.

That play we went to see, come to think of plays, was *Betrayal.* A subject, many people thought, Anna knew a whole lot about.

She was under five foot four, and those curves defied the rage for rangy people of the Kate Moss variety. Hers was a Snow White prettiness, with dark, expressive brows and raven hair and ruby lips to go with it. And those green eyes. The original witchy woman.

Six years older than me, she had turned forty the year before, an occasion marked by the Lordy, Lordy party to which we'd all been invited Chez Monroe.

She'd recently taken up running, maybe in response to that landmark birthday, and I can conjure a moving image of her even now, the dimpled white knees, the plump thighs emerging from her running shorts, legs pumping as she tried to leave behind those last stubborn few pounds. The flash of her expensive, colorful running shoes as she'd fly around the corner and disappear down Sheep Lane on her way to the river path. She would run along the west side of the river, then circle round the park, cross the bridge, and run back down the east side. She had told me she had lost seven pounds on this austerity regime. I could see for myself it was working — the jelly roll around her middle had shrunk by half.

I learned from the *Chronic* that she and I shared a middle name. I am Jillian Anna

Violet White nee Waterford, as in the Irish county. When Will and I married, I didn't even have to buy new monogrammed towels. Anna was Priscilla Anna Monroe nee Buckford. I'm assuming the *Chronic* got that much right.

As I had told Milo, Anna worked as an estate agent, and her day started early. In the past two years, more than thirty homes had sold in Weycombe for over one million — that doesn't sound so special until you realize we are talking GBP, not US dollars. All these years and I still have to translate the exchange rate in my head. So Anna, who had handled many of those sales, was doing well for herself and for Alfie, although how much Alfie's welfare figured into her calculations was anyone's guess. Most members of the Weycombe Court Book Club thought she might be tiring of the role of sole breadwinner. I thought she thrived on it; it gave her control. What was she supposed to do, stay home and experiment with squash recipes from the Women's Institute website? Anna the homemaker — that was not her style. Her job got her out and about.

Her job, let's just say it, got her out and about and under. Under men, I mean. Lots of men. It involved lots of dinner and drinks meetings, many late at night.

I'll mention that Anna's background was working class, not that that has anything to do with anything. But I cannot begin to describe what that means in this country, except to say it is a very big deal. More than one PhD has been awarded for research on place of birth and accent and education, and how these things unite to keep one in one's place.

Anna's stated goal was never to slip back into the class in which she'd been raised. The women she hung with were solidly middle class and had never known a day's worry over money: it was somehow always just *there.* Will, being aristo, was the neighborhood superstar. As an American I was tolerated as his consort if not entirely embraced as his wife.

Anna had made me her confidante, possibly as the one person in the Court indifferent to these social barriers. I came to think it more likely she didn't care if I judged her because she didn't care what I thought. She had been raised by a Catholic mother and grandmother in Bristol. Her father had not been much in the picture — something else she and I had in common. Her mother supported them all by working as a cleaning lady for the local church and its rectory. When the priest got grabby, her mother moved the family to London while she got herself sorted. One day she went to Brick Lane Market in Shoreditch and begged a job from a local greengrocer, a man she ended up marrying.

Growing up, Anna had impressed everyone with her smarts and her drive. While not possessed of a top-drawer academic brain, she swotted hard and ended up as a scholarship student at St. Andrews. She went there, she told me, in hopes not so much of academic achievement but of making a good marriage. She was attractive and she knew it — one of those women with a sturdy yet come-hither way of walking that always made me think of Helen Mirren. Men obeyed by dropping whatever they were doing and going thither.

She met Alfie at St. Andrews. He was a graduate student, already with a wife and baby boy. Like Anna he was working class and smart. Well, maybe not quite as smart as Anna. She may have had it in mind to marry up but she thought she saw in Alfie the pattern of someone very like herself. And marrying someone like you is far less stressful than having to keep up with the snooty Joneses all the time — trust me on this. In Alfie she saw someone also not willing to be poor, not ever again, and willing to do whatever it took to escape the large, deeply religious Methodist family into which he had been born. Moonstruck, he left his wife and child. Before long, he and Anna were married.

But first his family talked him into a stint working with a relief organization in Africa, where presumably he worked off his debt of guilt. After that, always good with numbers, he decided to become something in finance in the City. People tended to trust Alfie, which is even better than being good with numbers. But what neither Anna nor he could foresee was that during his time served in Africa he'd picked up a bug, some intestinal thing that would flare up unannounced and leave him horizontal for days. He was finally judged unfit for duty and given a small pension to go away quietly. It was small only by the standards of the African tribe that had shared its parasites with him, but it was nothing like the sort of money needed to keep the monthly Weycombe mortgage paid. This is where Anna stepped in, going to work for the local estate agent's office. In the UK the standards for this sort of thing are not too rigorous, but still, you need an aptitude and a can-do spirit, which Anna had in spades. She was soon the star earner for Desworthy-Neswith, or Des-Nes, as it was called.

I was so focused on my Anna bio that I started at a sound coming from behind me. Actually, I jumped about a mile — I imagine that like everyone in the village that morning, my nerves were shot; it was not a great time to sneak up on anyone. Will had emerged from below, probably to fill his thermos with coffee for the train ride into the City. I shuffled the notebook onto my lap so he couldn't see it. I'm not sure why, except that I knew he thought my journaling was a waste of time.

He was sober now, if looking like he'd slept under a tree in the garden. His rumpled shirt matched his expression. It seemed as good a time as any to ask where he'd been the night before, although why bother? I could guess.

I was amazed he took the trouble to answer. He seemed somewhat contrite and very subdued, a complete contrast with the night before. Some days I thought he might be bipolar.

"I was at the Bull," he said. "I ran into Andy on the train, and he told me what had happened. We stopped in for a quick one." His tie was loose, his hair still wet from the shower. He looked like he'd been caught in the rain. He looked vulnerable, like the man

I'd fallen in love with. There was a time I'd ache to reach out and hold him, but no more. He shook his head. "God, it was awful. The whole village was there. Everyone's hysterical."

I felt a twinge of envy. I so longed to be a part of that big gossipy village scene, everyone *tsk*ing and speculating in hushed, mournful tones about what had happened to Anna. Always the outsider, I wanted more than anything just then to belong. Somewhere. Anywhere. Will could have swung by the house to include me in this gossip fest. I was the one who'd found her, for God's sake; I'd have had a lot to contribute.

Of course he hadn't even called to let me know he'd be late. This sort of thing had somehow become the usual, along with the casual assumption that since I had time on my hands (in his view), my time was less important than his.

Never mind that I disliked the aptly-named Bull and Will knew it. It was the principle of the thing. Still, I didn't want to pick a fight; we'd had enough of that and it had gotten us nowhere but further apart. Besides, I thought he might have picked up some useful information about the investigation and I didn't want him to clam up on me.

It didn't used to be like this. This cageyness on my part, this wary stubbornness on his, that look in his eyes, as if I'd suddenly become a stranger.

This was our new normal and I hated it. Every minute.

Will seldom looked directly at me anymore, so I had ample opportunity to study the changes in him. Most days, he could have been a model for Abercrombie and Fitch, broad and tall and striking. He owned a collection of trendy eyeglasses and that day he wore the round tortoiseshell ones, which cost a cool four hundred pounds — Will always bought the best for himself. With his strong features and mop of hair he was amazing to look at, really, but the grave manner he wore like a second skin was what made him attractive to me. If anything, he had become graver since I was made redundant.

Why did he care whether or not I went out to work? Will was landed gentry. A minor nob in a land that grew them like turnips, but still. I thought him spoiled, entitled — but perhaps that was my perception as a yeoman by comparison. It had something to do with his upper-class drawl, so it may not have been entirely his fault. But it did seem to me nothing had ever *not* gone his way. The drawl, which had been a key selling feature in the beginning, began to get right up my nose within a year or two.

He didn't notice or care what I did, not really, not anymore, but I certainly noticed him. He'd been up well before I was, despite what had to be a world-class hangover. He'd seen me dragging myself out of the bedroom, knotting a chenille robe at my waist, and he'd turned abruptly to head into the garage, either to retrieve something or just to pretend he was on urgent business. The sight of me seemed to pain him.

"See you later," he said now. No inflection, no tone, no look in the eye. I think he was actually talking to the cat. He did not define "later" and I knew better than to ask. Our moment of détente was over.

"Okay," I said to his retreating back.

They say your gut doesn't lie but it had taken me longer to learn that lesson than it might have taken someone less besotted. Will wanted out. Any fool could see it.

"Goodbye," I said to the closed front door. "Have a nice day now." Part of me wanted to run after him, screaming like a fishwife, chenille bathrobe and all.

The larger part of me, by then having the upper hand, would never give him the satisfaction.

5

Kookie jumped onto my lap as Will left, knocking my notebook to the floor. The cat's full name was Kookie, Kookie. As in "Kookie, Kookie — Lend Me Your Comb." Most Brits didn't get it; Will did. We shared a love of songs with immortally awful lyrics, our favorite being "Leader of the Pack." We loved to shout "look out!" as his Rover rounded hairpin turns in the wilds of Scotland.

Nonsense was a real bond between us. Will *got* me in a way no man ever had. No straight man, anyway. I loved the British side of his nature that was always on the lookout for the ludicrous — that innate ability to see the absurd in everything. And he saw through most of my shit, which really impressed me to no end.

Now even Kookie looked put out by this frosty new regime. Cats can sense things, you know? Especially when something's up that might interfere with their food supply.

I had a return of panic at the thought of Will's never coming home, which every day felt more like a possibility. Of hearing from his lawyers, of having to live through deep dead space in the aftermath of divorce.

Of course he could always go home to mummy. She lived in a mansion with so many bedrooms she couldn't count them all. The pair of them could go for months without ever seeing each other.

But they'd see each other, all right. They'd have dinner together and discuss my shortcomings at length. And that was so galling I literally couldn't bear the thought.

I collapsed onto the sofa and held Kookie tightly against me, hiding my face in his fur until he wriggled free.

I sat twisting the neck of my robe at my throat, remembering Thomas Wyatt: *"They flee from me that sometime did me seek / With naked foot, stalking in my chamber."* They thought he was writing about Anne Boleyn creeping about his chamber, at a time before she had bigger (much bigger) fish to fry.

Just between us, Anne, was it worth it? The caskets of gold and jewelry in exchange for such a short but glittering career? And of course that gruesome ending . . .

She would always be remembered as a

sort of poster child for the other woman, but wasn't it better than being Catherine of Aragon, frumpy, sick, and old before her time, like her daughter Mary? Both of them earnestly clutching their rosaries and moaning over their loss of status? Of all the women in Henry's life, only Anne of Cleeves was truly sensible. She took the money and ran, glad to get away from him.

Sadly, I could relate to Catherine's desperation. There had been an evening with Will that still makes me cringe to think of it, an evening in which I disgraced myself, shrieking like a lunatic, totally losing it. I can't forget, even now, the look of contempt in his eyes. That was us done. Stick a fork in it; we were done.

I should have left.

Still I hung on.

For Will and me, the days of mind-altering sex into the wee hours, fueled by wine and interrupted only by meandering conversations about our glorious future, our travel plans, the big house we would build, and the extraordinary children we would create together, were long over. At one time I could barely drag my sleep-deprived body into work after one of these marathon sessions. This much I know: Will had worshipped the sight of me. It's terrible when that goes away, to be replaced by — what? Hatred? Scorn?

Those carefree days of our early courtship and marriage suffered at first a gradual fading away, then a steep drop-off. But that was only to be expected, or so I'm told. People fall into a comfortable routine with one another, and they leave the house properly rested, combed, and with their shirttails tucked in. And one day they have a child, and then another, and then a grandchild or two to spoil. That's the way it's supposed to be.

It was hard to let go of the memories, for once upon a time we were Will and Jill, a fairytale couple so perfectly suited our names even rhymed. We rarely argued and we lived our privileged lives on an even keel. Until I lost my job — I'll admit; my ego took a bruising. I'd also wrecked my ankle not long before, and that had laid me up awhile. So maybe I wasn't wonderful to be around. I guess before, we didn't spend quite so much time together. Busy, busy, all the time. Too busy to notice things weren't quite the same.

So, knowing exactly where I was — at home — and what I was doing — not much — all the time apparently didn't hold the same erotic charge. Okay, I got that. But there was more to it, and I started to wonder what would have happened if I hadn't lost my job. Would Will have noticed how unhappy he was? Would he ever have *been* unhappy or would we just have sailed along, oblivious, until we reached retirement age and noticed we had nothing in common?

At least these questions gave me something to occupy myself with in the hours I wiled away waiting for him to return from work. Which got later and later, nearly every day.

That's the way you boil a frog. Slowly.

I felt so very alone in those days. It was worse because Will was all I had in the way of family, not counting my stepmother, which I did not.

Will's mother and sister also did not count. As a people person, the sister in particular made Princess Anne look like the Dalai Lama.

I didn't notice my strandedness so much pre-Will, when I was living in London, a city I still consider to be the center of the universe. I was single, young, and free and had an office to go to each day. It was only at times like Christmas that things got rather strained. People would invite me to their homes for dinner with their families and I'd pretend another engagement rather than be the specter at their feast. More than once I'd had a marmite and cheese sandwich for Christmas dinner — alone, naturally, like Bridget Jones — and told myself that was fine. It was just another day on the calendar.

There was no one to visit back home in the US. There was no home, period. No kinfolk waiting hearthside with Tollhouse cookies for my return. I had one cousin who had notified me of her mother's — my aunt's — death in one of those photocopied Christmas letters, months after the fact. That's how close we were. Sometimes I wondered what it would have been like to still have my brother around, if only to have someone to buy ugly socks for.

No use going down that road.

I was relieved when the holidays ended and everything went back to normal. When the lights came down and the gift wrappings went into the bin and I could forget the whole thing and go back into work.

To take my mind off all things Will, I needed a distraction — and learning what could be learned about the investigation into Anna's death was tailor-made. Knowing what was going on would keep me occupied, keep my anxiety levels down. It's the not knowing that drives you crazy.

While there are times when you should leave things well alone — just let the gods of mischief handle it — this was not one of those times. I wanted to — *had* to — know. If at all possible, I could at least nudge Milo and Co. in the right direction, for cases had a way of going cold after a while. Ask any detective. Half my job at the BBC had been reenacting cold cases, of which there seemed to be hundreds.

I decided the best place to start would be Weycombe's gossip central.

I went to find my gym bag.

6

I hated the bloody gym. I really did.

I regarded it with even more loathing than most people. I had been a pudgy kid with pigtails and glasses and weird friends, and that trauma stays with you. Being shunned by the popular crowd in junior high finally drove me to start exercising and dieting in a fanatical way. Nothing at home was under my control except my weight, so I started to keep a diary of every calorie, every sit-up.

But in Weycombe, I just walked. If it was too cold and rainy outside, I would drive over to the gym and use one of the treadmills.

Now it was Anna sent me there. The path I normally would have taken was still taped off with blue-and-white crime scene tape and littered with blue evidence-collection boxes. I lingered a moment to watch the technicians still working the scene before I headed over to Miller Lane. I didn't see

Milo around but that was fine; I did not want to run into him just then.

The spot where the body had lain would be blocked off for several more days. The bicyclists were particularly upset by this; a lot of them commuted to work on that path and they were forced to return to their old car-polluting ways. The fact that Anna was found on protected land, which technically the path was, added a new investigative wrinkle. I gathered that pagans had lit fires, sacrificed animals, and thrown bodies into the river near the spot where she died. A territorial struggle among the various arms of law enforcement and preservationist groups ensued. Even contemporary pagan groups had their say about the desecration of the area but were roundly ignored.

It was finally decided to let the local police handle it unless the help of Scotland Yard was needed. The fear was of dirty tricks on either side contaminating the results of the investigation. Certainly that was the way the FBI and CIA would have managed things. It was not unheard of for evidence to disappear or be misplaced — anything was fair game if it could screw up an investigation for the other side. If you're planning to kill someone, be sure to do it on a spot of land where jurisdiction is at issue and you might just get away with it.

I walked everywhere in those days, lulling myself into exhaustion. Mostly I would just follow the river, seeing the hours pass and the steps add up on my pedometer.

FitFull Gym was a poor substitute. It was part of a chain that had spread across England in the past ten years. No pun intended on the word "spread," but the UK had an obesity crisis to rival that in the US, which helped explain FitFull's popularity. The top floor held the requisite machines and weights, the middle floor was used for classes like yoga and Pilates, and the ground floor housed the locker rooms. I knew no one in Weycombe Court who was not a member, although some rarely showed up while others, the gym rats and yummy mummies, made the most of their monthly, one-hundred-pound fees. One way or another, FitFull had encroached on the role in village life once occupied by the pub and the Women's Institute, the locker rooms becoming another center where information and gossip were exchanged.

The talk in the women's locker room that Tuesday was naturally about the murder, and I assume it was the same in the men's. Even the North Cliff woman who routinely spoke with no one outside her social set could be seen chatting with a group of personal trainers, excitedly discussing the case. Once you know that "we live in North Cliff" is shorthand for "we have money, very old money, and we have weekend houses, too; go ahead, envy us, that's why we're here" — once you know that, you will understand how Anna's demise had upset the social order. Possibly forever. Fear truly had gone viral in Weycombe if it had penetrated North Cliff. Once the plague of random murder burrowed its way in, presumably from London, it was a matter of months before desperate housewives would be found with their pearls missing and their throats cut. Or so the reasoning went.

I did learn that Anna had become a regular at the Pilates classes, part of her sudden devotion to health and well-being. It was out of character and I said as much to Becky, one of the trainers I'd hired for a few weeks last spring to check me out on some new equipment. Anna had gone from drinking red wine for her health to adopting a Hollywood starlet fitness regime.

"You're right," Becky said. "We usually get the sudden converts right after the holidays — New Year's resolutions and all." Becky was such an energetic, gee-whiz type

I could usually only stand a few minutes in her company. She stood feet apart, one hand gripping the other, flexing her biceps, a stance I knew was second nature. She was a devotee of isometric exercise and wasted no time just standing around like a normal person; she always had to be flexing something. She looked like she wanted to punch me but she always looked like that. She wore her hair in a braid that fell over one shoulder and she'd gelled her thick eyebrows into two dark wings, adding to her warrior princess look. She was rumored to be dating Frabizio, another personal trainer at the club. One could only begin to imagine the bouts of gladiatorial coupling that went on between two such perfect physical specimens.

"They say there's a witness," Becky added. "God, I hope they catch whoever did this. I told Frabizio I'm not going out at night again until they do."

Anna had been killed in broad daylight, but I let that pass. Besides, if anyone attacked Becky I had no doubt she could beat them senseless. "Really? Who says?"

She pulled the *Chronic* out of her gym bag — actually, a new, stop-the-presses flier with "facts" not yet posted on their website. The intern must have had trouble getting his retainer in or something, making him late for work.

"I wouldn't put a lot of faith in what you read there," I said. "They don't have a big enough staff to do anything but rehash hearsay." Some months before, they had rejected my application for part-time work, so I was not their biggest fan, true. But what I told Becky also was true. As mentioned, the police were not going to confide any juicy clues in those guys.

There had been nothing in that morning's national tabloids or broadsheets about a witness — I'd already stopped in at the village shop to buy whatever news was going. The bigger news guys had run with a short bio of the victim, with promises of more to come. How strange to hear Anna described as a victim, and stranger still to hear her called a "real property tycooness." Now here was the *Chronic* stating that "an eyewitness has reported seeing someone in a blue jacket or short blue coat having words with Anna amidst angry gestures." Which meant Garvin the tortoise had scooped the hares of London.

Who uses words like "amidst," anyway? It sounded like something Garvin would say, although I wouldn't credit he'd actually make up quotes. Mishear them, yes. He was notoriously hard of hearing, a fact reflected in some of his weirder stories, a hardship compounded by his scattershot efforts at proofreading. One locally famous headline had announced a reward for a lost doge.

But who had I heard using the word "amidst" recently? It had been one afternoon in the coffee shop . . . That's right: Frannie Pope, the owner of Serendipity, our local little shop of fashion horrors. She was the woman I thought I'd seen at a distance walking her dogs. Surely she had been too far away to see much.

Frannie was rumored to be in some sort of relationship with the doddering Garvin, which I tried not to think about.

I took the paper from Becky and read through it all again slowly. It was no use pretending indifference; I was as keen for news as anyone who knew Anna, which was pretty much everyone in the village. Just as I thought: the bit about the eyewitness was probably the purest wishful thinking on Garvin's part.

"A woman walking her dogs," I said. "That could be anyone, of course."

"You're right. The only odd thing around here would be to see someone not walking their dogs. Everyone but me seems to have one."

"And me," I pointed out. "I never had the time before. Maybe I do now."

I wandered off to do my routine — a few biceps curls here, and a stomach crunch there, and forty minutes on the treadmill. The dog walker was almost certainly Frannie, and dropping in on her to get her account firsthand would be a breeze.

Across the weight room I spotted our resident professional beauty, Macy Rideout, staring in the mirror as she lifted thirty pounds over her head. Every male eye in the place followed the way the movement lifted her boobs. Either Macy had adopted a "life goes on" attitude or she'd not yet heard about Anna. I thought I might talk with her at some point. She and Anna had once been close, although something had gone off there.

Back in the locker room, peeling Spandex away from my Jockey bikini no-shows, I stopped, one leg hovering in midair. My mind had lighted on the image of Anna as she lay dead, and on that glimpse of lace peeking out of her running shorts. For some reason that old Cole Porter "Anything Goes" song came to mind. Something about stockings . . .

And I realized what had bothered me about that flash of frilly lace at the time.

Who runs in expensive lace undies?

Where was she running to?

I got showered and changed and left the gym. As soon as I was outside and out of earshot of the late arrivals for the Zumba class (divorcees going through the spin cycle; you can always tell), I rang the person I most wanted to see right then, the one person I called "friend" in Weycombe. A woman trustworthy, reliable, and always up for a chat over tea or coffee and, with any luck, pastry. Rashima Khan.

7

The Great Book Club Schism began with Stephen Hawking's history of time. Or maybe it was a book by a British politician. Whatever. It ended on a night months later with everyone storming out in a strop. No one had the will to go on with it after that, so it was said. And no one was ever quite sure what had gone wrong, with the possible exception of Anna. And Macy Rideout.

The essential quarrel was not over the book itself but over whether we should all be forced to read it, a fight that shifted into a wide-ranging argument about freedom of speech. There was a camp that wanted to read something "nice," like the newest woman-in-jeopardy story, and a camp that was done with nice (*"Where Are the Editors?"* had been my quip, and "What's nice about that?" had, presciently, been Anna's) and had wanted to read a debate over the loopholes in the Magna Carta. Most of us, at the end of a long day, could not give a fuck about the Magna Carta. I think it was Macy, aka Racy Macy, who held out for a James Patterson.

I maintain that Hilary Mantel, a compromise choice, was the one who did us in. Not her, but the theme of high-stakes infidelity that ran throughout her tale of divorce. Her book ended the Weycombe Court Book Club — pow, just like that, a club that had been going for years — and looking back, I realized what I had only suspected at the time: the choice of book was a pretext, a way not to discuss the deeper, darker things scurrying beneath the placid surface of Weycombe. Things that lurked and wouldn't quite come into view, like those ghostlike ruins in the duck pond. These women — at least two of them — loathed one another and were in a never-ending struggle for supremacy over houses, cars, wardrobes, and most of all the men who provided them these things.

The final scuffle began almost immediately after the Rideouts' wedding announcements went out and reached a climax when Barry and Macy Rideout moved into their palace overlooking the Wey. Before, there had been very few problems. Half the books we read for club were crap but no one had minded much. We were there for the food and wine, anyway. Now suddenly we had ladies going to the mat over the selections, and, quite noticeably, the suggestions for upcoming choices were becoming very intellectual. Higher than Booker Prize highbrow. When Thomas Hardy and George Eliot were invoked, it did occur to me this might be a ploy to drive Macy out of the club, with Anna, her former champion, heading up the committee to oust her. Neither woman was a towering intellect — none of us were, really — but the choice of what to read next wasn't the point. The point likely was that Anna had reigned supreme for so long, and Macy had only just arrived, and she looked amazing, and she had snagged a millionaire on her looks alone, as if that were something new. And for some reason the force of her personality made the other women fall before her like bowling pins, a situation Anna could no longer tolerate. It may have been especially galling for Anna since she was the one who had invited Macy to join us, never dreaming.

Never dreaming.

Anna used to pair up with Macy for a morning run, but this was before Macy and her solicitor fiancé moved to their restored manor house in North Cliff. Both women had worn black spandex on those occasions, Macy looking like a black spider with boobs and Anna like a chunky house burglar. As the weather grew colder, Anna added a bright orange trackie to her wardrobe, an unfortunate choice as Halloween grew near. I'm sure she bought it intending to have lost fifteen pounds before she became a living reminder of the season. When she died, it was in a new blue outfit I didn't recognize, the maker's logo a shiny silver to match her shoes.

Not that this was one of those times when what you wore really mattered, but the blue had been a big improvement.

Anne did all her running and Pilates training in the morning, the only free time in her busy day. By ten thirty she'd be at her desk, or meeting potential prospects at a house that was on the market, or attending a meeting at a solicitor's office for the final conveyance of a property. But by the time she got herself murdered, she had long since parted ways with Macy, her running mate.

I couldn't pretend it was a big loss when Macy moved away. I'd gotten to know her and Barry only superficially before they left the Court for their even more impressive digs. I'd invited them to one of my summer cookouts, where I'd done my best to replicate the foods of my native land. What had started as a housewarming party became an annual event, but try finding anything like a hot dog bun in Waitrose; the closest I could come up with were baps cut in half. Hamburgers translated well, although the Brits did this weird thing of wanting "salad cream" on theirs, a sort of gelatinous faux mayonnaise. Dijon mustard was another of their innovations but I decided it was an improvement. The Court Cookout with its endless pours of wine went over well and became a yearly nod to Britain's brief summer.

In calling on Rashima Khan I was killing several birds with one stone. Not only had she been in the book club, but she'd known Anna for at least a decade. She also had a sharp eye for detail and an ear for nuance. Maybe she knew something that could direct the police to a theory of who had killed Anna, and why. The why was always so important.

I also just felt like a chat. The whole Anna business had left me feeling at a loose end. Will, of course, was useless for restoring my spirits. But I could usually count on Rashima. The ability to calm people, to put things into perspective, was her gift. She would sometimes comment on how together she thought *I* was, but that was just Rashima being loyal, another of her gifts.

Will did not really approve of my friendship with her. I felt it was some vestige of British Empire chauvinism, some bullshit like that, although he'd rather die than admit it. So going to see her always felt like a tiny, harmless, but liberating break for freedom.

The Khans' house was directly across the crescent from Anna's, and apart from the fact Anna had more of a mock Tudor vibe going with her front window panes, the houses were mirror images. Rashima's kitchen faced directly into the Monroes', and her master bedroom into their master bedroom. Rashima told me more than once she wished Anna would remember to draw the curtains.

"Good curtains make good neighbors," she'd say. "And I don't need to know every blow-by-blow in that marriage."

I took this to mean Anna and Alfie weren't getting along, which would now be grist for Milo's mill. I wasn't going to be the one to tell him unless for some reason it became necessary. I liked Alfie and wanted to protect him; he was already under suspicion just by dint of being the husband.

I pounded the lion's-head knocker on the Khans' door. Rashima would generally be working on her blog this time of day so she'd be wearing headphones, listening to the sounds of ocean waves or coffee shop noises or whatever gave her focus. But I guessed she would welcome the interruption. Rashima was tenderhearted — probably in mourning for Anna and not getting a lot of work done.

Work for Rashima was writing an online beauty blog. It was supported one hundred percent by advertising and in an ocean of such offerings, hers had risen near the top. Her stand against wasteful eye shadow quads, for example, was the stuff of legend.

Still, the *Huffington Post* had little to worry about. Rashima told me once that as sole proprietor she cleared about forty thousand pounds a year, after taxes, "but that doesn't include labor, which is nearly every waking hour." She was one of those who inspired me to go and do likewise but I could not for the life of me think what I was an expert on, enough to convince advertisers to support me or, better yet, buy me out within a month. And I was not really interested in working "nearly every waking hour." Sometimes I thought it might be difficult to say what I was interested in enough to work that hard. I was a skilled videographer, a talent honed at the BBC, but I had come to regard that as more of a pastime. I wanted to write — but what, I didn't yet know. Anna's death gave me the glimmerings of an idea.

Rashima and her husband, Dhir, a psychiatrist, were the only people of color living in Weycombe Court, and practically the only people of color anywhere near the village not in council flats. The depressing estate that housed those needing government assistance was hidden from yuppie gaze beyond a hill, far from the River Wey.

The Khans were in an arranged marriage that spoke volumes for the wisdom of the old system. Rashima had trusted her parents to find her a suitable mate, and they had done so. It was the same story from his side, presumably. They were compatible because it was in their natures, possibly, or because shrinks like Dhir always had happy marriages (a less-likely theory), or just because the fates had smiled on them both. I envied her the lack of strife and miscommunication in her courtship story, those staples of the romance novel, and what appeared, on the surface at least, to be the promise of a lifetime of emotional and financial security.

God only knows what my father would have chosen for me as a mate. Someone who would have sold me into white slavery, at a guess. Anything to get me out of his sight. My mother would have chosen more from the heart. And isn't that as bad as one's choosing for oneself?

Dhir was a hulk of a man working in what seemed to be a very profitable profession. Apparently there were a lot of disturbed but wealthy people in the world. I am judging by the fact the Khans' house sat on the largest lot in Weycombe Court, complete with a small swimming pool in the back. The Khans were well liked on their own merits as friendly, self-possessed neighbors, but people would spoil it by liking them in obsequious, toadying, politically correct ways. To be fair, centuries of discrimination needed to be made up for, and madly overcompensating seemed the least people could do.

Rashima had been a beauty editor at the *Globe.* Anticipating that her job would be outsourced to a syndicate, she had slipped easily into her new career at home. Some people are like that: cats who always land on their feet while the rest of us are stuffed in sacks to be drowned. Because she got a ton of free samples from manufacturers, her bathroom always looked like the cosmetics counter at Harrods. That she gave these samples away to anyone who asked made her very popular in the neighborhood. She had introduced me to Estée Lauder's "Madness" line, for which I'm still grateful. She made videos on how to apply makeup; I helped her light and edit them on occasion.

"People think beauty product reviews are a joke but people care about this stuff," she'd say. "And if readers even suspect I'm promoting a product only to get more freebies, I'm done. If a mascara brand smudges, it smudges, and I've a sworn duty to tell people the truth about it so they don't waste their money."

"I wish politicians had your integrity," I would say solemnly. Even though red lipstick and protection from search and seizure weren't comparable, she had a point. We all live downstream.

I picked up a tube of mascara and reared back when I saw the price sticker. *"Holy crap."*

"Yeah, I know. About the right price for an experimental cancer treatment. For a mascara, not so much."

"You're not kidding."

"From talking with Heather, I've been inspired to do a few posts on beauty solves you can find in your own kitchen. Using lemon as a clarifier and coconut oil to remove makeup are no-brainers, right?"

"If Heather has anything to do with it, I'd say that's a given."

Heather lived next door to the Khans. "Inspired" and "Heather" were not words often used in the same sentence. Heather had also been invited into the book club on her arrival in Weycombe Court, a kindness one and all had come to regret. She tended to plump for how-to books on how to build a compost heap.

This was the usual witless chitchat Rashima and I went in for. I'd sit at ease in the colorful, plush surroundings of her living room and feel time and care slip away as the aroma of spices and baked goods wafted from her kitchen.

But on this day we sat grimly across from each other at her breakfast bar, Rashima preoccupied like all of Weycombe with Anna's death. We dove into the sort of mournful speculation that would become a staple of village conversations in the days to come.

"Dhir doesn't think it was a random killing," Rashima finally said. "A crazed killer on the loose or anything like that."

"Really? How so?"

"He thinks he would know if there was someone like that living around here. They'd stick out like a sore thumb."

Dhir was pretty bright, so that was reassuring. "That's not to say it wasn't some crazy passing through," I said.

"I know. I suppose we'll all be looking over our shoulders now. The world is just so changed."

"I'm not going to get any sleep for a long time," I said.

"Me neither. By the way, did you see that person Dhir recommended? About the insomnia?"

As part of my enticing layoff package, the BBC had offered free counseling and job placement assistance. Dhir had endorsed one of the names on the list they'd provided.

"A few times, yes. It was helpful."

It was not, not really, but I didn't want to go into it. The gesture of asking had been well intended, but Rashima wasn't one to pry. She changed the subject.

8

"So, tell me what happened." Rashima clicked shut the lid on her laptop and offered me coffee, admitting she wasn't getting much work done. "Exactly as it happened."

I settled in to tell her as much as I could about the murder scene, tossing in a few theories. Finally I faltered, telling her I had no clue. "And I need to know. You know?"

"You're trying to find out who did it, aren't you?" Eyes wide and eyebrows up. This was Rashima's concerned face. Why would she assume I was snooping around in some amateur-sleuth way? Well, because she knew me pretty well: I had enjoyed my former job rehashing old true crime cases. I'd been good at it.

I pointed out that given I was the one to discover Anna's body, I had extra motivation. I didn't mention that Milo had found my presence on the path that morning to be a concerning coincidence, missing the point that I was always there at about that time of day. If anything, Anna's workout usually came earlier. I seldom saw her.

I said as much now to Rashima, adding, "I've been out walking every day for ages now and I know the regulars who head out when I do. She was not on her usual schedule. She'd been on this health kick for what — a few months?"

Rashima gave the question her most solemn consideration, her fingernails, painted white to match her computer, tapping on the computer lid.

"More," she said. "Anna had become way more interested in her appearance. She was always a bit like that, though."

"Vain," I supplied.

"Vain," she agreed. "Always shopping, with packages from high-end merchants being delivered to her door almost daily. Always in a new outfit with matching everything. And matchy-matchy is so last year."

"She was in real estate," I pointed out. "You can't show a house in ripped jeans and a T-shirt."

"True." Rashima paused. "Exactly how much did you . . . ? You know — see?"

"Of the body? Not a lot. She was mostly hidden by trees and bushes. Pure chance I saw her at all. Then . . . I saw enough to see she was dead."

"Dead, how?"

"Strangled, at a guess. The police were not in a confiding mode. Just by the look of . . . you know. Her eyes. I think she was strangled with that scarf she wore around her hair when she ran. That boho thing."

"She must have been so terrified." Rashima's slim shoulders moved delicately beneath the shimmering white fabric of her blouse. She was trembling, probably putting herself in Anna's runners, imagining her fear. That was Rashima all over.

"Must have been," I said solemnly. "It's a very — well, personal way to kill someone. You have to really hate them, I guess." I picked up another sample from the array scattered near her laptop — a salmon-pink eye shadow — and wondered what member of the human race that color would flatter.

"There was a certain manic quality to her behavior recently, I thought. Dhir thinks so, too."

I put down the eye shadow and looked across at her. "Manic? Manic how?"

Rashima shrugged. "Like there was something big on her horizon? Something that she wanted very badly? Someone in particular she was trying to impress? I don't know.

Anyway, maybe 'obsessive' is a better word. She started talking about plastic surgery and she was years away from needing that."

I nodded my agreement. That porcelain skin. It would be a sacrilege to start cutting into that before time.

"Maybe she had a younger competitor. I don't mean for Alfie's attentions — that's really hard to imagine. He adored her. I mean, a competitor at the office."

Rashima settled back into her chair, crossed her arms, and said, "Usually, when a woman is feeling insecure about her looks, she wears too much makeup — the worst thing you can do, of course. It ages you. I saw her one day the other week and it just looked ladled on. I told her to stop by, that I had some new samples she could try. I was trying to steer her toward a look that was less *Phantom of the Opera,* if you know what I mean."

I thought of one of my last sightings of Anna, outside of our early morning confabs over the recycle bin, when neither of us had anything on our faces but No. 7 night cream on mine and the high-priced spread on hers. She had been dressed for the office in a too-short, pop art wrap dress that showed off her chunky knees and too much black eyeliner, with fake eyelashes. Welcome back,

Mary Quant and the swinging sixties.

"I do know what you mean," I said. "So, did she come over for a consult?"

"No. You know how it is. No one has time to just drop in and chat. Present company excepted."

The blade on that point was unintentionally sharp. It must have shown in my expression.

"Sorry," she said. "I'd forgotten for the moment you were out of a job. I've been there. It sucks."

"But you landed on your feet. Overnight, practically."

"It just looks that way. I'd actually been planning my move for a long time."

Point taken — don't let anyone blindside you. Take charge; plan ahead.

She poured us both more coffee as we continued circling over the bones of Anna's life and death.

"Who would do such a thing?" Rashima asked for probably the twelfth time that morning. She looked as if she might have been crying earlier, and the fine skin around her doe eyes was crinkled with concern. It was not in her philosophy that human beings killed each other, and human beings known to her did not die violent deaths. She was genuinely shocked. Her small hands as she held her coffee trembled.

"I dunno," I said. "I think it could have been any number of people, don't you?"

"Oh, Jill, I —"

I waved away her protests. If we were going to get anywhere with this conversation there was no room for hypocrisy, and I told her as much. "I'm sorry to have to say it. But if anyone could provoke jealousy and envy, it was Anna. And it wasn't accidental or unintentional. She had to know someone was going to get hurt because of her sleeping around. I mean, come on. You know it; I know it. And the police don't need platitudes from us, not if they're going to solve her murder."

"I know. You're right. Of course you're right. But still, you should leave this to the police. You didn't even like her much."

"You don't have to like someone to be invested in solving their murder," I pointed out. "A lot of innocent people may get dragged into this." Rashima and Dhir in particular. Even though they'd lived in England for ages, they were outsiders, like me. How much would it take to start a witch hunt, I wondered? Not much. "And a killer remains at large in the village. Doesn't that worry you?"

"God, yes. It freaks me out. Dhir, too, if

you want the truth. He's getting a locksmith over to replace some of the locks." This idea made her look even more downcast. "But you are so good to be thinking of others like this. You should —"

I cut across this tribute to my goodness. "You caught her act at Racy Macy's garden party. The fundraiser."

The Rideouts had held a party for our local MP at their manor house not long after they'd moved in — a housewarming combined with a genteel shakedown for funds. This was, I believe, where Anna had met the candidate for the first time. By some quirk of fate or, more likely, a miscalculation of our net worth on someone's part — for this party was for the serious money — Will and I had been invited to the same party. That said, Will always got invited places because of his title. I saw the sparks fly between Macy and our man in parliament — no mistaking it.

"Flirting with Colin?" Rashima sighed — a big, penitent sigh at speaking ill of the dead. "Yes, you and I both saw it. It was most indiscrete of us to notice. And of her, of course, to carry on as she did. But then she had had a lot to drink, and —"

"The sparks were flying." I wanted to stop the flow of excuses I knew she would find for Anna's inexcusable behavior, as if being dead gave her a free pass. "And Alfie was right there. In fact I saw him watching, sort of hiding behind his drink but peering at them over the top of his glass. He looked gutted. Livid — for Alfie. Who doesn't really do livid."

I also had overheard Anna telling the MP that Alfie had said if anything should happen to him, she had his permission "to find love again." It was absurd. I would have been willing to bet Alfie never said any such thing — it sounded like something out of a telenovela script — but Anna had added that bait to her tackle box, alongside the false eyelashes. In case her intended target had any moral scruples about extramarital affairs, she'd been inching the door open.

If Alfie had said anything that even came close, he'd probably meant she should wait a decent interval before bonking someone else's spouse. I thought I'd ask Alfie about it one day, not that it mattered. It sounded like the convenient, self-serving sort of lie Anna would tell.

I felt bad tossing Alfie into it like that. The thing was, he was going to be the main murder suspect with or without my help. But this was Rashima I was talking to, not Milo. My plan was to shield Alfie from officialdom — at least for as long as I safely could without getting embroiled myself.

"You don't think . . . ?" Rashima began.

"Alfie? Right now I'm keeping an open mind." Spoken like a true detective. "But he has no alibi for that morning, I'm sure. He was probably just at home. He's always at home."

"You are starting to scare me," she said. The waxed brows over the soulful brown eyes again drew down in concern. "Whoever did this is dangerous — well, obviously. Perhaps mad as a hatter."

"No worries," I said. "I was just speculating."

"No, you weren't. I mean it, Jane Marple. People have been killed for less. They are killed every day over little things like designer shoes and jackets. We don't even know what this is about. Maybe she got on the wrong side of some bad people in a business deal. Mafia types. Maybe she cut someone off in traffic. Or maybe some lunatic who thought she looked like his ex-wife happened to see her in that ad — that video you made of her."

"Maybe it's an ex-lover," I said. "Now, there's a wide-open field for you."

"Yes, an ex-lover perhaps. A madman so full of hatred he doesn't even know what he's doing."

"Or madwoman. Most of her lovers probably had wives or girlfriends."

"Well, yes, of course! That is my point. It could be anyone."

I patted her arm reassuringly.

"No worries," I said again. "Say — didn't Anna broker the deal when Macy and Barry sold their old place and moved? I mean, I know she did. But weren't there some problems along the way?"

"I heard there were," said Rashima, "but I wasn't really plugged into all that. What I recall is that their old house sold well before the manor house was ready for them to move into, and Macy was really pissed off about it. It should have been built into the contract that they couldn't settle the agreement before a certain date — before they had a chance to pack up properly and move. But it wasn't and the contractor they sold to held their feet to the fire."

"That's right," I said. "They ended up staying in a hotel for six weeks. I guess that would tick me off, too."

"The added expense, sure. Plus Barry's dream of carrying his bride into the castle he'd readied for her was derailed, or at least postponed. Yes."

"And there was some tension over the asking price for their old place — Anna told them it was too high, and it was," I said. "Barry can be a bit full of himself. But that all got smoothed over. Didn't it?"

"Beats me. Macy and Barry gradually pulled up the drawbridge after that and I didn't see them as much. But killing Anna over a slightly botched business deal, if that's what you're reaching for? Not possible."

"Who else is a possibility then?" I asked, noticing that Rashima was getting into the swing of things, speculating right alongside me.

"Anna had been chummy with Heather lately," she said. "And I only tell you that because I can no more imagine Heather killing someone than I can imagine her, oh, I don't know. Getting a degree in astrophysics."

"I don't know," I said. "I think you can bore someone to death. Before you use them for compost, that is."

Rashima, knowing how I felt about Heather, smiled, but her face soon fell back into frown position: *This is no joking matter.* "I'm serious, Jillian. We must be serious. And you must be careful if you plan to go around asking questions. You never know when you might be asking the wrong person."

The Mafia hiding in plain sight in Weycombe, probably holing up in Riverside Park. Right. I nodded and looked her straight in the eye, as if I were planning to take her advice.

"Just don't corner anyone alone, all right?" she added.

"I'll be careful. But in your shoes, I'd be thinking what to tell the police, Rash. Your house overlooks hers; you saw Anna's comings and goings, her packages being delivered. You could even see right into her bedroom half the time, so the police will be asking what you know. It's probably best to say as little as possible."

"Well, unless they want to know she overwatered her plants, I've got nothing."

"Good. Okay." But did she hesitate for a moment? Yes, she did. "I'm not telling you what to do," I said. "I'm telling you what *I* would do. That's different."

"No, it's not. It's not different in the least. You may not plan to tell the police anything but you do plan to insert yourself into this somehow." The eyebrows settled back into a frown and stayed there. It was Rashima who had introduced me to the mysteries of things like eyebrow threading, not that I bothered to follow her more esoteric advice, but I was always fascinated to be reminded there was a world of women out there who had been born knowing this stuff. It was encoded in their DNA, and when my ancestors surely had been fighting over the last root vegetable in their barren plots of land, theirs had been lounging about harems or dancing with French kings. I envied them but I could never emulate them.

Now she said, "You will be drawing attention to yourself with this . . . this investigation. And you've no idea what might crawl out of that hole you're digging."

Okay, okay. "Anna is dead as in *murdered.* Aren't you at least a bit curious who did it? If only because there's a killer out there who for all we know may be randomly targeting women on the path?"

"No, I'm not. Because I agree with Dhir that this wasn't random. If you're smart you'll stay out of what you don't understand and let the police handle it."

She did know something, I was sure of it. Or had reason to suspect — something. I looked at her, trying to decide the best way to prize out whatever information resided inside that keen and very private brain of hers.

"Yes, yes, okay," I said. "Just tell me and

I'll leave you alone: who else crossed Anna's path, in a bad way?"

Rashima paused, stirring brown sugar into her coffee. "Arty Frannie would know a lot more about what Anna got up to. She was that dog walker in the paper, in case you didn't know."

"No, I didn't know, but I had a hunch. How did you come to find out?"

"Jill, you have got to get out more. She practically held a media conference at her shop this morning. Not with the media but with anyone who stopped by. She probably figured it would be good for business."

"She was probably right."

"Arty" Frannie Pope was the one I told you about, the woman who owned a boutique in the village called Serendipity. People made the necessary transposition of letters in her name, putting that *F* where they liked, as they felt pro or con about Frannie and her shop. Divorced, with dyed black hair skinned back from her brow, she sported a perpetual tan and the wrinkles that went with it. She looked mummified.

She also had a house in Weycombe Court — one of the more expensive units, which I thought impressive for a single woman. I always assumed she'd received a good divorce settlement because it was hard to see how her shop alone supported her lifestyle.

She had a seat on the parish council, and had bonded with Anna over some village fundraising event intended to save whatever was endangered and needed saving that week. Somewhere in her past, Frannie had worked as a professional moneymaker, organizing silent auctions, dances, and golfing events. She was the sort of person who was good at the "ask," which is the part most people — perhaps most especially British people — balk at. Asking for money is just not done. I wondered idly if she'd been involved in fundraising for our local MP and filed that question away for later.

I knew Anna was one of Frannie's best customers for the bohemian scarves and jewelry she sold in her shop, goods heavily imbued with a gypsy or Native American vibe. I would bet anything that boho scarf of Anna's, now stashed in an evidence locker somewhere, came from Serendipity. Frannie also sold a lot of turquoise jewelry she got from a wholesale outfit in Albuquerque, where she traveled once a year on shopping trips. Frannie was as indigenous to New Mexico as I was — which is to say, not at all. I think she was originally Australian. But with her black hair, dark eyes, and the tan, she passed pretty well, even with a last name like Pope.

"And then there's Heather," said Rashima. "It's an odd thing, but I did see Anna over at her house more than once lately."

"I know, and it *is* odd. What did those two find to talk about? Subprime mortgages?"

Rashima must have seen my eyes light up. "Be careful, Jill," she said again.

"You don't really think Heather . . . ? You said yourself, she —"

"I don't know what to think anymore."

9

It actually had occurred to me already that Heather might know something worth knowing (for a change). She was Rashima's near neighbor and a stay-at home mom. While she didn't have as clear a view into Anna's place as Rashima did, the fact she spent much of her waking life in the kitchen making porridge or whatever gave her more opportunity than Rashima to notice what was going on across the crescent. Like Rashima, I'd seen Anna going into her house a couple of times lately. Knowing the police would probably talk with Heather eventually, I thought I might get in there first.

Heather Cartwright had retired to full-time mummyhood from a brief career in human resources for a large retailer. Selfridges, I think it was. I can best describe her by saying that she patronized shops in Weycombe like the Cannery on High for herbs and jars and labels, as well as the Sew-Sew shop, where I understand you can buy calico and quilting supplies. I have never been entirely sure what calico is, but that's certainly where I'd go to look for some. It was Heather who introduced me to Mod Podge, saying it would change my life.

Physically, Heather was a big bear of a girl, flat-chested but tall and broad and imposing, with a habit of standing feet wide apart and arms akimbo, like a warrior queen atop a mythical lost mound in Ireland. You couldn't knock Heather over with a wrecking ball. It was as if she compensated for being so masculine in appearance by being determinedly domesticated, practiced if not skilled in all the womanly arts of hearth and home.

Philosophically she was a back-to-the-land type whose native habitat was the Saturday farmer's market on the green. There she would trot from vendor to vendor swinging a woven shopping basket covered with, I kid you not, a red gingham cloth, like a British Laura Ingalls Wilder. Her husband, Gideon, was the son of a well-known merchant banker in London; Heather was his second wife, playing against every stereotype. His first wife had been an actress who died in a freak accident playing Peter Pan — the wires holding her up had failed; big scandal — and the general theory was that marrying Heather not long afterward was rather like choosing comfort food over spicy takeaway.

What merchant bankers do all day remains a mystery to me. In the US they call them investment bankers, but it's no clearer what they get up to, and I'm sure they like it that way: better we don't ask too many questions as our money disappears down whatever sinkhole they've created for the world that week.

Gideon's father lived in nearby Watermill, and he and my husband knew each other slightly from being in the same profession. Will often would return from the Bull saying he'd bought the old man a beer, but possibly because they worked for competing organizations they kept a certain distance. They may have been worried about charges of collusion or something. As I say, that world is a mystery to me, and the spreadsheets I saw Will poring over might as well have been written in Sanskrit. It provided us with a comfortable if not luxurious income, and freed us from total reliance on Will's family, and for that I was grateful.

Apart from enjoying the occasional foxhunt, Heather's Gideon had turned his back on the world of his father to become a university lecturer specializing in foreign affairs. He had written a book I did not understand and would be willing to bet no one else understood either, but it was hailed as a masterpiece. "Makes accessible the recent history of the Middle East," as one reviewer put it, which, to give all credit due, really is saying something. Will and I went to Gideon's book signing on a boat chartered for the occasion and of course we bought a copy, but I don't believe either of us ever cracked the spine on it. It sat on our bookshelves making us look intelligent and concerned about the state of the world. I donated it to the library when I left Weycombe.

Gideon appeared on the BBC News in those days, sweating lightly through his makeup and pushing his Harry Potter glasses up his nose when he wanted to emphasize a particularly obscure point. The glasses I'd long suspected were less for viewing and more for enhancing the professorial stereotype. This included the standard tweed jacket with leather elbow patches. He was younger than Heather by a year or two, and how such an intellectual had landed himself with such a major twit was one of life's mysteries. Perhaps he found her company soothing after skirmishing with backstabbing eggheads all day.

He did travel a good deal for research, and I gathered his teaching duties were somewhat perfunctory and limited essentially to guest appearances. This left Heather with lots of time on her hands. Other women might seize the opportunity to have an affair or take up kickboxing. Heather knitted, canned, and cleaned. Too often she had only her child for company, and I don't suppose when Gideon *was* around Heather understood half of what he was saying.

I knocked at her door, not surprised to see she was taking part in the wreath-hanging competition that gripped the village each season. Right now every other door featured fallen leaves and small decorative pumpkins and the occasional bat with ruby eyes. Heather's contribution was an eyesore because she could never bring herself to leave well enough alone — a twiggy confection shot through with acorns and seashells painted brown and orange.

As I followed her into her kitchen I saw she was, swear to God, ironing tea towels as something like a witch's cauldron simmered on the stove. Nearby in an apple-green high chair sat one-year-old Lulu, engaged in her usual pastime of eating mashed something or other. If it wasn't mashed already you could be sure it would be by the time Lulu'd smeared it all over her face. This time it looked like oatmeal but of an *Exorcist* color and consistency — organic and all-natural, of course. Heather did everything but milk her own goats, and that was only because the homeowners' association forbade anyone's keeping livestock.

Before she'd put her people skills to use in human resources, Heather had been a retail professional. I think she worked behind the counter at Boots. That talent seemed to have carried over well into her life as Lulu's mother. There was a constant busyness to Heather's existence, and an innate order applied to everything she owned. While I had not seen her closet, you could be certain her sweaters were rolled just so and sorted according to season and color. Each spring, she would seal the heaviest sweaters and coats into vacuum bags and store them in the attic until autumn. I told myself I was way too busy for that but to be honest, I just did not see the point. A jumper thrown on a chair is still there to be found the next day. It's not like stuff moves around on its own.

A loom crouched in one corner of

Heather's living room, a great whacking thing of shuttles and knobs. I don't think she'd touched it for a while. At least, every time I saw it the same shaggy cloth was emerging from its innards. She made all her own Christmas presents from ideas she copied from Pinterest and Etsy, and if you were unlucky, she'd weave or decoupage something for you.

Lulu let out a giddy, ear-piercing shriek at the sight of me.

"Is it just me or is she just the cutest thing ever?" Heather asked of no one in particular (certainly not me), looking adoringly at her oatmeal-crusted offspring. She rested the iron on its heel while she settled a new dish-towel in place of the old one. I can't tell you the last time I ironed a blouse, let alone a fucking tea towel. I engaged in a mini-staredown with Lulu, who at that moment had a big drool of something coming out of her lopsided features. She looked like a miniature sumo wrestler clad in gingham and lace, and she seemed to be adding a few new rolls of baby fat to her middle even as we sat watching her, as if she were the subject of a slo-mo documentary on child-hood obesity.

It's just you, Heather.

"She's a charmer," I said brightly. "Reminds me of her dad." The last part at least was true. Her father had gifted Lulu with the chubby face, the Buddha-like build, and mounds of curly dark red hair. This last really was a gift, as Heather's own hair was stringy as a cobweb. But she was a busy mum, too busy to fuss with her hair, as she never tired of telling everyone who would stay to listen. She was also too busy to fuss with her wardrobe, which always looked like something knotted together out of dried rainforest plants. Lulu had a lot to overcome; I hoped I wouldn't be around to witness the teen years.

Of course, Heather and I had to spend the next five minutes discussing the mystery of birth, with particular reference to the miracles of reproduction and heredity and the DNA markers that had gone into producing such a specimen as Lulu, before I could finally get down to business. But while Heather seemed to be aware there had been a murder in the village — a murder of someone she knew personally, mind — she evinced more interest in her dishtowels.

"Did you get any sense," I finally got to ask, "that Anna was preoccupied in the days leading up to her death?"

I must have sounded even to Heather's ears like a documentary on police procedure, for she stopped making funny faces at Lulu and turned, giving me her full attention at last. Lulu aimed a cross-eyed look of unqualified contempt at her mother's back, then grinned at me as if I were her favorite co-conspirator.

"Preoccupied?" Heather repeated.

"You know. Worried. Sad. Distracted. Or happy, even. Manic. Was there something going on in her life, did you sense? Because — and forgive me, I may be wrong — I never had the impression you and she had much in common. And yet I noticed she was over here a good deal. I just thought she might have confided in you, given that you were so close."

"I wouldn't say close."

"Okay. What would you say?"

"Friendly."

I could see this was going to be a challenge, and I wished the police very good luck if they interviewed this doorstop. They'd have to take her to the station just to get her away from the ironing board. Lulu made some kind of choking, gurgling sound that pulled Heather's always fleeting attention back to her child, and before we were plunged again into one of Heather's digressions on the virtues of breast milk and whole grains, I said, "Look, let me speak plainly: Anna always had an angle. I mean, we all have one. We all want something from someone. It doesn't mean we're bad people. It means we're people."

Heather nodded along with this simple logic but said nothing, so I prodded her: "What did Anna want from you? Did you get any sense of that?"

"Hmm?"

"Did Anna seem to want something from you?"

"No. Not really."

Sigh. I wasn't sure why I thought she'd know anything. It was more her physical proximity to Anna. That and the occasional recipe exchange at book club, more out of politeness on Anna's part than a sudden interest in marinated tofu, I was sure.

"If you really want to know what's going on," Heather said, the beam of her focus returned to the precious Lulu — it was like trying to hold a conversation with a kitten — "you should talk with Elizabeth."

"Who?"

"Elizabeth Fortescue. I think she and Anna were friendly."

Knowing Anna, she had her eye on the elderly Elizabeth's cottage in case she decided to sell, or anticipated the day Elizabeth would have to go into assisted living.

Anna was like that, always one step ahead of the market.

Heather continued, talking to me but looking at Lulu: "Elizabeth knows where all the bodies in the village are buried. Literally, since she's on the St. Chrysostom's vestry. But you know what I mean. You won't have any trouble finding her — she's at the church every weekday afternoon."

A good tip. I wouldn't have thought of Elizabeth right away, but Heather was right: she was a busybody who had her finger on the pulse. Proving that even Heather had her uses beyond fermenting everything in sight.

"A village Iyanla," I said, nodding.

"Who?"

"As in, Iyanla, stay the hell out of my life."

"Who's Iyanla?"

"She's on Oprah. She's — oh, sort of an expert on everything. Particularly other people's business."

My eyes wandered over to the enormous pot simmering on top of the stove. The table was covered with Mason jars.

"I'm making jam," Heather said, going over to turn down the heat.

"Why? Did Whole Foods burn down?"

"Hmm?"

"Never mind. I'm sure it's delicious. Way

better than any store brand."

"I should think so."

"Although I bought a jar of blueberry preserves on sale at Waitrose last week and it was delicious."

Heather was aghast at this heresy, as I knew she would be. "I think a lemon is the last thing I bought at Waitrose," she said, "and that was months ago. Did you know lemon is a natural degreaser?"

"No. Myself, I prefer to use harsh chemicals that pollute the environment."

I gave her a moment to study my expression and figure out that I was kidding. Heather kept information like that stored in a tin neatly labeled "Social Interactions: Visual Cues."

I looked around as I waited for those gears to kick in. The kitchen was of course organized and homey, with each item in its own indexed container. It was as if a team of stagers arrived nightly to arrange the wooden cooking spoons just so in their white ceramic jars, to mist the leaves of the potted herbs on the sill, and to squeegee the sparkling windows. I wondered how long the perfection would last once Lulu began to walk and scream and pull things willy-nilly out of the lower cabinets, but for now her little toys were neatly contained in a single wicker basket in the living room. No surprise, Heather had woven the basket herself.

If I were leading the police investigation she would have my vote for potential suspect in the OCD category, but eventually I got out of her that she had an alibi. She was shopping at the Sew-Sew and had a conversation about how to make a French seam (don't ask, no idea). Then she'd tripped over to the yarn shop, swinging her little shopping basket, followed by a stop at the greengrocers. All easily documented, although in truth, one day's shopping for Heather was much like another. Would the shop owners even be able to verify this?

"Eliza had a sale on interchangeable knitting needles," Heather informed me. She zipped open a little container that held rows of what looked like something you'd see at the dentist's. I made suitable noises to show my awe, throwing in a tinge of envy when she added, "It was the last one on sale."

"Too bad," I said. "My husband will have to wait another year for hand-knitted socks."

It was the wrong thing to say. Heather did not have much of a sense of humor — at least, my comments tended to fly straight past her. As she was always looking for ways to increase her income and self-worth by selling her useless homemade crap, you had to be careful what you wished for. Her preserves for the church fundraiser might have landed a few people in hospital but fortunately the jars exploded prematurely. Before she could say, "I'll make him some if you'd like," I had to fess up that I was kidding.

Lulu had nodded off for a moment, so turning Heather's attention back to the topic of Anna's murder was easy, sort of like peeling open a little box labeled "Dead Anna." It was all anyone wanted to talk about, and that would be true for months to come.

10

"Did you need anything more, Jillian? Because I need to sterilize these jars and change Lulu in time for Baby Play, so I —"

"I guess I was just sort of wondering what your reaction to Anna's murder was. How you were feeling. You know." Even Heather looked a bit skeptical at my sudden concern, and I reminded myself not to underestimate her. Gideon was no dummy and he must have seen something more in her than I ever could. On the other hand, maybe she just catered to his secret bondage fetish. Still, I figured that with Heather, it was best to keep the questions open-ended and my motives for asking vague.

She put down her wooden spoon on a ceramic holder shaped like a little windmill.

"They're really certain it's . . . you know?"

She didn't want Lulu learning a new word like "murder." I nodded.

"I can't believe it. Right here in our

neighborhood, or nearly. What next?"

"I know," I said. "It's all way too close to home. I wonder if you'd seen her lately — to really talk to her at length, I mean? If you had any sense of what was on her mind?"

She shook her head. "Honest — I hardly knew her, really." I knew better but I let it pass. Keep her talking and something useful might pop out. "She was older than me, and interested in different things. You know how it goes."

I did indeed. I imagined that Anna had written Heather off pretty quickly — with Anna, it was always all about Anna, and advancing Anna's own needs and wants. Although she might have seen Heather's semi-famous Gideon as holding some romantic potential: I wondered about that. Just because I couldn't see the attraction in a red-headed Buddha didn't mean it wasn't there.

Heather was funneling something into a jar now. When she informed me she was making her own window cleaner I saw even more clearly why people like Anna had disowned her. I just hoped she didn't mix it in with the jam somehow. It was absurd — I mean, it wasn't as if Heather needed to save money by making her own Windex.

That was true of everyone in Weycombe Court, unless someone was going bankrupt I didn't know about. Anna, for example: she'd never let on anything was wrong but the real estate boom-bust had touched even Weycombe's strong market.

"Funny thing, though," said Heather, judiciously eyeing a measuring cup of white vinegar. "As it happens, I think I do know what was on her mind. Who, I mean." She reached for a bottle of rubbing alcohol.

I perked up. "Really?"

She began shaking the mixture in the spray bottle. "I've been wondering whether to tell someone. It's really none of my business. But if it helps them catch whoever did this . . ."

"Tell me and let me be the judge," I said, adding rather pompously: "It's your civic duty to tell the police what you know — of course you realize that."

"I know. But really, it's nothing specific."

"I was a reporter for ages." A slight exaggeration. "I know how these investigations work. What the investigators are liable to think is important may surprise you."

"That's just it. I really don't want to get dragged into it or drag anyone else in by mistake. It won't bring Anna back, will it?"

"Would you really want her back?"

She stared at me for a moment, letting that sink in. Then a surprisingly feminine little squeak of laughter escaped her. "Anna — yeah. She could be a real Miss Fitch." She casually leaned over and wiped some more effluvia off Lulu's face. "Or worse."

I took a wild guess Miss Fitch was cockney for bitch. Knowing I should not go down that road, I should just ignore her and plow on, I said, "Worse?"

"You know what I mean. Starts with C, rhymes with hunt."

I paused, pretending to have to search the windmills of my own mind.

"Oh," I said, wide-eyed as comprehension dawned. "Well, yeah. But she was pretty nice to me. When I first came here."

"She was nice to everyone. To their faces, anyway. Especially when they were coming or going. You never knew when they might want her to sell their houses for them."

"So, just tell me already," I said, trying not to throttle it out of her. "I promise you, pinky swear, that if it's important, I'll use my media connections to get the word privately to the police. You'll never even have to be mentioned. Unless you're, like, an eyewitness or something. Or you've found a signed confession in your kitchen."

She shook her head. "I'm an eyewitness

but there must be a dozen others. She was involved with . . . someone in parliament. Gideon knows about it, too. Can you see why I have to keep both of us out of it?"

Actually, I didn't see. Of course, I knew about Anna and the MP, but I played dumb. "You don't mean . . . ?"

She was looking really uncomfortable now, clearly wishing she'd said nothing. If her husband was pally with Colin Livingstone, our local up-and-comer and rider to hounds — so what? It was only natural. There was speculation Colin might one day lead his party. In any event, he fancied himself a big expert on Wither Britain, giving him and Gideon lots to talk about. He was an Oxbridge type and like Will he was the real thing, with a pedigree practically going back to King Canute.

"Colin and Anna had something going on," she said quickly, dropping her voice. She looked around the room, as if it might be bugged, or Lulu might be pressing the record button hidden under the seat of her high chair. "Something serious. Gideon is sure of it. And worse, Alfie found out about it."

Of course, I knew as much already, except for the part about Alfie's certain knowledge. How Gideon knew was anyone's guess, but maybe riding to hounds was just an excuse to brag about sexual conquests in the open air. In any event, Anna was not known for her discretion.

"Wow," I said. I wanted to encourage more confidences, not shut Heather down by letting on I knew much of this already.

"You do see the problem?" she asked. "I have to be discreet. At the same time, I have to tell what I know. Anything else would be wrong. Wouldn't it?"

The silence hung so long in the air I realized she was expecting an answer. I am so seldom the go-to person for parsing moral quandaries.

"Yes, that would be wrong," I said.

"But the thing is, I don't *know* know."

I emphasized it was her bounden duty to tell what she knew. "But not until you're sure," I added. "Lives could be wrecked, Heather. Murder investigations are like that. Everybody goes downriver with the victim. By the way, you weren't out walking yesterday by the river, were you?"

It was a clumsy segue in an attempt to test the strength of her shopping story. Because shops like the Sew-Sew don't open early on Mondays. They might not open at all on Mondays, now that I thought about it. Because most women in Weycombe didn't sew their own clothes; they went to London, like normal people, to buy them. I wanted to find out exactly where Heather had been, and when.

"Oh, yes, I forgot: I took the dogs for a walk while Gideon stayed with Lulu. I shudder to think . . . I might have seen something. Oh my God, if I'd known, I might have stopped her being killed. But I might have been killed myself. And then who would take care of Lulu?"

Good question; for sure not me. "You saw nothing of the — you know. Rhymes with herder?"

"I saw nothing."

I sighed. "Bummer."

She launched into a long description of the low-visibility weather that day, and the intermittent sunlight. Then she shrugged, topic closed. Heather was like that. The focus came and went. I decided to leave before she started measuring me for an apron.

"Here," she said, "Take some of this jam with you. I made so much we'll never finish it all."

I soon left Heather to her own early version of *Woman's Hour.* She was clearly anxious for me to go: I had put her behind schedule and she still had her daily wholegrain bake to do. Later that day I deposited her two jars of jam on a shelf at home, intending to wait a suitable interval before throwing the contents down the disposal and returning the jars. She'd made the jam from the berries of Chinese lantern plants, which even I knew was a dicey proposition if you didn't know what you were doing. I wondered vaguely where she'd got the berries from, as none grew in her garden.

11

Heather had given me a few things to think about. The weather had reduced visibility the morning Anna died, which had to be factored in. Heather was either a better actress than I could credit her with being, or, more likely, she had seen nothing worth mentioning during her walk Monday.

Now I was beginning to doubt my own eyes, my own timeline. Was it Frannie I had seen? Or Heather? I only knew for certain it was a rather large woman. Age differences at that distance aren't that apparent unless one of them is either sprinting or hobbling on a cane. If anything, Frannie was more on the spry side than Heather, even though she had a couple of decades on her. Heather tended to lumber about in her Birkenstocks like a groundhog coming out of hibernation.

Heather had two dogs just as Frannie did — medium-size furry things, also some version of golden retriever. Heather's dogs weren't around when I visited. They were elderly, like Frannie's dogs, and may have been at the vet's for a tune-up.

There was also that other person I'd told Milo I'd seen in the distance, making it a rather crowded field out there.

It wasn't yet noon, so I went home to kill some time: I'd decided to take Heather's advice and look up Elizabeth Fortescue that afternoon. I thought about reorganizing my CV in the meanwhile, wondering why I even bothered. I'd been trying to decide if a chronological format made me look more like a loser than a functional arrangement. I'd been in a hiring position myself and I knew the functional style was often used to hide big, ugly gaps in employment history. I hadn't had any ugly gaps until recently; I'd only had jobs I'd hated and didn't want to keep repeating. The problem being, as every job-seeker knows, once you are pegged as one thing you stay one thing. I'd once been a reporter, but a job on a fast-disappearing city desk was exactly what I did not want. If anything, I wanted my old job back at the BBC, and there was no other job like it in the UK. The equivalent slot at ITV was filled and unlikely to open up unless the current incumbent had a heart attack or something. Not likely at the age of twenty-eight.

I spent an hour cutting and pasting and "polishing," but it was no use. As I say, I would have given up the charade entirely if it weren't for the constant and not-so-subtle nudging from Will. ("So, any good leads today?" he would ask, like he was asking some punk teenager about her homework assignment.) Will had a magnificent disregard for the fact that connected though he was, and coddled by his old boys' network, this was not getting me any nearer to employment. He needed to be out there pulling strings for me, not nagging me all the time.

I began to wonder at his insistent harping on the subject. We were in okay shape financially and I knew he could float me a few more months. Years, if he gave up some of his expensive habits, like going to the pub to bullshit the night away. Of course, that was exactly what he did not want to do. My tentative attempts to open a conversation about how I was thinking about a new career path working from home went nowhere. Will considered the whole topic to be some elaborate ruse, a form of navel-gazing designed entirely to help me avoid working. Writing did not count as work in his eyes. To be counted as work it had to be highly paid work, in Will's World, and even I knew only lucky writers made a living wage.

But I'd been steadily employed since Will had known me, never once calling in sick, not even after leaving his bed so exhausted I could hardly blink. Did that count for nothing in his universe? Losing my job had been an unwelcome shock, sure, but I'd wanted — no, *needed* — to get off the hamster wheel for a while, anyway. Before I jumped back on, I had to figure out what I wanted to do for the next thirty-five or so years of my life. Now was the time. When, I wondered, had my dear husband become such a stranger he could not understand that?

I couldn't pinpoint the date, exactly. A year ago? Less. A year ago he had still been my darling William.

And then I'd twisted my ankle and lost my job three months later. Weird Will had come along somewhere in there.

The shrunken income worried him, sure. Being landed gentry didn't pay the way it once had. Sometimes I wondered if he'd lost money in the stock market, some loss I didn't know about.

Maybe he was just embarrassed to have a

wife hanging about at a loose end — a wife who had once been such a high flyer in a glamorous profession. Perhaps that should have worried me more, but what I worried about was that, approaching middle age, I was still finding myself. I felt I was becoming exhibit A in some sociologist's report on the extended childhood of the American post-adolescent. My first layoff back in the US had come as no surprise — anything having to do with the written word was in a do-not-resuscitate spiral. But, in all honesty, I had never given my all to the cause of saving that newspaper. What I most wanted, in my heart of hearts, was to write a book, just like half my colleagues. Up until now I had no idea on what topic, in what genre.

Now Anna, most providentially, had handed me my material. Now, I had a crime to keep tabs on. Could I not turn this material into a book? A sort of fictionalized true-crime story, like *In Cold Blood.* Why not? Who better?

I closed the CV file on my laptop and sat, thinking. Marriage to Will had become like an extended cruise that started out great — all the packing, all the planning, all the looking forward, which the experts say is the whole point of vacations, anyway. I'd once taken a cruise to Greece. It had lasted three weeks, and sitting in the sun for the first week had been just what the doctor ordered. But by the final week I was ready to catch the first freighter out of there.

What could be the problem? All the food you could eat, all the booze you could hold. Movies and a few live shows that passed for entertainment. It must be admitted the entertainment was aimed at some demographic I don't think has been invented yet.

The boredom level was off the charts.

Marriage to Will was like that. You didn't want to toss yourself overboard but you did want off this luxury cruise.

Half an hour later there came a pounding at the door so loud it made the pen fly out of my hand. Kookie bolted from my lap, not to be seen again for hours. I walked over and looked out the vertical row of small windows beside the door. There was my brawny policeman peering in, shading his face with one hand. I pasted on a neutral but obliging expression and opened up.

He was accompanied by the woman I'd seen him with at riverside — the fawning plainclothes cop. She stomped in on her black court shoes ahead of Milo and studied the pictures in the hallway before turning to face me. She wasn't tall but she looked like she could hold a miscreant in a headlock if she felt like it. Fireplug short and squat, she wore her blonde hair in a blunt cut across the nape of her neck and curled under along the jawline. It was a sixties look that suited her but I didn't think it was an attempt at retro irony, more a holdover from her school days. She introduced herself as Detective Attwater in what sounded like a Welsh accent, so I took it as given Attwater was a married name. I came to know her first name was Margaret but I was always careful to call her Detective. Her tight jacket highlighted a bad case of bra bulge, and under the jacket she wore an incongruous pale pink blouse with a pussy bow. She also wore way too much eye makeup and had had her mouth tattooed in permanent lip liner — big mistake.

And she seemed to view my presence in her country as deeply suspicious in and of itself.

But she also seemed to feel that Milo's presence in my living room needed explaining, as he was only a patrolman and this sort of thing was normally a job for the big guys. These police protocols were wasted on me but she spent a few moments clarifying that since he was first on the crime scene and had spoken with me already she had asked him to accompany her on this visit. For all I knew Milo was being groomed for higher office, but he didn't look the sort of man to ever be as happy at a desk as he would be behind the wheel of his little patrol car. I guided him to an easy chair and he sat on the edge of the seat like he might bolt at the first opportunity. She, on the other hand, settled in for a good long natter, accepting my offer of coffee and biscuits as she shoved her solid frame back against the sofa cushions.

Milo refused the coffee. My sense was that he was worried he'd spill it, having to juggle it with the notebook and pen I saw he'd produced from somewhere. Again I spelled my name at his request, and confirmed that I was the neighbor who had found Anna Monroe's body.

"You came to be on the river path how, Mrs. White?" Attwater wanted to know.

"I'm always there. I mean, I walk to Walton-on-Thames and back every day."

"Really." She seemed to think that an extraordinary thing to do, as if I'd admitted to swallowing live goldfish or stuffing clowns into Volkswagens as a hobby. "And do you do this at the same time every day?"

"Just about. I see my husband off to work, change into my walking gear, and go. Sometimes I do email or read the news for a while after he's left but generally I head straight out. I like to keep the momentum going. If I don't get the exercise in right away, I might put it off and never get back around to it."

She nodded. Judging by her muscular legs and her biceps straining against the polyester jacket, she was a woman who took her gym time seriously. A crumb of biscuit clung to her tattooed lips so I handed her a serviette.

"And so you saw Mrs. Monroe taking her exercise every day?"

I scrunched up my eyes as if to give this a lot of thought, wanting them to know I recognized the importance of the question. "Not really. I don't know for sure what her schedule was but it must have been earlier than mine because I seldom ran into her. I had the idea her running regimen was new. In fact, I'm sure it was." I turned to Milo. "I spotted her because of her new running shoes. As I told you. Well, you could see for yourself they were new."

He nodded but kept on writing, way past the point he could be quoting me verbatim. I wondered if he was editorializing a bit and if so, about what. That said, he seemed to be having a little trouble keeping up —

perhaps he was a poor speller — and I wondered why the police never seemed to make audio recordings of these occasions. I could think of a dozen reasons why that would be more efficient than old-fashioned note-taking. A video would have been even better, but things had not progressed to that point and it was very doubtful the Great British Public would have stood for it, anyway. As in the US, they seemed to veer between blind veneration of their police forces and fear that the police might be jackbooted thugs underneath it all. Looking at Milo, I thought he would be one of the venerated — brave and fearless, perhaps not too bright, but not-bright in a good way, if you follow. Stolid. It's the smart people who think they're smarter than they are who cause all the trouble, in my experience.

I turned my attention back to Attwater to find she was watching me closely. Maybe she was studying me for tips on the proper application of eyeliner. I should have sent her straight over to Rashima's.

"You were neighbors." Milo looked up from his notebook, a mild questioning look in his eyes.

"Yes, I've said."

"But not friends."

Since this seemed to imply the opposite

— if we weren't friends we must be enemies — I chose my words with care.

"We were friendly," I said. "It's just that we didn't see much of each other."

Milo leaned in, elbows resting on his knees, letting the notebook and pencil dangle between his legs. He sat on a chair next to his boss. He was too large for the chair and she looked like a child on the large sofa.

Milo didn't say anything, waiting for me to rush in and supply more detail. It was an old interview trick and I was glad to establish early on that I wasn't falling for it. It was also clear he had studied body language at Police U — it was probably some course they taught on gaining the cooperation of an interviewee, putting people at ease before you pounce and tear them to shreds. He pivoted his body toward me as he spoke and smiled after looking me in the eye, as if to highlight the fact that he liked what he was seeing, as if I were some old friend he'd just recognized. He maintained steady eye contact. He didn't fidget but sat firm, feet planted, rock solid. It was overall an impressive performance. Even I, who had studied these techniques, and had looked for them as I interviewed people for certain roles at the BBC, could only admire his technique.

It probably helped that my BBC job had included casting actors to portray real-life heroes, victims, and villains in the weekly docudrama *Bloody Murder: London.* The villains were the most fun of all to cast. They had to look plausible and normal, but with a tiny spark of madness shimmering around their edges.

"Do you have any idea, any at all, who may have done this? Or who would want to do this to Anna?"

This from Milo again. Don't you just love the open-ended questions? Police U again. Attwater looked content to let him run with it as she admired my arrangement of autumn flowers on the coffee table. I'd bought them at last week's market to cheer myself up and the water in the clear crystal vase was looking brackish. I made a note to take care of that once they were gone, recognizing that mentally I was leaping ahead to the moment these two were out of my sight.

I took a deliberate, slow breath to return myself to the crucial present. I knew that no matter what I said, they would go after poor Alfie first, so it might be better if they got it over with and eliminated him quickly from their list of suspects. I said, "Anna was in the business of being ingratiating. That's how you get people to trust you with your house listing, your money. She could also be, well, a bit bossy. That's part of the job, too, from what she told me. Getting buyers to make up their minds. Getting people to part with their precious junk so the house shows well. I gather that was the toughest part."

"It would be if it were my house on the market," said Attwater. "Three kids." Clearly, she was Good Cop and this domestic detail was supposed to endear her to me. She reached for another McVitie's.

"Were there any incidents you know of in her life, anything unusual, anything new? You live so near, and you share a common wall. Did you perhaps overhear something we should know about?" Milo again. Attwater continued to stuff her face.

I figured eventually I might have to tell them that I could often hear Anna and Alfie arguing through the thin walls. That sometimes the arguments were punctuated by the sound of a body meeting unyielding plaster. And that it was Anna doing the pushing — at least, I thought it was. And without one hundred percent certainty . . . well. It might become necessary for me to tell this story, ugly as it was, but I hoped I wouldn't have to. Alfie was Anna's victim. He along with so many others. I couldn't just throw him to this cookie monster and her creature Milo.

"Honestly, I wish I could tell you more," I said. "I just can't."

I really could hear nothing specific, not even listening with a glass pressed against the wall, which I did one evening when I was wondering whether I should intervene. It was the night I heard the sound of a plate connecting with the floor.

More ominous were the silences punctuated by slamming doors. Still, slamming doors told me everyone was alive.

Why didn't I do something? Because. I don't know. Because of who I was and who we all were in that neighborhood. This was hardly some low-rent district inhabited by Stanley and Stella Kowalski, although — yes, I know this — social class has nothing to do with these situations. Wife beaters don't all dress in wife beaters. Whatever Anna and Alfie got up to it never seemed to reach the point of anything more than yelling, and God knows Will and I did some of that, too. Once I became aware of the thinness of the walls, however, thanks to our quarrelsome neighbors, I reduced my voice to a low hissing sound, like a snake, or I stomped out of the room, keeping my thoughts to myself, and I never threw anything. (At least, not *at* Will.)

Their fights, on the other hand, were so noisy they sounded staged, perhaps fueled by alcohol. Clearly acrimonious but conducted in such a stressed, screechy register I couldn't tell exactly what was being said. I could hear the name "Jason" but I couldn't get much of the context, although given it was Jason they were arguing about I could guess.

All this was what I was not going to get into with Milo and his boss. Again, I had nothing against Alfie and nothing on him, and I was not going to have him dropped into it on my say-so. They could look closely at the husband without any nudging from me.

12

"Tell us about this book club you were in."

Milo had had second thoughts about the coffee, at a signal I'd picked up between him and Attwater. Now he was balancing my Alnwick Gardens souvenir cup on one knee, the notebook abandoned at his side.

"*Were* in, is right. The club disbanded some time ago. It happens. In fact, it happens quite a lot."

"Disagreement over the canapés," put in Attwater, with a knowing nod. What was she, some kind of idiot? Milo seemed to think so. He shifted a little way away from her. Now I was thinking I should send her over to talk to Heather, where they could swap recipes and poison one another with homemade preserves.

"We couldn't agree on what to read. That was all."

I didn't want to tell them the whole story. I thought it might be better to give someone else a chance to spread the gossip.

Milo asked me to name the members of the club. There were eight in all, give or take, but the faithful core consisted of me, Anna, Heather, Rashima, and Macy.

"They had a son, Jason," said Milo. "Anna and her husband."

It wasn't a question, but I treated it as such. "Anna's stepson. Yes." I hoped my reluctance to talk about him showed. I was still holding Jason in reserve.

"Living in London."

"That's right. As I mentioned, I think he lives somewhere around Catford Bridge or Ladywell."

"It's Shoreditch, actually."

Fine. Shoreditch. Why ask me then?

"That's a nice area these days," said Attwater.

I remember thinking if I were ever murdered, I hoped Attwater wouldn't be put in charge of the investigation.

However, it was news to me that Jason had moved to Shoreditch, which was in those days a bit of a hipster haven. Not all that long before, I'd lived there myself. The Brick Lane Market near my old flat was where I could be found on a treasure hunt most weekends. Escaping for a few hours from Ken, my boyfriend at the time.

"Did they get along? The boy and Anna?"

"Aren't most stepchildren just crazy about their stepparents?" I asked. "Seriously, I think they got along better than most. Mostly because Anna left Jason alone as much as possible. She didn't bug him, I mean. She was considerate that way." From the tiny smirk at the edge of Milo's lips, he didn't buy it. I didn't expect him to. Anna left Jason alone because she couldn't stand the sight of him, and the loathing was mutual. I guessed Milo had already met Jason.

Attwater looked confused, as if she'd missed something. I would bet she wore that look a lot. I could have added that Jason was hardly a boy, but apart from the drug use and the fact he liked to sunbathe, that was nearly the sum total of my knowledge of him. My second-floor dining room window (first floor, in Brit-speak) overlooked the Monroes' back garden, so I knew they had a pool no one but Jason seemed to use — Jason and the pool cleaning services guy, a sort of dim bulb who had let a summer job become his life. It wouldn't surprise me to learn he was Jason's supplier as well. I only had visits from the Orkin Pest Control man to liven my days, a slender Somalian, unfailingly polite, but I would have traded a few spiders for a dip in that pool on a scorching hot summer day. England did have them, alternating with monsoon-style flooding, more and more as the planet seemed to tilt the wrong way on its axis. Anna had never invited us over for a swim.

Jason had spent some time as a teenager in South America, volunteering as part of a school project in some place flattened by a hurricane. He came back fluent in the language, so it wasn't a total waste. He also came back addicted to something or other. To a lot of somethings. He soon found a home in the drug world, bought into its warped paranoid philosophies, and set out to do its bidding. I had seen my own brother start down the same path, so this was nothing new. I have always hated drugs, pushers, users — the whole scene.

Milo must have been a mind reader. "How did you and Jason get along?"

"Fine. I seldom saw him."

Again with the skeptical look. It was clear Jason was prime suspect material.

Along with Colin Livingstone, MP. But they never asked about him and I didn't tell. I was saving that bomb for when — if — something really needed shaking up.

Milo and Attwater left about a half hour later, taking with them my assurances I would call if I thought of anything else. They thanked me politely for my cooperation but you could tell they'd been hoping for more. I, on the other hand, felt I had gained a good sense of where they were in their investigation. It had been a morning well spent.

I put their coffee mugs in the sink, combed my hair and put on a cardigan, and went in search of Elizabeth Fortescue.

St. Chrysostom's Church had existed since the days when Sundays drew such big crowds they'd had to enlarge the building, twice. It was sad, given how much the Church had once been the center of all things British, to watch it waste away. Even a nonbeliever such as me could feel the weight of history and beauty in the monuments and crypts.

I searched the side chapels for Elizabeth as apostles and lambs followed my progress from stained glass windows. I found her arranging flowers in enormous Grecian urns on two pedestals near the altar. She held aloft a stem of gladioli like a scepter as she turned at my approach.

Elizabeth fit right in with the tomb art. She had a long, el Grecoish face with a receding chin and an elongated figure, all wavy distorted lines, as if some giant had grabbed her by her head and feet and pulled hard. I suppose I was most reminded of Virginia Woolf, she of the hooded eyes and a nose that went on a fraction of an inch too long. I almost wondered if Elizabeth could be some distant relation to the writer. Her countenance simply blazed with intelligence, so much so it was hard not to want to avert your own gaze. It was as if she could beam those eyes like torches to see through you.

That intelligence made me hesitate. How to start asking questions that I had no business asking? But her concerns were apparently more spiritual and having to do with the state of my soul. After we had exchanged the preliminary greetings and I had given her a sort-of explanation for my presence, she asked, "You're not a member of our church, I take it? At least, I don't recall seeing you here before."

"No, no," I said, adding, "I was raised without any religion in particular. I'm told I was baptized in the Episcopal Church but I was never confirmed. My grandmother was quite religious and I think that was sort of a trial to her — that no one apart from her was observant."

As if she hadn't heard the "no, thanks" in

that speech, Elizabeth said, "If you want to become a member, just submit a copy of your baptismal certificate to the vicar. Nothing to it."

I shook my head. "There's no record of the baptism. The church burned down a few years later and all the records were lost."

She was staring at me with such a peculiar look in her eyes, perhaps thinking the rules and procedures in the US were vastly different from here. This sort of sloppy carryon would never be allowed to happen with parish archives in England. In the event of a fire, Elizabeth would no doubt hurl her body on top of the records in hope of saving them.

"We weren't religious," I emphasized, hoping she'd drop the subject. I would no more allow myself to be confirmed at St. Chrysostom's Church than I would volunteer to join the Chinese army. Or the Women's Institute. "My father wasn't around much, and my mother was too busy." That was the short story for public consumption but I realized as I said it how perfectly it summed up my childhood. My mother was always working, or always worried about losing some stupid little job on some assembly line — we moved so often that was the only kind of work she seemed to be able to find. She was nervous by nature, and in a way that I thought almost guaranteed she'd be caught up in the next round of layoffs. They can smell fear, these corporate bully types. Ability and knowledge, it seemed to me then and now, had nothing to do with it. And of course what confidence she had ever possessed had drained out of her with age. My father saw to that.

"Too busy. I see," Elizabeth said in her sharp way, but not unkindly, and clearly deciding to skip any homilies about how God is never too busy for us. Which is good, because I'd be prepared to argue the opposite any day. "So. How can I help you?"

"Actually, it was Heather Cartwright who suggested you might be able to help. I was thinking of getting involved with volunteer work. Give back, you know. Now that I have some free time. And she seemed to think you were someone who could point me in the right direction." I was winging it, of course, as I'd learned in Improv classes, and I think I said it because I knew instinctively she would approve. She was the type of earnest good-body who would devote most of her boundless energy to good causes and could not see why everyone didn't follow suit. "I even thought of joining a political campaign — helping someone else get elected, I mean. Not me."

Did I imagine it or was there a sudden frost in her voice as she said again, "I see." Perhaps she thought, and rightly, that politics were not a worthy cause, and was hoping for something more along the lines of wrapping bandages for soldiers or feeding the poor.

"I've always thought Heather Cartwright was rather a ninny," she said, out of nowhere. Since that of course exactly matched my own sentiments, I warmed considerably to Elizabeth. She spoiled it by adding, "God forgive me."

"Yes," I agreed.

"I suppose you have in mind Colin Livingstone," she said. "Our local MP."

Softly now. I didn't want to be too obvious, but we'd arrived at the object of my visit. I decided to play my foreigner card.

"I don't really know the system too well," I said. This was certainly an understatement. The electoral college back in the US was a model of logic and transparency compared with British politics, to my mind and many others. Only cricket could compete for its ludicrous rules of order. But I couldn't pretend not to know something of whatever it was the man stood for.

"Ah," she said. "I shouldn't be surprised."

"Yes," I said. "But I admire what he's done for the preservation movement. Anna Monroe used to speak most highly of him."

"Ah," she said again, but this time with a far more weighted emphasis.

"Poor Anna," I added.

"Hmm."

There was condemnation in that *hmm,* in the lift of one dark eyebrow that accompanied it, and in the sharp stab of the next chrysanthemum into the vase, but she was not going to be drawn into speaking ill of the dead, not she. If Elizabeth Fortescue thought Anna, too, was a ninny — or, more likely, a slut — I was not going to hear it from her. At least, not directly. Fortunately, she had fewer qualms about commenting on how the living were managing their lives, as she began to reveal with her next sentence.

"He went through the discernment process at St. C's," she said. "Years ago."

"What's that?"

"It's a vetting procedure they put religious candidates through. In the case of clergy, they can't be too careful who they let in. There are all sorts of steps to discernment."

"And?"

"And I guess they discerned he was — unsuitable." Had it been anyone but Elizabeth I would have sworn she was about to say "an asshole." She smiled a secret little smile that highlighted the creases around her eyes. "At least I never heard any more about it. The next thing I did hear, he was running for parliament. Where he could be among his own kind."

It was interesting that someone besides me, someone with obvious brains and some authority, felt that way about Colin Livingstone. I began to think I might look into joining St. C's myself one day if this was the caliber of bright spark it attracted.

"What exactly did they discover?"

"Discern. And I tell you, I have no idea. I'm only on the vestry. Word gets around but no one ever confides details like that."

Well, it hadn't been a fondness for choirboys, not if his relationship with Anna was anything to go by. "You didn't like him either, I gather."

"No. And it was nothing I could put my finger on. If I could I would say. You can't be in public office and not expect people to comment on your suitability to govern." She paused, considering, and finally said, "It's so subtle, what he does. So nebulous, it's difficult to come up with an example. He liked to tell people this story about his being at a child's funeral. A four-year-old who'd died from a rare blood disorder. And how God spoke to him, to our Colin, right then and there and told him he could alleviate suffering like what these parents were going through. That was when he said he'd got the call to serve — first in the church, and then when that didn't work out, in public office. Oh, I'm not telling this right. But Colin is the last person you'd want to talk with if you'd just lost your child. His tendency was to make himself the middle of every story."

"Including being blinded by the light at a child's funeral."

"Precisely. Like he was the Virgin Mary or St. Paul or something. You do see?"

I did. I felt I'd come across that brand of narcissism before. Mostly, it was benign, and in the case of someone bitten by the religious bug it could at least be put to good use, given certain strict parameters and a watchful committee or two. But there was a line that could be crossed, unwittingly, without anyone noticing until it was too late. People started to believe they could heal, or raise the dead, or found a new church, or whatever loony thing they thought God was calling them to do. In the case of someone with political leanings, it would not require much of a leap. Having failed in one arena, the political showground would beckon even brighter. Much more money and power and prestige involved there, anyway. A clergyman is seldom offered the best table at a restaurant, when you think about it.

I was just collecting my things to leave when she said, "You could ask Macy Rideout." From the knowing Miss Marple twinkle in her eyes, Elizabeth knew exactly what I was after. And who would likely have no qualms about speaking ill of the dead.

13

The next morning I stayed out of Will's way, pretending to be asleep until I was sure he had left to catch his train. Then I jumped into the shower, a hedonistic black-tiled cave with multiple water jets that tempted you to linger far too long. Will once had called it our secret Victoria Falls. We'd stay in there until both Will and the hot water ran out.

I didn't linger, for I had work to do. I washed and towel-dried my hair, fluffed out the curls, pulled on jeans and a cowl-neck, and headed for the Rideout place for my pre-arranged chat with Racy Macy. I decided against taking the car; it was by my standards a short walk to her house. It was, besides, a beautiful day. The odd thing about Anna's murder was how lighthearted it made me feel — just grateful to be alive to see another sunny day. Soon snow would pelt the windows of the darkened houses, and the lights of Rashima's kitchen across the crescent would glow like a safe harbor for me and all who sailed on the good ship Weycombe. It would be beautiful then, too, in its way. Weycombe was never not beautiful.

My grandmother used to drag me to this place in West Virginia, a religious retreat in the woods that became a camp for kids during the summer. For very little cash you could stay in a rundown log bunkhouse, eat starchy food in the main lodge, and listen to lectures in the woods about the nature of the Trinity. Needless to say, I hated it. It was like *The Hunger Games* with camp counselors.

The most marginal kids imaginable were there — kids no self-respecting teenager would want to be caught dead with. And they made us do "spiritual exercises" like walking the labyrinth. At night that became a metaphor for something else among some of the older kids. But one day as I was tracing a path between the rocks I very nearly got the point. My heart lifted *up* and I saw my brother. He was right there, hovering just at the edge of my line of vision, standing with his hands on his hips, the usual know-everything smirk on his face.

I wasn't frightened; I'd never been afraid

of him in life and I wasn't afraid of his ghost. I remembered running back from the car the day he died, my breath coming in ragged gasps, reaching him too late, too late to save him.

That day I stood stock still under the sun in complete and utter peace, and I knew I was forgiven. I had failed to save my brother — from himself, from our parents, even from me — but that was okay: I forgave myself. And as far as the universe was concerned, it didn't matter, anyway.

It was the only experience of my life that could remotely be called spiritual. It was also my first step on the road to freedom — a leaving behind of everything adults had told me I must believe. I knew then with certainty the universe had no system of checks and balances. Except for the parts I could control myself, it was completely random.

It had been unseasonably cool on Nerd Mountain, and the weather in Weycombe that had called it to mind as I walked to Macy's was likewise flawless — a perfect autumn day. Sunny and warm and the air as crisp as apples.

I could see a plucky paddleboarder, far out on the river. In winter the water would freeze, sometimes becoming thick enough to skate on, and even now a paddleboard was optimistic, pushing the season. At least in a kayak your feet and lower body had some protection from the elements.

Was I unfeeling about Anna? Hardly. I was disturbed by her murder, and sorry it had happened, a regret shared by the many people she'd shafted, I'm sure.

But if I'm honest, I have to say before long I felt a ripple of excitement at something this huge unfolding right in front of me. I think most people feel this way about murder. It's why crime novels are so popular. People want to be a part of something bigger than they are, bigger than their petty lives. Something more epic.

My life in Weycombe until Anna was killed had been circumscribed by the boundaries of what was, however upscale and prettified, just a poky little village. I had been reduced to noticing which workmen had been called in to repair a leak, and who was planting tulips already, and wasn't that the Myers' dog, the one developing a limp?

Some days, I was bored — most days. I refused to turn on the telly before four in the afternoon, just on general principle. That was a slippery slope to the fat farm and the loony bin or some awful hybrid of the two. If you know anything about British television you know it's not all mind-expanding drama anyway, not by a long shot, certainly not during the day. You are much more likely to find hour-long footage of a pond being drained, or of a bird building a nest only to have its eggs stolen by predators. The British are very big on nature shows that are nothing if not bloody and true to life. Sometimes they save this type of show for the dinner hour, God knows why.

So it was with this hint of excitement and joie de vivre that I headed into my meeting with Macy Rideout. She and Barry, her newish husband, lived in that honking great manor house I told you about outside the village. Built centuries before on top of a hill, and shored up with rock for impregnability, these days it was reached by a long, winding asphalt drive, at the top of which was a wrought-iron gate and intercom. Together Macy and Barry lived an artfully curated life, routinely pruning away unnecessary people, cutting them off the same way you'd deadhead a rosebush or remove Brussels sprouts from the stalk.

I, apparently, was one of those unnecessary people, which had made it difficult to know how best to approach Macy. I was only slightly acquainted with her to begin with — those superficial book club and Court Cookout encounters. I'd rung her first, of course (I wasn't going to get past the gated entrance without that) and I think she was so surprised she forgot to maintain her distance. So much so I wondered if the distance hadn't been Barry's idea more than hers.

I needn't have worried. My discovery of the body, of which she was by now fully aware, had sprinkled me with celebrity stardust. She gushed a bit when I rang her, as if I were a long-lost friend. Apparently we were going to pretend she hadn't dropped me months before from her flawless new life.

"Here's the thing, Macy," I had said when I got her on the phone that morning. I'd left a message (I was probably interrupting her manicure) but she'd called me right back. "I've remembered something odd about Anna."

"Everything about Anna was odd," she said acidly. "Except the parts that were just plain rotten. And mean." I'd guessed right about the manicure; I could hear little puffing sounds as she blew the paint dry. "And self-serving. You know that book we read? *The Devil Wears Prada*? Like that."

"I meant, odd about her body." I waited for Macy to ask why in God's name I would call her about that, but no. This seemed to make perfect sense to her. "When I saw her that day. She was dressed in exercise gear —"

"That unspeakable orange horror? I tried to tell her —"

"Blue, actually. Macy, stay with me here. Under the running shorts she was wearing this lacy number. I could see it wasn't the normal sort of thing you'd wear jogging. I mean, would you? Did she?"

"God, don't ask me. I mean, I never watched her getting dressed. Except at the gym but I wasn't watching her, if you know what I mean. We didn't have that sort of —"

"So, Macy, she normally wore the same type of underwear any woman would wear to run in. A support bra and industrial-strength panties. Not some flimsy thing designed for a man to peel off with his teeth during a midnight tryst. Macy, think about it. Who runs in lace knickers?"

There was a pause as she thought it through. I gave her a moment to engage the gears.

"No one," she said at last. "Not me. Probably no one."

"So this was unusual."

We both agreed it was ("She wouldn't bother for Alfie, that's for certain") and that this deserved further exploration. So at the pre-arranged time, I appeared at the gate and was duly admitted into the plush embrace of Rideout Manor. They had had the name of the house changed officially, causing no end of fuss. God only knew how Barry rammed it past the parish council, the historical society, and all the gray buns in charge of flying the tradition banner. Barry might be nouveau riche, but riche talks.

The door was opened by a young, curly-haired blonde most women would have barred from the house rather than risk the inevitable complications. In a thick Eastern European accent, she invited me to wait in the parlor for her mistress, asking politely if I "vood lak anysing to drank." I asked for some water, just to see if it would turn out to be Perrier. I was so wrong. It was Veen, from Finland. I looked it up later. It cost about fifteen pounds per 750 milliliters. Thanks, Macy. Apparently, I was worth bribing. More likely, it was just what they kept on hand at Chateau Rider.

Macy did keep me waiting for nearly fifteen minutes, but then I'd arrived early for our talk. And for Macy, somehow you always made allowances. That level of perfection took time to achieve.

She finally descended on a cloud of perfume known only to the twelve Olympian gods. And only they knew what it cost.

Macy had struck gold on her third marriage (much like my stepmother, gold being relative; to someone like Tralee, my father looked like a billionaire). Other comparisons could be made with my stepmother, except that Macy was a genuine knockout, not the dime store version, as well as being about a hundred years younger.

Physically she was all chest and tiny waist, a tanned blonde Barbie brought to life. She had been a flight attendant before she retired to attend to Mr. Rideout's every need. She liked to wear white to offset the tan and to match her wide peroxided smile. Her hair nestled at her collarbone and never grew an inch longer — the whole time I'd known her the hair had never changed. For all I knew she'd been born that way. It was not a wig, either; it was weekly attention from Maurice de Fortuna (nee Stanley Bobienski). She was on the waitlist to get into Rossano Ferretti, where it was said Duchess Kate got her hair done.

Since Macy could hardly disguise her

good looks, she compensated for the mayhem she caused by being nice. Not pretend-nice or icky nice — one of those people driven by guilt to donate excessively of their time and money to charitable causes, a type of which the village had no shortage — but genuinely kind, which no one, especially me, could understand. Where had the compassion and awareness come from, if not from being one of the world's outcasts? I would swear she had no mean bone in her body, this woman for whom men flung themselves across rooms for the honor of opening a door or holding out a chair for her.

It also made her dropping me from her life all the more puzzling. It had been nicely done, you understand, so nicely it took me months to notice the ruthless efficiency of it. In the US, we grow our own version of women like Macy. We call them Southern Belles.

Now she seemed genuinely happy to see me. That was part of her charm, professionally honed in the friendly skies of British Air. It is said of former flight attendant Carole Middleton that she is more beautiful in person than her photographs convey. I believe this. I also believe if you could photograph the inside of her head you'd find an array of computer chips. That may also have been true of Macy but if so, she kept her brains better hidden, distracting the viewer — the male viewer, in particular — with a shot of cleavage that stopped them in their tracks. Why she wasted this firepower on me I can't imagine, but perhaps she had an engagement later that day. She wore a white scoop-neck sweater with crocheted lace around the low neck, and skintight white pants that suggested she wasn't wearing underwear.

That thought, of course, pulled me back to the image of Anna as she lay half in and half out of the water.

Something stark must have shown on my face, for Macy said, "You poor thing. It must have been terrifying. Please sit down. Tell me all."

So I did tell all, or nearly. I left out the part where Milo looked suspiciously at me. It's a funny thing, but once people get it into their heads that you're a suspect, just because you were neighbors with the woman, for God's sake, it colors the entire conversation. So I gave Macy the short version, concluding: "But I'm confused. I thought you two were jogging buddies. And there she was, alone on the path that morning."

"We were. We were for a long time. But it's been ages now."

I waited for her to expand on that. Most people do rush in to fill the silence, as Milo clearly knew, and someone as eager to please as Macy was no exception.

"Once we moved away, it became more difficult to meet up."

"I understand. You grew apart?" I kept my tone light and friendly. It was not an inquisition, but from the pretty pout on Macy's features, the wrinkling of her powdered button nose, she was enduring a mental struggle of epic proportions. She knew and I knew: the two women could so easily have met up about a third of the way along their regular route, keeping up part of their running routine together. And yet, they had not. The runs had stopped as if overnight.

At a guess, Macy's husband was at the center of it. Somehow, some way. Anything dodgy in the neighborhood, he usually was.

I actually knew Barry slightly better than I knew Macy. For several years, Barrymore Rideout, Esq., had lived alone in the house catty-corner from ours. It came as a surprise to many in Weycombe Court when he no longer lived alone, that the rumors of his gayness were evidently not true, and that he and Macy, every woman's basic nightmare, were an item. It was about the time she moved in, I noticed, that remarks began to be made about Barry's commonness. Comments of the "of course, his father was a butcher" variety, showing how quickly they forgot how many famous Brits had working-class fathers (*Wolf Hall,* anyone? Cardinal Wolsey? Cromwell? Not to mention Shakespeare). I guess Barry's prole background and rise to success in spite of it all were okay with them so long as he didn't breed.

I think it was his choice of bride that cemented his fate in terms of his place in Weycombe society. Macy's looks were so much of the Vegas showgirl variety. Even at the gym, it was full makeup, push-up latex, and that precisely coiled hair. Needless to say, she did not perspire. She'd probably had surgery to remove her sweat glands and seal her pores.

And there the rest of us would be, in at best some BB cream and yesterday's smudged mascara, hair in a ponytail, and wearing, in my case, a Wellesley T-shirt and yoga pants.

Problems in Weycombe Court began to simmer from the moment the wedding invitations to Macy and Barry's nuptials landed in the postbox. Macy had made it to the top of the financial ladder, an achievement undreamt of by her grandparents, who ran an off-license in Newham or somewhere with a similar crime rate. She and Barry living together was fine with everyone, that's what commoners do, but making it official crossed some sort of line, exposing the fault lines running beneath the village.

Barry was head of a firm of solicitors which he was said to rule like a warlord. Stocky and swarthy, he oozed testosterone and carried himself with the swagger of a footballer. He looked the type of man who needed to shave twice a day, and now that we knew the Neanderthals bred successfully with Homo sapiens, it was clear his family had participated in these mergers. He did the "seduce with the eyes" thing with every woman he met, just to keep in practice. But there was no doubt in my mind or anyone else's that Macy was the catch of his life.

His accent was a bit common, even to my ears. His bigger crime may have been that he socialized at all levels — he was as friendly with the milkman as he was to whatever lordship crossed his path. But apparently this democratic attitude masked a thuggish, no-holds-barred way of dealing in the courts, much of it behind the scenes. So his marital happiness upset the social order, and Weycombe's job was to keep him firmly in his place, no matter how rich he was. If he had been killed instead of Anna, my money would have been on the members of the Weycombe Court Book Club as suspects, following the plot device of *Murder on the Orient Express* and working out the assassination plot over wine and toads in the hole.

Come to think of it, it wasn't impossible that Anna had been targeted in similar fashion. But every group needs a leader, especially for a murderous enterprise, and Anna would have been that leader.

14

Macy and I went a few rounds until finally I said, "Macy, was Barry another reason you and Anna stopped running together?"

"What exactly do you mean?" She wasn't making it easy. I didn't think she was stalling: it was more that she seemed genuinely perplexed.

"I mean, whose idea was it that you drop your daily runs?"

She thought some more, staring into space, her face a picture of pretty concentration. In an old Victorian print, the image would be titled Beauty Bewildered or some such.

"I guess it was hers."

"She wanted to be free to meet up with someone." It was not a question.

"You think so, too?"

"Yes," I said. "Knowing her, I do."

Macy examined the silver sheen of her manicure, in case something in the conversation was causing it to tarnish. With a visible struggle, she said, "You don't think it was Barry she was running to meet? In Riverside Park, maybe?" She wanted to know, and yet she didn't want her suspicions confirmed. They should issue a permit for this kind of denial with the marriage license.

"Maybe," I said. I was a bit surprised to have my own hunch confirmed by such a noodlehead. But truly, I thought if Anna was meeting up with Barry, it was more likely some financial skullduggery was afoot, not romance. Barry would have to be crazy to jeopardize his relationship with Macy. He'd never again get that lucky. "If it helps put your mind at ease, Macy, I think it could have been anyone she was meeting. Any number of people."

"I hope you're right. There could be a thousand reasons . . . Maybe she just didn't want my company."

And maybe I was looking at this the wrong way up. Had Macy dropped Anna? Somehow I didn't think so. By Macy's standards, Anna was royalty. Besides, Macy needed some friends, even in her new exalted state, and Anna had played that role for a very long time. She had nearly stepped in as matron of honor at the wedding when it looked like Macy's sister was going to go into labor right about then. What Anna and Macy ever found in common I wasn't certain, but a fondness for clothes and makeup and apple cider slimming regimens and discussing those things at length probably passed for a close sisterhood in those parts, in those circles. I wouldn't know.

"It's just that," I said, following up the thought, "she had once been so close she had nearly been part of your wedding party."

Macy nodded. "Krista's timing was always bad. The baby ended up being so late they had to induce. Whatever was I was going to do with a matron-of-honor dress, size elephant, for heaven's sake?"

Krista at the altar had been a sight to see. No one in the pews could take their eyes off of her, in case she doubled over in pain behind the baptismal font. She looked like Exhibit A in some medieval pageant on the wages of sin.

"There would barely have been time to cut it down to Anna's size," Macy continued. "Even though she was no gazelle, mind."

"This is true."

"And her coloring was all wrong, with that dark hair. She'd have been the only brunette on the altar, apart from Barry."

"Mmm. Yes."

"You have to think of the photos. For pos— pos— posterior?"

"Posterity."

"Right. You are so smart. I wish *I'd* gone further in school."

It was a snarky comment on its face but with Macy, you never felt that snark was in her repertoire. Along with "posterity," it just wasn't in the database.

I smiled. "I still have the student loan debt to prove it. Anyway, I did not get the sense from Anna that there had been a rift. You know, living next door to her as I did, I picked up on a lot. Still . . ."

I let Macy's mind drift over the possibilities of what I might have picked up on. Which was not much about the Rideouts, truth be told. But from the stricken look in Macy's eyes, I might have been Anna's closest confidante, engaging in soul-baring conversations over hot cups of cocoa before the fire, just us two girls in our footie pajamas. After the slightest hesitation, Macy seemed to opt for admitting to the truth of what I might already know.

People are funny that way. It was something I learned in my time as a reporter: they always assume you know more than you do. And they are so anxious to get their side of the story out, they end up revealing more than would ever have come out on its own.

She looked at me, assessing me for — what? My ability to be discreet?

"Would you like something to eat?" she asked. "C'mon, let's have a bite. Like old times. It's almost time for lunch. Bonita does a mean tuna salad."

"Bonita?"

"Her grandmother was Spanish."

So we continued our conversation over a staggeringly good *salade niçoise.* We sat at a round table in a warm pool of sunlight before a picture window overlooking the back garden.

"She, well. Hmm," began Macy, taking a sip of Veen and replacing the bottle with care. "It's wrong to speak ill of the dead. But Anna was not what she seemed."

I wanted to say she seemed to be an evil, double-dealing, bloody-minded slut, but instead I shoveled in a forkful of tuna and waited.

"She set her sights on Barry. Well. You can see for yourself what an attractive man he is. But I wasn't having any of that."

Again I was left wondering, this time at Macy's view of her husband. I supposed he was attractive to women with Neanderthal DNA, which on the surface fair Macy did not seem to possess. Still, we're talking more than three hundred thousand years ago. A lot could happen.

"It's the reason we moved out of Weycombe Court so suddenly, you know," she offered. "We had planned to stay longer, take our time finding and renovating the perfect place, wait and see what the market did. We weren't in any rush."

"I thought Anna was the broker on the sale of your house. And the purchase of this one."

"Yes, she was, and it was right about then the trouble started." Macy had a trace of salad dressing at one corner of her lips, marring her lip gloss. At my signal she dabbed it away. "We were playing it safe and cautious. Wanting her to get us the best deal. You know. But then . . ."

"Trouble?" I asked silkily. I could see she was ready to spill and I didn't want to spook her. I took a swig of my drink to mask any signs of too-avid interest.

"Barry. Well. Barry's meetings over the state of the housing market were taking a little longer than I thought they should. And they were running late into the night." She ducked her head, and the impeccable hair swung forward to hide her expression. It was a handy hairstyle if you were easily embarrassed. "If you know what I mean."

I could guess. But I had no idea why she was confiding in me like this. None. We had gone from being — not enemies, but very distant acquaintances to confidants in a heartbeat. I guessed that life at the Petit Trianon was a bit isolating, especially if you'd excised almost everyone in the village from your guest list in some desperate social-climbing attempt to separate yourself from the herd.

"I can guess," I admitted. "But surely Barry — well, I mean, you're so beautiful, Macy. And he's besotted with you. Everyone knows that."

"Do you think so?"

God. How pathetic. How could she not know — really know — the impact she had on men? On everyone?

"Yes, Macy, I think so. What makes you think Anna would make any headway there? Even assuming she would dare."

"Dare? I think she'd *do* it on a dare. For Anna, that was half the fun. She and I were friends — *were* friends, before all this started. Once we'd hired her to represent us, we had a business relationship that we really couldn't call off, as much as it galled me to pay that woman a commission. Barry said we'd lose too much in penalties to just walk away. There was a lot on the line. I think in some perverted way knowing we were stuck just added to the thrill for her."

I knew people like that. Don't look for the logic or you'll go crazy. They do it because it's there, because they can, just to see what will happen. What kind of chaos they can create. I was starting to believe Macy's view of things. "So you confronted Barry."

Again she hung her head, letting the hair shield her expression. "I just said I wasn't comfortable with Anna. I made up some story about how I questioned her honesty. Well, I did, but in a business sense I guess she was being honest with us. It was everything *else* she was dishonest about. Like other people's fiancés."

"And what did Barry say?"

"He blew up — went completely crazy. Without my even asking, he denied anything was happening, or had happened between them. He got so angry with me for doubting him, I just dropped it."

A classic legal tactic. The good offense being the best defense. In other words, he bullied her into silence. Macy didn't dare anger the rich fish she had angled so hard to catch. Jesus, did this woman own a mirror? Of course she did, but she had somehow convinced herself that at the ripe old age of forty, the best she could do was Barry.

My best guess was that Barry and Anna had been in cahoots over a deal that was in some way illegitimate. If I had to choose in which direction Barry would stray, it would be that; he would be fiscally unfaithful, unscrupulous in his dealings. He was famous for it already, in a quiet way.

Anna had been beautiful, yes, but Macy was the bomb. For a man who assessed his womenfolk according to their marketplace value, that would have tipped the scales. Besides, he had just put a ring the size of a grape on Macy's finger. Would he really screw it all up so soon?

Macy asked Bonita to open a bottle of *rosé* and began pouring with an open hand. She honestly seemed glad of my company and especially thankful for my tribute to her looks. This was taking candy from a baby.

We lingered over the meal, staring out the window at the flagstone patio and the manicured garden beyond which colorful Chinese lanterns were nearing the end of their season. I may have solved the mystery of where Heather got her berries, although it was news to me she and Macy were close. Perhaps Heather had climbed over the fence to sneak some. But Chinese lanterns grew everywhere in the village; I had heard people complain they grew like weeds and once they took hold, they couldn't get rid of them.

In the vast distance of the Rideout estate a man could be seen riding a mower. Twirling the stem of my wineglass, I thought how best to approach the subject of exactly what uses Barry might have found for Anna. Macy saved me the trouble.

"You know," she said, "at one time I thought Barry had some sort of agreement with Anna. Something to do with property titles."

"Really?" I said. "To be honest, I never heard Anna was anything but straight in her business dealings."

"Well, maybe I was wrong. Can people be dishonest in just one area of their lives? Can they compar— compart— ?"

"Compartmentalize?"

"Right. Maybe it's dishonest in one way, dishonest in all ways."

It was an interesting philosophical point. God, the money I had wasted on higher education, not to mention self-help books. People like Macy seemed so shielded from the world. They spent their days happy, sitting in huge mansions having splendid wines with lunch, with nothing to do with their time but decide what to wear next, and whether that nail polish really went with that day's outfit. I suspected Macy's real value to Barry, apart from the obvious, was her groundedness — her warm-heartedness, and her common sense, and the fact that there were so few edges to her generous personality. Her general cluelessness probably helped with someone who sailed as close to the wind as Barry. I decided to forgive her for shutting me out for a while, realizing it probably had more to do with cutting ties with Anna and anyone in near physical proximity to Anna. Macy had been fighting to save her marriage, or so she thought. And before that, her engagement. It was not rare in these cases for other people to be jettisoned like so much ballast. I've seen the same thing happen when the grandchildren come along. Everything suddenly has to be perfect, perfect, perfect. It's a control thing.

I guessed the police might wonder how far Macy was willing to go to save her marriage. If I'd been tempted to wonder the same thing, a few hours in her company had ended my doubts.

Macy was if anything too nice for her own good.

15

On my way back from the Rideout palace I stopped along the High at the Coffee Pot to clear my head of wine with their high-octane brew. A handful of people were there, including the Ichabod Crane-looking guy the villagers called Dr. Odd. He liked to prescribe bizarre home remedies for any ailment, to anyone who would listen, often complete with healing incantations. I knew that he and Heather, despite the age difference, got on like a house afire.

Bathsheba the cat lounged as usual before the fireplace, at a distance nicely judged to prevent her fur bursting into flame. There was often cat hair floating in the coffee but no one seemed to mind.

The Coffee Pot had become my home away from home. Sometimes I'd put in my earbuds ("I Think Ur a Contra" was a current favorite) and tune out the world. Sometimes I'd eavesdrop — actually, I did that more often than not: I like to know what's going on. It is not true that eavesdroppers only hear bad things about themselves, by the way. One day I overheard two women talking about me, not realizing I sat right behind them: The woman from the dry cleaners said she admired my can-do spirit, but she added she'd been worried about me since I lost my job. Her friend said, "Nah, she'll be fine, she's American, they bounce back." I felt great about that all day. It is nice to be admired. Of course, they'd never seen my kitchen.

On occasion, I would strike up a conversation with Dr. Odd about native plants and wildlife. He was the reason I recognized some of Heather's deadlier concoctions.

The door swung open and, speak of the devil, there she was. She blocked the doorway for a few minutes, struggling with Lulu's baby carriage. She gave me a friendly wave but settled at a table with Dr. Odd. Some minutes later:

"Bath! Come down from there, you!" This from Greta the proprietor, who always wore her hair in swirls like cinnamon buns, one over each ear, like a woman in a Grimm's fairy tale.

Heather looked over and said complacently, "You can always tell when they're pregnant."

"That tom of Margaret's has got out again, then," said Greta. "Lord, I hope not."

I had taken my usual corner table and pulled out a notebook, intending to be professionally systematic, jotting down the date and time and the high points of my interview with Macy.

But our conversation had brought up some things I didn't want to dwell on, for naturally, Macy had wanted to hear all the details of my discovery of the body. Now I blinked away an image of Anna's dead stare, and shaking my head as I sat with my notebook, a small "no!" escaped me. I looked around to see if anyone had heard — it wouldn't do to let them think I was coming unhinged — but beneath the sound of the espresso machine and Heather's prattle I might have been alone.

For a while I simply devoted myself to eavesdropping. Someone's daughter wasn't doing well. Someone else's "dogs were barkin' from the new shoes, and serves her right." Someone named Maxwell was just having trouble finding himself, and the new girlfriend — no better than she should be — wasn't helping. Someone's Hughie with allergies had "nearly died — the lads hid his inhaler from him as a lark." Because of my brother, I knew too well how that could happen. I fought back another horrid image surging to the front of my mind.

Then I heard Heather say, "I did wonder when I saw Anna leaving the doctor's." That made me tune back in. Surreptitiously, I made a note to ask her more about that later.

My eye roamed to a nearby stack of trashy magazines and newspapers that reflected the owner's taste in news. Headline news like *ROBERT DOWNEY'S BACK.* And *BRAD AND JOLIE: CALLING IT OFF?* Sometimes I'd borrow a copy of a particularly juicy old issue to take home.

Children from St. Clement's primary passed in front of the shop, followed closely by the gooseberry butcher — still my top pick if I were profiling someone to be the village killer. The children always walked through the village on their way home, cute as buttons, starchy in their little uniforms. I liked to assign them character traits and futures as bankers or film stars. One of the little girls had the most complicated plaits you've ever seen, different each time I saw her, and I thought of the love and care that went into their creation each day.

The children were totally unlike the weekly boarders from St. Felix's, the private girls' school. In that case, being forced to wear a uniform had with the advent of the teen years encouraged gaudy flamboyance in hair and jewelry. St. Felix's was a refuge that allowed the wealthy to avoid letting their daughters mingle with the great unwashed at the local comprehensive. It was necessary to keep these kids on track with relationships and associations that would get them into the right universities followed by the right jobs and marriages. I certainly could see the sense in that.

I often wondered what it would have been like to have been born and raised in the village. I wondered, moreover, if living that sort of cosseted life might have made me a different person. It was an unanswerable question — nature vs. nurture — but in my heart of hearts I believed the answer was yes. It would all have been different and I would not have been sitting there alone apart from Dr. Odd and the cat and assorted strangers. Oh, and Heather, of course.

Wasn't it Lady Astor who said most women marry beneath themselves?

That evening with Will . . . It's not worth writing about but I suppose, in the interest of accurate notetaking, I must.

Wind had whipped the trees in our garden as night came on, throwing droplets of a late afternoon rain. It seeped in at the base of one bedroom window, making the blinds rattle like a Halloween skeleton. I'd woken from a nap — the alcohol; those memories — as thunder rumbled in the distance, coming nearer.

Someone was in the house, moving stealthily, but I knew Will from the footfalls, the pacing of his steps, even his scent being transmitted to me subliminally. I got up to check my makeup. Panda rings under the eyes and not a trace of lipstick — your basic Alice Cooper makeover.

I'd opened the Crown Royal for a mid-afternoon sock of oblivion and that was the last I remembered. I found Will in the kitchen, holding my glass to his nose. The great detective.

"You've been drinking? Really?" he said. "It's six o'clock."

So? The sun was over the yardarm now. And I hadn't had a drink in forever. Besides: *hello?* Kettle/black. I didn't answer, since it wasn't really a question, and he knew everything already. He always did.

"I'm making eggs and sausage for dinner," I said. "If you want some. I didn't have time to shop." It was a favorite meal of his, nursery food, really. I was determined we would just be normal for a while — coast along, no major eruptions, see what developed. Although my every instinct was to tell him if he wanted dinner he could take me out to the gastro pub. I just didn't want to be alone.

"I'm meeting someone at the pub," Will said. He was rifling through some paperwork I'd left on the coffee table, which included the latest version of my CV. None too gently, I removed it from his hands. "You've been out of work for almost a year," he said. He'd spent the last year complaining that we needed to tighten our belts and cut back on our spending. How that fit in with going to the pub all the time wasn't clear to me.

"Nine months," I corrected him. *Someone? Who, someone?*

"Closer to ten. Whatever." He gave me that look, the kind of look you reserve for someone you might have crossed paths with in a mental ward. I hated that look — was it fear? Distrust? Or contempt? If so, what did he have to be contemptuous about? "You need to start pulling yourself together, Jill." He stopped, peered at me, and said, "What have you done with your hair?"

So he'd noticed, at least peripherally, that

despite the current panda eyes I'd been trying to pay more attention to my appearance. I'd also mastered coq au vin, but he'd yet to comment on that.

"I thought I'd try highlights." I'd had them done weeks before. Did he never look at me?

"Good to know you have time for that."

I looked out the window. Some star was spinning, twinkling, turning its face from me. A dog barking — that godforsaken dog of the Westcotts, left alone again. Some people don't deserve the animals they've got.

"Look, it gives me confidence. When I go out for interviews and things."

"When's the last time you went out on an interview? And whatever happened with the voiceovers? All that money splashed out on equipment, just sitting there gathering dust."

That really was the worst thing he could have said. It was unfair, the whole conversation, and he knew it. The truth was, it's a cutthroat world out there in London and Americans need not apply. I was an alien. Even married to a Brit, I was and would forever be viewed as an alien. I had tried explaining this to Will, to no avail.

"I've got an interview next week," I lied.

"Really?" The skepticism in his voice, habitual now when he spoke to me, was still there, but now he was less sure of his ground. "Next week" was more a concrete concept he could cling to. Will liked absolutes. "Who with?"

Annoyance inspired me. "Whom. With whom. Well, it's sort of an interview. You remember Oscar? Guy I used to work with?"

"Oh, man. Oscar? Really?"

"Yes, Oscar." I found myself getting defensive on Oscar's behalf, although I totally got Will's take on him. Oscar was perhaps not the world's most reliable person, but still. The fact that Oscar fancied me and made little secret of thinking my marriage to Will had been a mistake might have factored into Will's cynicism.

"What's Oscar's last name, anyway?" Will was not being ingenuous here. He simply didn't remember or care to. "What kind of job?"

"Mayhew."

"Oscar Mayhem. Right, I remember now. You're wasting your time."

I decided to let that go. If Will had a better connection, now would be the time to mention it.

"Oscar knows everyone," I said. "I thought if I reminded him I was still on the market he'd have some ideas." I was completely forgetting by this point that I had no appointment to meet with Oscar, but that could easily be remedied. More importantly, Oscar was bound to have one ear to the ground on what had happened here in Weycombe. Someone like Anna being murdered would be right up his investigative alley. The BBC camera van and crew had already trundled through the village; the wide-angle lens shots of our historic market town as it sat twinkling in the sunlight, festooned for harvest time, had been featured on the evening news. There had also been a close-up of the spot on the river where Anna had been killed, and establishing shots outside the estate agent's office where she had been employed. Best of all, there had been stills of her desirable house in its exclusive enclave. I could write the voice-over introduction myself with my eyes closed: "Beautiful Anna Monroe, rich and successful, the envy of her neighbors. The envy of everyone who knew her. But was it envy that led to her brutal murder at a bend in the River Wey, just outside her postcard-perfect village? Or was it something else? The police are baffled by this crime — a crime that has shaken bucolic Weycombe to its core." When they ran out of things to say there would be archival shots of the Bull, probably with my dear husband sitting at the bar, and of the farmer's market on a Saturday morning, bustling with people like Heather buying flowers and cheese and free-trade coffee.

This sort of thing had been perfected by US television producers of true-crime reenactments — the type of show that makes you wonder just how many people are actually murdered every year, because there seem to be an awful lot. They also make you wonder how the justice system ever got to be so screwed up. These shows tend to feature an overblown narrative style and an awful lot of repetition, and the victim is always beautiful and wealthy and envied — or at least, very young. Ugly and poor don't sell. Anna fit all the requirements, except for the young part. I wondered briefly who might play the role of Anna, and an image of a somewhat zaftig Catherine Zeta-Jones floated before my eyes.

The UK version of this stuff was *Bloody Murder: London* — as I've mentioned, I'd done much of the casting for that show. So when I say Catherine Z-J, I know what I'm talking about. Sooner or later, Anna's death would be featured, no question about it. I figured maybe I could wangle a comeback when it was. Now that would be interesting.

Having "promised" Will I would go and talk to Oscar, I figured I might as well make good on it. It might prove useful, and Oscar — well, at least Oscar was never boring.

"Besides," I added, letting Will in on some of my thinking, "I need to talk to someone right now. And Oscar's good at getting me out of a slump."

"Is that what you call it?" he said, not completely unkindly. Not completely. There was a shade of old Will peering out from behind fed-up, up-himself Will now. And there was a softening in his voice that allowed me to say, "The thing with Anna. It reminds me of my brother somehow. She . . . it's so . . . awful. I don't know if I can stand to relive it. But I don't seem to have a choice."

He nodded. I had told Will soon after we first met about my brother, and I could see how it got to him, the pity in his eyes. Pity is such a dangerous emotion; it can masquerade as love. I told him how I did everything I could to save my brother, and how I still felt the most terrible guilt.

"Of course you did everything you could," he'd insisted. "You were only a child yourself."

I knew my face now reflected some of my turmoil. His was pale, devoid of color. He looked like he'd aged ten years. He also looked as if he might have been crying.

The uncaring Will of recent weeks was gone and for the moment, my Will was back. He reached out and drew me onto his chest, holding me and kissing the top of my head. It was so unexpected, so tender; the treacherous tears I had banished forever, ages ago, sprang to my eyes.

This is what kept me off balance — this thing Will was doing, right there and then. He could not bear to see anyone suffer, you see. Especially when he was the cause. Otherwise Will was careful to avoid any scene with the potential to turn emotional.

Eventually, he extricated himself from my grasp. Furiously I dug my fists into my eyes to quell the tears. I didn't want his sympathy. What was wrong with me?

"Look, I'm going out," he said. "I have to go out," he amended. "I'm meeting Gideon's father for a drink." This was a huge concession; Will seldom bothered anymore to tell me where he was going or who with. "You'll be all right on your own?"

I nodded mutely. Wasn't I always? All right, and on my own?

"Look," he said. "Just — try to be . . .

calm. Relax, if you can. And no more drink, at least for tonight, all right?"

I almost laughed. It was so Will. So very British. Just pull your socks up, stay sober, and everything will be fine.

"Are you happy?" I asked him. "I mean, despite . . . ?" It was a ridiculous question, given the circumstances. We barely spoke anymore; it had all broken down. Why would I care if he was happy?

But I wanted to hear what he'd say.

Predictably, the question embarrassed him. "You mean, despite all this." He swept his hand vaguely about the room, and I was reminded of the Monty Python line, "What, the curtains?"

I wanted to laugh but I just nodded.

"Not happy," he said. "No. Dazed would be a better word. We'll — we'll sort it all out. Just give it time. Let's . . . For now, I'm content to wait and see."

The way he said it, I could hear things unspoken. "We'll sort it all out, and then . . ." And then what? Goodbye?

I decided not to press. So long as Will was content for now, I thought, that's good.

That was all that mattered.

Part 3

16

I am a stranger in a strange land. As much as I love England, apart from the soggy winters, I know I will always be a stranger; I will spend my entire life on this island peering into others' lives from outside. Perhaps that's just what writers do, anyway.

But at least living in the UK expands your vocabulary with words like "bedsit" and "chunder" and phrases like "two up two down." There's that.

I still don't know offhand the difference between icing sugar and powdered sugar, or my way around frosting and butter icing and royal icing and just plain icing, not to mention caster sugar, and whether you pronounce scones as "scons" or "scoans" — the British don't seem sure of that one, either (Will's mother pronounced it "scons," so we can probably take that as gospel). Then there are muffins and crumpets; there are cookers and stoves and ovens. These are just the problems I've had in the kitchen. The universal language of love is not, I've found, all that universal.

Celsius versus Fahrenheit, millimeter versus ounce — once you've got that down, as well as the wardrobe, particularly the shoes, you're a native. The accent is harder to pass off and I never wanted to join the pretentious who try to adopt the posh version. Even trained actors fail here; we've all heard some calamitous bits of miscasting on the silver screen. This crosses both ways: I kept wondering why Rosamund Pike kept sneering and whining through her nose throughout *Gone Girl* until I realized that's how we sound to the British.

Will had the most desirable accent of all; he went to Eton. *And* he had the hair — mountains of thick wavy hair cut in that voluminous, floppy Etonian way. They all look alike, these boys of privilege: they talk alike, they walk alike, they talk about all the same things, and the best-trained actor can't begin to imitate them.

Will told me something of his life at Eton, which I gathered was not always a laugh riot. That constant if unstated pressure to be better-than, which pressure I understood completely. The fact that showing weakness was never allowed, even though you were just a kid of thirteen. You had to be a man. I felt a bit sorry for Will, hearing this. This was before I knew about pity, how it can be confused with love, and how dangerous that is.

Apart from that sense of being an alien, the real problem I had in Weycombe was that I was bored, depressed, and down on myself for being made redundant (that lovely British euphemism meaning canned, your key card confiscated, your computer locked). Although for a while there I'd enjoyed my freedom. Early on I literally ran about the house hugging myself (once Will was safely on his way to the train station), so happy I didn't have to trail along beside him in heels, clutching my leather tote with its laptop and iPhone and all the toys grown-ups play "business" with. None of that for me, the pointless shuffling of papers and creating new problems to solve. I was going to make money on my own terms, answering only to myself.

But doing what, exactly?

I only wanted to write and I kept circling back to that.

Write what? That I didn't know.

It is possible recent experience with Will contributed to my utter inability to write erotica but I didn't want to think too much about that. I did try writing a Regency romance, but that stalled out at fifty pages.

How did these superwomen do it? The ones who found time away from playdates and diaper changes to do something dynamic and financially rewarding *inside* the home, avoiding the commute, pausing only long enough to be interviewed over Skype about their amazing success. I didn't even have the excuse of childrearing to fill the hours that began to stretch from ten a.m., when I returned from my daily walk, to five p.m., when I would start to cook dinner. Or three p.m., when I might sometimes have a glass of wine. Will wanted to wait to have children "until we were more settled." Something told me not to push too hard on that subject. What if I asked him point-blank and his answer was no, never — or worse, not with you? I want children but not with you?

What else was there to engage me, then? Writing a memoir? My memoirs would fill at best a few paragraphs: I, Jillian Anna Violet White, was born with an ability to memorize almost anything you put in front of me. Any scene, any page. That was my one gift, my ticket to a scholarship at Wellesley.

Nothing in my childhood had prepared

me for life with blue-blooded Will. My parents briefly separated when I was fifteen and my mother and I went to live with my grandmother, who was the antithesis of upper crust. In my memory she is always in her lavender stretch pants from Sears with a starched white top tucked into the elastic waist. She dotted vanilla extract behind her ears for scent and always looked clean and neat and dirt poor. I tried to picture my grandmother sitting in Will's mother's tufted sitting room and it was impossible.

She was for me an oasis of sanity. She lived in Virginia, in the sort of little town that made you think of endless summers and apple pies and white wicker rockers on the front porch. It had rows of nineteenth-century houses and shops; to kids from the nearby farms it was the Big City. The last time I went to see her was just before the Parkinson's took hold and she found it difficult to walk or talk. The conversation, as usual, turned to my brother. Which is kind of why I started avoiding her. She got morbid in her old age, paranoid and rambling, turning on people. Turning on me. The doctor said that was a normal part of the disease, only to be expected.

I'd been brought up on or around military bases stretching from California to New

Hampshire, living with a constant background hum of jets flying overhead. It made me feel safe, knowing someone was always patrolling the skies on my behalf, especially since no one on the ground could really be bothered.

Then my father retired and moved us to Maine, in what was clearly a midlife overreaction to the rules and regulations of military life. It was at this point he began falling apart, becoming enamored of hunting and little else. Without someone to tell him what to do and when to do it, he was lost, and what really pissed him off, I think, was finding how hopeless he was at life. My mother was not strong enough to fill the void or create the structure that he needed. My grandmother tried but she was too far away. She'd send these little care packages, tins of homemade cookies cushioned in popcorn.

My father began to drink once he retired. Or maybe he'd never stopped and it just became more apparent he was drunk once he was underfoot all the time. I suppose it is just possible he was on his face all day on the job and nobody noticed. Because he was in intelligence — the irony, I know — they did random drug testing on all those guys. But my dad was in charge of his squadron and maybe it never occurred to anyone to test the boss. If that makes you sleep less well tonight, knowing someone with his finger on the button might be drunk off his ass, well — yeah. It should.

I had to get out or turn into them, into my parents. That fear guided my every move.

My looks helped. I was aware of that from about junior high on, once I'd shed my ugly duckling carapace. But it was my brains that got me out of Dodge.

My looks don't matter to my story, except that without them, Will would never have noticed me, I would never have married my titled almost-prince, and I would never have had Weycombe to write about. If it matters to posterior, as Macy would say, I had brown hair falling past my shoulders and light brown eyes, and a heart-shaped face with a widow's peak. I carried just 125 pounds on a five-foot-seven-inch frame, although under stress I weighed less. At the time Anna died, my Bugs Bunny pajama bottoms were barely clinging to the tops of my hips, and I knew I'd probably have to go to the next size down.

I wondered if the local lingerie shop, In-time, carried Bugs Bunny PJs.

17

It might have been smarter to stay on the sidelines than investigate Anna Monroe's death. But I had always been fascinated by crime — by murder, to be specific. Not by court dramas: by the time lawyers get involved the truth never comes out. But by the people who commit crimes. By the reasons behind premeditated crime, domestic crime, malice foreign and malice domestic. And all the ways a killer can get away with it — or thinks he can.

At the BBC I started out doing broader categories of show but soon all my assignments were for *Bloody Murder: London.* It was an enormous hit from the day it launched, and I'll take credit for that. I even wrote the scripts for some of the better shows. What I learned is that people don't half get up to some crazy stuff, and they always get caught because they do one stupid thing that gets them caught. In domestic murders, especially, the necessary detachment is missing.

I learned a lot about forensics doing the *BM:L* gig. For instance, did you know a tongue print is as good as a fingerprint for identification purposes? That everyone's teeth are different — that even identical twins have different teeth?

Also, FYI, if you're going to do away with someone, just do it yourself. Hiring a hit man is never the way to go. Those cheap losers who hang around bars trying to find someone to kill their spouse for five hundred pounds — those are the ones who always get caught. The police even send out people to hang in bars, just trolling for malcontents.

I remembered a conversation I had with my *BM:L* boss. A lecture, rather. He actually wagged his finger at me. "This isn't fiction, Jillian," he said. "It's supposed to be true crime." In my experience, true crime bears less relation to reality than does fiction, but I didn't argue with him. The show's sponsors were unhappy and that's what mattered.

Now Weycombe villagers would be starring in *BM:L* or some other British version of *Dateline on OWN* and here was I. How could I not want in?

My parents once lived off-base near a

house where a woman had been murdered five years earlier. I passed that house on my way to and from school — it was yellow, two stories with a red door — and every day I pictured the woman who had died there, lying mutilated in a pool of her own blood, sprawled at the foot of the stairs in the dirt-floor basement until someone at her job finally wondered where she'd got to. A boyfriend did it, they said. Her married lover. They never were able to pin it on him, if he did it. He was rich. He was connected.

You just know that sort of thing happens a whole lot more than people think it does.

How I landed that job at the BBC is difficult to explain, because to this day I don't know why they thought I was qualified to do it. I applied not exactly as a lark but not expecting much, either. I seriously needed to find a job in the UK or be tossed out as an illegal alien, so I was applying for everything going, in scattershot fashion, only to be pipped at the post by some less qualified but native-born applicant. The only good thing was that the British have a wonderfully fair and polite system whereby if they call you for an interview, they pay for your transportation, realizing, as their American counterparts should do, that the expedition is costly and inconvenient to the applicant who most likely, being unemployed, is broke. In this way I traveled for free a good bit to and from London and Oxford, stopping in after interviews to see every play I could. This went on for months before I took my degree. While it was a good deal for me I was, as I say, growing increasingly worried that no one would hire me and I'd have to leave.

The day of my interview with Eric Avalon, the man I'd soon come to think of as Beelzebub, I was let into his office by his assistant, Noelette Minon, whose finest quality as far as I ever was concerned was that wonderful, toady name. In addition to kowtowing to Eric she acted as his spy, reporting back on infractions large and small.

It turned out that what made me perfect for the job in their eyes (Noelette stayed for the interview, glowering suspiciously throughout) was my Americanness, which they seemed to define as outgoing, friendly, and ballsy. I will own to the latter but not to the rest. I am in fact an introvert. People exhaust me and I am happiest in my own company, where I can withdraw and assess what happened during any unavoidable transactions with the outside world. But

Eric had got it into his head that I would be able to draw in the right people with the talent and knowhow for any upcoming production. Finally I realized my spell of employment with Hollywood Green Productions had created this misapprehension. HGP was a deli in Wellesley, Massachusetts. But my experience in amateur theater at Oxford may also have helped.

Of course I did what I could to foster this illusion of vast expertise — I knew I'd learn on the job once I'd landed it. That part of my confidence was, I suppose, pure American. And I had screwed myself up to a fever pitch over this. There was a letter from my Oxford college officials sitting on my desk, asking me to vacate my rooms by the end of summer so they could be readied for the next influx of graduate students. They'd let me overstay by several months after I'd completed all the work for my degree, drag it out as I might, being aware as they were of my circumstances. I had thrown myself on the mercy of the bursar, but even he did not have the authority to let me stay forever. I had to get out of there.

So when Eric asked what I had actually done at HGP, I had done enough research on talent scouts to be able to describe my work at the deli in human resources terms, throwing around words like procurement and interview and due diligence, grinning at him with what I hoped was an energetic, can-do Yankee attitude.

I glossed over the fact that my stint at HGP came just before I was forced to endure death by teenager at a newspaper, a gig that came along when I already thought life had kicked the last bit of stuffing out of me. I was working in a deli, for God's sake — a college graduate who had gone heavily into student loan debt so I wouldn't have to work in a goddamn deli.

My journalism career didn't last long, either. My boss at the small daily was a senior editor by virtue of being old — Mike had to be over sixty-five — and of having survived several past pogroms. The rumor was he had something on the publisher, some dirt or other that allowed him to hang on to his head while those around him were losing theirs.

He and I once had a conversation where he told me he found me alarming.

"You are smart and charming when you want to be," he'd said. (I let that "when you want to be" slide.) "You have something that makes people want to open up to you, to spill all their secrets. Don't abuse it. Don't abuse that power."

"You're talking to a journalist and telling me not to get people to open up?"

"I'm telling you to be more careful how you go about it. I'm telling you not to lie to them. It'll come back to bite you."

"But schmoozing is okay," I said. "Got it."

A fine distinction, but whatever. I'm sure he meant well. Finally the suits sent him to that elephant's graveyard where old newspaper editors stagger off to drink Mojitos and pretend they could have been Hemingway — if only.

And then — just as I was beginning to taste freedom, *then* they promoted this girl-child in Mike's place, and I was asked for several months to endure life under this teenage potentate. It was like building pyramids for a female King Tut. Until finally, mercifully in fact, they let me go, too.

Whenever I relived these job memories, I was overcome by waves of special loathing for Eric, who had assured me not three weeks before canning me that my job at the BBC was safe. *Probably* safe. But he was so busy by then shagging the married copyeditor (Coleen, Our Lady of the Possessive Pronoun), I should have known this man's word was not his bond.

18

The night before Anna's funeral the kitchen phone rang, just as Will was saying, "Jillian, we need to talk," in the deep, dramatic voice he'd honed in local theater.

It was his mother on the line. Of course it was his fucking mother. It was the only component of disaster missing from that evening. Will and I had quarreled and I had ended up slamming down a plate of spaghetti Bolognese that splattered all over the tablecloth. I forget exactly what the fight was about, but it didn't take much anymore to get us started.

I signaled to Will (a sort of begging gesture with my hands) to call his mother back later. He ignored me. But given the threat I felt looming behind his "need to talk," it was just as well. It may have been the first time I was grateful for one of Rossalind's interruptions.

The Dowager White detests me, of course.

She is the biggest snob since Queen Victoria and her son's taking up with an American nearly did her in. I didn't even bring great wealth into the marriage in the time-honored tradition set by the Vanderbilt girls. I brought nothing but myself, and she quickly made it clear that wasn't enough.

They say men fall in love with their mothers, but Rossalind and I were nothing alike. Nothing. She was very tall, although she'd shrunk an inch or two with age and was tubby around the middle. Her large bones were spaced wide apart at shoulders and hips, and she had that rather equine look that seemed to go with liking horses and always being around horsy people. She wore her hair in the same style she'd adopted in her twenties; going by the family photo albums, what had once been blonde strands had lightened to gorgeous white hair that she wore tightly curled around her ears. The Queen Mum had probably been her model for that. She had crooked teeth, in the way of people of her generation, even those who could have afforded a good dentist. What was it with the British, anyway? Are the Middletons the only millionaires in Great Britain with a private dental plan? But she had kept all her teeth, it appeared; in fact she seemed to have more than the allotted thirty-two, slightly bucktoothed and buckled as they were.

She could talk all day about what bulbs she was planting and where she'd got them and what kind of soil was best and on and on until you just wanted to kill yourself but she never seemed to notice her audience had tuned out. She simply took it for granted I'd be fascinated, as her friends were. It was another thing that was a fence between us, my lack of interest in mucking about with bulbs. Ascot was different; here and there I could inquire intelligently about Ascot. She went every year. Only Will was invited to accompany her. Not me. The excuse given was how difficult it was to get an invitation. Maybe for the run-of-the-mill masses it was. Not for someone with her connections to that world. It was bullshit and even Will acknowledged it.

"What can I do?" he would say.

"You could call her on it. You could say if Jill can't go, I can't go. Try that."

But that only drove him into a sulky silence. You do see, I couldn't win and I decided to drop it. She couldn't live forever, after all. Fingers crossed.

When Will took me to meet her for the first time, it was a fiasco — from her standpoint. The meeting was a sure sign Will and

I were an item, that Will was looking at the long term. He was crazy about me. It didn't really matter — then — that his mother seemed to dislike me on sight: I would prevail in this contest for her son's heart. And perhaps that realization is what made her so hateful.

And maybe that's why Will's kowtowing manner with his mother always drove me batshit. I could only hear his side of the conversation when she phoned, but still. His little heh-heh laughter at whatever she was saying — so unlike him with anyone else. This guy did not suck up to anyone — not me, not anyone. Whatever I said, however hilarious, seldom earned the heh-heh, but everything *she* said was apparently straight out of a comedy skit. If she happened to interrupt us during a fight, which was more and more likely to happen, he was perfectly capable of stopping his rage, as if he had a pause button, and continue to rage at me when the call ended. And she never once asked after me or asked to speak with me. Never. It was like I didn't exist.

Things rapidly went downhill with Her Loathsomeness after that initial frosty meeting. Before too long I'd misspelled her name on a birthday card, and I never heard the end of it. She completely overlooked the fact that I had paid too much for a hand-painted silk scarf I thought she'd like. Instead she went into a decline over the inscription on the card. You tell me: Wouldn't anyone else in the world spell it Rosalind? Was it not in fact rather *common* to spell it Rossalind with that extra *S*? And no, I didn't do it on purpose, which was what she implied. Will at least pretended at the time to believe me incapable of such a petty revenge.

Anyway, she would much have preferred some gift for her horses, unless I miss my best guess. Hay or a bridle or something. She kept four horses in a stables on the grounds; in the early days, Will and I used to travel to Wiltshire on a weekend to ride.

But, that *house*. I could not believe my first sight of Will's ancestral home. I thought we had made a wrong turn into one of those safari parks like Longleat. The place was an Anglophile's dream come true. I felt like Rebecca seeing Manderley for the first time.

You couldn't take in all of White-Ashby Hall at once; you sort of swept up to it. Rather than sitting exposed to the world, like Highclere Castle of *Downton Abbey* fame, it was shielded by trees. Much better that way, because when you rounded a corner, just as you were wondering if you were *ever* going to get there, there it was, on a slight rise of the ground. And it was stunning: it literally took your breath away.

Palladian in style, it grew out of the footprint of a much older Tudor house dating back to 1548. It was huge, sprawling, and open to the public five days a week in peak season. Even the dower house where Her Wretchedness now lived, effectively pensioned off by the National Trust, was a five-bedroom behemoth that could have housed far more people than the acidulated, poisonous lady it did house. Once she was gone, Will had explained to me, his last ties with the house would likewise be gone. The arrangement with the trust was that she be taken care of for her lifetime. I wondered if they rued the deal, because she seemed likely to live to be a hundred and haunt the place thereafter.

The progenitor of the Whites came over if not with William the Conqueror then in the next wave. And from that point on they tended to pick the right side in any war or political struggle. They were savvy enough to keep their heads down in the religious skirmishes while others were losing their heads over which books of the Bible were apocryphal. I suspect this was because none of the Whites were particularly religious to begin with. They were also very lucky their lack of devotion did not, in and of itself, invite uncomfortable scrutiny. That they did all this while continuing to amass a fortune is miraculous, and it wasn't until wars and taxes began to chip away at their fortunes that, like the Crawleys, they lost some of their luster.

The magnificence of White-Ashby Hall did beg the question: What was posh Will doing with an American mutt like me?

It was a question I'd asked myself a lot. A question Rossalind, needless to say, had asked from the very beginning.

I was such a thorn in her paw, the unlooked-for sorrow of what would otherwise have been a golden retirement from doing nothing to a retirement of doing more nothing, only with titled grandchildren. She was appalled that Will had not married someone of his own kind, and came very near to saying so to me on more than one occasion. But that would be common and Rossalind was many things, but never that.

In my own defense, I never pretended to be other than I was. This scored me no points with Rossalind, who had had several titled young women lined up for Will when I'd come along and snatched him from her clutches. My lack of pretense only made her more convinced my family and I were beneath her. She seemed to have gained her knowledge of North Americans via a cursory reading of Fanny Trollope and regarded most of us as one step up from slave-owning pig farmers.

What really got me was that Will never defended me to her, not once, despite the many opportunities that presented themselves. It's not as if she would cut him off without a penny for taking my side, for in her widowhood especially she worshiped him. Besides, the terms of the trust under which they all thrived prevented that sort of dramatic renouncing gesture — he'd have to be a complete wastrel in nineteenth-century fashion for the trustees to cut him out. But his real security lay in the fact that he was the adored son — the only son — and much like my sainted brother he could do no wrong.

So even though there would be no consequences, Will never spoke up for me. I came to believe he was afraid of her — possibly because she saw through him. She had few illusions about her son. She saw through most people but in Will's case she didn't seem to mind what she saw.

Of course I made a point of calling her by her first name because really, what else would I call her? Mother? Not even. Lady White? She was lucky I didn't call her Rosie. We were family now (like it or not, and despite her energetic attempts to prevent the marriage, including hiring a private eye to have me checked out — truly) and she was not, as I explained to Will after one icy visit, going to get away with making me feel inferior, even if I didn't descend from landed gentry. (My father did own the rundown farm in Maine, but that was decidedly not the same thing.)

While I was always introduced to Rossalind's friends with my university tags attached ("Say hello to Jillian, she was at Lincoln in Oxford, however she did not matriculate in the same year as your Biffy"), it was awkward to toss all that into a conversation. Even she barely managed it. Often she would wedge in the fact that my room overlooked the Garden Quadrangle, which was a thing that seemed to thrill her to her very core — never mind the fact that I was only housed there a few months when my actual "outside walls" room was flooded by broken pipes. Had she been as familiar as I was with the equally appalling state of the plumbing in the quad she might have been even less thrilled. Her horses lived better than I had in that freezing pile but it was, I had to admit, as historic as could be. When I had first moved in I spent a certain amount of time trying to pry the wood off the walls to make sure a student from the Middle Ages had not been walled up alive in there. It had that sort of atmosphere, riddled with ghosts of the past. Rumor had it that a student had hanged himself in the room when he failed his exams and I totally believed it.

At least my Oxford degree was something I'd done right in her view, Will's choice of me being so inexplicable otherwise. I made sure to tell Rossalind my father had served honorably in the military, since the men on both sides of Will's family had some tradition of that sort of thing. I left out the part where he fell apart later.

Sometimes I wondered: Was I Will's one stab at rebellion from his upbringing, even though it was a rebellion quickly crushed? Because the more I thought about it, the less I could see what he had seen in me in the first place, compared with the Debrett's debutantes he could have had. Obviously, his mother had the same problem.

Will's father was seldom mentioned, however, and it was a significant omission. He had been sent away for some unspecified treatment to clinics a few times over the years. Whatever was wrong with him — drink, mental illness — it apparently killed him in the end.

My employment with the BBC, of which I had been rather proud, also was a source of embarrassment for Rossalind in the stately circles in which she ran. It was akin to being in trade, like being a fishmonger or a saddler. The fact that Will and I had met in a bar, a fact he mentioned to her in some careless moment, sealed my fate in her eyes. I thought of telling her that was how my parents met also. She was set against me, anyway. If I had rescued a train full of orphans it was not going to change her views one jot.

But. You could tell what really, *really* bothered Rosie was that her grandchild, the heir to the throne, would be a mongrel. That's how she would look at it. Of course, that only made me redouble my efforts to get pregnant. And it tripled my dismay when I failed. Any idiot can get pregnant, I told myself; look about you for the evidence. The gynecologist said there was nothing physically wrong. Will refused to get tested, but it was early days yet. I would wear him down: he could not be the one to let the family tree die out.

I tried every folkloric cure: ginseng sprinkled on my cereal, tanking up on folic acid (me) and caffeine (him). For a while, I practically hung upside down after sex to give Will's sperm every chance to survive their swim north. Or south, in this case. Nothing happened, month after long month of anxious waiting. There was a miscarriage early on but the doctor assured me that was common and normal and nothing to worry about. But I did not get pregnant and it became a thing, the way these things do. The more I tried the more I cared the more worried I got the smaller my chances seemed to be. It did not help that Rosie's relief at my failure to conceive as time went on was palpable. I grew to loathe our visits. I grew to loathe her. I considered faking a pregnancy just to piss her off — clearly too short-term a revenge, though.

It really did not help that Will's impatience — at first — grew along with mine. I was starting to identify with Anne Boleyn.

I used to wonder if Rosie had the power to make her son leave me. If, like a steady drip-drip on a rock, she could recall him to his privileged roots, to long summer days playing cricket, to boarding in public schools with all the other privileged fluffy-haired toffs. Never mind that he claimed to despise the memories of those days. I didn't, for one thing, believe him. He was the head boy, not some scrawny weakling tormented by the other boys or molested by some pervy headmaster with a whip. It was possible Will had been a main tormentor, in fact. The ringleader. The one they all looked up to. A leader of men, even at a tender age.

I wondered often what it would have been like to take for granted that sort of upbringing. The old-boy and old-girl networks. The unthinking wealth. The tea parties on the lawn in summer, with the dogs and children running about, the swarms of bees after the honeypot. The instinctive knowing what to wear — there was never a frantic moment in Rosie's life of picking out what she would call a "frock" — buying something on sale at the last minute, to regret it ever after. She just wore the same dress or suit that had been tailored for her years before. Not Chanel — I think Chanel had become so common she regarded it as off the rack. Something bought at some secret atelier in Paris. Somewhere in a Paris attic there might still be a tall, wide dressmaker's dummy with her name on it.

I had wanted so much for her to like me, until it became apparent that was never going to be. It was not so much jealousy I felt, this I know. It was fear.

One of us was going to die on that hill and I was afraid it would be me.

It was odd how a visit to Rossalind made me wish I still had some sort of relative left who might have defended me. It could have made all the difference. But my brother died one sunny fall day and — well, the difference to me. To all of us. It was like a curtain dropping between acts. My parents never got over the loss; in fact they dined out on it the rest of their lives. No one is ever going to hold you to the same standard as the rest of the world once they hear you've experienced such an unfathomable heartache. You can walk in and set fire to someone's living room carpet and people will say, "It's understandable. They lost a son, you know."

The same went for me. My high school teachers tiptoed around me from the day he died until I graduated. It was my first experience of being apart, of being special. "She just lost a brother, you know."

My parents never met Will, of course, which was too bad. He could have been their son restored to them, clothed in glory, hallelujah.

19

The funeral for Priscilla Anna Marie Monroe was held at St. Chrysostom's Church. It is doubtful she ever set foot in the place apart from the occasional wedding. She had long since abandoned the vestiges of a Catholic upbringing and become the most nonreligious person I ever met. Most people believe in something, if only in a superstitious way. Step on a crack, break your mother's back. A lucky charm or necklace; a lucky dress you wear on a first date. But Anna believed you made your own luck. I guess that didn't really work out, in her case.

I couldn't do more than mouth the responses to the prayers for the repose of Anna's soul. I didn't know if she had one, or if she was now in a better place; I could not begin to guess or even to care. Inside the elaborate white coffin Alfie had chosen for her did not look like a better place to me.

Just so long as she didn't come back to haunt the village. I overheard in the coffee shop someone was claiming to have seen her floating in the river, or running through the forest in a long white dress. If she'd been seen wearing the jogging outfit I'd found her in I'd have been more inclined to believe that one. Or does heaven require a change of costume into something more dignified, more spectral?

The air in the church was heavy with the scent of garish flowers, and the priest droned on and on, extolling the virtues of a woman he clearly had not known well. "Devoted wife?" I think not.

The Anglican service involved a lot of books and a lot of mad switching back and forth of pages, and of trying to find the right spot in the hymnal and whatnot. I finally gave up when they'd reached the end of "Immortal, invisible, God only wise" and I was still nowhere near finding it in the hymnal. I noticed Will next to me was not employing the lovely deep baritone voice I knew he had: he used to warble at full volume in the shower.

I stole a look at him and saw his face was flushed a deep red, and a tear had escaped from behind his glasses to roll down his cheek. *Pull yourself together, Will,* I wanted to say. There were sure to be police in the congregation. That's how they always worked these things.

Afterward there was a "Celebration of the Life of Anna Monroe" and although I felt I'd celebrated quite enough there was no way to pretend a more pressing engagement. I could tell Will felt the same, but we sloped along to the circa 1930s village hall with everyone else. Huge black clouds squatted on the distant hills as the coastal towns took a beating that day. The internment of the body was to take place later, in private, and outside the village, as there was no more room in St. Chrysostom's wee graveyard. I'd heard Alfie had wanted to cremate her but the authorities wouldn't allow it under the circumstances.

As I passed by that graveyard nearly every day, I was glad she'd be elsewhere.

Out of sight, out of mind.

The village hall is one of those institutions difficult to explain to anyone outside the UK. It bore no relation to the ugly community centers to be found across the US, built of surplus concrete blocks or whatever junk an enterprising contractor had been able to foist off on gullible or corrupt town fathers. The Weycombe Village Hall was, for one thing, the center of life for the local

Women's Institute, another of those thoroughly British inventions that for whatever reason had not gained a foothold in the States. Which was a shame, as in addition to demonstrations of corn-dolly making and canning, the women managed to do a lot of good, raising funds to feed the homeless and save the planet. Despite recruiting efforts aimed at revamping the WI's image of stodgy domesticity, the Weycombe branch remained stubbornly in the vein of the inbred women of *Harvest Home,* and I would resist joining with my last breath.

Will had once asked me why I didn't go to their meetings just for the networking opportunities, a theme that became more woven into the rich tapestry of our lives the longer I remained unemployed. He could not understand my aversion to hanging out with so many women like Heather, who went through life, while living just minutes from every convenience money could buy, as if she were homesteading on a Kansas prairie during tornado season. I was very afraid that if I got sunk into that world there would be no escape. I would end my days poring over knitting patterns and worrying that my cakes wouldn't rise, and my book or books would stay unwritten.

". . . she won't take pictures and she won't be me!"

At the celebration of Anna's heartless existence, I felt I knew most everyone apart from people connected with her job. That had always been a bit of a closed door to me, anyway, what estate agents did. If the movie *American Beauty* was anything to go by, they obsessed over feng shui-ing houses to ready them for sale. Despite her agnosticism, Anna had probably lit candles and, for all I know, performed animal sacrifice in the hearths of homes on the market for more than ninety days.

Anna's mother and father were at the celebration, looking pretty much wrecked. Alfie had told me once they "dressed funny," a statement I didn't bother to question at the time. But their fashion sense might best be described as Reformed Scottish.

Anna had seldom talked about her background. If asked, she would say she was from Bristol and change the subject. Half the population of Weycombe seemed to be from Bristol but to me it was like saying they were from Dunkirk or Glasgow. I had very few preconceived notions about the things that seemed to exercise the British the most, like class. I think, if I'm honest, it was my saving grace. Americans can be snobbish, in our vast country, about people from the Deep South, and sometimes about people from Texas, but even then, we are not particularly all about keeping them in their places based on their accents. Their race and sex, sure. Otherwise, we thrive on the rose-from-poverty stories, all that Horace Greeley stuff, and we love to have people who came from nothing regale us on talk shows, telling us how we can do it too, if we just start a vision board and kick all that negativity to the curb.

Sometimes, we raise people up just so we can tear them down again, it is true.

Anyway, Anna's parents were dressed in plaid, both of them. She in a skirt, he in a matching jacket, both in white shirts with ruffles down the front. Maybe they were going to be in a parade after the wake. It was a dark blue plaid, shot through with black. I had no idea if it was a mourning tartan or even if there were such a thing.

Her mother had been pretty once and had taken good care of her rose-petal skin; her father was a homely man, stunningly so, with an enormous putty nose stuck to his face, riddled with veins and broken capillaries. His eyes were bloodshot to match. I remembered he was technically the stepfather, which explained the gap between him and Anna, who had been so exquisitely assembled.

I offered them both my condolences, explaining that I had been Anna's friend and neighbor. I threw in the "friend" so they might let down their guard, but grief had barricaded them behind a drawbridge. Anna had been an only child. They thanked me with a stiff courtesy and went off to refresh themselves some more at the drinks table.

There was a woman there I learned later was Jason's mother, Alfie's ex. A peroxide blonde wearing a black bandage dress, she seemed to be delighted by Anna's disappearance from the scene and was not good at hiding it. Surely, please — surely she wasn't thinking Alfie would give her a second chance with Anna out of the picture?

Looking across the room, I saw Will in deep conversation with Frannie Pope, the woman who owned Serendipity, where she sold scarves and statement jewelry — gigantic necklaces and pins with slogans like "Just do it" or "Dance like no one's watching" picked out in rhinestones. Boiled wool hats in mimsy shades of lavender and, for the summer, straw hats rimmed with fabric flowers. Drapey, menopausal garb in taupe and tan with odd seams and hems that fell at odd angles, most of it appliqued with cats and butterflies — stuff like that.

I thought most of her merchandise appalling but she had been in business a long time, so what did I know. Something must get into women on holiday that would make them want to wear affirming slogans over their hearts and don night shirts decorated with cats. Who knows what their husbands thought but if I had to guess, Frannie's target market consisted largely of widows and divorcees.

At the celebration, Arty Frannie wore some crepe number in shades of mud-brown that fell in folds to her Mary Jane–style orthopedic shoes. She had piled her hair in a topknot for the occasion, gray tendrils spiraling about her face. There was something in Will's stance and hers that held my attention as they stood to one side, away from the crush by the buffet, talking practically nose to nose in hushed voices. I stepped behind one of the pillars in the room to study them from over the top of my wine glass. Whatever was going on, it wasn't sexual, God knew. I mean, the woman had thirty years on Will — definitely old enough to be his snippy mother — and she was a very odd duck, besides.

Will drank at the gathering in a way that told me getting blind drunk had been his plan from the first. It was not a matter of loosening up or of drowning sorrows: he drank with the determination of a man knowing there was hemlock in that glass and he was going to drink it to the dregs, anyway. He looked forlorn, bereft as a kid whose dog has just been run over. At least he wasn't crying anymore but I did hope no one else noticed his reaction to Anna's death was a bit out of line for someone who was, you know, married to me.

I had put away a few drinks myself on an empty stomach and I started silently to cry as I walked home from the Anna celebration, alone in the dark and well over the walking limit. A strong, manly arm to lean on — any arm — would have been welcome. There was no one to see the tears as they coursed down my cheeks, and I didn't care if they did. I wasn't crying for Anna, of course, but for myself; funerals bring up all the stuff you don't ever want to think about in the course of a normal week. Or lifetime.

So I was indulging in a rare, gooey sentimentality. I wished fleetingly there really was an afterlife so I could see my mother again. To explain to her the why of my choices.

In days past I might have shared these sentiments, however sophomoric, with Will.

Of course, he was now the last person who would tolerate listening to all that. The fact was, he'd never seen me break down. Well, maybe the once. I'd been angry, lots — there was plenty to be angry about, Rosalind just for a start — but weeping and carrying on? Never.

It still raises the hair on the back of my neck to remember this: As I felt my way home from the celebration, blinkered by the darkness, I thought I saw Anna drive by in her white convertible. She was dressed as I'd seen her a thousand times, in a too-tight navy blue suit and white blouse and with big chunky jewelry at the neck — the uniform of her profession. But she was a corpse, dead at the wheel. She turned her head and stared in my direction out of those dead eyes. "Made my flesh creep" is an exact description. So is "my stomach churned." Mercifully, the car sped off and only then could I see it was not Anna. It was some dark-haired, hollow-eyed woman, perhaps the woman who lived over the linens shop a few streets over. I had to get a grip.

Investigating this case . . . Rashima was right. I needed to leave it alone, for my sanity's sake.

I went inside and poured a tumbler of

scotch from Will's stash of single malt.

I told myself it was fatigue, it was fear, it was knowing this thing with Will was hanging over my head and I would have to get through it somehow. We were coming apart — fine. Okay. But we would part on my terms. And that required a certain shoring up of defenses.

It was the not knowing what came next, the not being able to control for everything, that was freaking me out. But by halfway through the second glass, I'd calmed myself down. And I kept a tighter rein from then on.

The next day I asked Will what was up with him, waiting until he looked slightly sobered up. He said he didn't know why the whole thing had hit him so hard. He'd slept in his office again, emerging just long enough to pour some emergency coffee. I could almost have felt sorry for him. That dangerous pity again.

"It's just . . ." he tried. "It's just that I just *saw* her, I just had seen her, and she was so alive. Not just talking and walking around but *living,* the way few people are, smiling, happy — full of it. Brimming over. You know how she was." Yes, I knew. "I guess," he continued, "I had a 'there but for the grace of God' moment."

"Understandable," I said. "Me too."

"Let's not talk about it. I really don't think I can bring myself to talk or even think about it anymore."

True to his word, he seemed to let all thought of Anna go. Three days later, it was as if she had never existed. Sociopaths can do that. I'm not sure about the rest of us.

There had been plainclothes cops at both the funeral and the celebration, I was sure of that. Too young and bright-eyed; too alert, too not grief-stricken to be mourners.

A lot had been going on, for sure. I had also seen a look pass between Alfie and Heather, and I'd seen her start to ask him something, then think better of it. I asked Will if he'd noticed it, too.

"No," he said firmly. "I saw nothing whatsoever. You have too vivid an imagination."

While he didn't mean it to be, I found that rather flattering. A vivid imagination was way better than the "reliable" label my teachers had attached to me. I read that as dull and plodding, when what I wanted was to be wild and free and — above all, once I reached my teens — sexy. Reliable was for bus drivers.

Of course, then Will had to ruin it with a snipe about how I had too much time on my hands and that's what was leading to all this wild speculation. I refused to be drawn. I had many potential suspects to write up, to get down on paper. Everything and everyone by that point was material. I was itching for Will to go away so I could get to work.

Anna's stepson had been at the celebration, but just barely, and he was worth many pages as a suspect. Jason — gangly, almost feral in appearance, looking nothing like his father. He was the sort of aggressively artistic kid you'd find working in a movie theater that specialized in indie films, with a scraggly beard and Celtic tattoos and jewelry stuck all over him.

He had slipped away early, barely acknowledging anyone who approached him with condolences. His father seemed too out of it to notice. I suspect both of them were on something to dull the pain. The scotch looked like a bad idea on top of that but it was not my place.

I'd decided the police could learn all about Jason with no help from me. The usual sense of entitlement disguised as "a struggle to find himself." For Jason, finding his own ass was a struggle and would be until he made some different friends and put away the drug paraphernalia for good.

Briefly, I wondered how Anna's death would affect him. Financially, I mean. Emotionally, I'm not sure it even registered.

He had inherited a small amount of money from a great-grandmother when he turned eighteen, but he'd blown through that quickly. Snorted through it, traveled a bit. "Learned how to abuse me in three languages," as Anna had told me. He'd lived out in Oregon for a time, starring in his own version of *Portlandia* and routinely predicting the end of the world. All by way of dodging the question of when he was going to get a steady job. Why bother with jobs when the world was coming to an end?

Actually, it turned out he had had a steady job all along, and once they legalized marijuana it cut into his profits so much he had to return home. He paused only long enough to top up his allowance on the way to South Africa, Alfie being ever a guilty soft touch for his son.

Six months later, Jason was calling from Cape Town, astonished to learn his credit card no longer worked since Alfie and Anna, after fair warning, had stopped paying the bill for him. He'd come home for a brief, raucous visit that ended with another flare-up of his father's illness. Jason had flounced off and hadn't much been seen in the neighborhood since.

I knew him mainly from Anna's rare outbursts of frustration with him and from his boyhood photos scattered about her house. From these photos I'd gained an impression of a gangly four-year-old with a toothy grin who had survived a fraught adolescence of facial hair experiments to become a surly young adult male of the kind often described in police bulletins. He seemed to have got into some dicey business arrangements, either to fund his drug use or because his judgment was so impaired by them. As a teen he frequented Riverside Park, a common scene of drug busts. You'd think they'd learn but anyone who would take drugs in the first place is probably incapable of setting new memories.

Anna had told me all this late one night, finishing off a bottle of wine after the others in the book club had left. I had a feeling she was confiding too much and might come to regret it, not that I was going to tell anyone. Even after she died, I never told Milo everything I knew.

Anna had clearly been at her wit's end or she would not have confided in me. We were, as I say, not exactly close.

20

The day after the Anna service I paid a visit to Arty Frannie's kaleidoscopic shop. I could think of no way to ask what she and Will had been so cozy about, but that question was not my top priority. What had happened to Anna was, and what Frannie might really have seen that day.

Everyone called her Frannie, never Frances or Fran. Over her drapey dresses she was given to wearing capes and shawls, dramatic, curtain-like things she could swish about her shoulders to knock knickknacks off of tables. She often wore her hair in an intricate braid and she had the kohl-lined eyes of a mystic, a look which she used to good effect in her shop, selling in addition to her unique line of fashion all sorts of candles and incense and New Agey gimcrack.

Physically she was all bust and belly like a fertility goddess; mentally she was an alumnus of the Shirley MacLaine School of Karma. She was also a bit of a busybody, if likable enough. When I saw her with Will at the village hall, I remembered thinking his own mother had never looked at him with such real concern.

I had never set foot inside her house in Weycombe Court, which I imagined was furnished a lot like a sultan's harem, smelling of incense, all beads and candles and embroidered tassels.

The dogs stayed with her in the shop all day, occasionally nipping at the heels of customers they didn't like. They observed me closely for between-meal-snack potential as I entered. Like many dogs in Weycombe, Buzz and Armstrong had been to the Weycombe Academy for Dogs (WAD) and were spoiled rotten. In winter Frannie dressed them in little sweaters, different ones each day, another outlet for her uncertain fashion sense. She came into her own at Halloween, when she sewed their costumes. They often won the annual Dog Days of Autumn competition; the year before, she'd dressed Buzz as Princess Leia and Armstrong as Darth Vader.

She'd been divorced so long ago she couldn't be bothered to mention her former husband. She might even have forgotten his name: I always suspected that despite hanging out with Garvin, the village scribe, she was one of these women happier on her own. She was happy with her work, content with her lot, and had the wisdom to shut up and be grateful. I should have suggested she embroider that on something.

She did not seem to have a dread of growing old, or of living like a character in some Anita Brookner novel, drawing out the long days in a sort of pointless shuffling about. You saw lots of those Brookner women in London: they worked for the Department of Something Boring and took pottery classes and hung around galleries and so on but it was all a pretext to find a mate, or at least to keep busy-busy until a mate came along. Or so it seemed to me. I had vowed I would die before I joined their legions.

As I walked in, the bells over the door chimed, a curtain leading into the back of the shop parted, and Frannie breezed in like a vaudevillian stepping onstage.

"You're famous," I told her.

"So are you." She pulled her shawl closer, bracelets jangling. "Not in a good way, sadly."

"So it *was* you. You were mentioned as a woman walking her dogs. I know of only one other person it could have been, out there at about that time."

"They didn't use my name!" she said. "I hope not. They'd no right. The police promised." She was being more than a bit disingenuous here. Rashima had told me Frannie had broadcast her involvement to everyone who would stay to listen. It made me wonder how far she could be trusted.

"Don't worry," I said. "I just put two and two together. They said you — someone — saw Anna go by and then, as you were turning back with the dogs, at the top of the hill, you saw her stop to talk with someone. The police put out a call for that someone but no one has come forward. The logical suspicion is that Anna was talking with her killer."

"They said as much to me." Frannie looked alarmed, uneasy. She'd been dragged into something really ugly as a witness, so no wonder. But she was, on some level, excited by it, at being the center of attention. It positively shone out of her eyes.

I saw little point in beating around the bush. We both paid our respects to Anna's memory ("Shocking!" "So sad." "So young . . . ish") and then I said, "Am I remembering right, that Jason worked for you once?"

She was sorting through something in a

drawer and gave the drawer a harder shove than was needed to close it.

"Yes. I gave that little son of a bitch a job for the summer. Did you see him at Anna's wake? You could tell he was stoned." Then her expression froze as her brain caught up with her mouth. "I mean — meaning no disrespect to Anna, but you know what I mean. He wasn't literally a son of a bitch, he was only her stepson, besides —"

"I know what you mean. Go on."

"He stole from me. He took from the till, which was stupid of him — of course I'd notice during the end-of-day tally and it could only have been Jason. Probably he thought someone my age was too senile to notice. Presumably he stole to support his habit. One of his habits. I believe he also rifled through my purse one day. I had a prescription for sleeping pills and about a third of it had disappeared."

"You're sure it was Jason." It was not a question. "The purse rifling."

"Not one hundred percent, but near enough — yes. I left him alone to run the shop while I popped out for a sandwich and to run errands. I don't believe people will behave in a trustworthy fashion if you treat them as if they're untrustworthy. I'd never had a serious problem operating under that principle until Jason. It still makes me angry to think about it. I trusted him because I didn't think he'd be that dumb — I knew his parents. It's not as if he had wandered in off the street."

"I think he was past caring," I said. "Addicts lose their reason."

She nodded. "I guess. At some point last year, the story went round that he had traveled to North Africa for reasons unknown. Some were rather hoping he'd become a suicide bomber. One of the stupid ones that accidentally blows himself up before he reaches his target. More likely he was on a drug expedition." She held out a hand and began distractedly to check the state of her manicure; her nails were painted a blackish red. I noticed she had the beginnings of arthritis in her thumbs.

"He vanished almost as soon as the wake started," I said.

"Making a run for it, do you think? What a foolish thing to do."

I shrugged. "I'm pretty sure they'd have stopped him from flying out of Heathrow. The police looking for his stepmother's killer, I mean."

"Would they stop him?" she asked. "There's no warrant been taken out that I'm aware. But I think he'd go to ground somewhere they'd never think to look. Someplace with no extradition treaty." She seemed certain a guilty conscience was at work. Maybe she thought it was Jason she'd seen that morning at a distance. That was interesting, right there. Jason did have a way of turning up like a bad penny. But when I asked her, she shook her head.

"I couldn't say," she replied. Whatever that meant. British reticence? Or she wasn't sure what she'd seen?

"Hmm," I said. I decided not to pressure her. As to Jason's making a break for freedom to parts unknown — it was a theory, but it was likelier he would pop in and out of the village to see what pickings he could glean off his father. If he ran, he'd run for the nearby hills. Scotland would be a good guess, or Wales. Anna and Alfie had a house out there in the wild, as I recalled. Some unpronounceable place. I supposed Milo and Co. knew all about that but I might point them in that direction when I saw them again.

Gently, I guided the conversation back to that day by the river, what she'd seen or thought she'd seen.

"Are you sure about the time?" I asked. "The paper said it was nine o'clock."

She sighed; her exasperation with the

Chronic was plain. Garvin, her geriatric paramour, was thought to drink or be losing his eyesight, or both — possibly related conditions. "Then the paper got it wrong. Honestly, Garvin needs to hand the reins to a younger person. The dogs always get their walk at nine before I open the shop at nine thirty. I reach that part of the path by nine fifteen. Not more than a minute or two off either way. It wasn't nine."

"Nothing delayed you that day? Or threw you off your routine?"

"No. The police asked me the same thing. It was a normal day and I have to keep the dogs on their schedule. I'm religious about it. Otherwise — accidents. You know."

I looked over at the dogs, who managed to look embarrassed.

"And you saw someone with Anna?"

"Yes, I did. I saw them from the back, though. I never saw the face."

"Man or woman?"

She shook her head. I noticed her hands were trembling even more as she played with one of the long silk scarves at her neck. Nervousness? Parkinson's? Or lying?

"A man."

"Are you sure?"

"I'm pretty sure, Jill. Everyone on the trail wears jogging pants and hats and scarves and jackets. Sometimes a balaclava when it's really cold. It wasn't a large person. So perhaps a woman."

"Jason," I pointed out, "isn't a large guy. What was this person wearing?"

"The usual black Lycra pants. A jacket. A hat. The jacket was blue."

"The hat?"

"It was gray."

"Could it have been someone with gray hair?"

She paused, considering. "Well, I suppose it could have been. From that distance, and looking down, a gray hat could look like gray hair."

"Could you spot the brand of any of this stuff? Generally there's a logo."

Again she shook her head. "Too far. The police asked me the same thing. They were so insistent, my head started to hurt."

That seemed like a hint that I should back off, so I did. I started wandering about the shop, inspecting items at random. She had a gift for choosing things a tourist might buy on impulse, even though the tourist could buy the exact same thing back home, probably for less money. But they would always remember that they bought that candle or incense or whatever on their vacation to historic Weycombe.

As I shopped around I reflected that Frannie might make a compelling witness, despite all the black liner and mascara and the head scarves and stuff that made her look like a fortune-teller. A life-size scarecrow sat on a chair in one corner, part of a seasonal display, and whether or not Frannie realized it the scarecrow woman was dressed just like her.

She seemed sure of herself but her memory was largely based on her daily routine. She struck me as a bit persuadable, a bit bendable, wanting to please. It was hard to see which way she'd bend but for now, I'd say Anna had a good and observant witness on her side, at least as far as pinpointing the time.

"Good," I said. "That's good that you're so sure, I mean. I was a reporter. I've seen the most competent witnesses torn to shreds by a good prosecutor. You're sure it was a blue coat? Dark blue, was it?"

Now she looked doubtful.

"Not purple?"

She squinted up at the ceiling fixture. She'd painted her eyebrows into an unhappy clown expression, like a mime.

"Maybe purple blue. Purplish."

Maybe she was not the unshakable witness after all. "They'll want you to be consistent," I said.

"It was dark blue." She nodded her head, having settled it in her mind once and for all, nailing down that feathery testimony.

"Did you see anyone on the water?"

She started to shake her head, but then she said, "Not then."

"Not then?"

"Later that morning, from the shop window. I saw someone in a kayak. I remember thinking it was too cold for that. There've even been paddleboarders out there. It's ridiculous."

My heart gave a hard thump, the blood catching up to a missed beat. I thought of the person I'd seen on the river as I headed to Macy's that day, and how I'd had the same thought. Sports enthusiasts knew no common sense.

"Man or woman?"

"I don't know. A woman, I think."

"Could it have been the same person?"

She shook her head decisively.

"No. They were wearing a red jacket."

She seemed satisfied with that logic, as if a person could only own one jacket and never change it.

"The news report said it was probably a male you saw."

This seemed to confuse her. "It did?" she

said. "Garvin again, I suppose."

"You know the sun was bright that day. It had to be in your eyes."

"Ye-s-s-s. Whoever it was, was sort of silhouetted against the sun. You're right."

Her eyes danced across my face and would not meet mine. Every actor I'd ever hired to play the shifty-eyed villain had had the same look.

Frannie was lying. Interesting.

"So it could have been a woman."

She seemed to be recalled to some warning, probably from Attwater and Milo, that she wasn't to talk about what she'd seen. They knew witnesses could mess up their own testimony, shade it and color it in the retelling. They knew that all witnesses are unreliable, the more so as time passes.

"Really, Jillian, I'm not at liberty to say. Anyway, it's too awful. I don't want to talk about it now."

Again I decided I'd be wise to back off. I feigned interest in a tray of reading glasses.

"It really was a shame," she added. "About Jason, I mean." She was sorting baubles by color into a tray. "He was a natural at sales."

I'm afraid I snorted at this. "I'll bet," I said.

"I didn't mean that exactly, the drugs. It's that women trusted him, you see. Trusted his taste."

"Mmm." More fool them. I was looking at a necklace that wasn't half bad, though, and thinking I should buy something to show my goodwill.

"Still, he could be a bit of a lad."

Such a useful phrase. We don't really have the equivalent expression in the US. Our "bad boy" carries heavier connotations. "Bit of a lad" covers a wealth of wayward behaviors like a tent dress.

But Frannie was getting jumpy again. I finally asked her if something was wrong.

"Wrong? Jill, I just witnessed a murder. What could be wrong?"

Of course, of course. But did I imagine it, or was there more, something beyond that?

I tried a long shot, a test of how much she knew of the intrigue that tended to bubble around Anna. "There was some sort of tension in the book club, before it disbanded," I said. "Any idea what that was about?"

"You're asking me? Ask Heather or someone. I thought it was *your* book club. I wasn't a member; I was never invited to join." *Ah.* It was clear this omission had stung. Book clubs were tricky things. I knew of a club that ran for decades until it blew up over an infidelity in the ranks. One member had dropped out, as it turned out, so she'd be free to meet up with one of the other women's husbands. I knew this because the dropout had become my stepmother.

"But you were so busy running the shop," I said diplomatically. "I don't suppose it occurred to anyone you might be interested." In fact, Frannie was never a candidate, and it had nothing to do with her busyness. It was feared her taste in literature would mirror her taste in clothes and jewelry. Danielle Steel meets Alexandre Dumas. "I was ready to quit myself but it disbanded before I could. You didn't miss much, trust me."

She didn't look mollified. For some reason, the snub still bothered her.

"But," I added, "maybe I will have a word with Heather. Another word, I mean. She and Anna were not exactly close, but Heather saw a lot more of her than I did. Thanks for the idea."

"Don't mention it," said Frannie, again with that skittish look. Some gadget for attaching price tags fell from her arthritic hands; I swooped in to catch it before it hit the floor.

That really seemed to unnerve her. It was clear she couldn't wait for me to leave. It was almost as if she was waiting for someone else to come in — she kept checking her watch, like she had an appointment.

I decided to end her misery; I could always come back.

"Well, bye," I said. "See you around. If you think of anything else . . ."

"If I think of anything else," she said, with some asperity, "I'll call the police."

That was me put in my place.

21

Of course I had no intention of talking with Heather. One visit to *Little House* a week was my limit. I had said whatever came into my head to calm Frannie. It seemed to work. But my leaving worked even better.

I stopped at the coffee shop for a soy latte and to jot down as much of the conversation as I could remember. Frannie's jittery body language said plenty. But what, exactly? Still, I wrote it all down, in no particular order. One day — I hoped — this would be part of my story.

As usual I was in no hurry to return to an empty house. I sat at my favorite corner table, recalling Frannie's weird demeanor and appearance, as Bathsheba slept nearby. Then I cast my mind back to the last book club. The last intact book club, that is. It happened to have been held at Macy's new place.

We'd been on *Wolf Hall,* and the whole

subject of adultery and Anne Boleyn's reaction when Henry's wife Katherine had died. Her undiluted joy that her nemesis finally was gone, legitimizing by her death Anne's own marriage to Henry. Henry had shared Anne's joy, short-lived though it turned out to be.

Heather's take on this had been surprising. She felt that Anne had been unjustly stigmatized as the other woman. Heather was a second wife herself, and this was my first inkling that perhaps she had not met Gideon after his first wife died, but before. This cast her in a new light for me: not the goofy queen of homespun naïveté, but a potential homewrecker like Boleyn.

"Easy for some to say," Anna had said, turning to stare at our hostess, Macy. She held the stare until Macy, realizing a strange hush had descended on the room, looked up. Anna had muttered the words almost under her breath, but they were audible.

As they were meant to be. This was the Weycombe Court equivalent of throwing plague-infested bodies over the wall into Macy's garden. (I was constantly thinking in terms of Borgia metaphors in the days when the book club began blowing up.)

Anna had turned away with a sniff and made a covering dive for the nacho dip.

Macy actually grabbed Anna's arm, forcing her back into the sofa. It was not a wise move. Anna jerked away abruptly, teeth bared. Predictably, the nacho dip fell onto her white skirt. Macy released her but continued to hold that frozen blue stare. The soft overhead lights were reflected in her eyes, contributing to the impression of a malevolent force having taken control of her brain.

Anna stared back, wiping furiously at her skirt with a serviette the while. It was then that Macy crossed the line, although half the people hearing this exchange didn't understand what was going on.

"You treat him like he's not even there," said Macy. "He needs to prove, if only to himself, that he's alive."

"Who?" This from Heather. The rest of us knew without asking.

"You have no idea what you are talking about," hissed Anna. "And it's no fucking business of yours, anyway. How dare you? Who are you anyway?" She paused for a deep breath, then fairly shrieked, "You are nothing but a trollopy little stop-out and the whole village knows it."

Wow. While I and some others might have felt this was Anna calling the kettle black, it was time to break the two ladies up before a hair-pulling catfight got underway. What had been said so far was already so terribly non-British, you could hear a pin drop as people waited for the next round, wondering what on earth to do. It was hard to imagine where it might lead if cooler heads did not prevail. I don't normally do cool head but this time it seemed to fall to me.

"Come on," I said to Anna. As I was nearest her, and she lived nearest me, I got to play the peacemaker. Simultaneously, Heather latched onto Macy. "It's okay," she kept saying, like she was talking to Lulu. "It's okay. Come along with me now. We'll have some nice tea, shall we?"

Tea. A line of coke might have been more like it, but the words had the desired effect. Macy stepped back from the brink and followed Heather meekly into the kitchen.

Having little choice, I left with a still-fuming Anna.

The drive back from the Anna-Macy playoff had been about as uncomfortable as it gets. Clearly, Anna was as ill at ease to find herself in my Mini — being escorted home like someone tossed out of a pub— as I was to have her there.

"Can you tell me what that was about?" I ventured, partly because my apparent cluelessness might add an air of normalcy to the ride, which was otherwise suffocating in more ways than one. The warm air outside had come up against a cold front, resulting in the densest peasouper fog I'd ever experienced on these shores. I wasn't sure whether to turn the heat up or down against the windscreen to combat the blinding mist, so while I experimented, nearly running us off the road in the process, Anna took a moment to consider the question. And to dial it down a notch, as I was relieved to hear in her voice when she finally spoke.

"What really fucking goddamn galls me," she said, as if continuing a previous conversation, "is her presumption. That she knows all about my marriage, and what my husband needs and thinks and feels, and I — just the wife, you know — have no clue. Well, walk a mile in my shoes, bitch. If you can fit your size forty-one Louboutins in there. You ever notice how big her feet are? *Cow.*"

I nodded, still fiddling with the dials. Mercifully, the bottom of the screen started to clear, so if I ducked down and drove like a ninety-year-old Floridian, I could just see my way ahead. Anna's language alone was a barometer of her state of mind — she seldom swore. Professionally, she had to keep it clean so as not to offend potential clients. She dealt with so many types of people, she had adopted an excruciatingly polite, bland, yet la-di-da way of speaking. I always thought she might have been over-compensating for her background.

"When Macy lived over in the Court," she began, "she'd come over every ten minutes with some lame excuse. She couldn't find the valve to turn on the water to the patio outside. Did we have a chainsaw she could borrow. Did we —"

"A chainsaw?"

"Yes, God knows what for. She didn't have any body parts to dispose of that I'm aware of, although I wouldn't put it past her." Anna paused to push glossy locks of dark hair away from her face, using both hands. The movement pressed her large breasts against the thin white fabric of her Oxford shirt. Even dressed down for a book club with a bunch of other women, Anna was stunning. Sexy without really trying, damn her — unlike Macy, whose every moment and every available fund were devoted to enhancing her allure.

I forget what I was wearing. Jeans, probably. Some no-iron shirt, fresh from the dryer. Will was right. I was in a rut.

"I mean, you don't get where she is

without being out on the pull most nights — if you get my meaning." I had no idea but I nodded sagely, not wanting to stem the flow. "Hanging around bars was the only way she was going to meet someone with Barry's cash. She could hardly enroll in law school, now, could she? She came from nothing and now she practically lives in a fucking palace."

As Anna's vocabulary continued its descent, traces of her Bristol accent came creeping in. I thought it was funny that she considered Macy to be a social-climbing bimbo when she could so easily have been tarred with the same brush. Me too, come to that.

"Well, none of us are actually going without, now, are we?" I said. "We don't have the manor house but loads of people would envy us."

She turned in her seat to face me. "Oh, *shut* it, Mary Poppins."

"Sorry," I said mildly. I lifted my hands from the steering wheel in an appeasing gesture. "Didn't mean to condescend."

Sitting back now in my worn chair in the coffee shop, I thought: So. Anna had thought Macy was after Alfie. And Macy thought Anna was after Barry. Interestingly enough, Macy had not brought up Anna's accusations the day of the *salade niçoise.*

I watched the rise and fall of Bathsheba's rib cage, remembering one other thing about that book club night. The wind had roared for hours, clearing away the fog as it lifted some of the tiles of our roof. It was a huge storm, and probably a metaphor for something but I had been too tired to think about it.

Will had not come home until midnight. I heard him head downstairs and later I thought I heard him throw something against a wall, a book or something, which he sometimes did when he was angry.

It was crazy, I know. Crazier still that I put up with him for so long.

22

After a reasonable amount of time, I went to make a condolence call at the home of Alfie Monroe, widower. At least I hoped I'd waited long enough. Ten days might have been more like it but I didn't feel I had that long. I bought a gluten-free casserole from Waitrose and popped it in the oven, hoping it was something Alfie could eat. I could hardly show up with a tub of yogurt. When I saw his car pull in, I gave him ten minutes to pour himself a drink and then I went over with my offering. He had been to and fro a lot since Anna's death, I guessed having things to do with winding up her estate. And talking to Sergeant Milo.

I hadn't been in the Monroe townhouse since the last time Anna had hosted the book club. I'd forgotten how over the top it was: Imelda Marcos might have been the design consultant. Anna was big on brocade and satin, so at the book club sessions held in her parlor, as she called it, it was a challenge for the more inebriated participants not to slide off the sofa onto the floor. I had taken to wearing high heels whenever Anna was hostessing because they allowed me to brace myself against the rug the way a mountain climber might cling to a sheer rock face.

The fabric that predominated in the room, covering the chairs and sofa and windows, was a pale green textile she'd had imported from France. I'm sure the fact the color perfectly matched her eyes was the purest coincidence, right? But why not play up that striking coloring? I remembered her as she had sat on her usual chair, curled up like a cat with the firelight throwing shifting haloes and shadows at her back. She was so *alive.* Just as Will had said. I'd taken advantage of that relaxed setting when I made that video of her. Subliminally, it suggested that if you allowed Anna Monroe to broker your house deal, you would find yourself living in similar comfort and luxury.

Just then something nudged against my knee and I practically jumped out of my skin. It was Georgina, their dog. I forget what breed it was — the kind with Rastafarian hair. I reached down absentmindedly to stroke the top of its head. It occurred to me

I might offer to walk her for Alfie.

I crossed the room to look at the collection of framed photos, Georgina trailing me. There was one of Jason as a rebellious teenager, looking pissed off and ready to bolt, taking his bad complexion with him. The photographer didn't have to be a genius to capture the fact that Jason was wishing himself anywhere but at the studio, posed before a phony backdrop of the Roman coliseum. This surly Jason was lined up next to playful, happy Jason: Jason as a toddler, tightly — too tightly — hugging a long-ago family cat. There was also a photo of Anna that I'd seen many times, the backlit glam shot that appeared in all her realtor ads. She looked like an angel, but then again, that photo was at least ten years out of date. There were no family group photos and none of Alfie, not even of Alfie before disease had begun ravaging his frame. I suppose staring at photos of yourself as you used to be and never would be again was best avoided. He had only to look down at his arms and legs, which showed little sign of fat or muscle, the raw-looking, age-spotted skin stretched over tendon, to see the damage done.

I heard the sound of a door opening; Alfie had returned from depositing the casserole somewhere. God knew, he might have a dozen such meals crammed into the fridge or the rubbish bin by now, but it was the thought that counted. I couldn't show up empty-handed, and there are times when a card just doesn't cover it. It's a missed opportunity but card manufacturers haven't produced anything to moderate the mind-blowing loss of a loved one to murder.

For many reasons, I liked Alfie, as I've said. People did. He had kept his nickname despite its less-than-aristocratic associations, for one thing. Anyone with a shred of pretension might have insisted on Alfred. But Alfie suited him. Friendly and approachable. Put aside images you may have of Michael Caine in the role of the callous scoundrel who seduces his way across London. This Alfie's defining characteristic was his humility, whether a legacy of his religious upbringing or some genetic marker — who can say. But what struck me most about him was his gratitude to Anna and to God, presumably, for Anna's having married him. He truly worshipped her and could not seem to believe the good luck that had brought her to him. Or, presumably, the bad luck that had taken her away.

He wore small dark glasses that, along with his wizened physique, made him look like a blind beggar in some Dickensian drama. They — teams of white-coated specialists in tropical medicine — had never been able to sort out exactly what was wrong with him, but the bug he'd picked up in Africa made recurring appearances, rendering him periodically useless. Anna would complain and I couldn't honestly blame her — the frustration of not knowing or being able to fix what was wrong must have been colossal. Alfie had this philosophical, "whatever God wills" sort of resignation to the situation; Anna, not so much. I think she felt she'd bought a cat in a bag, as the French would say. Because the National Health wasn't well equipped to cope with long-term cases such as Alfie's I'm sure the couple's finances, substantial though they appeared to be, took a hit as well as their marriage. Vacations had often been planned when Alfie seemed to be on the mend, but more often than not had been cancelled last minute when he just could not manage the strain of air or train travel. What their sex lives were like (and on this subject, Anna did not share), I didn't care to dwell on, but "sporadic" is probably the best way to describe it.

Alfie indicated that I should sit on one of the slippery chairs, so I did — tentatively, hoping it would keep me in its embrace.

"How're you holding up?" I asked him, plumping a tasseled pillow behind me and planting my feet on the rug.

He just shook his head, his expression bleak. It is unfortunate but true that you can't choose where you love, and he had loved Anna. It's like there is a little department in the human brain, the Department of Bad Choices, and when it spots a likely target it says, "There's a really selfish jackass, made just for you. Go for it."

"I'm so sorry," I said. I determined to keep this as brief and painless as I could. "Have the police been awful?"

"Apart from having decided, on the basis of nothing whatsoever, that I probably killed my wife? Because it's always the husband, you know. They've come close to trying to nail me a few times, but having no, like, evidence, they've snapped shut their notebooks and gone the fuck away. For now." He stopped, took a big gulp of air, and said, "Sorry. Sorry for the language. Just . . . sorry."

"Oh, please," I said. "I can't imagine what you're going through. Say what you want and don't edit for the likes of me. I just wish . . . you know."

"You wish you could help. Yes. Half the

neighborhood has been by to offer little pep talks about time healing all wounds. What is flaxseed, anyway? Heather came by with this brick made of it. I'm not sure if I'm meant to spread it with butter or wait for her to bring more over so I can cement the bricks together. Anyway, being the police's main suspect is no joke. Correction, their only suspect. The only person they can be bothered to question. But at least the neighbors don't seem to share their opinion."

"I've spoken with Sergeant Milo. Honestly, he seems, well — he's no Rhodes Scholar but he might be a bit less inclined to fall for clichés than most."

"You think so? Really." Alfie was not actually listening. He had brought out some water and glasses on a tray and busied himself trying to pour me a glass. I was surprised he didn't offer me tea, that British solution to everything, including Zulu uprisings. But that's how far standards had fallen at the Monroe house. He probably didn't know how to boil water. I finally took the pitcher from him; his hands were shaking so hard with the effort it was a very good thing it was only lukewarm water.

Inspired, I asked, "Would you like me to make you some tea?"

"Oh!" he said, as if realizing for the first

time it was the one thing he did want in the way of help. "Yes, please, would you? I'm afraid I'm hopeless. Anna always . . . She always made us tea right about now. When she was home."

Which was practically never, but you could see how that little lie comforted him. Anna, domestic goddess, adoring wife and stepmother, putting aside her dreams of world conquest to make tea for her happy family.

The dog and I followed him out to the kitchen, with which I was only fleetingly acquainted from the nights when I dropped off my contribution to the book club. We drew lots for what to bring and somehow I most often drew the dessert card. Once I no longer had a day job I'd arrive laden with something I'd slaved over literally all day. The last meeting — the one where it went irretrievably to hell — I'd brought individual ramekins of chocolate panna cotta. The ramekins were still over at Macy's house — I kept forgetting to ask for them back.

Alfie pointed out where the tea things were kept — his best guess, in some cases, including under the sink — and stood back while I filled the electric kettle before setting it back on its base and turning it on. I busied myself with tea cups and saucers before finally turning to him, asking, "Are you really their only suspect? That's absurd." And it was. There must have been a hundred people they could pin this on.

"I think so. And I agree that it's absurd." He ran one hand through hair that looked like it would soon be in need of a good wash. This time with shampoo. "But there was someone —" He dropped a spoon, interrupting himself.

"Someone?" I prompted.

There was a long, heavy pause at this. He put the spoon back on the saucer. I removed it, replacing it with a clean one.

"A witness, I guess. Because they kept asking me if I owned a blue jacket. I asked them if they knew anyone who didn't own a blue jacket."

"A blue jacket," I repeated. "Nothing more? I mean, they didn't say why they were asking?"

"They didn't confide their strategy to me. No."

I felt a twinge that there I was, pressing him. Then I reminded myself that this was a way I could help him — by pointing the police in the right direction and getting them off Alfie's back.

The one person in the world they should probably be open with, I thought, and they were playing games with the guy. I knew Alfie didn't do it; he couldn't have done such a thing in a million years. They were just being dense. And lazy, wanting to wrap this up as soon as possible. But then, they didn't know the man as I did. He loved Anna, as I've said, and not in a "if I can't have her, no one can" sort of way. He just did.

23

I stayed nearly an hour at Alfie's, doing what little good I thought I could: just sitting there listening as he praised Anna's many virtues, which to be honest, wasn't easy. I left promising to pitch in with walking Georgina where needed. He didn't seem to have any better idea than I did where the police were in their investigation.

I thought Oscar Mayhew, my old colleague, might have ways of finding out. That evening I shot him a test email. Oscar changed jobs often and there was no guarantee he'd be in the place where I'd left him. I soon received a reply with one of those paranoid legal disclaimers four inches long at the end, as happens whenever you communicate with any corporate email account, demanding that I delete any messages received in error and notify the authorities, or something. I thought it rather sweet that they imagined I was going to trash any juicy emails from my system just because they asked. But given the level of distrust under which news organizations operated, email didn't seem the best forum to discuss a murder investigation. So I simply asked Oscar if he could meet me over drinks or lunch as soon as possible. He knew I lived in Weycombe; I figured he'd know what it was about.

We arranged to meet at Murano's near St. Bride's Church — known as the journalists' church. If that isn't an oxymoron, I don't know what is. Anyway, the restaurant was hidden in a ganglia of lanes behind Fleet Street, where Oscar was now plying his trade alongside the other ink-stained wretches. He gave me good directions, saying he wanted to meet close to his offices to allow us time to talk. Not that it mattered: Oscar was the kind of reporter who set his own rules, seldom bothering to tell anyone where he was. He was known for turning off his mobile when he didn't want to be disturbed. He might be out chasing a lead or getting blind drunk. With Oscar, the result might be the same — he'd get the breaking story no one sitting at their desk had even heard about until they saw the words running under his byline. He was a legend in the business, as much for his personal life as for his nose for news.

He'd run through three wives already. I'd asked him once why he bothered to get married and he'd said they all looked like different types before the marriage, and had all turned out to be the same woman afterward. This confession would have been more appealing had a couple of the previous wives not told me the hair-raising stories of life with Oscar, when he was seldom home and seldom sober — or alone — when he was. Still, he arrived on time for our meeting and as he politely pulled out a chair for me, he signaled the owner to bring the wine he'd already ordered. He'd not drunk a drop, awaiting my arrival, but I knew from experience we'd make up for lost time quickly. I was fine with that. Over drinks was always the best way to tease things out of Oscar.

The kitchen at Murano's sounded like a construction site. *Bam bam bam!* Someone was making veal scaloppini. I took advantage of the distraction to study my former colleague across the starchy white tablecloth.

Oscar was the kind of guy who looked like he might have taught surfing or TM somewhere in his checkered past. He wore his hair long, often pulled into a Samurai-type folded ponytail at the nape of his neck. He was thirty-four years old but looked about twice that age — Philip Seymour Hoffmanesque, with everything about him as rumpled as a used paper bag. His shirt today looked slept-in; when he hugged me in greeting, I caught the faint smell of whiskey and cigarette smoke. He wore a tie in a concession to the occasion, loosely knotted. The jacket I'd seen on him many times, an old houndstooth check with what I imagined were real and necessary patches to keep the lower halves of the sleeves from falling off. It was pockmarked with burns from cigarette ash. More than once during our meal he excused himself from the table to stand outside the nonsmoking restaurant for a cigarette. If he'd taken advantage of the break to snort a line or two I wouldn't have been surprised. He always looked a little too lively on his return.

He seemed to be emerging from one of his recurring bouts of catatonic stupor, which were interspersed with fits of manic hyperactivity. He had been totally out of place at the BBC, which, despite its finger-on-the-pulse pretensions to the contrary, is conservative to its core.

Oscar's brief bursts of genius were the only reason the BBC had continued to employ him long past the date when saner heads would have had him committed. Just as they might be getting ready to give him the heave-ho, he would bring home the scoop every other news outlet had missed, for Oscar could find a story the way a dog can find a cadaver. He knew who to talk to, and who could get him in to talk to the source — the real source. God alone knows why, but people trusted him. It was said he'd been responsible for putting more than one criminal behind bars, and that there was a price on his head as a result. I guess I'd drink, too, if I had to live like that. And do coke: Oscar's all-nighters were not possible without it, and he was not alone among his colleagues who had discovered better living through chemistry. But truth to tell, if it weren't for people like Oscar we'd all end our days in some frozen gulag.

He'd come to the BBC from a rival program that had refused to air one of his documentaries charging corruption in Parliament. I gathered his whole career had been like that: once upper management bowed to pressure from an advertiser or anyone with deep pockets, he'd be gone. It was what I liked about him, of course. What everyone in the trade liked about him, even though the paranoia that stoked his personality could be trying to deal with. He claimed he'd been threatened, which I believed, and that he'd been wiretapped by Buckingham Palace, which I did not. At least, not entirely. His specialty was the time-consuming investigation and he had the patience of a spider, spinning an invisible web and sitting beside it for months or years, awaiting his prey. He'd been barred from more than one news conference for being disruptive — a code word for asking the questions nobody wanted to answer.

I hadn't seen him since early summer, when I had called him out of the blue for a lunch date and been surprised to find him available — his assignments often took him overseas. The Monroes had been renovating their patio — Anna had designed, all by herself, an Italian Renaissance addition to her Tudor-style house, which as it turned out required jackhammers to be deployed round the clock. By week two of construction the noise had reduced me to a gibbering mass of creative profanities, most of them suggesting what Anna could do with her jackhammers. The resulting addition to her palazzo was lovely if incongruous, and more than one fence had needed mending once it was done. So Anna had thrown a huge party for the neighborhood. She was like that: do first, apologize later. She always thought she could charm her way out of anything. But by the time her invitation arrived, I'd had enough: I told her I was coming down with the flu, and Will went in my stead. He reported later that Anna had got very drunk on wine — Italian, of course — and that a few people had jumped into the pool in their underwear. I had mixed feelings about having missed that.

Anyway, because of the construction noise I'd taken to calling up old friends at random, seeing who was available to get me out of the village for a day before Anna came to grievous harm.

The waiter came to offer a tasting of the wine, and the cork, both of which Oscar waved away. "Just pour," he said. He turned his attention to me and said, "Weycombe has its own hashtag on social media these days."

I waited for the waiter to take himself off.

"It's been . . . unreal," I said.

"First tell me, how goes it with his lordship?" he asked. "Are you still finding it worthwhile, selling your soul to the peerage?"

Oscar did not like Will, and, as I think I mentioned, it was mutual. It wasn't jealousy, as far as I could tell, even though Oscar had made it clear a few times he would be there to pick up the pieces if I needed someone. It was more a working man's outlook, a class-hatred thing. Then again, Oscar hadn't liked Ken, either, my boyfriend just before Will came along.

"He's doing well," I said. "He's being groomed for promotion. Which is good. We could use the money. I did a lousy job selling my soul, you see. Will is only land-rich."

This was true, as it happened. Will had inherited almost nothing when his father passed, apart from a few hand-me-down war souvenirs. I gathered there had been a bit of a sell-off of property to pay death taxes.

"Yeah. I'm sorry. About the job thing — sod the peerage's land-rich problems. Anyway, I've got one ear to the ground for you, job-wise, but nothing has come open. You know I think you got a raw deal."

"Thanks." I took a long sip of wine. It was awkward, because I didn't much want Oscar championing my cause. A referral from him, in many circles, was more of a condemnation.

We turned our attention to the lunch menu, both ordering the leek soup served with fresh-baked rosemary bread and topped with a slick of olive oil. We shared a soft buratina tied up like a bag of money with strands of celery. I chose pasta; Oscar ordered the veal.

It was the kind of place where the service was so unobtrusive you never saw a waiter unless you wanted one, and plates seemed to magically appear and disappear. A reviewer recently had called the place the best Italian restaurant outside of Sicily, and it was jumping with customers.

I'd told Oscar at the time about Anna and the jackhammers. Now he said, "So. I hear the jackhammer problem has been solved for good."

I paused for a moment in spreading about a million calories of cheese on half a million calories of bread. The bread had seeds and nuts embedded in the crust and if I'd been smart, I'd have stopped with one slice. But Murano's was the kind of indulgence I didn't allow myself often. Weycombe, for all its five-star foodie posturing, still had a way to go to match London. I'd just walk further and faster the next day.

Settling my bread knife, I answered him. "You laugh, but you should see the village — hashtag Weycombe. People are terrified."

"Why? From everything I know, and a few things you've told me, they're better off without her."

"They think they could be next."

"Oh, *not* the serial killer theory. She was a thoroughly selfish woman who deserved to be shot. You said so yourself during the jackhammer jamboree."

"I did not," I mumbled through a mouthful of bread. I paused to wash it down with wine, a red from Palermo, plush with tannins. "I said someone should shoot her. I didn't offer to do it for them."

"No matter. She was strangled. And stabbed."

I stopped the glass midway to my lips. "That's certain, is it?"

"I thought you were the one who found her."

"Yes, but I didn't, you know, do an autopsy. At a glance she'd been strangled, yes. But she was stabbed?"

"Maybe they used a jackhammer."

"Please. Would you be serious? Anyway, who is your source? Not the guy who runs the local paper, for sure. He's still figuring out how to spell her name."

Oscar smiled, a slight twist to his cupid's-bow lips. "You know, you do have a bit of a wicked streak."

I nodded, acknowledging the compliment. Coming from Oscar, it *was* a compliment. "You have someone in the police you're talking with?" I asked.

"Yeah. And someone at the coroner's. An acquaintance from school days."

That absolutely figured. Oscar really did know everyone. He told me he had once dated the woman who measured the Queen for her bra size.

"And?"

"You think I'm going to tell you which way the wind blows? No way. At least, not yet. My sources will dry up the second they think I'm talking with anyone in the village. I don't have to tell you that."

"Yes. I see that," I said obligingly, nodding. I'd get it out of him eventually. That and more.

"Besides, I saw loads of people murdered in Bosnia that no one gave a shit about. I'm not particularly interested that a village socialite got herself murdered, probably for leaving someone off her dinner party list."

"But your readers will be interested."

He shrugged. "Which is why I may do a little snooping around. But you really should stay out of it, Jill."

This was like talking with Rashima. "Who says I'm into it?"

That earned me a "come *on*" look while he paused for a sip of water. He saved his hardest drinking for after hours, but the preliminary rounds started early.

In spite of which, Oscar was going to be a hard nut to crack.

24

"Okay," he said ten minutes later, humoring me. "Let's shake the snow globe a bit."

It was a favorite expression of his, meaning "let's throw stuff in the air and see what sticks." He was good at this, as many people had learned to their dismay. I thought of the blameless villagers of Weycombe and for a moment I felt a twinge on their behalf, picturing Oscar swaggering down those cobbled streets in search of gossip. I thought of Will: I was unleashing the hounds on him, for sure.

"Who were her known enemies?" Oscar asked. He took out a notebook that looked like something he'd retrieved from a shredder.

I named a few people, male and female. The males were mostly Anna's ex-lovers and the females their wronged wives or girlfriends. Anna never seemed to go after single men, not that there were many of those of the straight variety in Weycombe.

At the end of this recital I shrugged and said, "I'm not sure it rose to the level of 'enemy,' in every case. It really was on the level of social snobbery — as you say, who was left off the guest list. All of this carried out in accordance with some finely calibrated system of etiquette, or whatever you'd call it, to which only Anna held the key."

"You were off the list?"

What the hell . . . Oscar, I swear, could read minds.

"Yes," I said, "and I don't mind telling you, and you alone — it was galling to be dumped. If only because, really, who died and put Anna in charge of the fucking book club?"

Oscar smiled. "People have been killed for less."

"But not in Weycombe," I said.

"No. Probably not in Weycombe."

"You see?" I said, taking another sip of wine. "Now I sound like a moron even to have mentioned it. They count on that embarrassment, people like her. But it stung to find out the club didn't end, as I was told. It simply carried on without me, at least for a couple more months. Which involved more than a little skulking around, believe me. They were all in on the secret. They had to have been."

"Not necessarily. If Anna cut you out, she might just have told the others you'd dropped out due to time constraints, and no one questioned it."

I hadn't considered that. Of course, Rashima would never have been part of this deception — I should have known. She'd bought into another of Anna's lies.

"All of which does beg the question of why you were included in the first place."

"Oh, that's easy. Because I'm aristocracy. Minor, but with that thrilling aura of glamour. I guess I was included out of curiosity. And then I was found wanting."

"You're right," said Oscar. "They're petty little bitches. Let it go. You need better friends, that's all. Speaking of which, who was Anna's best friend? That's always a good place to start when there's been a catfight."

"Funny you should mention . . ." I told him about my recent visit to Macy's manor house.

"Well, there you have it," he said. "A lover's triangle. Or is it a quadrangle? Anyway, between the husband — first suspect, always — and this Macy person, the police will make a short job of things."

"A short job of jumping to conclusions, you mean."

"They go on statistics," he insisted. "And if it's not the husband, it's a jealous rival."

"You're hearing this from the detectives on the case?" Oscar just shook his head and smiled: *Nice try.*

"Alfie would not be up for murder," I said. "The pure energy required for it. He's really ill and I don't think he's faking it. One look should convince anyone."

"Jealously is great at giving you that needed adrenaline surge. What's he got to lose if he's as ill as you say? Maybe it's something terminal and he doesn't give a rat's arse anymore. Besides, he may have hired someone to do it for him. Maybe he knew someone from a place where they don't get worked up about the sanctity of life — not if enough money is on offer."

Like Africa? I said slowly, "I suppose Alfie and Macy could have teamed up together." That was a viable theory, to anyone who didn't know Alfie.

Oscar nodded. "There you go. Spoken like a true detective."

We hashed over more theories for the snow globe. There was always the possibility Anna had been killed over some financial skullduggery with Barry or some unknown person. A barrister would have an embarrassment of ways to divert a jury if it came to defending almost anyone in this case. The prosecution would need a case much closer to airtight.

"What about the neighbor who thinks she's living in a Viking settlement? Or her husband?"

"Heather? Yes. But I'm sure that's a nonstarter. It's hard to imagine a scenario where Gideon would be involved with Anna or in her death. He's barely around, for one thing."

Still, even as I said that, I began to revise my opinion. Never say never. Gideon probably was a contender. I should mention that our globe-trotting expert on global affairs had a roaming eye. I'd seen it roam over my breasts and I'd chosen to pretend a sort of hysterical blindness, like one of Freud's early patients. He also had, possibly related, a drinker's nose. It was Shakespeare who wrote that alcohol paints the nose and takes away the performance. But Gideon had somehow managed to bestow on Heather the miracle that was Lulu, so I guessed things were working in that department.

Gideon's survey of my anatomy had happened at a party — I think the Rideouts' housewarming — when I wore a dress that was cut slightly low in front. Not low enough to drive anyone wild with lust; I'm not well-enough endowed for that. It seemed almost an automatic response on his part, to keep the old libido in tune. You have to wonder if there is an academic anywhere out there whose eyes do not roam when he — or she — is not fighting the good fight over the serial comma. But I always thought they saved that sort of thing for impressionable undergraduates. Heather had been one of his students.

It was at this party Anna probably had hooked up with her MP. I started to write *our* MP, but that would imply I voted for him or he was in office for the sake of humanity, and I was fairly certain that was not the case. In the same way Cesare Borgia was probably not the best pick to wear a cardinal's hat, so Colin Livingstone, MP, might have been better employed selling reverse mortgages to credulous old people.

"Gideon's a possible, but I can't really see it," I said. I looked around, adding, "I think this is the best Italian restaurant I've ever been in, including in Italy," because I didn't want to waste time on Gideon. I'd keep him in reserve on my list of suspects — there was a case to be made that Anna might have responded to his advances. She didn't seem to have a highly developed sense of discrimination. My doubt came in more because Anna was twenty years too old to be Gideon's type.

We bowed our heads reverently over our main courses. During a pause for water I asked, "Are you still seeing Karen?" Karen McQueen often played the crime victim in *Bloody Murder: London,* a fact more than one viewer had picked up on. Karen the exhibitionist, the showoff, the makeup expert and player of many parts.

"God, no. There's barely room in a relationship for two people, let alone thirty. I swear to God she has multiple personalities." Oscar paused, staring into the dregs of the wine in his glass. "Can I ask you something?"

"Sure. I might tell you."

"What ever happened to Clarice?"

"Will's old girlfriend?" Clarice was one of the anemic blonde blue-bloods Will's mother was always shoving under his nose during our courtship, hoping to distract him from red-blooded me. "I've no idea, Oscar. I like to think she couldn't stand the competition and finally just got out of the way. Will never talks about her. Neither does his mother, thank God."

"He never talks about her? Interesting.

Because I've got to tell you, the way she just vanished makes you wonder."

"What, you think Will stuffed her in a trunk and tipped her into the English Channel?"

"No. Well, yes. But really? No, of course not. Maybe."

I laughed. "My guess? She ran off to Majorca with that guy she was seeing. Jose something. Will says she always had a thing for Spanish men."

This was one of those topics there was no need to revisit, so over coffee and Italian brandy I brought the conversation round to where I wanted it to be. I shared with him Elizabeth Fortescue's views on the character of the local MP, concluding by asking, "Do you have Colin Livingstone in your file of people who owe you favors?"

"No. But I have him in the file of those who fear me, and rightly so."

"Really? What's he done?"

"Who hasn't he done is more to the point."

"Really?" I stopped mid-stir and thought about this. It certainly matched my impressions of the man, and those of Elizabeth Fortescue. I would put her in the camp of people who have a low opinion of most people all the time and are right in their opinions half the time. In Colin's case I'm sure she was spot on. "Well, he hasn't done me, for one."

"Put on some makeup and quit wearing your hair in a ponytail, and he'll try. If that's what you want."

"Of course it's not what I want. Fuck's sake. I want information."

"Such as?"

I centered my cup carefully in its saucer before replying. We were now engaged in a negotiation, much like a transfer of prisoners. I didn't want to give too much away. At the same time, I wanted Oscar's help. "I think he knew Anna," I said. "I think he knew her quite well, if you follow."

"Sure. No surprise there. But before we go further, let's have a serious word about this detective drama you're playing at." He took a large sip of his brandy and ordered another. I wasn't really up on my Italian brandies but I suspected a slug like that midday would put most people on the floor. "Do I need to tell you how dangerous it can be?" he continued. "What if he's the killer? What if he actually killed Anna, for reasons unknown? Although blackmail would be my guess — she knew too much. Then again, what if your friend Macy killed her?"

"She's not my friend," I told him. "My friends don't ask the vet to Botox their dogs. My friends have brains. Like you."

He nodded, a slightly tipsy nod, accepting the compliment as his due.

"But that's all the more reason I want to meet Colin in his offices in Whitehall."

"Meet him in —"

"It's extremely unlikely I'd come to harm there, unless he stuffed my body parts behind the walnut paneling or something. Even then, there would be a record that I'd gone in there . . . *and I'd never come out.*"

I'd dropped my voice to a low, growling register. It was a pitch-perfect imitation of the man who narrated *Bloody Murder: London,* if I do say so myself. It made Oscar laugh.

"All right," he said, giving in more easily than I'd expected. No doubt he saw advantages to my getting the inside track. "I do see your point. And there's nothing easier to arrange. All that's left to talk about is what's in it for me."

"You want an exclusive, right?"

"Of course I want an exclusive. I'm not running a charity here."

"Then I'll see what I can do."

He drained the last of his brandy and started looking for the waiter. "We'll strategize how you're going to get him to open up. Let's start with the hair and work our way down to the shoes."

"What's wrong with my shoes now?" I looked down at my ballet flats — my go-to shoes for walking around London.

"Nothing, if you're trying out for the Royal Ballet Company. But if you're going to get Colin to reveal anything, you'll need heels. It also wouldn't hurt to wear something a little tightfitting."

"What's any of this have to do with —"

"By the way, whatever happened to Ken? More brandy?" he asked.

"No," I said. "I really have to get going soon."

Catching the waiter's eye, Oscar signaled for the check. Knowing him, he'd spend the afternoon going from one pub to the next. He called it networking. Most people would call it getting drunk.

"Ken?" he repeated.

I shrugged. "He went back to America, I guess."

"I always liked him. You two were good together."

"Because we were both Americans? That's a tight bond, all right. We both liked baseball but so do the Japanese. And you *never* liked him."

"Seriously, I think it helps, don't you? Like backgrounds. Similar tastes and memories. Shared language."

"Ken and I," I said firmly, "had zero chance of making a go of it, especially once I met Will. I've told you that a hundred times. I met Will and my fate was sealed. There was nothing I could do about it."

He looked at me for a long moment, studying me as if for a portrait. "Men always go for you, don't they?" he said. "You just pull them, without even trying." He shook his head. "Amazing."

I shrugged. That description sounded more like Anna to me.

25

A year earlier, the most fortunate and photogenic people of Weycombe had celebrated the Autumnal Equinox at the home of Colin Livingstone, MP, in one of his more blatant attempts to curry favor with the moneyed constituents who could stand to be in the same room with him. So it wasn't as if I didn't know the guy; it was more that the chances he'd remember who I was were small. There is nothing memorable about me unless I make a huge effort to stand out. That chameleon quality came in handy when I was auditioning for stage roles: I could become anyone I chose. But even playing a part I am not an attention seeker. I prefer it that way.

There was, of course, an enormous security hassle about getting into the houses of Parliament. Even with Oscar smoothing the way for me, I had to book an appointment well in advance while they tapped my phones or did whatever they had to do to ensure I hadn't stuffed my bra with explosives.

You might think someone as inflammatory as Oscar would be a hindrance to my gaining access, but everybody owed Oscar something and it was best not to ask what was owed in return. I arrived at the prearranged time at the visitor entrance and was led away from the tourists to a staging area for special guests. There my name was ticked off a list after I'd shown my driver's license to the uniformed policewoman. She made a photocopy as I sent my handbag down the conveyor belt to be x-rayed and then walked through the scanning station. I've no doubt I was watched by the surveillance camera from all angles.

Before 9/11, it was a simple matter to visit your MP. He or she is, after all, for better or worse, yours, and access to lawmakers is written into the Magna Carta, or it should be. With all the terror alerts, I couldn't casually wander the corridors of Her Majesty's government, knock on Colin's mahogany door, and inquire as to the exact nature of his relationship with Anna. No. This was going to require a little more finesse.

The runners Anna had been wearing on her

last day were a hint to her ties with Colin.

They were a brand called JoySports, imported from the US, making them insanely expensive. Wearing them was supposed to be a punch in the eye for China and whoever else flooded the UK with cheap goods. In the US, the congressman most involved in getting a factory for knock-offs of these shoes installed in his district ran on the slogan, "On your feet. Support your country." Which, once you got past the shoe-insert associations, was not a bad slogan.

Still, only the upper one percent could afford to buy these shoes with their cushy insoles. The push now was on to get them manufactured in the UK. Our local MP was heavily invested in this effort, perhaps even financially; I'm sure I couldn't say. But he probably had a closet stuffed full of free samples in all sizes and colors, men's and women's.

The fact Anna was wearing JoySports the day she died I might more easily have written off to coincidence had I not seen her at Macy's garden party having that smoldering *tête–à–tête* with Colin.

I was met by one of Colin's protégés as I emerged from the body scanner and was ushered through the back ways of the famous old building. It is typical of the English that a building Americans would attempt to preserve in aspic is in daily use in London, and has been in daily use for centuries, its artwork largely unprotected from theft. It was overwhelming, and for me, a lover of all things British, a paradise. I could thank Anna, in a way, for getting me inside.

I had looked Colin Livingstone up online, of course, and could not make head nor tails of his various titles. He'd been shadow secretary of this and that for nearly twenty years, finally in the past few years achieving the title of minister. I gathered this was a reward of sorts. I am the least political person alive, and if I can't understand US politics you can be sure I've no idea what in fuck the people of Westminster get up to. I did finally figure out that the main job of a shadow is to take potshots at the sitting cabinet. There is nothing that resembles a schoolyard so much as the houses of Parliament.

Colin's fortune was inherited from his father, who invented a popular condiment, a fact Colin tried rather desperately to play down. You will have heard of Hotsy Topper? — made with the secret formula the family refuses to reveal. I suspect grain alcohol is added to offset all the corn syrup, but his opponents swear it's made from the blood of newborns.

Anyway, he was born rich, and rather than sit around being the son of privilege he decided that interference in other people's lives might get him laid more often, or something like that. And so after his failed attempt at piety, he ran for office.

Physically, Colin was larger than life, which we demand of our politicians. Whatever the phrase means, you know it when it hits you. Livingstone (no relation to the one you're thinking of) had a huge physical presence that seemed to suck the air out of every corner. He was a man who might one day look good cast in bronze as a park statue, a pigeon sitting on his shoulder.

At the Equinox fundraiser, a literal shock had gone through me as he clasped my hand in both of his. He had looked deep into my eyes and said how *wonderful* it was to meet an American cousin. His large hands were as warm and soft as mittens and, as he continued holding my hand, speaking of his delight at seeing his heart's desire at last, I had the queerest sensation of energy being passed from him into me, like he was some sort of faith healer. If he'd told me to pick up my bed and walk it would have fit perfectly with the tone of our meeting. Instead he asked me what part of the US I was from and actually seemed to have some passing knowledge of the country. It was a geographical sort of knowledge of Maine's major export (lobster) and industry (healthcare), but that he knew so much about it from memory impressed me not a little.

He had a Bill Clinton-ish reputation already. I don't mean just *that* reputation, necessarily. I mean he had that charisma that made people like him and made them want to buy whatever he was selling. He also was all teeth and starched hair, tie knotted just so. The tie only came off when he traveled to the rural parts of his constituency, where he became a man of the people. His website had a gallery of photos of him standing about in fields or surveying England's mountains green from a hilltop, and looking at these photos you might be forgiven for mistaking him for a prosperous farmer with lots of time on his hands.

Like my husband, Colin was of a type that must be issued in boxes for later assembly by public schools all across England. He did not get where he was by being bipartisan, and he was loathed and envied by his opponents for his hair, his big teeth, and his wealth, pretty much in that order. To all appearances he was securely married to his childhood sweetheart, a washed-out wraith of a woman who was seldom seen in public, and all attempts by reporters to prove otherwise had proven fruitless. I know because I knew some of those reporters, whose job it became to stake out his London pied-a-terre when he hired an assistant who could neither type nor spell. It was not clear she could read, either, but that may have been because she had difficulty seeing over the top of her enormous chest. It appeared she had no difficulty reading the instructions on her can of hair spray, however.

One day soon after he took on this assistant, Colin had announced he was going hiking, alone. Already by this time, "hiking the Appalachian Trail" had become Washington-speak for having it off with someone not your wife. A fit reporter (they could only find one — it's a drinking, smoking, and snorting profession) followed him to Wales and sure enough, hiking was what Colin was doing. Building a fire, alone with his thoughts, only small forest creatures for company, like Snow White. The guy was as untouchable as Mitt Romney, and it was finally decided to leave him alone and spend the editorial budget on more likely targets. The thing about both Whitehall and Washington, though, was that these guys never learned. Leave Colin alone long enough and temptation would find him.

I believed Anna Monroe had found him.

26

The hallway to Colin's office was as long as an airport runway, giving me lots of time to rehearse what I wanted to ask him. Well, it would have given me lots of time if not for the chirpy intern or PA or whatever at my side who never stopped talking for a moment.

Colin stood up politely as I entered and ushered me to a plush seating area across from his desk. The intern's almost imperceptible lift of eyebrows was met with a small shake of his head. Refreshments were not to be offered. I was to say my piece quickly and leave.

"This is a rare pleasure," he said, smiling and oozing bonhomie. His veneers made his teeth look four times their normal size. "To see such a beautiful woman in my office." The intern smirked a farewell and walked out, closing the door sharply behind him. No doubt he'd heard this hooey many times before. "To what do I owe this honor?"

I opted to speak bluntly. "I am here about Anna Monroe," I said, watching for his reaction. Nothing hostile in my demeanor, just a look of innocent, wide-eyed curiosity.

"Anna Monroe," he repeated. "You're not — tell me you're not the young woman who found her body that terrible day? I hadn't connected the name."

"I'm afraid I am. That's why I'm here. The suspicion in this kind of case — well, you can imagine. It sort of *spreads.* In addition to losing a friend and neighbor, I've got the police looking very closely at me. It's most uncomfortable."

"I can see why it would be. I don't, however, see how I can help you with that. Just answer all their questions. They'll go away eventually once they see they're wasting time talking to you."

"That isn't always how it works back in my country."

"Well, it's how it works here, I do assure you."

Before he could add "now if there's nothing else, I'm terribly busy," I said, "As I mentioned, I was a friend of Anna's. She confided in me, you see." This was a slight exaggeration, to say the least, but it worked.

He got very, very still, his expression frozen, and the look on his face was one of polite inquiry. But I thought I could smell fear beneath his citrusy aftershave.

"Ye-e-s-s-s?" he said.

"Yes." I went for it now. "She told me you and she were having an affair."

His hand shot out to the intercom on his desk. For a second I thought he might call in guards to haul me away. A wiser, or at least a more innocent, man might have done so. But when he said, "Hold my calls, please, Alice," I knew I'd scored. His face now carried a curdled look.

"It's not blackmail, if that's what you're thinking," I said quickly. "Nothing remotely like that."

"What is it you want?" The geniality, so second nature to the political beast, had completely vanished now. I was seeing the face behind the mask, the face of a man who had risen to such giddy heights of power by playing hardball. I didn't know about Anna — she clearly felt differently — but I would have given him a wide berth. But it's not news that power is an aphrodisiac.

"I want information, that's all."

"What is this? You're not with the police. I don't have to talk to you." He might have added "you weren't even born here," and looked like he was thinking of doing so, then thought better of it. I was a constituent, just one with a grating accent.

"Information," he said, winding down and allowing a hint of sarcasm to creep into his voice. The silly little housewife wanting information, that was me. "Go on." He could barely get out the words through his gritted, enameled teeth.

I was still making it up as I went, and I decided that playing to his ego was the way to go.

"She spoke very highly of you. She did nothing but sing your praises, really."

"Anna? Now you do surprise me. That's very flattering, but I still don't see h—"

"She told me she was meeting someone that morning."

"Well, it wasn't me."

"She didn't say it was. That's why I'm here. The police are talking to me, as I mentioned, asking me questions. I have to tell them what I know, obviously. Everything I know. But before I do that . . . you see, I'm not interested in tossing anyone into it. Anyone innocent, I mean. The problem with murder is it drags everyone down, even people who don't really deserve to be dragged down. You do see?"

I was doing my best Miss Marple imitation at this point, dithery and twittery as if I didn't know what I was about. I was even clutching my handbag in my lap with both hands.

"I agree with what you say but I don't see what I can do about it. If Anna was meeting anyone, it wasn't me. In fact, I can prove it."

"You have an alibi?"

"What a dreadful term. But yes, as a matter of fact, I do."

"That could make all the difference," I said. "A solid alibi. Like mine — I was seen by a dozen people walking up the path that morning, walking toward where Anna already lay." "Dozen people" was another slight exaggeration, but I felt it might make him unbend a bit to hear my impeccable bona fides. "I might not feel obliged to tell all I know, you see, if I were certain you couldn't possibly be involved." Here I sort of convulsed into some more Jane Marple twinkle.

I may have overdone it a bit. He studied me, never taking his eyes from my face. My gaze roamed about the room, that bastion of privilege. The dark paneling, the gold-leaf frames holding historic faces I didn't recognize, and scenes of historic wars — ditto. I was affecting a wait-all-day nonchalance I didn't feel. This was one dangerous guy and I was playing a treacherous game. I didn't think he'd snuff me out or anything, pull a gun out of the bottom drawer and let me have it. That would really screw up his chances for re-election. But he might tamper with my ability to stay in the UK. I was legally married to a British citizen but I had the fleeting thought Colin might drum up drug or terrorism charges or something else undesirable that could get me deported if not thrown in jail first. God only knew what kind of connections someone like this had.

But I was here to play the game and play it I would. I really did want to know exactly where he was at the time Anna was killed, and when. Once he told me, I'd go away.

"It's none of your business," he said.

"I know that," I replied, waiting as the seconds passed.

"Cow," he muttered, almost under his breath.

"I beg your pardon?"

"Anna. She was nothing but a jumped-up, overreaching cow. I was supposed to give up everything" — and here, he swept his arm out to encompass the tables with the inlaid designs, the sofa cushions embroidered by the tiny fingers of Chinese orphans, the window dressings that made the whole place look like the setting for a regency play — "for some woman from Cardiff with ambitions high above her station?"

"Bristol," I corrected automatically. His sweep did not, I noticed, include the photo of the washed-out wife and the two pasty-faced children.

Ambitions high above her station? Ambition summed up Anna, all right, overreaching and all the rest of it, including cow, but what century were we living in? This was rich, anyway; coming from a man who had run for office on a platform that played up his vague and likely imaginary working-class roots. It was another case for Sigmund Freud, but right now I had to get what I wanted from him before he went into a full-tilt panic.

"Alibi?" I repeated mildly, like a gentle suggestion.

"I was visiting a school," he said, biting off each syllable. *Temper, temper.* "As it happens."

"That's nice," I said. "I didn't know schools opened that early around here. It explains so much, though. Bright little buggers, aren't they? Quoting Shakespeare while they're practically still in nappies."

"I wanted to be there when it opened."

I didn't have to ask what school. Or even what time. This was public information, verifiable. Just like the royals, these guys had a schedule, and their every move was documented so the taxpayers could see how their money was being spent.

"Wonderful," I said. "That's all I need to know then! I won't trouble you further."

"Good. See that you don't."

I got up to leave and when I reached the door, I turned around.

"One more question," I said. Now I was Columbo. "Did you drive yourself? To the school?"

From the look on his face it was clear he had, which meant he had no witnesses to his every movement. He said no more, just continued to glower. If anything, he turned a brighter shade of red.

"Okay," I said. "Well, I have to be off."

"Sit down," he said.

"Sorry. No."

And I left, closing the door quietly behind.

Well, that was future invitations to fundraisers for Colin Livingstone, MP, stuffed, which was fine with me. I fairly danced down the corridors of power on my way to Westminster Underground.

For Colin Livingstone, MP, had no real

alibi. I was a little surprised someone at his level did not have a car and driver at his disposal, but he would surely have said so if that were the case. I decided to treat myself to lunch at a nearby bistro while I did a little research on the school where Colin claimed to have been. I pulled up his public diary for the day on my mobile, and it was all there: he had been scheduled to appear at St. Hildegarde's School for Girls and cut the ribbon on their new gymnasium at nine thirty that morning. As an alibi it was crap. The school was about ten miles away from Weycombe, no distance at all, so his being there did nothing to prove his innocence. It was a straight shot up the motorway for most of the way, and even the curvy bits of road at either end wouldn't add that much to his time. I made a mental note to drive out there and see for myself, maybe even talk with the headmistress if I could get near her, but Colin had had acres of time to do away with Anna and not be noticeably late for his ribbon-cutting duties. He was the perfect suspect — if it turned out I needed one.

I did another search and saw the school opened at eight thirty. So "I wanted to be there when it opened" didn't add up. What did he do for an hour? Hang upside down on the jungle gym? It was a crazy lie to tell, in fact. The kind of lie a habitual liar might throw out there, never thinking anyone would check up.

The only questions that remained for me were when, how — and whether — to let Sergeant Milo know.

27

I needed to go about this investigation systematically, and — above all — quietly. I could no longer write whatever I was thinking in a notebook Will might stumble upon any day. I'd already started jotting only the sketchiest of notes, leaving things out, in case he did find it. What I needed was the freedom to write the truth and nothing but.

That truth was bubbling up more and more, becoming by some weird process material for a novel. My purple notebook was filling up, but not with my usual venting. It was becoming a whole new *thing* with a life of its own. Base metal turning to gold. Alchemy. I was writing a novel now, *without even trying.* It was intoxicating. I only needed to change a few names and, here and there, rearrange the order in which things happened.

I had a large collection of paper notebooks, too large — not even Joyce Carol

Oates could fill all those pages. They sat taking up space in a desk drawer, nagging reminders of the novel not written: leather-bound notebooks, and ones handmade from cotton rag paper. Cheap spiral-bound notebooks and exercise books. All sizes from A2 to A8 in every color. I'd spent untold hours in the WHSmith on the Cornmarket in Oxford, near the New Theatre, when I was supposed to be revising.

But now it only made sense to write on my MacBook rather than leaving bits of paper scattered around like bullet casings. Will had zero interest in what I got up to, but why take chances? I spent half a day scanning in the pages I'd written in recent months and saved them in an encrypted file labeled "Recipes" on my computer. I shredded or burned the actual notebook pages in the fireplace (that hurt, but it had to be done). And then I began to use the computer as a diary. Password protected, of course.

The day I returned from talking with Colin I got to work in earnest, organizing random thoughts and insights and character sketches, and wondering: Was everyone living in Weycombe at it? Having it off as I sat staring at my CV, trying to turn my time at the BBC into something romantic and dashing, myself into someone innovative and imaginative, eating my way through bags of Cheetos I bought from an online UK deli?

Now I sat trying to think as the police would think. To make it all into a story I could package and sell one day.

Opening a new document titled *Suspects,* I wrote:

- Colin Livingstone, MP, the married man
  - — Motive: His involvement with Anna is an embarrassment as he climbs the ladder.
- Alfie, the husband
  - — Motive: Obvious
- Jason, the delinquent son
  - — Motive: I don't think people like Jason need a motive, they're just plain crazy, but it's probably something to do with inheritance or insurance.
- Racy Macy
  - — Motive: Jealous rage. Had Barry been

romantically involved with Anna?
— Financially?
— Had they quarreled further over Alfie?

- Heather Cartwright

  — Motive: None. As tempting as it is to throw her to the wolves, it's hard to see a motive. Maybe Anna had stolen one of her recipes. Nah, this one just doesn't fly.

- Elizabeth Fortescue

  — Motive: Religious mania?

- Milo the cop

  — He was the first on the scene for a reason. Others arrive and he inserts himself into the investigation.

A gang-related killing was always possible, if highly unlikely. I didn't know enough about gangs to speculate.

The last item with Milo struck me as genius, but the devil to prove. Agatha Christie could have pulled it off, but reality, I was finding, was different from the preposterous connections and magic tricks Agatha could pull off. In real life, anyone attempting one of her crimes would be caught within minutes, as they still stood holding a knife dripping with blood.

So for Milo to be involved, I would have to dream up some ancient connection between him and Anna, and although it was true Anna had done half the men in town, the chances she would have singled out a lowly policeman for her favors seemed a stretch. Unless she was trying to get out of a parking ticket. It was more of a stretch that he would kill her over it. He wasn't married — no ring, anyway — and he didn't seem like the type given to jealous rages. (Although, from my experience, you can never tell about that. Still waters.)

He was certainly handsome, in a footballer sort of way, and people who know the system know how to corrupt the system. So I kept him on the list. I thought I might need a cast of characters to keep everyone straight. I opened a new file called "Cast" and started the list. I'd rename most of them before publication, of course, with a search and replace.

What stones, I asked myself, had I left unturned? What remained for me to learn? I wished more than ever to be a fly on the wall of the police station, to be able to get to Milo's desk and read the reports, see who their suspects were, who they'd been talking to, what *their* working theories were.

I worked for an hour before turning on the evening news. The TV newscaster was someone I knew from the old days at the BBC. She looked about eighteen although I knew she was closer to thirty. She also looked like she was going to a party after the broadcast, all silky dress and statement necklaces and chandelier earrings, despite the early hour. Someone, I told myself, nibbling the edge of a Ryvita Multi-grain, should tell her never to wear a big necklace like that with chandelier earrings. If they got tangled together with the mic, they could make an unholy racket while you were on the air. Learn from my experience already.

I sat through the whole broadcast and not a word was said about Anna. It seemed as if the investigation was already losing steam as the national focus shifted to the immigration and Euro crises. I turned off the set and, looking around, noticed a stack of newspapers had started collecting.

Nothing new in there, not even locally reported gibberish penned by Garvin. I turned to the engagements column, always my favorite light reading. There was an especially rich crop at that time of year, to allow lots of planning time for June weddings. Today we had an accomplished retail professional, possibly Heather's cousin, who had landed her man approximately three years after the birth of their son, who appeared with the happy couple in the engagement photo. How much the world had changed. I thought I might begin keeping a scrapbook of these things. No reason, just that the great messy sprawl of how people live their lives was fascinating. Happiness so often was in the form of another human being, even though women especially should know better. Not a job, or a stellar career, but some funny-looking IT professional who happened to stop your heart each time you saw him.

I was beset by a memory, a surge of yearning that made me reach out a hand as if I could pierce time and pull that moment back in from the past: a group of us in Oxford, piling out the stage door after a late Improv performance, the light from inside spilling out onto the alley, the night cool and all of us laughing with giddy relief at the end of what we knew had been a spectacular show — no script, and so much to go wrong, but it had gone off without a hitch. By that point, after so many performances, we could almost read each other's thoughts, anticipate the next bit of nonsense. It was the last time I had known camaraderie like that, a sense of belonging to anyone or anything. In fact, I couldn't recall having that exact same feeling since. Love for Will, excitement over the wedding, the new house, the kitchen fittings, all of that. But this was a distilled whiskey shot of joy, chased by a heady sense that all that had come before had been surging toward that moment, and all that came after would be a slow slide down. We were strong and alive and we could feel, taste, touch, and see, and that was all that mattered or ever would matter.

The theater attracts all sorts, mostly misfits, but it mainly attracts people who like living in their imaginations because they like what they see in there. It's not cold and ugly inside the imagination. Or if it is, there's nothing in there that can harm you.

They were my tribe. And once you find your tribe, you are home.

Will was so late coming in that night I kept thinking it might be the night he would vanish completely. I guessed he'd stayed late at work and then gone to the Bull again — I could smell the beer, an odor I'd come to hate — but I no longer cared. By that point I much preferred my time alone. I also feared where conversation might take us. Some things were best left unexplored.

I suspected he came home only to shower and change — it certainly was not a haven for meals or conversation or, God knows, for sex. With a few notable exceptions, we had been living like brother and sister for a long while.

Jason stopped by about nine to return my casserole dish. Somehow I was not surprised to see him: I hadn't seriously believed he'd do a runner. I offered him a drink, and he ended up staying a while, talking about Anna. I remember he said he was sorry she was gone, and wished he'd been nicer to her while he had the chance. The usual stuff people say in these circumstances, sentiments I didn't believe would last coming from him. He left with a mumbled, graceless "thanks" and without meeting my eye.

When Will returned, I was reading a Garvin article in the *Chronic* about a poisoning that had occurred in a nearby town. The speculation was that the man killed had crossed some Kremlin types you wouldn't want to mess with. The article went on to say that lots of people are poisoned every year, especially the elderly, with nobody the wiser. That I believed.

Garvin stated in a sidebar that at least five popes in history had been poisoned. Arsenic, a byproduct of copper smelting, was a popular choice in Italy. The best way to deal with anyone who bothered you in the days before forensic labs was to have them over for dinner.

But this Kremlin-style murder had been caused by a rare plant toxin called gelsemium, found in Asia. They call it heartbreak grass over there.

In England we are short on heartbreak grass but not on divorce, and arsenic, harder to come by, is easy to detect. At least Alfie could take comfort in the knowledge that someone had done the job for him. I wasn't sure he saw it that way.

Who would credit this wayward love for Anna? Despite the betrayals, despite the lies, she had a hold on him. Some people are born with that ability. They're usually sociopaths. Sometimes . . . sometimes I even wondered at Alfie's mysterious illness, if Anna weren't behind it somehow. A modern-day Lucretia Borgia.

Reminded of something that had been nagging at me, I powered up the laptop again, looking up the Chinese lantern plant — called Japanese lantern in the US. My mother had hated them because they grew like kudzu. The poison garden at Alnwick Garden in Northumberland had a specimen in its collection. According to Wikipedia, it was a member of the nightshade family, and the unripe berries and leaves were poisonous. "Highly toxic and possibly fatal." Symptoms of poisoning included headache, stomachache, vomiting, diarrhea, and breathing problems.

Heather was, I trusted, using ripened fruit to make her jam, so it should be okay. Still, I reminded myself to get rid of that jar she'd given me. Weeks before I had thrown away mushrooms she had gathered and made into a chutney, for the same reason. She might know what she was doing but why take chances?

28

Milo paid me an unexpected visit the next day. I was putting away a few things in the garage when, through the row of small windows running across the top of the garage door, I saw him emerge from his car across the road. A BMW this time. He was flying solo. I wasn't sure if Attwater had let him off his lead or if he was doing some extra-credit sleuthing. I thought cops always worked in teams but really, that's telly knowledge. They do what they can get away with, as we know.

He wore an off-the-rack suit that might have come from Marks and Sparks. Where he'd found the tie I couldn't guess, but I remember it had shiny orange stripes on a brown background. He and DCI Attwater, despite the age difference, surely were meant for each other.

I was warming to him. He had an easy manner that was only partially for show with the public. Most men are paranoid about women, because most men know that at heart they are shits. Will is the exception. His belief in his lovability was total. Milo was a lot less complicated.

"Shouldn't you be in uniform?" I asked, inwardly shielding my eyes from the glare of that tie as I ushered him inside.

"I've been promoted," he said.

"That was fast. Does this mean you've solved the murder?"

"They had me in uniform for a while. Now I'm back on the team. It's a new initiative meant to give us broader experience working with the public."

Right. I wondered if he'd pissed someone off, or broken some rule, or both. Been spotted rifling through the drug locker or caught fixing parking tickets — either of which, I realized, would mean he was off the force for a good long while, if not serving time somewhere at Her Majesty's pleasure. And so far as I knew, they didn't put you back in uniform and send you out on patrol and then change their minds. The whole thing was odd. But surely whatever his misdeed, it had been something petty.

Unless being on patrol had been some undercover thing.

Whatever it was, I was sure he had not

rushed over to my house wearing his awful tie to share it with me. He wasn't particularly welcome at that moment. I'd told him what I could tell him, at least for the time being. When I was ready, I planned to spoon-feed him some tidbits.

His training showed in his every move. He walked over to the window overlooking the back garden and the river as if admiring the view, but my sense was that he was casing the joint — checking out the view from my place into Anna's back garden. He then planted himself in the middle of the living room, where he carried out some sort of visual appraisal, hands on hips and biceps flexing. The bookshelves seemed to hold a particular fascination for him, but the contents were as blameless as could be: A collection of leather-bound classics imported from Will's ancestral home. A stack of *Country Life* magazines. Gideon's unread book on the Middle East.

I had read an article not long before about how you could count the number of civilians killed by British police forces on one hand, while all across America the police seemed to be on a crime spree of their very own. The article explained that firearms were not handed out in the UK to anyone who thought they might make a good cop;

instead there was a rigorous vetting procedure that included psychological testing, along with plenty of time spent just walking the streets unarmed, learning to deal with people rather than thinking largely in terms of self-defense.

Milo turned and gave me a fleeting grin of — what? Reassurance, I guess. He never in all the time I knew him — and I came to know him well — looked like he might lose it with me, or as if he were capable of that. This self-possessed calm seemed inborn, as much a part of him as his hair color, while training had further drilled into him that he was there to help people get themselves sorted, not to punish them senseless. If he had to take some guy down, someone violently drunk or strung out on drugs, he'd probably apologize first, like Colin Firth.

I could tell he thought I was cute, but honestly? I didn't need the complication.

I indicated a chair for him at the breakfast bar and offered him coffee.

As I put the cup and saucer before him he peered at my face and asked, "When are you going to tell me what happened to your eye?"

I put up a hand to where a shiner of moderate proportions had begun to glow. I would later successfully hide it with one of

Rashima's miracle concealers.

"I ran into a door," I said, and I didn't plan to elaborate. Not even if he promised to burn the tie. Off his look, I added, "Really. I did." To change the subject, I said, "To what do I owe the honor?"

"Actually, there's been a complaint."

"There's been a complaint," I repeated woodenly, although I could guess.

"Colin Livingstone."

"MP," I said. "Don't forget the MP. He loves titles. On that topic, Sergeant, do you have a first name?"

He hesitated, clearly weighing whether becoming too chummy with a witness in an investigation was a good idea. The police couldn't get rid of helpful citizens and grieving families once that door was opened. "It's Andrei," he said. "But everyone calls me Milo. My parents were Russian. They immigrated here."

Ah. That might explain why Milo struck me as sympathetic. He was only one generation away from being a foreigner himself.

"I see."

"Mr. Livingstone says he feels you've harassed him." Milo leaned back in the chair and reached for his coffee cup. The wooden slats made a creaking sound against his weight, just as they did when Will sat there. I had a wild image of the chair collapsing and Milo disappearing from sight like Wile E. Coyote falling off a cliff.

So Colin had ratted me out, a good and fast offense being the best defense. I should have known. This was a man who thrived on backroom politics. He would try to silence me by intimidation. But I wasn't intimidated, not by a long shot. In fact I felt he might have played into my hands.

"Did he tell you about his relationship with the victim?" I asked. "With Anna?"

"He did. He made a clean breast of things. Said he wanted it all out in the open, nothing to hide, etc."

"Did you believe him?"

"It's neither here nor there if I believed him or not. You are playing a very dangerous game, Mrs. White. He may be innocent. He may be guilty. But he's already brought you into a situation that doesn't involve you. And that part is dangerous. For you."

I would maintain that I brought myself in with my visit to Colin, but I pretended not to see Milo's point.

"What do you mean, doesn't involve me? I found her body. Anna was my friend. Sort of. She was my friendly neighbor. And her living — *having* lived next door means I might be in danger from whoever did this.

A sort of double whammy of involvement. So I'm sorry if Mr. Livingstone, MP, doesn't like it but I don't like my neighbors being strangled, either."

Milo looked at me a very long time. I couldn't read what was in his eyes. Compassion? Concern? Exasperation? All those. And suspicion: *What was I up to?*

"He doesn't have an alibi, you know," I said. "Not really." I told him about the school visit.

Milo took out his notebook and made a show of writing that down. But he must have known about that already, if Colin had indeed bared his soul to him. He was probably just jotting down a reminder to buy aspirin.

"We've got only his word for it that he and Anna were no longer a thing," I said.

"We?"

"Maybe she was trying to shake him off. She and Alfie had a bit of an unconventional relationship, you know. Maybe Colin was in love and thought she would leave Alfie for him. But lots of people probably thought that."

"Lots of people?"

"Anna got around — anyone can tell you that. She was a highly sexed woman married to an invalid. The suspects here are without end. And that's just the male suspects."

"I can see you've given this some thought."

"It's the new sport in Weycombe," I said. "A sort of 'pin the tail on the donkey' guessing game. I used to see her with the pool guy, you know. But that was years ago."

"The pool guy?"

"Yes, the guy from the pool cleaning service. I could see them from the first floor window at the back. I mean, I'd see them go into the pool house and I wouldn't see them come out again for ages. Could mean nothing, of course."

"Maybe they were just straightening out the hoses."

I couldn't quite believe he'd said that. I breezed on. "By the way, I've remembered something from that morning."

"Oh?" He drank coffee with his left hand while his biro hovered over the notebook.

"Something about the man I saw in the distance. He looked like he might be a vagrant — shabby clothes and shaggy hair and beard, as I said. He also walked with a pronounced limp — there was something wrong with his right leg. I would bet it wasn't an old polo injury."

"How old would you say this individual was?"

"He might have been forty. Fifty. It's hard to tell with someone like that. A beard hides a lot. And it was at a distance."

"It sounds like Roger. We'll look into it."

"I just saw him in the vicinity," I said firmly. "I didn't see him do anything."

"Got it."

"I've seen him before, in fact. In the village. He seems to be like the token poor person."

That made Milo laugh; it was a good, rumbling laugh that made me like him more. I pushed the plate of biscuits I'd unearthed from the cupboard closer to his reach.

"Got it," he repeated. "It's Roger. He's a schizophrenic and he probably should not be out on his own. But so far as we've ever known, he's harmless. He comes to us all the time to report angels are living inside the post box. He refuses treatment, if there's any to be had. Won't go into the shelter, not willingly, even when it's cold; he says they rip him off, steal his kit. The system's broken as far as people like Roger are concerned."

"It's the same back home. Anyway, I thought you should know."

"Where was home, again?"

"You'd never have heard of it. Augustus, Maine. It's in the rural part of the state. Way up north. Past Bangor."

"Ah. Stephen King," he said.

"Yeah," I said. "Stephen King." Why does everyone assume everyone who has ever been in Maine knows Stephen King? Like he sits on a bench in front of the local bait-and-tackle store whittling ducks and swapping jokes with toothless yokels all day long. Assume, while they're at it, that he's the only writer the US ever produced, apart from Mark Twain. Because Maine's population is so low-density, I guess. Where I had lived, no question, you could disappear forever into the forest and the trees and never be found. I did love that about it: the loneliness, the rugged individualism that was the hallmark of the place. In my memory, it was a perfect place to grow up, wild and free and anonymous. But you could go quite, quite mad living there as an adult, and if you wanted to make anything of yourself, as I did, you had to get out. You first had to have the smarts that would carry you out on the wings of a scholarship to a high-toned place where, if you couldn't read a menu in French, you were considered unfit to join the human race. But I got through that; I excelled. I showed them all. Didn't I just?

Milo wrote down my date and place of birth, which was Kansas. I had to spell it for him, seeing him start off with a "C." His jotting all this down kind of freaked me out. What was he going to do, put out a request for information on me through Interpol? Did Anna's death really rate that sort of international scope? Well, good luck finding anything of interest; I was clean as a whistle apart from some traffic citations, but still, it was disconcerting to be reminded I was in the thick of a murder investigation and likely to remain there until they made a good arrest for this.

"Will I have to testify?" I asked him. "When you find the guy, I mean."

"Probably," he said. "Let's worry about that when it happens, all right?"

His manner was so Mayberry reassuring, so calm and matter-of-fact. Murder was just a routine disruption like a traffic jam, nothing to worry about. I was beginning to see why they were likely fast-tracking this guy, despite the little detour to patrol. His good looks probably didn't hurt, either. I mean, when you think about it, you don't want some ferrety-looking creep covered in hair and tattoos investigating crimes for you. You want Superman. As mentioned, Milo was heaven-sent as far as the police's public relations department was concerned, and might one day be great in front of the TV cameras reassuring the Great British Public about whatever it was they needed reassuring about. This was, you may recall, my job in my former life. Sizing up the talent not just for their expertise but even more for the way they came across. Did they seem trustworthy? Believable? Like someone you would want to have in your living room for an extended visit? Go on vacation with; climb a mountain with? If they were nervous in front of the camera it was not necessarily a deal-breaker, so long as they didn't positively collapse with fear, of course. Anyone could be coached. But my assessment was that Milo would, in a self-guided sort of way, go far. He would regard the camera as just another challenge to overcome, another skill to master. No problem.

Curious, and seeing no reason not to ask, I said, "Where is your boss today?"

"DCI Attwater lets me out on my own once in a while. When she thinks it's a routine visit."

Something in his voice made me ask. "And isn't it? Routine, I mean?"

He didn't answer directly. In fact, I wasn't

sure what unasked question he was answering when he said, "Attwater isn't as dumb as she acts. I wouldn't underestimate her."

"Meaning what?"

"She comes across as not the brightest, but they don't promote dummies to her position. Not often."

"Sure. Okay." *Why tell me this?*

"What makes you think Anna was strangled?" he asked. His deep voice was casual, melodious, but I didn't think the question was casual. It was a reminder that Milo, while he might be officious, was also not as dumb as *he* seemed, and a sign that this was not the casual drop-in for a chat he'd led me to believe.

"Anyone could tell. From her eyes, the way they were, you know . . . bulging. Why?"

"You could see that through the trees?"

"I went a bit down the slope so I could peer over but yes, I had a clear view of her face through the trees. Why?" I was getting a bit het up at this point, as my grandmother would have said. Exactly what was he implying? "I thought I saw red marks on her neck. And those eyes . . . God. Those eyes . . . I mean, I just assumed."

"Okay, that adds up," he said evenly. They could have saved all the money they'd wasted on the autopsy. "Just checking. We have to cover every angle."

I thought about taking his coffee away from him. All thoughts of providing more biscuits for this little coffee klatch vanished, too.

"Good," I said. "I'm so glad you're being thorough."

29

When the BBC handed me my walking papers, I went to a therapist, a service provided by the company, which practiced only the best and most advanced Human Resource techniques. I said this already, right? If Rashima's husband hadn't endorsed her I wouldn't have bothered.

I'd been down this road before and I was getting used to the process. Maybe everyone in Recession World was. As my newspaper back home was slowly dying, they had brought in professional vultures to sit by the windows and talk ever-larger groups of people out of jumping whenever more layoffs were announced. Private counseling was offered to those who wanted it and golden parachutes were offered to those who didn't deserve it. We had one jumper in all that time, actually an overdose, a hyper girl in marketing who, in turned out, was only pretending to be engaged to some made-up boyfriend or other because she thought it made her seem more stable or more interesting or something. That was one of the worst stories ever, and her death (which in fact was mourned by no one, her entire family having been lost in some foreign war or another) amped up the already rampant paranoia of the place.

I survived several rounds of layoffs at that paper before it was at last my turn on the wheel of fortune. Toward the end I stopped believing, as we were told repeatedly, that these group therapy sessions were part of the corporation's deep paternal concern for its employees. By then I had stopped believing in a lot of things, and only the youngest employees were dumb enough to believe they had a sort of second family in the corporation, where we celebrated diversity on a daily basis. Anyway, the counseling was meant as a safety valve in the case of employees who were ready to explode — the therapists served as a sort of early warning detection system in the cases where someone left destitute might be at home sharpening the knives with a former supervisor's fat neck in mind.

Anyway, I went to the three BBC sessions. I figured it wouldn't hurt to maintain a semblance of normalcy, to board the train to visit an office in the city before returning home to the hopeless task of finding a job comparable in pay and prestige to the one I'd lost. I was sensible enough to realize how lucky I was — thanks to Will, I wasn't destitute. He was not a make-believe husband, and I had a roof over my head and food in the fridge. And several business suits dry-cleaned and ready to wear to interviews, should there be any of those. To keep busy I developed hobbies: I started to take more interest in the kitchen arts, in baking pies and cakes and experimenting with gourmet meals, as a way to compensate for being at home all day and not bringing home the bacon. To make it up to Will. To stop what soon became his harping on the subject. I began to frequent the local kitchen shop, buying lemon squeezers and other gadgets I never knew I needed. I ended up with three types of garlic press.

As it turned out, Will was less interested in my cooking than in my monthly paycheck, which came as a huge surprise to me. Didn't all men secretly want someone like our neighbor Heather waiting for them at home? Well, maybe not someone like Heather, but someone whose only focus in life was cooking and sewing and in general tending to her man's needs, especially in the bedroom? But it was about this time his interest in sex became sporadic, too.

All this was especially galling because, in the very back of my mind, with the encouragement of the therapist, I'd started to think of the layoff as a blessing in disguise. We could try for that baby now. No pressure, lots of time. All I needed was a willing partner. I had even, in an idle moment, visited a few baby naming sites; I was thinking Natalie White had a nice ring to it. But something told me not to mention that plan to Will just yet.

The name of the therapist whose job it was to Marie Kondo the closets of my mind was Dr. Dray. I thought of her as Dr. Dre: I would settle into the chair in her office and put on earphones, metaphorically speaking. I usually left her presence with the sense of a burden shared and lightened. I never got around to telling her about my plans to add to my family, somehow, but she had a calming demeanor and I left feeling that things would be all right. The feeling lasted about an hour and then it wore off, like painkillers, and I was again left alone with myself.

I did tell her I had started a regular fitness routine, without mentioning it was part of my plan for a healthy pregnancy. I had already cut back on my drinking, figuring this was not the time to let some depressive episode with alcohol get its nails into me.

She gave me a prescription "to treat your anxiety." I didn't have it filled right away, of course. I looked it up online and saw it might harm the baby. Besides which, I wasn't anxious. Scared and majorly pissed off, yes. The juddering waves of anxiety came later.

Anyway, this was the same woman who thought my walking every day might be "obsessive." I ask you.

We wasted an inordinate amount of time talking about my stepmother, it seemed to me. Thank God it was three sessions and I was done.

I loathed everything about my stepmother, beginning with her name. I tried for all of five minutes to like Tralee but it was doomed from the start. She was like the Yoko Ono of Four Corners. What was my father thinking?

Another saying of my grandmother's was that the first woman to the front door with the casserole gets the widower. My father had been a widower for about twenty seconds when this predator, all boobs and hair spray, swooped in with a whole lot more on offer than tuna casserole. She was white trash out of Carolina in a big way. It took me longer than it should have to realize she'd been in the picture with my father for a long, *long* time before my mother died, biding her time and waiting like the spider that she was.

He sent me to live with a big Catholic family for my last year of high school, so he could live with Tralee. The O'Brians had seven kids and he figured they wouldn't notice one more. He was right. I soon moved out and got a shared apartment and a job at the local deli. Later I put myself through college with a combination of the scholarship and working at Hollywood Green Productions, which as I've said proved to be my launching pad into the BBC.

Was I angry? You bet I was. None of it would have happened if my brother had been alive. My father would have stuck around for *him,* not dumped him on that tribe of well-meaning religious nuts.

It's pronounced Trah-lee, if you're wondering. She could be sweet but only when she was getting her way. My father was besotted with her and I came to believe he was some sort of masochist.

This was not just my opinion: everybody in my parents' little town saw what was going on — what had been going on for years. Everyone hated her, especially the women, and many hated him. Just take my word for it. As a couple, they were shunned. I can only think he was reverting to type, sinking to the easiest level, letting Jack Daniels do all his thinking for him.

She always wore a diamond big as Texas from her third husband on her right hand. That's right — my father was husband number four. Spineless and at a loss as my mother's health failed, he grabbed onto Tralee like a drowning man. They eventually got married in a hole-and-corner civil ceremony befitting the occasion. My father, with his usual impeccable timing, died soon afterwards. They were married just long enough to screw up my life.

I was not invited to the wedding but I wouldn't have gone in any case. I had some fun considering what I might send them as a gift, but — no.

Tralee had two grown daughters, Marla and Brandee. Seriously. Because *"Streetcar* was my favorite movie *ever."* She was not aware *A Streetcar Named Desire* had ever been a play and she was shocked when I told her. (Was I sure? Yes, I was sure. She was delighted to learn Brando had starred in both versions.) I thought she should have named her daughters after characters in *Star Wars,* like Jabba and Jar Jar. I don't think Will would have married me if they'd been blood relatives, or if he'd met them or even seen photos of them. They were embarrassment enough at second hand.

At some point I had to return to the US to deal with stuff it was costing me a fortune to keep in storage. I had time to kill before my return flight so I decided to go see the new beach house my stepmother had bought with my father's life insurance money. With what should have been *my* money. I still don't know why I did it. It was salt in the wound. An impulsive giving in to curiosity, it was also a final gesture; I knew I'd never see her again. I guess I was hoping I'd find her failing, finally succumbing to one of her many illnesses, melting like the bad witch she was.

Will wasn't with me, of course. I had only just met him, and — well, see above: Tralee and her daughters would have had him running for the hills.

When I called she sounded suspicious, paranoid — why would I want to see her, after all? Maybe to steal something I could use in a satanic ritual to make her bleached hair fall out? But after filling me in for a few minutes on her medical conditions, she told me I could come for lunch. I declined lunch, but I arrived to find she'd made tea and Ritz crackers with artistic little swirls of Cheez Whiz — sharp cheddar with pimento. Yum. I drank the tea.

She was older, and, of course, when you finally face the dragon in her doily-dotted cave, not as scary as you've built up in your mind. She was moving slower and seemed to have trouble focusing, if the nail varnish was anything to go by — it looked like she'd painted her nails in the dark. We spent half an hour talking about her vast array of fascinating medical problems; I hoped even half of what she claimed to be suffering from was true. Pretending to listen, I scanned the room for belongings she'd stolen from me and my mother. Every vestige of my childhood had disappeared, to be replaced by tacky crap that looked like it had all come from a garage sale.

Finally she surprised me by moving on to a topic beyond her high, but not high enough, LDL cholesterol levels. She asked me if I was seeing anyone. I told her a bit about Will, keeping it vague. I told her him name was James le Blanc in case she looked him up. I wanted this woman nowhere near my life.

Tralee said, "Well played. A highness, no less."

I nodded. I could not be troubled to explain British titles to this peasant. I sat staring into her gleaming little blue-lined eyes as she replayed the story she had already once told me of her third husband's dying wish — his heartwarming desire that Tralee should find someone to take care of her and their two little orphans when he passed. That she should not mourn him forever (as if).

So touching. And doesn't this Make-a-Wish scenario sound familiar? I mean, please. Did he also desire that my mother should suffer so horribly, waiting at home for my father to come give her her medicine?

So this monster and I sat and drank tea and I watched her lick the Cheez Whiz off the crackers as I wished arsenic was easier to come by. She wanted to reminisce over pictures of the funeral. Of course I declined. The person buried in that box was not my father, not the hero he'd been. He'd thrown all that away.

She always had a parting shot.

"I think you're making a big mistake," she said as I rose to leave. "He's miles out of your league. You should stick with your own kind." She said this not particularly with spite, but more as a point of information.

It was this kind of thing . . . I don't know how I stopped myself from choking her or throwing something at her head, maybe one of her bargain purchases from the Shopping Channel. There was a heavy glass paperweight on the table I stood next to and my fingers itched to throw it at her like a baseball. Then I realized it had belonged to my mother. I pocketed it instead. At least the visit wasn't a total loss.

If Will was out of my league, my father was for sure out of hers. How fucking dare she? I literally bit the inside of both cheeks until I tasted blood. Then I spun round and stalked out the door without another word.

These memories, these blasts from the past. What was the use of them, and why did Anna's death seem to dredge up all this crap? It was nothing to do with her . . .

Ken, for instance, the guy Oscar was so exercised about — why think of him now? I'd allowed him to move into my place in London to save money, which proved to be one of those false economies you could kick yourself for, like buying the second-hand car that leaves you stranded when you could have afforded better. For a while after I tossed him out, Ken became a bit of a stalker. He had thought his moving in was a prelude to forever, it seems. But I met Will and that was that. Bad timing, that's all. Too bad. Ken had to go.

I didn't remember a whole lot about him, to tell you the truth, apart from the way we parted. He's a vague, large blonde shape in my memory, a sort of Ken-doll in looks and name. He had some adventure TV show about exploring the Amazon jungle that he was trying to sell to the BBC. I suppose I was really only seeing him because he was American and I had fallen into a sort of nostalgia for people who sounded like Ken, who looked and acted like him: all puppyish exuberance and not a lot of forethought. But then Will came along, handsome in that pale, long-nosed British way; Will had a British passport and a title. And, oh my lucky stars, Will was smitten with me.

I spent half a day, while Ken was out, packing his belongings for him to save on the drama — he didn't have much, as his major stuff was back in the US. He walked in to find his bags stacked in neat rows by the door, his coat folded on top of the largest case. I even had my phone ready in my hand to call him a taxi. Yes, I waited until he got home, even as I wondered if that was wise. They always say it's when things end that the guy gets violent, if he's going to.

But I'd never seen a sign of that sort of temper from Ken. I almost wondered if he wouldn't have been more interesting to me with that edge. The edge that Will had, in spades. Poor Ken. He couldn't help it that he was boring.

He bleated for about five minutes, and finally said, "Did you ever love me?"

Why pretend? I shook my head.

"No. Of course not. I don't think you're capable . . ." His voice wavered, and he must have sounded pathetic even to his own ears. But his gaze never left my face, in that hopeful, puppy-dog way of his: Surely I was joking and we would go for the walk I'd promised after all? I looked away, the way you turn from a car wreck once you realize it is way worse than you expected.

"No, not really," I said, to make sure he got this. "I didn't really love you. And before you say it again, whether you loved me or not doesn't matter, don't you see?" More quietly, I repeated, "It doesn't matter. It's just over. It never started." Really, I thought to spare us both further embarrassment, truly I did, but Ken did not seem to take it that way. I suppose I should just have just left him alone to sort himself out for an hour, but I wanted to feel I'd behaved well, cutting him free to find someone else: It just didn't work out, blah blah blah. Best of luck for the future.

I also didn't quite trust him not to set the place on fire, lovable or not.

As I'd told Oscar, I don't know what happened to Ken.

Or maybe I don't want to remember.

30

There was a woman on one of those true-crime shows on the telly who had cut her abusive husband up into a curry. Seriously. Well, several curries, presumably. A squeamish BBC had declined to dramatize that one for *BM: London.*

The night of Milo's visit, Will started to get up in my face about something, but he stopped when he noticed I was cutting carrots and parsnips into a one-inch dice. Maybe he'd seen the show. Instead of going out of his way to provoke me, as was his wont lately, he got himself a gigantic pour of something and went off to the living room to see what was on TV. I had started doing all the cooking but honestly, it was better that way. Will had once been good about helping with the cleanup. Now that had become my job, too. I reminded myself it was only temporary and not worth fighting about.

I liked to have classical music playing in the background during dinner. We had a built-in stereo system that could pipe music into any room in the house. All very civilized, plus it hid the fact that my husband and I had nothing to say to one another. Without music to fill the silence, there was only the sound of the scrape of knife and fork against the plate.

When did this start? Six months ago? More?

I wondered what it was this time. Anyone could see the tension in the man, in the way his head jutted from his shoulders, in the way he stabbed his fork against the plate. I knew better than to say a word. I wondered if anyone from Milo's team had spoken with him yet.

Half the time I didn't even know what Will's problem was. Lately I could guess: a guilty conscience makes the best people behave badly.

How had we got to here, me and Will? It had started so well. We had been one of those golden couples books are written about.

I had been at a wine bar with some people when I spotted Will having a drink. The mirror over the bar reflected the aristocratic lines of his face — not Prince Charles aristocratic; more Jude Law with hair — but what really captivated me was the way he carried himself, his relaxed posture as he chatted with the bartender. He radiated man-of-the-world confidence, that self-assurance that comes naturally to people of his class and background, to men who are born to lead. It's attractive until you have to live with the accompanying sense of entitlement every day.

Anyway, I reapplied my lipstick and headed straight over to order food for my table from the bartender. *Carpe diem.*

Much later I ended up making excuses to the friends — BBC coworkers celebrating something, some engagement or promotion long forgotten — and I left with Will.

Not that anything happened that first night. I'm not stupid, and besides, Ken was at home watching telly, waiting for me. In hindsight, Ken-as-barrier was a good thing, making me a little more elusive in Will's eyes. We went from the wine bar to the cozy basement of a restaurant on Great Titchfield Street for dinner — Will first picking up the tab for the appetizers I'd ordered for my table. Yes, he was all that — thoughtful, generous, *and* good-looking. This one act won him many fans among my colleagues, apart from Oscar, who saw it as some toff showing off.

I had the Ken situation to get out of first. This had to be clear sailing, for I was just as smitten as Will was. I found it hard to *breathe* in his presence. Ken would have to understand: it was just one of those things.

Of course I pretended not to be too interested in Will at first, but I did look for a wedding ring and saw none. That didn't mean he wasn't taken in some way. It turned out he was. One of his mother's finds. He told me the whole story over more drinks, then, still the perfect gentleman, he put me in a cab and sent me home.

The next day he was ringing my doorbell. A bit awkward, that, because of course he didn't know about Ken. I told Will over the intercom, politely, that I was busy and I'd ring him later, which just whetted his appetite. He never guessed about Ken. Sometimes jealousy over a rival works for you but in Will's case, I had a feeling it would backfire. Just being unavailable to Will now and then was all it took.

Will's girlfriend later ran off, to all appearances disappearing with her Spaniard, as I'd told Oscar. Will swore it was nothing to do with me.

"It had been over a long time," he said.

Exactly what I wanted to hear.

I've had some amazing luck in my life — things that seemed just handed over because I wanted them so much, so intensely. Will was one of these things.

To avoid talking about Anna that night of the parsnips, I kept jumping up to refill Will's wine glass or get more bread from the oven. Getting him plastered was always a dicey proposition: sometimes wine would calm him down; at other times, it was fuel to the fire. That night I made sure it calmed him. A little something added to his drink, that was all.

He grabbed the remote, dropped into a chair in front of the TV while I did the dishes, and promptly fell asleep.

I know this sounds like a marriage in the death throes, and of course, it was. But meanwhile, an uneasy truce was preferable to the endless rounds of fights. Least said, soonest mended. I needed calm and space to think, to be ready for whatever lay ahead. I decided to pretend, to keep on pretending. Keep him from doing anything rash, and calling on whatever skills I possessed as an actress. I couldn't quite pull off doting wife, but I could do patient and long-suffering wife.

Around eight Frannie Pope stopped by. She did this occasionally — she was lonely, I guess, and would turn up once she'd closed the shop with some feeble excuse to talk. Generally, it was Will she wanted to take financial advice from. I took her coat and scarf to hang in the hall closet and sent her off to bend Will's ear — he'd been awakened by the doorbell. I offered her wine and said I had something to finish up in the kitchen.

She was a welcome distraction. From what I could overhear, she was nattering at Will about some investment or other — was it a good buy? Was gold still a safe bet? She'd come into some money, it seemed. A small bequest from Anna, of all people. I tuned out at that point and continued fussing around, wiping down the kitchen counters.

When she got up to leave I went to fetch her coat from the hall closet. She stood there saying endless goodbyes, complimenting me on my hairstyle and my watch, and then, in her dithery way, she dropped her purse. Half the contents spilled out and coins went rolling across the wood floor, so we spent some time getting her sorted. She seemed flustered, but then, she always seemed flustered.

What the hell, I asked Will once she'd left,

was *that* all about?

He shrugged and turned the set back on.

I resumed organizing my Anna case file. Drag and drop, drag and drop. I had started keeping the writer's equivalent of a double-entry system: the whole truth, and the truth in its fictionalized version. The story was taking shape, the pages adding up, and I had started keeping a page-count spreadsheet to document my progress.

I made fun of the OCD tendencies of my neighbors but in truth, while the rest of the house might be a shambles, my office was generally shipshape. I'd spent a certain amount of time each day getting even more of my files in order, shredding and condensing. Tidying my life for posterior.

By this point I'd realized there was a good chance Will had been reading my stuff. That my assumption he didn't care enough to bother looking was risky. Every once in a while he'd refer to something he shouldn't have known about — something he couldn't have known otherwise than by snooping. For a long while I'd been a little too open in writing down my thoughts, which was foolish of me. It was particularly foolish to continue operating under conditions of trust when trust was gone. Where Will was concerned, I had been far too naïve.

Then there was the problem of my computer itself. I worried Will may long ago have figured out my passcode — which would be easy to do, as I used the same code at the ATM. He may have been looking over my shoulder as I withdrew cash from the bank. So I started changing the MacBook password daily, and I changed my phone so it could only be accessed with my fingerprint. I supposed he could still drug me and wait until I passed out and use my print that way, but hey. You can't control for everything.

I only needed to control the story.

I needed to be in charge of how it ended.

The last time Will and I had had a romantic getaway was when we'd gone hiking in the Lake District, staying at night in one of the rustic, fire-lit inns that dotted the area, roughing it yuppie style. We'd hired a Sherpa service to carry our bags ahead so we didn't have to carry much and we weren't rinsing the same clothes out in a stream at the end of the day. Leave that for the back-to-nature diehards.

Had that been the start of the troubles? Because Will had not wanted to go, and I'd had to talk him into it. Normally I'm not one to nag, but this seemed like the only chance, the best last chance for us to make a go of it, late in the spring.

"Would you really like us not to go?" I finally asked, exasperated by yet another winding conversation on the subject. Will could be crablike in his approach to things, so polite you barely knew what he was saying. I was always the more direct of the two of us. Well, not always:

"Yes," he said. "I would really like not to go."

"Fine, then."

Of course, I sulked the rest of the day. I mean, he'd promised and I'd made all these deposits, some of which were nonrefundable. In the end, I wore him down. I hated it when he didn't just agree in the first place and save us all the fucking drama.

The last time we'd really been together before that had been when he'd been promoted. We'd had dinner to celebrate at our favorite place on Walton Street near the V&A, and rented a hotel room. That night he grabbed me before the door had even shut behind us — just like in the old days. We were out-of-body drunk on champagne; when we made too much commotion some old codger actually called downstairs to the desk to complain. It was a very good night; Will had picked up a few new moves from somewhere, I noticed. It may have been the last of what I would call a good night for a while. After that, he was gone more often, the new job "bringing new responsibilities." And then I lost my job, and the contrast (no responsibilities, unless you count coping with his insecurities) became too much. Perhaps that was it. I try not to think about it.

So the walk in the Lake District was a big deal. A chance for us to be alone and make a fresh start.

But there had been one incident during that trip that, looking back, was a major crack in the ice. It happened the last night of our trip: We'd walked the route full circle, having left the car at the first inn, staying at other inns as we looped our way back. We felt fit and hearty, our legs on fire from the unaccustomed tromping over uneven terrain, and by day three we'd quit the testy squabbling over trifles that had become our standard mode of communication. The dead silence was only broken by bird and squirrel chatter and the sound of our shoes on the leaf-strewn path. The green hush reminded me of my weekends roaming the woods in Maine, gun at the ready. You never ventured into those woods back then without a gun, and even now, with developers moving it, a gun was a good idea.

The one useful thing my father had taught me was how to shoot. He loved to fish and hunt and kill things, skin and gut what had been living moments before. One time he killed a bear cub and was overjoyed. Who does that? Me, I could never kill, except to save my own life.

That last night in the Lake District we ate in the inn's dining room: candlelight, firelight, gleaming glasses and pewter. We were too full and tired afterward for sex — nothing new there — but this was a good tired. I was happy in this Camelot, for one brief shining moment. I thought Will was, too.

As I headed out to the car after breakfast, backpack slung over one shoulder, I saw him talking to the inn owner, pointing at the bill.

"Two drinks, not three," said Will. The men put their heads together, scanning the lines on the paper. The man got out a ruler so the items could more easily be seen as they lined up with the costs.

"I guess that's right," said the man. "Hard to be sure now."

"I only had two drinks," Will had insisted, politely but firmly. "I know my wife didn't have any."

"I'll get it fixed, no worries."

I asked him as we drove away, "What was that about?"

"He'd overcharged us," he said briefly.

"I had water at dinner."

"I know that," he said. He had the "not amused" look on his face so I said no more.

The thing was, Will had started noticing when and what I drank, literally keeping tabs, and I guessed he'd figured out it had something to do with when I was ovulating. I wouldn't drink for the two weeks spanning just before, during, and after. And when it all came to naught and the home tester turned the wrong color, I'd be so depressed I'd binge until I was on my face.

In other words, he'd begun to suspect I was trying to get pregnant. I'd started pretending to drink wine when I was only having grape juice; that worked for a while. I could get away with it at home, but not when we ate at a restaurant. So we stayed home more and more. At least, I did.

This probably sounds bad, right? Dishonest and underhanded. But I was desperate.

Will was no longer my friend and partner, coparent of my future child. He had slowly become the enemy, him and his fanged mother. But all the more reason I was determined to take something away with me from the marriage, should it come to that. I set my heart on getting pregnant, on carrying the titled legacy of the Whites into the future. Will was . . . on the fence, let's say. From once being an active participant in the whole process he had become undecided, then opposed, then outright surly whenever the subject came up. I stopped bringing it up.

At first I thought he only needed a little nudge into fatherhood. Most men are like that. Then I would take over. Nothing for him to worry about.

So what right did he have to deny me what is every woman's birthright?

The love I once had felt for him, which had beat through the very heart of me, had gone. I was married to a control freak, a man who had the nerve to monitor what I drank, and when. To monitor my every move.

31

The next day came the call from Rashima.

I had just returned home from a walk in the freezing cold and was boiling water for green tea when my mobile buzzed.

"Hey, Jill." I should have realized from the tone of her voice — straining high and nervous, without her usual warm singsong notes. "I was wondering if you'd like some tea. If you'd like to come over for some tea."

Well, that was nothing if not clear. I started to invite her over instead, but she added that she was making a Swiss roll using Chetna's recipe from the *Great British Bake Off,* and I could not resist a little stress eating. A Swiss roll might be exactly what the doctor ordered to take my mind off things, if only for a few blessed moments.

"I'll be right over."

"Give me ten more minutes to let the cake cool so I can frost it."

It sounded just like a normal visit.

The cardamom, pistachio, and coffee Swiss roll was beyond perfection. Rashima knew that woman doesn't live by bread alone: cake is what makes it all worthwhile.

I'll always remember her doing that, making the roll especially for me, to soften the blow. Not everyone in the village was up themselves. Rashima was one of the good people.

The sweet, lovely aroma hit me as I walked in the door. I sat at her kitchen island as she worked, flipping through one of her magazines ("Six Ways to Tell He's Lying"; I dunno, is he breathing?) as she made the icing of double cream, sugar, instant coffee, and chopped pistachios. She didn't talk as she worked, but she was an artist and I dared not disturb her.

Suddenly she put down the spreading knife, a look of dismay on her face.

"I forgot to make the little chocolate flowers to decorate."

"Well, that's it," I said. "I'm leaving." Rashima could be a bit literal-minded, so I was always careful to smile to make sure she knew I was kidding. She returned the smile but it was not her usual sunny offering. More like the smile you get when you've made a joke in poor taste. I wondered what could be the matter.

"I can never tell when you're joking," she said.

"No kidding."

She cut two generous slices of cake and poured the tea before leading the way into her living room, where we settled on a sofa in front of a glass-topped bamboo coffee table. Her home was like a sanctuary, all light balsam wood and wicker, with plants on every surface. From one corner came the soothing drip of an outdoor fountain. The Khans' place was a refuge from the relentlessly tartan-or-chintz-covered horsiness of the rest of the village.

"I think I can always tell when you've got something on your mind," I prompted her.

"Please," she said with a small laugh. "It's bad enough being married to an all-seeing shrink. I don't need one for a friend, too." She hesitated, then said, "It's because I'm your friend, you see, that I . . ." She began to separate the icing from her slice, shoveling it with her fork to the edge of the plate. I supposed she was trying to save calories but what a waste.

"That you what?" I prompted.

She began stabbing at her slice of cake distractedly. I was busy discovering it was the most delicious Swiss roll ever made.

"I put myself in your shoes," she answered obliquely in her honeyed voice. "If you knew something, something like what I know, something that affected your whole life, would you be obligated to tell? As a friend? Or would it be a true act of friendship never to let you know, and to hope the whole thing would blow over and you none the wiser?"

"Rashima, I —"

"Let me finish. If I don't say this in my way, I'll never get it said."

I nodded solemnly. Reluctantly, I put down my fork.

"But now the situation is so serious. I mean, it was always serious, but . . . now there is a sort of — well, I can't say a moral angle. There was always that."

For God's sake.

"With Anna dead, you see . . . I can't not tell you. I can't see a way to not telling you. And I can't not tell the police."

I thought I could see for sure now where this was going. "Will," I said.

And her face crumbled into what I can best describe as a mashup of gratitude and wretched misery. Those theater masks depicting comedy and tragedy? Rashima managed to achieve both simultaneously. Gratitude that she hadn't had to say the name of the villain aloud, or to spell out his crime. She knew I meant Will as in William, my husband. And I knew that she knew that I knew — and how she knew that, I don't know. Except Rashima was one very savvy lady. It probably helped that I didn't reel back in disbelief, that my shoulders sagged with unhappiness, and that there were tears at the corners of my eyes. There was that.

"Jillian — Jill — I am so sorry. How did you find out? *When* did you find out?"

I could have asked her the same questions, but I said, "Not long ago. Quite recently, in fact. I found some credit card charges that couldn't be accounted for in the normal way."

"For *her*?" I nodded. "He bought her *presents*?" This seemed to horrify her — to horrify her even more than the thought of my husband shagging Anna every spare moment God sent. The presents elevated it to the status of a love affair for the ages. Bless her simple little heart, she got it: that was the real betrayal. The whole time he was making small talk about the stock market, and giving me vague answers to inquiries as to how his day went, and putting celery in the vegetable drawer, he was probably fantasizing about how his life would have been better if only he'd met Anna first, his head stuck inside some porno fantasy only Anna could fulfill.

"Well, yeah. But not roses and perfume and books of poetry, at least not that I'm aware. He bought her some things from Intime."

At that she, God bless her further, screwed up her little face into a moue of disgust.

"He bought her *knickers*?" She didn't ask the question so much as spit it out. "What a creep. I'm sorry. Should I have said that? He is your husband, but —"

"For heaven's sake, Rashima. He's a dishonest, lying, sneaking fuck. Creep is probably one of the nicer terms you could use."

She nodded, agreeing almost happily. Her husband would probably approve of the appropriate display of anger as a healthy release.

"How long?" she asked. "How long were they . . . ?"

"How long were they at it, my dear friend and dearer husband? I'm not actually sure. I only noticed the receipts about three months ago. It might have been going on a year or more — I can't say without access to his account."

"Wow," she said. "That really sucks. I'm sorry."

Anyone else saying that, I might have gone all prickly. I can't bear to have anyone feeling sorry for me. I got my fill of that when my brother died, and my mother, and when my father married Tralee. But since it was Rashima, the empathy was like a balm. The tears began flowing in earnest now, on both sides. She went out of the room and returned with a box of tissues.

"Thanks. I thought I was all cried out, but . . . You're so kind. Always so kind."

"Never mind that," she said, suddenly all business. "We have to decide what and when to tell the police." Notice she didn't say "if." "I don't want to push Will in front of a train," she continued, "no matter how much he deserves it, but they will surely see this as important. They must, however, keep in mind that 'unfaithful' and 'murderer' are two different things."

I felt I could debate that, but I let her go on.

"I just can't, you know, withhold evidence."

This was what I had been afraid of. While she was out of the room retrieving the tissue, I'd been busy thinking what to say to her. Rashima was the most ethical person I think I ever knew. God fearing, authority fearing, a believer that the police were just doing the best gosh-darn job they could in an evil world full of hijackers and terrorists. It was a wonder she hadn't rung the station already; I knew only her sense of loyalty as a friend and neighbor had stopped her. As well as a certain fear of the unknown: there would be no way to stuff this particular genie back in the bottle.

"No," I said. "You can't. But you can let me tell them, in my own way." Whatever that way was. I only knew that I would be shut out from the case entirely once the police knew how close to it I was — how the case was actually in my basement, in a manner of speaking: I had finally realized it was Anna's perfume I had detected there on a few occasions.

I wasn't ready to have all the avenues of information closed to me. Heck, they might decide I was a suspect in killing Anna — what more logical leap could they make, after all? Except the logical leap to Will's having done it.

"How did you find out, by the way?" I asked.

She actually hung her head and would not meet my eye, as if she were ashamed for me of the dirty rutting scoundrel that was my husband.

"It was Dhir. Dhir saw them, you see."

I sat back, the image of what Dhir must have seen splattering across me in a dark spray of tangled memories.

"Really?" Was there no end to the number of people who knew what my faithless husband got up to? Did the police know already? "When? When did he see them? Where? Come on. Spill, Rashima."

"This is so awful. I am so sorry, Jill."

"Never mind that," I said, all business in my turn now. "Just tell me, okay? It can't hurt any more than it does already."

Well, it could, but I'm a great believer in pulling the plaster off in one rip.

"He saw them on the train together."

"Really? Were they snogging or something? In public?"

"Yes, actually. And holding hands. I'm so, so —"

"Honestly, if you tell me again how sorry you are, Rashima, I will scream the house down around our heads."

"Sorry." She was crying — I'm furious, raging within and without, and she's crying. Typical. But I softened my voice in case my anger made her retreat into silence. I needed to know what she knew, and, as she lived by some byzantine code of honor I could not for a moment begin to understand, I was afraid she'd clam up.

"What else did he see? What did Dhir see?"

"Will got off before she did. The train, I mean — oh, God, I didn't mean . . . anyway: he got off the train at the station just before Weycombe. I don't know how he got home — cabbed it, I guess. I suppose the idea was that they couldn't be seen arriving in the village together."

I didn't give a shit how he got home, of course, but it was curious. Just a curious sidebar in the action-packed romance of Bond, James Bond.

"So," I wondered aloud, "while Anna was busy owning her sexuality and being brought to fullness as a woman, where was her husband? Where was Alfie?"

" 'Owning her sexuality'?"

"It's something I read in a women's magazine. They must think we're all morons."

"Besides," said Rashima, "maybe Alfie was looking for someone to bring him to fullness as a male."

"Huh?"

"Haven't you seen the way he looks at other women? I mean, like, all the time?"

"He never showed the slightest interest in me, so, no. And besides, he's sick all the time."

"Men have to be dead to stop being interested in sex."

Well, yeah, there's that.

"You're *not* jealous," she said. "Say it's not so. Alfie had a roving eye, nothing blatant or creepy, but — oh, *aware,* somehow. You probably just didn't notice. I'm sure he looked at you too."

"Thanks. I guess."

The next question was the hardest to ask, but I had to know.

"When?" Meaning, how long had these two, Dhir and Rashima, known and kept quiet? A corollary question was, of course, who else knew? In such a small place as Weycombe, the fact that Garvin hadn't put a notice in the paper's gossip column might be down to sheer forgetfulness on his part. "When did Dhir see them?"

"When? See them, erh . . . ?"

"Yes. Snogging, on the train. When did Dhir see them doing that?" That still got me. Will was not a kid anymore, and neither was Anna. Not even hardly. That they could not contain themselves, given the chance of being seen in public (a one hundred percent chance, as it turned out), spoke volumes for the lust propelling them into this idiotic display. Did Will actually think he was Lord Byron or something? I almost couldn't credit him with it. It was so outside the staid, boring (yes, boring; boring as fuck) man he was, deep down. I suspected that the fact I knew how boring he was lay behind the infidelity. I knew too much. Or he had too much to prove.

"It was six months ago." Off my look, she rushed to add: "I only just found out."

Meaning, Dhir saw it as a guys-must-stick-together thing.

But, wow. Wow wow wow. So it predated Anna's politico affair? Although maybe it ran parallel. I wouldn't put it past her.

Rashima had been doing the same math I had.

"It was just before what we saw at the party. You know, at Macy's party. Dhir sort of thought she'd moved on so no need to say anything to you."

"Yes," I said. "No doubt Anna thought our MP was a leg up on the power ladder."

"A leg over, more like."

I looked at her and despite it all, despite the anger ricocheting inside my head, I managed a smile. She returned it, soggy with tears though it was. Good old Rash.

"Exactly," I said.

"You don't think . . ." she began. Her slice of cake was reduced to rubble, like a demolition site. I had absentmindedly hoovered up every bite of mine.

"Don't think what?" I put my teacup on the table, a bit too late. Tea had sloshed all over the saucer during these revelations.

"You don't think Will, um . . . ?"

Of course I knew what she was getting at but I wanted her to say it aloud. I needed her to say it for me.

"It's just that, he was at that party, too. And if we saw, and we think Alfie saw, don't you think Will saw, too?"

"It's a thought," I said neutrally. It gave Will one hell of a motive. I was sure he *had* seen Anna and her latest conquest. I hoped it cut like a knife. "You didn't see?"

"See Will seeing them, you mean? No. No, I don't think so . . ." But her voice trailed off uncertainly.

Given time, her memory might improve. Me, I was busy remembering yet another party, one of my Court Cookouts, where I saw a smile pass between Will and Anna. This would have been in August, well over a year before. These events had grown to include nearly everyone in our circle. The village doctor, the woman who owned the flower shop, friends from work willing to make the trek out from London. As I recalled, Macy and Barry had been there; Frannie Pope had even closed up her shop for the occasion. All the usual suspects.

It was just a smile, I'd told myself, that was all. Innocent. You know, the way a baby smiles not because something's funny but because it's got gas. Okay, bad example, but you know what I mean. *That* kind of smile. An involuntary reflex. Someone smiles at us, we smile back. We humans have been doing that since we first swung down from the trees.

And yet . . . And yet. Didn't their eyes meet and linger for just a moment? Yes, I knew they had: sort of locked, just holding the gaze a second too long. Hadn't it been a meaningful glance, an exchange with notes of banked passion, passion delayed or denied?

Why was Anna smiling at my husband?

Smiling what looked like an invitation at my husband?

Stop it. Stop! I had ordered myself at the time. Their eyes met, the way your eyes will meet someone's as you scan the room looking for the canapés, hoping for someone to talk to besides the software engineer you're landed with at the moment. Will didn't even like Anna. He'd said so often enough. Said he couldn't stand pushy women like her. He'd been saying that since she sold us our house.

And yet, still . . . Wasn't there in her eyes that sort of yearning — that same look I'd once had for him? And he for me? And he, didn't he sort of stare coldly, in that way he had that struck fear into my heart? Until suddenly that stare would thaw into a smile, a very sexy smile and my heart would thump into life again.

Rashima tried picking up her own cup again with shaking hands and gave up the effort as hopeless. She clasped her hands tightly in her lap instead. Finally, she asked, "What will you do?"

"Rashima, I only wish I knew what in hell to do. I suppose I should be packing or something."

"No, I meant, will you tell the police?"

I shrugged. "Now I'm trying to think what to say. I can only repeat what you told me. After that, they'll want to hear it direct from your husband. From Dhir. Will he do that? I mean, Dhir really can't not tell them."

She looked a bit startled — this was moving fast, and I don't think she'd thought much beyond putting me out of my misery by filling me in on the doings of my faithless husband. Of course she knew the police had to be told about their new suspect, but she probably hadn't expected me to capitulate so readily to the idea.

Besides: "I think Dhir planned to tell them today," she said. "Since there's been no arrest, knowing all this started to make him uneasy."

So that was that. It was out of my hands now.

Que sera, sera.

32

I seldom dream, and I envy people who have those rich nighttime experiences, those movies playing in their heads in which they're warned of disaster or told where to find the promised land. Or even where they left the car keys. How lucky dreamers are.

I would like to have that. Some channel into the inner workings of my mind. A message direct from the other side with stock tips would also be nice. But I can count on one hand the dreams in my life I can remember, and none of them foretold great fortune.

Frannie Pope was found dead the next day, however, and that night I spiraled into a clammy nightmare of a dream. In this dream I saw blood, rivers of blood, pouring from beneath the curtain that led to the back of her shop. I saw the shop itself, a chaotic mess of beads and sequins. I dreaded looking into her face in this dream but I had to, there was no choice; I'd been asked by the police to identify her and I couldn't refuse. I began forcing my head to turn and I saw a knife sticking out of her chest and that was what finally woke me, my heart pounding so I could only think heart attack; I'm having a heart attack. I must have been thrashing around in my sleep; the bedclothes were flung everywhere. I reached for Will but he was of course nowhere to be found.

It was Heather who found the body this time. She was standing on the village green when I came along on my way to do some shopping. She was surrounded by a group of people, none of whom seemed to know what to do for her. Elizabeth Fortescue was practically holding her up as she sobbed.

Heather saw me approaching. "It's Frannie," she said in a scalded sort of voice, her face awash with tears. "She's dead. Someone *stabbed* her. Where the scarecrow was."

What this turned out to mean was that Heather had found Frannie propped in a corner in place of the shop's scarecrow. Someone had put a Venetian mask over her face.

Heather sobbed as she said this, great honking sobs, the freakish nature of the find having completely undone her. She said she'd walked in with Lulu and begun idly shopping around, looking for something to buy for her mother, never realizing the scarecrow in the corner was now in fact a corpse. Then she started to notice that straw had been scattered about everywhere and when she took a closer look at the scarecrow's should-have-been-straw hands, realized it was not a scarecrow but a human being, and whoever it was wasn't breathing. She saw the blood — she told us blood was everywhere, "bucketfuls of blood" — so of course that's what turned up in my dream that night. She was smart enough not to touch anything but instead went screaming with Lulu down the High to the coffee shop, looking to find someone with a phone. Heather didn't believe in mobile phones; they caused cancer.

Heather yammered out this story in bits, but we got the picture. She said she would have to move; she would go to the mountains and get Lulu to safety. Elizabeth finally walked what was left of Heather and her child home.

The next day's paper was full of the tale. Garvin was now beside himself, which was understandable. It was a wonder he didn't pass along the reporting job on this particular case to someone else, anyone else, but instead he took it upon himself, putting his emotional involvement on bald display. I suppose in his shoes I'd have done the same, not trusted anyone but myself to the report, but it made him mix his metaphors with a certain gusto:

> "In a vile defilement of our precious village, and in a clear shot over the bow at the forces of law and order, Frannie Pope, one of our most beloved citizens, was found murdered yesterday *inside her shop,* Serendipity. In a morbid, obscenely callous act, her killers had dressed her in the scarecrow costume of one of her shop's Hallowe'en displays. The grim discovery was made by a longtime customer who asks to remain anonymous."

Well, that wouldn't last. Before long, Heather would be repeating the story she'd already told to all and sundry, complete with lurid embellishments like the buckets of blood.

The thing was, I had just seen Frannie alive, not half an hour before Heather arrived on the scene. I would have to tell Milo that. I supposed he would also want to hear about Frannie's rather mysterious late-evening visit to Will, and there went Will, landed in the thick of it again.

As for me, I could only say with certainty that Frannie and I had had an innocuous conversation, that nothing was said out of the ordinary — certainly she'd said nothing to indicate she was waiting for a visitor with a sharp knife — but Milo would be trying to establish a timeline of what she did and who she saw in her last hours. At least I could tell him she'd been absolutely fine, no worries. She and I had talked about Anna, of course. We'd speculated some more as to who could have done such a thing. Of course, I hadn't mentioned Will to her as a suspect.

Frannie was thinking of taking in Anna's dog, as she wasn't sure Alfie would be up to walking him — a typical thoughtful gesture on her part. After I'd left her shop — I'd been there no more than ten minutes — I'd gone into the butcher's and chatted with old goggle eyes for a bit, haggling over the price of the lamb chops I wanted for dinner.

I returned home after witnessing Heather's meltdown, poured myself some coffee, and pulled up the Anna file on my laptop. I looked back over the clues, looking at everything from the perspective of the police. What was missing? What was obvious? Who was the obvious suspect?

And, who benefits? As far as Frannie was concerned, there was nothing that tied her with Anna, apart from that unexpected small bequest in Anna's will. It wasn't a large enough amount to be a clue, I didn't think.

I sighed. Agatha Christie would have seen *lots* of clues here. I used to read her all the time on the train to and from work. The situation with Anna and Frannie made me think of *The Moving Finger,* I suppose because that story took place in a typical little English village, like Weycombe, and described so perfectly the poison that bubbles beneath in places like this. The petty grudges that turn into life-and-death struggles. The closeness to nature and all that really entails. I don't mean the cleaned-up animal parts that get shipped to Waitrose, wrapped in cling film. I mean the gritty awfulness of farm life, such as I had known. Lambs weren't cute and fluffy; they were dinner.

Frannie Pope had had no close relatives but in true Agatha fashion there might be a distant relative in Australia who had fallen on hard times and had come to England disguised as a maid or something, worming her way into Frannie's household and good graces. I'd have to remember to suggest the lost relative theory to Milo, because Frannie was said to have a pretty penny set by. She had no particular expenses, apart from her house. She seldom traveled, except on business; she drove an ordinary little energy-saving car. She worked all the time and seemed to have few social outlets to spend her money on — dinners out or visits to the theater and such.

But the lost-relative angle would ignore the fact that her death was tied to Anna's death — it had to be. That would be the angle the police would be working, and of course they would be fools not to. Murders, as I've indicated, just don't happen in Weycombe, especially one murder piled on top of another like this.

The most likely connection they'd be working was that Frannie knew something, and that that something had got her killed. Classic Christie stuff.

Frannie had been the one, after all, who had been a witness of sorts to what happened with Anna that day by the river. If she had seen more than she knew she'd seen, if she had later pieced together two bits of the puzzle that had been missing before — well. Agatha would be all over that. The police would take longer to catch on. In fact, in real life, the killer would get away with it. It happens every day.

There can always be that one person taking advantage of an existing situation. Someone Frannie had offended who saw a chance to do her in and make it look like a serial killer was on the loose. That was another theory to set before the police.

The possible scenarios played themselves out in my mind. I found I was enjoying this, jotting down notes and connecting the dots, but it was a strange exercise, writing page after page without knowing the purpose. Would anyone ever read my notes, besides me? Could I somehow turn it all into a finished book? While I hoped the world would read it one day — whatever *it* turned out to be — there were other people's feelings to consider. I knew enough about the laws of libel and slander to avoid the biggest pitfalls.

But writers live in hope, buoyed by the smallest encouragement; we live on air and nothing is ever allowed to go to waste; to us it's all inventory, transmogrified into a tale to tell at fireside.

The intellectual exercise was taking me back to my days on *BM: London.* I used to watch the various shows being filmed, watch the actors filling out their roles. I don't think

I ever got it wrong in choosing the person to play the villain, and that generally was the most difficult role of all. Anyone can play the victim: a general air of cluelessness, a belief that no matter where they went or what they did, they were lovable and would never come to harm. It's not that they were easy to cast, but they were, underneath it all, the same person. The same type. Another thing Agatha knew well.

It was different with the killers. They were all charming, or at least plausible, in their own ways. And as I say, they had to have that look in their eyes. Nothing too obvious, nothing that shouted, "Yes, I'm a lunatic!" But that look, it was always there, and the good actors knew how to capture it.

Jason Monroe had that look. Plausible, charming when he felt like it, deadly. Should I tell Milo I had seen Jason at Frannie's the morning of her death? Really, I had no choice. What I couldn't decide was whether to tell him I'd also seen Will in the village when he had no business being there.

I'd had some errands to run that fateful morning, and the bells of St. Chrysostom's rang ten as I left the village shop with some Gruyère and biscuits. As I approached the High, I saw Jason leaving Serendipity. From a distance it was hard to say for sure but — yes, it was Jason. Knowing that he and Frannie had parted on bad terms, this surprised me.

"She told me she'd had to fire him for theft," I told Milo later that day. He'd given me his direct phone number, not just the general exchange where they weed out the cranks, and he'd told me to call anytime. Little did he know how often I'd be taking him up on that offer.

When he arrived I had the kettle ready. He turned down the offer of tea until he saw I had McVitie's digestives to go with it. It had begun raining hard and his pants legs, not shielded by his umbrella, were soaked. I handed him a dishtowel to mop up.

Once again he settled his weight on a chair at the breakfast bar. "Could you see inside the shop?" he asked, leaning over to pat himself down.

I shook my head. "I wasn't near enough, and I was headed in the opposite direction. But our cul-de-sac intersects the High, as you know, and Frannie's shop is to my right. I only happened to look in that direction to watch for traffic before I crossed."

"And that's when you saw Jason."

"Pretty sure it was him. Yes. Oolong or

green?" I showed him the tea caddies.

"Whatever you're having. So, how did Jason look?"

"Normal, really. For Jason. If I'm honest, normal for him is skulking. He sort of creeps about."

There was more to tell Milo, but I hesitated, and in the end decided I'd said enough for a while. If he caught the hesitation he chose to ignore it, engrossed as he was in his dark-chocolate biscuit. Too bad I didn't have any doughnuts.

"What time was this?"

"Ten?" I said. "Ten-ish? I needed a few things for dinner, and I had an order to pick up from that guy at the butcher shop. Have you talked with him yet? He knew Frannie pretty well, his shop is so near. Anyway, I just grabbed a coat and ran out. I wasn't thinking of the time, it didn't really matter to me, so I couldn't say except it was around ten o'clock. I heard the church bells ring but the church clock is usually wrong, have you noticed?"

"Your husband was at work, right?"

"Well, um. I assume he was. Yes."

Milo gave me a funny sort of look. Of course. He'd have heard from Dhir by now.

Milo ended up staying a very long time that day.

That evening I went next door to Alfie's.

The situation with Frannie had jacked up everyone in the village, of course. People went from concerned and frightened to crazy and frightened. There's a big difference.

I assumed Alfie would have heard by now about Frannie and would be more affected than most anyone. He had to figure there was a connection between the two deaths. It was either that or all the villagers had turned into pods and were killing one another at random. I first went out into the front garden to peek over the fence to his house. I don't know why, but I half expected it to be cordoned off, or for there to be a flock of patrol cars parked in front. Instead it looked as it always did these days. Empty and forlorn. With Anna gone, there was no question the life had drained out of the place.

Jason came to the door.

"Jason," I said. "Hi." Even though he'd just been at my house, returning that dish, I always felt that with Jason a reset was needed: "Jillian. From next door."

"Yeah."

"Is your father home?"

"Yeah." A beat, then he added, "Where

else would he be?"

Oh, I dunno. Out rollerblading. Or behind bars. As tempted as I was to match the snarkiness of his tone, the general smarminess of his demeanor (so utterly lacking, by the way, in his father), I simply widened my smile and played the age card. I had more than ten years on him, which made me a wizened matron in his eyes.

"I need to see him, Jason," I said. "It's important."

"He doesn't want to see anyone."

"I'm sure that's true. But he's expecting me."

Not true, of course, but since Jason didn't much care either way, it made him step back from the door to allow me in. He shouted up the stairs for his father, then headed for the kitchen. Of course, I didn't mention seeing him at Frannie's shop. I'd decided it was better to let Milo deal with Jason.

I closed the front door behind me and went into Anna's harem-inspired gaff to sprawl among the satin pillows. The cat glared at me, like it was willing me to die, before taking itself off somewhere. It used to give Anna that look all the time. Maybe the cat did it.

When Alfie dragged himself into the room I felt bad about interrupting him — he looked like a man stuck permanently in the depression stage of grief.

"You've heard the news, of course," I said gently, indicating a seat across from me as if it were my living room and not his.

"About Frannie. Yes. They rang me, the police."

"Alfie, do you have any idea?"

"Who killed Frannie? No. And I don't care right now. I'm sorry — I know how that sounds. I'm sorry. So sorry. For her."

I had to interrupt this recording. I began to suspect Alfie wasn't going to be a whole lot of use, but I wanted to make sure he had no further clue. Frannie might have confided something to the police when she'd been busy putting herself front and center of the investigation — something that they'd relayed to him.

He looked at me with that bleak, beaten-to-death stare that by then had permanently creased his features. "You may as well know," he said. "If it's not already common knowledge it soon will be. Once the press gets hold of it."

"The press? You mean Garvin Barnes? Honestly, Alfie, I wouldn't worry about that. He can hardly find his toupee these days." Off his look, I added, "But what do you mean? Might as well know what?"

"They called me to say . . . to talk about the doctor's preliminary results."

He still couldn't bring himself to use the word.

"You mean, the autopsy results," I said. "And?"

"She had —" Alfie stopped and swallowed hard, as if the words had clumped together in his throat. "She had this, uh, medical condition."

What was he saying? Anna was ill? Dying? I almost said aloud: it might have saved someone a lot of trouble if only they'd known.

But I wondered: if you layered illness on top of a basically greedy and unstable personality, what would you get? Some people might turn to religion, but Anna might have gone to the devil, thinking it didn't matter anymore and wanting to extract every thrill she could mine from her life. Breaking bad, girl style. It would explain her promiscuity. It would explain Will.

"She was dying?" I hazarded my guess. "Anna was dying?"

"No, it's worse than that," said Alfie. "I mean — I don't mean that. That didn't come out the right way. I meant —"

I waited as patiently as I could, breathing

softly, afraid of shifting the ions in the air or something in the moment that had brought him to the brink of confiding in me.

"Anna was pregnant when she died," he said at last. His hands worked against his thighs as he rhythmically opened and closed his fists, weapons in search of a target.

"Oh, my God. Alfie, that's —"

"There was semen found in her 'vaginal cavity,' they tell me. They use phrases like that."

God. She *had* been keeping busy. But oh, sweet fuck, why was he telling me this? I guessed I'd walked in before the shock had worn off, before he'd had time to concoct a story, to even see the wisdom of concocting a story, if only to salvage a scrap of dignity.

"Oh, Alfie —" I said.

"And I —" He spoke over me, as if afraid he'd lose his courage if he didn't just let the words tumble out. "I happen to know I'm not the father."

33

"The police know, of course," Alfie said. "The au— the au—"

"Autopsy." I spent a moment sharing the image that must surely have been spooling through Alfie's brain: Anna naked on a cold silver metal table, her entrails spilling out and the top of her head sliced open. The wages of sin, after all: I hurriedly erased that from my mind.

I said, "I am so sorry, Alfie."

"For what — my wife's death? Or for my wife's being pregnant by another man?" His eyes, I saw, were rimmed with red, his face white and drained of color, like a man made up for a Kabuki performance. He looked, truth be told, a little mad about the edges. A touch insane. For the first time ever, I was a little afraid of Alfie. I had the fleeting thought that whatever was wrong with Jason, perhaps it was hereditary.

"I don't know. Both. Either. I'm so sorry,"

I repeated.

"The joke is, I was worried about her health. I couldn't help but notice the food cravings. The obsessive exercise — she was overdoing it most days. The sudden aversion to eggs and alcohol. I thought it was — oh, I don't know, a faulty thyroid or something. I urged her —" He stopped and a strange sort of laugh escaped him. "I urged her to go to a doctor. What a fool."

I knew the feeling.

Alfie and I sat and talked until there was nothing more to say. The fact he had confided in me made me feel I had to stay and listen until my presence was no longer needed or wanted. It was past nine when I returned home. I could hear Will in his office, snoring to wake the dead over the blare of the telly. I looked at the papers spread on my desk and sat before them, head in hands, unsure how to go on. I felt so bad for Alfie.

Anna had really done for him.

And for Colin.

And Will.

Could they compel a DNA test from everyone she'd been intimate with? Stand in line, guys. Take a ticket until your number is called.

I picked up my pages and clippings about

the murders, sorting them into random stacks.

I realized that of all people it was goddamn Heather I needed to go see. Interrupt her stirring and spinning and weaving for a few minutes.

Because what kept playing in my mind was her saying in the coffee shop that day, "You can always tell when they're pregnant." She was looking at the cat, so I'd assumed she was talking about the cat. Then when I tuned back in later I'd heard her say something like, "I did wonder when I saw Anna leaving the doctor's." Somehow I thought she was still talking about the cat, maybe about Anna taking her cat to the vet.

But of course that made no sense; that was not what Heather had said at all. Why would Heather give a shit about Anna's cat? The smug look on Heather's face had said more, and I should have stopped to fathom what.

Heather joined the book club about the time she knew Lulu was on the way. She told us she thought the fetus would find it educational. When we got down to reading *Fifty Shades of Grey* I had to wonder. But she'd arrive at the meetings in some enormous homemade maternity smock and ostentatiously sip a Perrier while the rest of us got shitfaced. We joked that she was the designated driver but in truth, until Macy moved away, we'd only had to stagger next door or across the crescent to get home.

I made no apologies to Heather for interrupting her session of herb drying or whatever she was up to that day. Actually, from the evidence of the packed suitcases by the door, she was preparing to flee, which she confirmed by telling me she was just waiting for Gideon to get home. She'd given the police a statement and now was taking Lulu "somewhere safe" until all this blew over.

It did strike me that I never saw Heather not in motion. Always doing, always going. Busy, busy. It was exhausting to be around. Lulu, apparently feeling the same way, was passed out in her carrier.

"You honestly didn't realize?" Heather asked, not bothering to hide the little note of superiority in her voice. "The signs were there if you knew where to look."

"Well, the first place I generally look is the stomach area. But no. I really didn't." Not at the time — I didn't connect Anna's health kick with anything except a desire to shed some weight. And I wasn't around her enough to notice she'd stopped drinking. "Not a clue," I added, shaking my head, confounded by my own denseness.

Heather gave me a complacent, pitying smile. I was of course not part of the great sisterhood of the have-been-pregnant. The sisterhood of the pants that no longer fit their fat asses.

I smiled back. "When did you guess?"

"It must have been — oh, I don't know. About two, three months ago."

"Clever you. Well, it's certainly a new wrinkle in the case."

"Case?"

"The police case. Of course." It was my turn to sound superior.

"They must know for sure by now. The autopsy." She paled a bit, her hands clenching as she held a sprig of rosemary. "Ugh."

There's rosemary, that's for remembrance.

I nodded. "Exactly. Ugh." I stood up, slapping my knees in that way that says "well, thanks, gotta be going now." As I've made clear, a little Heather and *fille* went a long, long way with me. And with most right-thinking people, I would imagine.

Even so, Heather did seem to have a lot of friends. A troupe of grotty-looking, bespectacled young women beat a path to her door routinely, wielding knitting needles and an electric contraption I later learned was used for canning. I had heard someone describe

Heather once as "a real mover and shaker," which completely floored me. I guess you had to be on her wavelength, if your dial could spin that far.

"Of course, I suppose I'm especially sensitive to the signs right now. Gideon and I are expecting another visit from the stork."

Oh, great. Just great. I pasted on a big smile, feeling like Dexter Morgan mimicking normal human emotions. "Wonderful!" I said. "Gosh. What fantastic news!" It just wasn't fair. It was *my* turn. And besides, the world didn't need any more versions of Heather. Or Gideon, come to that.

"Look," she said, "I hate to ask but I've seen that detective at your house a few times."

"Just routine," I said smoothly. "I've been helping with police inquiries." My conversations with Milo were not for Heather's ears.

"Well, I have Anna's phone and I've been wondering what to do about it. If I should tell someone."

"Anna's *phone*?"

"Mmh hmm."

"Wait a minute." She'd turned away from me to dribble water on a plant from a decorative watering can with *Land's End, Cornwall* painted on the side. "You did say Anna's phone? You mean her mobile?"

"Uh huh. Can I give you the orchid to water while I'm gone? I don't know how long we'll be, and Gideon —"

"Sure. Now, Heather. I would like you to tell me more about the mobile, please."

"Oh! Well, you see, she'd gotten rather chummy, Anna. I think she wanted to list our house if we decided to sell — she knew we were planning an addition to the family and might want a bigger place. She was over here one day and asked if I'd keep her mobile — she was always asking favors and doing stuff in return, of course. But there was that one time she borrowed some flour and never repaid me. Hers had gone bad, weevils, you know, flour bugs, so I —"

"Wait!" I nearly shouted. I sat back down. I didn't point out that this hardly meshed with what she'd told me before: that she'd barely known Anna. "She asked you to keep her phone? Where? I mean, why? Why would she do that?"

Heather thought, fumbling for the light switch inside her head. Watching Heather think was a lot like watching a squirrel trying to outfox a squirrel-proof bird feeder. It always got there in the end but it took a while. At least it stopped her witless chatter for a moment.

"I think . . ." she began. I waited encouragingly, fingers itching to grab her by the shoulders and shake it out of her.

Finally: "Do you know, she didn't say? I guess she was afraid she'd lose it and wanted me to have it for safekeeping."

I drew a deep breath before plunging in. "Does that really seem like something she'd do, Heather? Something anyone would do? I mean, if you think about it, does that make any sense at all? She was an estate agent; she needed a mobile for her work. Why not just leave it in her car? Or her own house for that matter? It seems to me — and I'm making a big leap here, but it seems to me she was trying to keep the phone a secret. She didn't want someone, probably Alfie, to know she had it. She must have had another phone for business use."

Heather pulled her attention from Lulu, who was now awake. Screwing up her eyes, Heather sought the answers in the ceiling. This was beyond her powers to imagine.

"Alfie? You don't think . . . ?"

I shook my head sadly. "I don't know what to think. Certainly I don't want to jump to conclusions."

"No, she's dead now. What good would it do to speculate?"

Apart from helping catch her murderer? Sweet merciful Jesus. "So, Heather, what did you do with the phone?"

"It's in the kitchen. On the shelf with the canning jars."

"It's in the —" Really. No words. "May I see it, please?"

Heather considered this. "Anna asked me not to tell anyone."

I could picture me flinging myself across the room, arms out, fingers poised to grab her throat or scratch her eyes out.

"She's dead now, Heather. She won't care, I promise. And the police will want to know about this. Absolutely, no question about it. I'll have to tell Sergeant Milo."

Reluctantly, she dragged her gaze toward one of the cabinets. Lulu and I eyed each other while she rummaged about; Lulu seemed to like me better than Anna's cat did, anyway.

Heather returned clutching a phone that was a twin for one I'd seen recently. No surprise there. Heather having handed it over, I flipped it open to access the screen options, pushed a few buttons, and saw the expected calls to the expected number.

Part 4

34

I hadn't told Rashima everything, of course.

No, not even her, although I trusted Rash as I had trusted few people in my life. I was too aware that her innate honesty would in the end trump friendship every time, making her, paradoxically, untrustworthy.

I'd missed so many signs about the imminent collapse of my marriage — denial is such a bastard. There was that time he made dinner reservations that didn't include me. A confirmation text from Alexandra's Bistro arrived on his mobile, which he'd left charging on the breakfast bar. The problem was, we had no plans for dinner together that night. I was meeting an old colleague — part of the never-ending job search — and Will's stated plan was to stay home and ring for pizza. But when I asked him what was up he laughed it off, said he'd got the dates wrong and added it was meant to be a surprise date night. Just for us. Right.

And I believed him. Mostly. God, but this guy was one good actor. Or bad, depending on how you look at it.

Then there was my birthday present. I'd been expecting some antique jewelry, you see. Because of the receipt from a London jeweler for £200 I'd found in his pocket.

It still makes me cringe to think how dumb I was in those days.

What item the receipt was for wasn't spelled out, so as my birthday approached, my vision for this gift grew from a charm bracelet to an emerald ring I'd once admired in a magazine to a diamond tiara.

What I got was an embroidered sweater, two sizes too large, in larvae green. I happened to know it had gone on sale at Frannie's shop the week before. At the time I figured he'd changed his mind and returned the jewelry and got this thing instead; it was during the phase where he'd started talking about money all the time.

I never did find out exactly what the receipt I'd found in his pocket was for. I only knew it wasn't for me.

I quickly learned I had bigger problems with Mr. Control Freak than his watching what I drank and when. Will's purchase at Intime, the one I'd told Rashima about, was one of the more defining moments of my marriage. I'd told her because I didn't want her head filled with any true-romance ideas about Will and Anna. I only wanted her to know the sordid bits, so she'd hate Will as much as I did.

It happened like this: Will and I had been legal adults for years when we met and melded resources, so of course we had our own credit cards and histories. We were both too used to being single to instantly merge into a couple where money was concerned. Our groceries came out of a joint account, but Will made three times what I made, which made me less willing to hand over my entire paycheck to the mortgage lenders. Will was fine with this, at least while I was still employed, and I spent my job income on clothes and haircuts and helping to pay for the occasional fun vacation, like that Lake District hike. Anything left over I banked in savings.

We each had our own Barclays credit cards. Will had a few other cards for whatever reasons, but I was a firm believer that the credit card companies needed me, I didn't need them, and I tipped all those glittering offers from American Express and Mastercard straight into the bin. So when a bill turned up from Barclays, I tore it open, expecting to see nothing worse than a charge for my latest splurge on bath salts and eyeliner at Boots.

And there was the little item that signaled the end of the world as I knew it. At the top of the bill was his name, clear as anything. As I stared at it, I could almost hear the tumblers click into place.

I had suspected all along. Of course I had. Even so, there was a sort of tawdriness to this discovery that left me stunned. Reeling. Speechless. And somewhere in a very cold icy place beyond anger.

I started to tear up the paper, with its assurances of how much Barclays cared about their customers' financial security; my hands moved to do it, and then I stopped myself. I thought: Evidence. You will need this as evidence.

Evidence for what? For divorce proceedings?

Of course.

Did I even want that?

No.

Did I have a choice?

It didn't feel like it.

What I saw was a charge for £124.95 to Intime, a women's lingerie shop on the hidden alleyway in Weycombe that was Weaver's Lane. A place that sold everything from bustiers and garters to granny cat jammies. So by itself this purchase didn't seem suspicious.

My birthday was many weeks in the past. Maybe Will thought cat pajamas would cheer me up. Or that a balconette bra might cheer him up. But if so his dates were off by three weeks, when Barclay's seemed to think this purchase was made.

It would be dumb to assume this purchase had anything to do with me. And still, my mind reached for ways it could be so. It sure as hell had nothing to do with his mother or any other female relative. Will would, in normal circumstances, rather die than be caught shopping in a place like Intime.

Round and round I went in a sort of fugue — that crack state of mind where you feel your head has exploded into bits and that shards of it appear to be missing. They might be stuck to the roof of the galaxy, for all you know; you're so angry you might just have burst through into another dimension. I couldn't see, I could hear nothing, and if you asked me later what I did in those long minutes I couldn't have said.

The odd thing is, I had suspected *something*. In that indefinable way when you don't want to know, you can't be bothered to know, you're too busy to notice — you know already, you know just the same. The spouse is the first to know, really, but the spouse is too afraid to take a closer look.

I had been uneasy around Anna for a long while without understanding why. Well before I found that credit card bill, I was subconsciously picking up clues. Like the flowery perfume I'd detected in the basement of my house. Like her attitude, that look on her face, superior and knowing, with a hint of pity — or was it scorn? And when I was with her, wasn't I picking up on traces of Will's soap, his aftershave, the cologne he'd suddenly started wearing? I was. And I got very busy telling myself I was imagining things.

By the time their affair was in full swing, I was seeing less and less of her, however. And I remember being relieved that I didn't have to deal with Anna, I didn't have to see her at book club anymore; I no longer had to feel odd, inadequate, somehow less-than, around her.

I didn't feel jealousy, not then.

The full flight of jealousy came later.

35

I spent much of that day of the Barclays discovery pacing about, staring at that piece of paper as if the ink would move around and form itself into something more bearable — a charge for sushi from Wasabi, or for a hammer and box of nails from the ironmonger's.

But, no, there it was. Nearly £125 worth of male-fantasy lingerie from Intime. For in the helpful way of computers, part of the description of the purchase appeared in truncated form on the statement. "Saucy Blk Kitten, Cami Set — L" came through clearly, along with the stock code.

Eventually the blood stopped pounding in my ears, my breath settled into something like a normal rhythm, and, hands still shaking, I forced myself to think. What were the possible explanations for this — explanations I could live with, that is? That Will was a victim of credit card fraud — a possibility, except wouldn't there be other and more extravagant purchases listed? There was only the one sexy kitten thing in a long list of mundane purchases, most of which I could verify had entered the house.

That he had bought this for my birthday and then, changing his mind, had returned it. Yes, that was it. Surely that was it. Yes, sure . . . surely.

Size large. "L" for large. Not in a million years would my sexy kitten lingerie be in a size large.

Was Will a secret cross-dresser? That would almost have come as a relief. My mind played awhile with a picture of him as saucy kitten and as angry as I was, a ragged, hysterical laugh at the absurdity of the image escaped me. No way. As gullible and naïve and just plain *stupid* as apparently I was, that much about him I would know.

I sat there holding the shreds of envelope with the distinctive blue Barclay's logo, and I wished I could just hit reverse and see the envelope glue itself back together. I would undo having this knowledge if I could. Which tells you right there I already knew this purchase had nothing to do with my birthday, or with Halloween, Christmas, or New Year's.

The fact that I was still considering going

straight upstairs to shred both the bill and the envelopc also should tell you I was a coward. No way could I confront him with this.

It is evidence, I kept thinking. Keep it.

My heart thudded with anxiety and anger — and a real, shuddering fear for the future. But — there were other explanations, I reminded myself repeatedly. And maybe he had returned the items for whatever reason. I would worry later about why he would return such a gift. He thought it would offend me? He realized it was the wrong size?

So why did I find the whole idea of just showing him the bill and demanding an answer so repugnant, so impossible to do? I will leave that for a shrink to decide. I will only tell you that to buy some time, I hid the underwear bill in my underwear drawer, under my fucking Jockey for Women guaranteed-no-panty-line bikini briefs.

At least they didn't have the days of the week on them.

After that I steamed open his mail routinely, with particular attention to the Barclay's bill, but I found only routine purchases or innocuous items like notices of the card company's change to its privacy laws. Fool that I was, I also looked for a refund from Intime, in case he had returned saucy kitten after all. No luck.

That day I opened the envelope, the bad, very bad day, I even played with the idea that I had deserved this somehow. I had simply not been good enough, so this betrayal was due me. My mind chased that thought for a while. I wondered if a simple saucy kitten purchase, if I had been the one to make it, could have saved us.

I thought about that for all of two minutes. And I decided I was not taking that trip.

Instead I walked to the cupboard, grabbed the ugly soup tureen Will had inherited from someone, raised it over my head, and smashed it to the floor as hard as I could. It was priceless. I hated it.

A shard made a gouge in one of the cupboards that is probably still there. I suppose I was lucky not to have lost an eye.

I was out of control — just for a moment. Then I got it back.

I got out the broom and dustbin and went to work.

I decided to have a look at Will's new favorite shop. Salt/wound. I wanted to remember this pain, in case I was ever tempted to change course and forgive him.

Ostensibly, I was there to inquire about the kitten line: "I want a set in a size small for a bachelorette party gift. You know. Fairytale wedding." Like mine. Our wedding ceremony had been held in the chapel where all Will's ancestors had exchanged their vows. It had been the most perfect day of my life. Now I showed the woman behind the counter the statement, using my thumb to hide the name of the purchaser. I wasn't sure I was fooling anyone, but I didn't suppose it really mattered.

I waited, drowning in a foamy sea of Fleur of England camis and knickers. She came back holding an example of the offending item in size small, black lace. It also came in other colors, if I was interested. White was popular for bachelorette parties.

It was about what I'd expected. The sort of bordello number a besotted lover would buy. I couldn't really reconcile this thing with the urbane man I knew Will to be. And yet, there it was.

Squinting again at the statement, the woman told me the purchase had included a free pair of stockings of the kind that needed a garter to hold them up. Garter stockings, they were called, she explained. They'd been having a special promotion that week. Sadly, that promotion had ended.

I assumed from the woman's appearance and demeanor she was the owner, for she gave off a Long Branch Saloon sort of vibe: kindly, war-torn, seen it all from behind her heavily kohl-lined eyes. She was dressed like Miss Kitty, too, with a low-cut frilly bodice above a full patterned skirt. Her breasts were, needless to say, up and out to the wall, a walking advertisement for the robust, suspension-bridge construction of her inventory. You could have wrapped her bra around my torso twice and there would have been fabric left over.

"Item number 496BZ," she read, pronouncing that *Z* as "Zed," one of those Britishisms I never got the point of. "They're very popular in red with black lace trim, also." Classy. "An old-fashioned look that never goes out of style."

"Nothing else? Just the camisole and . . . and bottoms? And garter stockings?"

Why was I even asking? What did it matter exactly what he'd bought?

It mattered. It just did.

Miss Kitty shook her head, peering at me, and seeing — what? Was I one in a long line of wretched women who came creeping into her shop clutching evidence of their husband's foul betrayals?

"So, no bra or anything more with this sale?"

"Not on this statement. I think I remember the gentleman who made the purchase, though. He'd been in before."

Really. Wonderful news.

This was all before Anna died, of course, or I would have asked about white knickers like the ones she'd been wearing on her last and final run.

I told the woman I'd think about the kitten thing for my bride-to-be friend and I walked out, clinging to the few scraps of dignity I had left.

I already knew I wouldn't confront Will. I didn't want a confession, or even an apology, and anticipating what his lies or excuses might be made me start to spiral. He'd say he'd bought that stuff for me and then had thrown it away, feeling foolish and realizing it wasn't my style. Right. Oh, and he'd accidently bought the wrong size: he was no good with sizes for women's clothing. He'd say he'd been too embarrassed to return it to the store. He'd be mumbling, his face red. Like maybe he *was* a cross-dresser, caught in the act. He would say, "That shop is, well . . ."

Yes, I knew. I'd seen that shop.

That day I went through every hiding place in Will's drawers and closets but the Saucy Black Kitten cami set was nowhere to be found. I didn't expect it would be. I did find the garter stockings, however. Will must have been keeping them back as a surprise gift for someone special.

Had Will come to feel he had chosen wrong? At one time my Americanness — my folksiness, if you like; my down-to-earthiness — had been an attraction. I guess the novelty wore off and he began to long for his own kind.

Perhaps Will felt that with me he'd been slumming the whole time. Maybe he'd come round to thinking that mother knew best after all.

Or maybe he was just born a faithless shit. The simple theory, in life as in quantum physics, is always the most likely.

I struggled with forgiveness. And went to the mat with that concept, and I lost.

What Will had done was a betrayal, not just of our marriage vows — who cares about vows anymore — but of my trust. Finding out about this sordid secret life of his, I knew I should pack and be gone before he got home from work. That's the kind of advice I'd get from women's magazines. Actually, the magazine hacks would whinge on about marriage counseling. *Stuff* that.

To leave would mean I'd end up alone in

some grotty London bedsit while he continued living the life, with *her.* Unemployed and lonely, just me and the cat living a worse than Anita Brookner existence. If I could even afford to take Kookie with me. If I'd be able to afford cat food while the divorce ground on and the solicitors got paid. There was, in fact, no way I could afford decent representation. Which would mean I would get screwed in the courts. I'd seen that happen too often to let it happen to me.

It was so goddamned unfair.

We hadn't been married long enough for me to claim extra privileges, according to the prenup — yes, that mother of his had talked him into a prenup. While a sympathetic divorce court might have given me more, I wasn't going to chance it. Those of us who have gone without know what without feels like and we can never go back to it. Will might have played poor when he vagabonded around Europe in his gap year, but he'd always known mummy and her lawyers would be there to catch him if he fell. It was what made him a child, no matter his age, and it had kept him a child. A greedy, uncontrollable child, as it turned out.

I looked at the palm of one hand where

I'd dug the nails in deep enough to cut the skin in four perfect, bloody half moons.

I told myself then: He could not know that I knew. I had to be calm and pretend all was well. The same way he had done with me for how long — weeks or months? Years? Surely not years. We had been happy together, especially when we'd first been married. We'd been happy together before we got married. But then, we'd been happy together last *week,* or so I'd thought. Off and on happy, but still. I began to wish I'd never opened that Pandora's box of an envelope.

I poured wine into a glass big enough for a goldfish to swim in. Then I turned on the fire, sank into one of the chintz chairs, and sat staring into the flames. I turned my focus inward, remembering. It was a trick I had practiced forever: I could will myself into stillness as everyone else was raging, as my parents fought and sobbed over my brother — focusing on my breathing, the rise and fall of my chest, until there was only the now, the right now. And the past would come into view more clearly; I could recall every moment, with no emotion to cloud it.

I started to remember all the little things that did not add up. If I inserted one and only one name into the equation, those things did add up.

Anna.

Case in point, that phone call.

What was memorable about Anna was not just her zaftig physical presence, imposing as it was, but her voice. Glossy and sultry and compelling as a voiceover announcer. "Just sign here. You're so *lucky.* You're doing the right thing; you won't regret it." A saleswoman's voice.

I thought back to the last time I'd heard Anna purring over the phone. She used to call the house pretty regularly, to chat about this or that or to discuss arrangements for some get-together or other, but she hadn't called in a long while.

I had picked up the landline receiver and heard the stuttering dial tone that told me there was a new message in the mailbox. I'd punched in 1571, put the phone on speaker, and started unloading groceries into the refrigerator.

"Hi," I heard. "It's Anna." I assumed it was something to do with the book club. "Look, love, I need to talk to you. I —" *Click.* She'd somehow been cut off and apparently had not called back, as BT had no further messages on our answerphone service. I used the feature that allowed me to press "3" to return the call. There was no answer at the other end and I didn't leave a message.

I finished putting away the groceries before I put my coat back on and went next door to her house, but she didn't respond to my knock. I thought no more about it, and when I saw her in the village the next day she told me she'd been interrupted by someone at the door as she'd been leaving a message. So she'd rung off. "It was nothing important," she assured me. "Just that I wanted to borrow that recipe of yours for — was it candied yams, you called them?"

"Yes," I said. "Glad to oblige. I'll email it to you." But you know, even then, I didn't believe her. Her voice on the answerphone had sounded urgent, and it did not suggest to me an emergency yam situation. It suggested something quite different.

And she had never called me "love" before.

One day weeks later, I punched in the speed dial to talk to Rashima. I hung up quickly when I realized I'd called her mobile by mistake, when what I'd wanted was her home number — I knew she'd be at her desk that time of day. I hung up and started to dial the right number, then stopped, finger poised over the keypad.

That call from Anna.

She had rung our house phone rather than Will's mobile number — I was sure of it. It was Will's voice on our answerphone, and if you weren't paying attention you might not have heard him say "You've reached the Whites." When she'd realized her mistake, she'd hung up. She'd made the same mistake I'd made with Rashima's numbers, only in reverse: mistaking landline for mobile.

Around the time I realized that the jewelry receipt I'd found wasn't for a gift intended for me, I decided that keeping an eye on Will's mobile phone couldn't hurt. I did find an old message on there from Anna, but it was so innocuous my suspicions were allayed. "I'm having trouble reaching Jillian," it said. "Have her call me, okay?"

Only trouble was, that message was dated weeks earlier and Will had never passed along the message to me. He had "gone out to the pub" for an hour or so after dinner that night. He'd done the same on a few other occasions that I thought might line up with Anna messages. But I remembered that one in particular; we'd had a major fight on his return because he was so much later than he'd said he'd be.

Coincidence? I asked myself.

Don't be an idiot, I answered myself. There are no coincidences.

36

There were signs and portents galore, harbingers of things to come.

I didn't leap to conclusions. Conclusions were handed to me.

One day late that summer I was in the garage, hoisting the kayak back onto its rack — Will had a tendency to just dump it somewhere when he was through with it. It was then I spotted the mobile phone tucked behind some old rags. It wasn't mine; it wasn't his. Someone had dropped it in our garage somehow? The workman who'd installed the shelving, maybe. I turned it over.

It was a plain black phone that looked like the sort of thing they sold at convenience stores — not a real phone connected to a monthly service. I'd never held a burner before but I knew what it was. A disposable phone, used by people with bad credit and by drug dealers.

And by cheating spouses.

Immediately, I got on my alternate theory hamster wheel. It was a habit of mind I didn't seem able to break. Anything to dodge reality for a little while longer.

Was Will a spy? Was he MI6, recruited at university like the Cambridge Five? Or maybe he was spying on another corporation, trying to learn insider secrets.

Would you need a secret phone for that? Wouldn't you just meet in a pub and exchange views?

Maybe the phone didn't even belong to Will. Maybe someone had broken into our garage and left his phone behind.

I chased down every ridiculous scenario, including Will White, Drug Runner. And not one of them made an ounce of sense.

The phone was one of those designs that folded in half like a taco, hinged from the top. Cautiously, I flipped it open. It was branded with a logo I recognized — I'm not sure what I expected, maybe something Russian or a Chinese character meaning good luck. If you are not into this sort of thing, you just don't know, and my mind was still on the spy-go-round wheel, hoping to escape the obvious truth of what my dearly beloved husband had been up to.

I pressed a few trial buttons. Not being

familiar with the model, I didn't want to accidentally erase something. I also didn't want Will to know I'd found his secret phone. It might come in handy. It might help me keep tabs on him.

The voicemail queue was empty, but there was a list of calls made and received, with their dates and times. The calls were all to one number, but it was a number I didn't recognize.

A number for someone I didn't know?

Just as likely, the calls were to another burner phone. They stretched over the past few months, those calls, all to the same number.

In my heart I knew already, that number would connect me with Anna.

There was only one way to find out: to call the number already, but using another phone. If anyone answered, I'd hang up. I'd have to call from a phone box, and good luck finding one of those left in England.

I made a note of both numbers, and a list of the dates and times of calls. I planned to check against my calendar what I knew or could remember of Will's activities. The calls were in most cases made at night. Probably he was sneaking into the garage to call. Why he didn't just keep the thing with him at all times I couldn't imagine, but maybe he thought I was more likely of an evening to search the briefcase he took into work each day. As if I would ever do that.

I put the phone back where I'd found it.

First I wiped it clean of prints.

That weird calm stayed with me as I planned my next move. The marriage was over, of course, but I wanted Will to believe for now everything was just fine, that he could have his cake, etcetera. So I cooked his meals and did my best to be agreeable when I couldn't avoid him entirely. And I kept busy. Busy, busy.

Would it have made a difference if it had been anyone but Anna? I'll never know. Apart from Rashima, Anna had been as close as I'd come to having a friend in posh, let's-do-lunch Weycombe. Friend and confidante. At least, I'd thought we confided all in each other. Obviously, not quite all.

I'd spent hours listening to Anna as she detailed her unhappiness with Alfie and Jason, her frustrations and yearnings, her attraction to Colin. Was all that just meant to mislead me? Worse, to play with me?

I remembered one time, she'd started to name her current lover and then she'd caught herself, corrected herself. Had that name begun with a *W*? The chances were looking good it had.

Later, when Anna was killed, there were plenty of men who made good suspects — Colin, to name one. But Will had "Likely Suspect" written all over him. And a prize catch for any policeman working the case would be landed gentry like Will.

Fine with me, I'd decided. I could help with their inquiries. And whatever happened to Will, happened.

The day after Frannie died I found a letter mixed in with the ordinary mail. It was in an ordinary WHSmith-type brown envelope among all the other mail, but without a stamp. It was a warning, created in time-honored tradition with words cut out of headlines. It read, *BACK OFF.* Just those words, nothing more. *BACK OFF.*

I called Detective Milo, a tremor in my voice. He was there in ten minutes.

I heard him talking to someone as he stood outside the door, concluding with, "I'll see you back at the station." I opened after a suitable delay. I projected composure, a woman worried but totally in control, as if finding warning notes on my doorstep were an everyday occurrence.

Whoever he'd been talking to had vanished. Probably he'd sent someone to case the back of the house.

"You didn't see who left the note?" Milo asked.

"No," I said. "It could have been anyone. The walkway up to the door is partially hidden by those bushes in front. And almost no one is home this time of day. I happen to know Rashima from across the street is out of town until this evening."

He looked around. "You've been busy, I see," he said. "The place looks nice." I had spent the morning cleaning; the aromas of glass cleaner and furniture polish filled the air. I'd be putting the house on the market soon; Anna would have approved of my efforts in getting it ready. As a bonus, it might get Will off my back for a while, and I needed to keep him sweet, or at least in the dark, awhile longer. What happened next had to come as a complete surprise. As big a surprise as that Intime bill and that burner phone had been to me.

It was during this conversation Milo talked to me about his son, who as it turned out had some rare cancer or other. Which explained why Milo often looked so worn away at the edges. The only treatment for the disease was an experimental gene therapy that cost a king's ransom. It wasn't covered by the National Health, of course.

Sometimes I wonder what is. My heart went out to Milo, it really did.

I offered him coffee and a blueberry pastry from the local shop, and as had become our wont we settled across from each other at the kitchen bar. It was homey there, with the sun sieving its way through the German lace curtains. I would miss the house but it was time, past time, to start a new life. To set down roots elsewhere. I had put on a new blue dress that morning to cheer myself up, to signal that things were changing.

Milo finally gave the pastry a rest and looked at me expectantly, as if I'd invited him over for a chat about my plans. In a way, I had. He had already slipped the poison pen letter into an evidence bag. To his questions I could only answer, "No idea."

I asked after Detective Attwater. "Your boss sent you here on your own?"

"Technically, she's not my boss. I don't work Murder, as a rule."

"I see," I said. He might have been there in some special capacity. Or he'd gone completely rogue and was making a break from standard protocol. I half wondered if he was going to ask me out on a date or something.

"We seem to have hit a bit of a wall," he said. "And I'm wondering if you've thought of anything more about Anna, something you may have forgotten when we spoke before. Sometimes neighbors see or hear things that they don't realize at the time are important."

"Sure, I get that," I said. He'd completely sidestepped my question: Where was Attwater, anyway? I decided to play along. If he pressed me on things I couldn't talk about yet, I'd ask him to leave — or so I told myself. Could he refuse? Not really. This was England. So I sat back in my chair and relaxed, at least as much as I was able under the circumstances. Only I could hear my heart hammering away, on high alert. I said, "Speaking of walls. Although these walls *are* thin, you have to understand there was nothing much to hear from next door. At least, not once Jason moved out."

"There were quarrels over Jason?"

"The quarrels were more *with* Jason. He would turn up and, so I gathered, ask for money. But I got that knowledge more from conversations with his mother than from anything I overheard. It's just . . ."

"Go on." He'd been eating the pastry with one hand, ignoring the fork I'd provided. I noticed he kept his hands neat, the nails smooth and squared off. He set the remaining pastry down on the plate and, wiping a smudge of frosting from his lip, gave me his full blue-eyed attention.

"I don't think Jason could have done this," I said firmly. "Killed his stepmother, I mean. I don't think he was even visiting here at the time. He was in London, wasn't he?"

"We think so. Yes."

"So — what is it?" I asked. There was clearly something on his mind and he was having trouble finding the words. Or deciding whether to tell me at all.

"That scarf she was wearing," he said at last. "It was not what killed her. She was choked with a woman's nylon stocking. The scarf obscured it."

Holy gods. Had the police traced it to Miss Kitty's Long Branch? To Will's credit card? These were questions I didn't dare ask.

"We're keeping these details away from the media, you understand. We may use them to trip up a suspect during questioning. That is, when we have a suspect."

I wondered at this new open, sharing phase to our relationship. He was telling me things that certainly should have been kept back, in case of false confessions and what not. *BM: London* had taught me that much.

"Yes," I said. "I mean, I noticed it, the scarf, not the stocking. And from the way she looked . . . it had to be . . . that she was — you know. Anyway, she often wore that scarf while she was running. Blue background with a flowered print. A boho scarf, they call it. A single piece of cloth that goes in a continuous loop around . . . around the neck. Like an eternity scarf." Just then the implications of "eternity scarf" struck me. I vowed I would never wear one again, so long as I lived. Who was that dancer who was strangled when her scarf caught on the spoke of a wheel? Isadora Duncan? "How awful for Anna."

"I wasn't clear," he said, cutting across my babble. "What actually killed her was a knife wound. A knife aimed at the heart, from under the ribs. But first they tried to strangle her from behind, using a stocking. That gave the killer the advantage."

I paused, smoothing the fabric of my dress, to show the gravity of the whole thing was not lost on me: someone had really wanted Anna dead, choking *and* stabbing her. I shook my head in confusion. "Sorry? How do you mean, advantage?"

"The element of surprise. If you're being strangled while you're facing your attacker, you have at least a fighting chance. You can land a strategic kick or scratch his eyes out. This way, you can't do much to defend yourself. Victims tend to panic, to claw instinctively at their own necks, to relieve the pressure on the windpipe. The fight for oxygen becomes their only priority. The experts think she was choked until she was unconscious or nearly so, then she was stabbed. At that point she was an easy target."

"Don't," I said. "Jesus. Please, stop. It's too awful." And why tell me?

"By the way, Roger is in the clear," he said.

It took me a full beat to remember who in fuck Roger was. The vagrant I'd told Milo I'd seen near Anna's body that day.

"He was locked up at the time, our Roger. Drunk in public. They let him sleep it off inside. So unless he managed to tunnel his way out, we have to cross him off the list."

I wondered at that "we," and then realized that of course he meant himself and the crack team of detectives on the case.

I was reaching for my coffee when he said, "A video has surfaced. It might give us something to go on."

"A *video*? No kidding." Suddenly I couldn't take my eyes off him. "A video of what?"

"Some tourists were out early wandering about — Japanese with jet lag, internal clocks shot to hell. They were documenting every moment of their holiday with a camcorder and happened to aim it at the river. They didn't hear about the murder until long after they got home. Their lawyer got in touch with us, thought we might be interested."

"What luck," I said. "What did they record?"

"Unfortunately, they didn't have the lens pointed right at the spot where Anna was killed. They were more interested in the scenic river and the trees, and a kayaker on the river. We're following up on that, anyway, putting out a call for information. He might have seen something."

Or done something. "So that's how . . . ?" I let the sentence hang, but of course, I was going to say that must have been how the killer got away. How Will got away.

He nodded. "The footage is grainy and taken from a distance, so it may not be a lot of help. A logo on the jacket the kayaker's wearing can be seen, and a flash of a watch or jewelry in the early light. And the time the video was recorded, of course, which may be useful. The kayak itself has a logo and a distinctive color. Would you mind if I took a look?"

He stood. For a second I didn't realize he was asking if he could look in my garage. I nodded and pointed him the way. I stayed where I was, waiting for the verdict.

He was back in less than a minute. "It looks like a match to me. Someone will have to come over and photograph it to make a comparison."

"Okay," I said.

He sat back down, pushing his plate to one side, and folded his hands in front of him. Clearly this was his getting down to business pose. "I'm very sorry to have to tell you," he began, "but we've heard rumors. It looks as though your husband had a relationship with the victim. An, erm, inappropriate relationship."

Good old Dhir. So male solidarity had in fact gone by the boards.

I shook my head. "That's impossible," I said. "Will would never . . ."

I'd already decided to pretend this was shocking news. Impossible to take in. I'd had some time to practice a look of stunned dismay.

He proceeded, oh so gently, to give me the details. Some of it *was* news to me, so I didn't have to pretend a keen interest. I had pieced together that the affair had got going about the time I'd been laid up with a sprained ankle, giving them freedom to meet pretty much whenever they chose. Once I was laid off but was walking again, it had really put a cramp in their style to have me around the village all the time.

According to Milo, Will and Anna had worked out a strategy for meeting in which she, in the middle of preparing dinner, would pretend to have run out of goat's milk or quail eggs or whatever and would send Alfie off to Whole Foods — a thirty-minute round trip minimum. Then Will would pop over when she rang him with the all-clear. It was the very definition of a quickie, wildly reckless. I'm sure the risk of discovery was all part of the thrill. If Alfie had returned mid-romp, they would have had a French farce on their hands. In a narrow four-level house there is really no way to sneak out the back door. If you can't climb out a window, you're likely to be trapped in the bedroom closet until dawn.

I did gather, however, that the English basements in both houses came in handy in a pinch — so to speak.

Milo told me all this, or a much more dignified version, trying to spare what sensibilities I had left.

How could he possibly know this? I demanded of him.

From Alfie, of course. Alfie had known all along.

What the hell, I thought. *Tell him.*

Tell him the whole story, what you know, what you suspect.

Just do it now.

37

I settled back into my chair, feeling about a hundred years old. I had wanted to be surer of my ground first, but hey. There would never be a better time.

I poured Milo more coffee and said, "I think I should come clean about something. I saw Will the day Frannie died, here in the village. Not just Jason — Will, too. And he wasn't supposed to be here. He should have been at his offices in London. I knew it would look bad for him, so I didn't — I couldn't just toss him in like that. After all, he's my husband. I wanted to give him a chance to explain."

"And did he?" Milo wanted to know. "Did he explain?"

I shook my head, the picture of misery. "I chickened out, didn't ask. I didn't want to know."

"Most people do that."

"Do they? It runs big in my family, that's

for sure. It's like a giant hole in the brain where we hide things, where we hide the fact that everything's coming unstuck."

"Did you really think he had anything to do with Frannie's death?"

I shook my head, but my expression was full of doubt. It was important he understand that I was at best a reluctant witness. "Not really," I said. "That's why I didn't tell you. I just couldn't figure out what he was doing there, otherwise. Why he was even in the village. Or even why he seemed so friendly with Frannie at the wake for Anna. I couldn't make sense of it and until I did, I didn't want to make wild accusations. Especially against my husband. I just didn't want to be that person." I jutted out my chin. This he had to get straight. "I am *not* that person."

Milo did not look much concerned about my ethics or my moral quandary. But he did look sympathetic, his face creased with concern. He pushed aside his coffee mug.

"Where is your husband now?"

We'd arrived there at last. I shook my head. "He left early this morning. He didn't say where he was going. Just 'out of town.' "

That earned me a look.

"Did you notice if the envelope was there when he left?" Milo asked.

"No. I had no reason to go into the hallway until later."

"So the real mail might have landed on top of it. He might have left the envelope there as he was leaving."

I shrugged. *I guess so.* "It was underneath the regular mail, yes. I *think* it was."

"Your husband. He travels a lot." Again the look of unease. I imagined he was wondering why I put up with Will's absences and disappearances, his happy hours. I couldn't say. You sort of get worn down. You get used to it.

Will's travels used to suit me, or they did for a long while. He'd go to Berlin or somewhere for days at a time and I'd stock up on gelato and queue up the On Demand service with all my *Breaking Bad*s, my *Better Call Saul*s, some *BM: London,* plus a movie or two from the girl channel. I wish I could say I used my time wisely, reading the great philosophers, but this sort of film fest was my escape. I'd open a bottle of wine and sometimes the contents just seemed to disappear.

So I didn't mind the absences, at least not at first. But slowly, something changed. His disappearances in the evenings became a different story. One night he said he was going to the Bull for a drink with Gideon's father on some pretext of important business to discuss. He may have used that excuse one time too often, and that night curiosity and boredom got the better of me. I wandered over to the pub on my own.

He wasn't there. *Duh.* I looked in the nooks and crannies where he might be and finally I sat at the bar and had a drink alone, like this was what I'd planned to do all along. The knowing looks, particularly the bartender's, said it was obvious I was checking up on my husband. Those looks of pity were enough to ensure I never did that again. It wasn't until later I wondered if they'd all already known what it took me so long to tumble to.

Now I sat with Milo thinking about marriages, especially the arranged kind like Dhir and Rashima's, and feeling bereft, cut loose, adrift — all the words we use to mean nothing much matters to us anymore. I realized that of all my family, only my grandmother would have had the intelligence, the emotional IQ they talk about, to pick someone compatible for me. Someone, as no doubt she would have put it, who could see through my nonsense. Whether that would have worked for me and Will is anybody's guess. If it were left to his mother to play matchmaker he'd certainly be with Clarice now.

Milo sat quietly, waiting for the dark clouds to pass. He said at last, "I'll put a watch on the house. And I'll have them keep a lookout for his car, just so we know where he is. But to be honest, we're stretched thin and I can't have the house watched all the time. Could you go away until this settles down? Stay at a hotel, perhaps?"

I shook my head. "No. When will it settle? Next year? Next decade? Hey, life goes on. I'm staying here in my own home, even with the doors and windows locked, and sleeping with one eye open."

From his resigned expression, he knew I'd say that.

"Don't let anyone in. No one. Do not open the door to anyone."

"Including Will?"

"Especially Will. Of course Will."

I nodded. "Okay."

"And get the locks changed. I can recommend a bloke who can get them fixed today."

I hesitated. This was all moving so fast.

"Your husband is violent," he said. "Do you think I don't see cases like this every day? Putting aside the question of murder, he's violent toward *you.* Did you really expect me to believe your story about that shiner of yours? And now he's abandoned you."

I was shaken by his words. More than I wanted to let on. The thought of a pissed-off Will popping back in without warning unsettled me now. But I said, "That's overkill, isn't it? I mean, excuse the expression, but somehow I doubt he'll be back. Knowing Will, if he thinks you're looking for him he'll turn himself in at the station. With his solicitor."

"Maybe he will, maybe he won't. But he's gone off and not said where or when he's coming back. You've every legal right to secure your house. Whether he had anything to do with these killings is another issue — we've no proof."

"No," I said. "No proof at all."

He looked at me for a very long time. Then: "We could get proof," he said.

"What do you mean?"

"Would you be willing to wear a wire?"

"Get him to confess?"

He nodded. "To the affair. To the killings, if he did them. Yes."

I shook my head doubtfully. Not convinced, me. But clearly excited by the challenge: "Do you really think it would work? He's not dumb."

"You'd be surprised. There is a certain . . . mentality at work sometimes. A certain caliber of man who can't keep quiet about what he's done."

Milo didn't leave for ages that day. My, but tongues would wag now, particularly over at Hacienda de Heather. Milo was trying to prepare me, taking extra care to let me know what I was letting myself in for. And wanting to make sure I would stay the course. That I wouldn't freak out or freeze up or in any way disrupt the plan to get the goods on Will, if goods there were to be had.

He said something odd just before he left. I thought he was talking about Attwater but maybe he meant himself: "The thing with being police, there's no one to stop you if you go to the bad. That's when they circle the wagons — isn't that your expression? To protect the team. To protect themselves."

I just looked at him like I knew what he was trying to say. I didn't suppose it mattered.

Once he left, I wandered into Will's office, the one room I hadn't purged in my frenzy of cleaning that morning. Will had long since reverted to the halcyon days when a scout at Oxford would clean up after him. I was now, presumably, the scout. But the police wanted him sent down for good —

another of their charming euphemisms. You aren't expelled for criminal misdeeds, you're sent down. It all sounds so much nicer that way.

Could I really do this, I wondered?

I must, I answered. Not just for my safety. For my sanity.

I decided I'd bin his stuff tomorrow, once I'd had a good search through the drawers and pockets. I looked first for the gun I knew he'd inherited, a Browning his grandfather had smuggled back from service in Cypress. Will kept it in a locked drawer — technically it was illegal to have it without a firearms certificate. That drawer was unlocked. And there was no gun.

This didn't particularly alarm or surprise me. He liked to keep the gun with him when he traveled by car, in case he was set upon by motorway bandits.

I would have pitied Will if I didn't loathe him so much for getting us into this mess. For hitting this replay button of my father and Tralee, making me relive all that. Those memories were what had had me pacing the halls and stairways of the house for weeks — and walking, walking, walking along that river — trying to exhaust myself to sleep. Booze and the occasional pill weren't helping anymore.

Anna and her enormous self-regard, her reckless disregard for anyone's happiness but her own. Couldn't Will see it? Tralee at least had her fascinating medical complaints. For my father to have cheated on my mother, there had to be some touching human component, you see, some justification for the bad behavior. It couldn't just be about sex. Oh, no. That would be too ordinary, too common. Theirs was a love to last the ages. Right.

I realized Anna had probably made Alfie's condition her pity play — not pity for Alfie, of course, but for what his illness had done to *her*.

I went to have a look in the attic for Will's favorite suitcase. It wasn't there. I hadn't really expected it to be.

I decided after all that I'd start binning his stuff in bags right away. I wouldn't even bother setting some of it aside for Oxfam.

Clean sweep.

38

I had an MRI test done once after I injured my neck in a fall. Not watching where I was going, I fell over a tree root and landed hard against one shoulder. The resulting pain lingered and it got so I couldn't turn my head to drive. The MRI never showed a reason for the pain but it did find I literally had a hole in my head, at the base of my skull. There is some Latin name for it I can't recall now. The doctor said that while it was a bit unusual (less than one percent of the world's population has it, according to Wikipedia), it was nothing to worry about. It was not in the realm of something wrong that had to be fixed or plugged or sewn back together.

I wonder if maybe that's where most of my dreams go, pouring through that black hole in my brain.

I wondered too if that's where odd moments of my life in Weycombe got to.

Sometimes it was as if the days just disappeared and one day maybe a package would arrive of stuff I didn't immediately recall ordering: vitamins from Boots, or a dress I saw online, or shoes to go with, or a necklace. That I had nowhere to wear such an outfit, especially when I was just wandering around the village all day, didn't enter into my thinking. If you build it, they will come. It might be the navy blue interview dress that would land me the job, or the black satin nightgown that would make Will look at me the way he once had. That would make him love me again.

That ever happen to you — ordering stuff you don't remember ordering, I mean? It's like being gaslighted. As it turned out, it *was* gaslighting. Usually I didn't bother to call to complain because if the dress fit, and was a good color, it was just not worth the hassle to pack it up and return it.

But those gaps in my memory in the Will days . . . I did start to wonder.

Was it stress, plain and simple? The occasional drink (or two or three), and the pills?

Knowing Will was lying and not knowing about what? That right there was enough to drive a person round the twist.

At last — finally — I began to suspect

something more was going on, something truly sinister. That Will might be tampering with my vitamins, or with my food or coffee. Substituting something that was making me groggy, that was causing memory loss. Could he do that? Would he do that, to give himself more freedom to see Anna whenever he liked?

Well, the Will I was coming to know was more than capable of it.

I threw out all my vitamins one day and bought new. I saved one each out of the new bottles, to have a sample to compare against in future. And I paid close attention before just popping anything into my mouth.

And I started doing all the cooking.

That seemed to do the trick, and the fuzziness gradually went away. I was sharp as a tack from then on. It was proof not only that Will could not be trusted: Will was dangerous.

There was comfort in knowing he was guilty. The uncertainty was gone, any doubt I was doing the right thing was gone. Will was a monster and I was free to act on that knowledge accordingly.

I began to think about my life without Will, planning it like a long-awaited vacation, daydreaming of the trips I would take around the world, the men I would meet and never, ever get too involved with, in a vampy Colette sort of way. I would visit Paris all the time, and I would dress in black, head to toe — not in mourning, of course. I would take up smoking, and sit at outdoor cafes writing poetry and drinking coffee or champagne.

I would never grovel in some "let's be friends," divorce victim way, the way I'd seen too many women do. No, I would run with it. I would crush him. As Stephen King has Dolores Claiborne say, sometimes, being a bitch is all a woman has to hang on to. I resolved to expand on that philosophy. I would be a bitch and *enjoy* myself.

In "Live Free or Die" New Hampshire, where we lived just before my father moved us to Maine, there was a high bridge over a fast-moving stream near our house. I used to declare in my teen-drama way that it was handy in case I ever decided to jump. But the truth is, I've been down and out but I've never once considered taking my own life.

He killed himself, did I tell you that? Yes, I see I have failed to mention that my father, officially diagnosed manic-depressive, finally ended it all. The depressive part I could see for myself, but he did a good job of hiding the manic side, which at least would have made him interesting to be around. My mother always thought he might do it, but her fear also was that he'd wait until after a divorce so he could leave it all to someone like Miss Trailer Trash. Which of course is what he sort of did.

My mother was of her generation. She got pregnant with me and had to get married, although neither of my parents would own this. My brother came along two years later, so they hadn't learned their lesson yet. They quarreled all the time, agreeing only that my brother was perfect. He was the one thing they'd done together that they were proud of. If I had been their only child the marriage never would have lasted. I was the starter child, the one to practice their mistakes on. As a girl, I just didn't count. Not even up against my druggie brother.

We never discussed anything as a family, it seemed, but my brother's addictions. Once he hit the teen years he just kept going, trying to jump straight off that bridge. Since he was our official sick family member anyway with his allergies, it really seemed too much to hand him official druggy status, too. To worry and quarrel and wonder if doctors and clinics could save him.

The focus was always on him. *Always.*

Sending him to rehab, lashing out money over it, too — borrowing money they didn't have. Wringing hands, staying up late drinking coffee, waiting for him to come home, wondering whether or not he was using again. (Yes, he was.) Running the gamut from fear he'd kill himself with an accidental overdose to worrying if any college would accept him if he got into legal trouble. As if it weren't money down a rat hole anyway to educate such a fool.

No time was wasted on the good kid — me, the kid who was perfect all the time, who stayed out of trouble. Not on the straight-A student with the scholarship to Wellesley. Not on me in that constant, nonstop look-at-*me* way my brother had perfected. Not on me, who quickly learned to avoid the whole drug scene in college. If I wanted to hang with addicts I'd go talk to my brother. He had gone to his reward by then but you know what I mean.

If anything, the more my parents worried about him the more perfect a child I became. It never occurred to me to just take up using drugs myself — as an attention-getter, it seemed to work for my brother. It wasn't compassion for my parents that prevented me. It was the certainty they wouldn't notice or care if I did.

The expectations for him were so high he'd never have made it as a normal person, anyway. His death spared all of us his mediocrity, his inevitable slow decline.

This makes no sense if you come from one of those happy families that go on ski trips together and gather round the tree to sing carols. But our dynamic was clear from the beginning, from the time they brought him home from the hospital. I tried to like this change; I tried to play mother with a new baby doll. But I took one look and I wanted that little bastard gone. I said so out loud, in so many words, which everyone thought was cute. How could they not realize? I meant it, even then.

My parents spoiled him, of course. He blamed them for his addictions, and you know, he may have had a point. They spoiled him not because he was bright or special or gifted in any way, a star on his own merits, or because he had achieved great things under his own steam. There was nothing special about him. He was spoiled because he was a male. Because he was the first born son. The only son.

Living in that family was like living in some sort of caliphate. They tried to hide it, they tried rather extravagantly to be fair, in an overcompensating way, but it made their preference for him more obvious. My only recourse was to beat him at something, and he was so stupid that beating him academically was the best way. Because of his allergies, I was also able to best him in several sports. If you are a glass-half-full type of person you might say I would not have achieved what I did without my parents' benign neglect to goad me on. If so, you'd be full of shit, and not just half full.

His allergies were a constant source of worry to my parents. After a few midnight runs to the hospital his early demise became their biggest mutual fear, possibly the only thing they had in common by that point. He was barely left alone for an instant. No doubt this explained the insufferable entitled little jerk he became. Speak no ill of the dead, they say — but why not, if they were insufferable? It's like trying to whitewash the Borgias. Death doesn't change what they were.

39

The thought of Will and Anna together may have unhinged me for a while, I know that. I wanted revenge that even her death couldn't satisfy. I wanted revenge on her *corpse,* her head on a spike, the way they did things in the Middle Ages. Now, that was a great tradition. They should bring it back. I could have stuck her head on the archway leading to Weycombe Court.

Her betrayal and Will's infected me like a virus in the blood. I staggered through the days and weeks before her murder, blind with rage and confusion. Afterward I wanted her back, just so I could punish her. It was a wildly frustrating time.

The suspect most likely to have killed her, my own dear husband, deserved to die, too. If only the UK had a death penalty.

I knew what it was to see red. I read somewhere that if your blood pressure skyrockets high enough, the eyes will extend from their sockets. That's what happened to those airmen they used as guinea pigs in those rocket sleds in the desert. They tested them for what the human body can endure in outer space.

Will and Anna put me over the limit of what the human body, and the human spirit, can endure. It's as simple as that.

The police sent me out to meet Anna's killer: chin up, brave, biting my lips to keep from trembling or showing any fear. I used Audrey Hepburn in *Wait Until Dark* as my model. I really was scared, so it wasn't all acting; I was afraid if I let my nerves show too much, the police would cancel the whole escapade. There was a lot to go wrong — the definition of wrong including my getting caught in the crossfire. Any failure of resolve on my part would be calamitous. If ever I were to be cool and calm, this was the time.

Milo's final instructions were still running through my head. I'd heard them two dozen times by then and anyway, I already knew what I had to do.

In the end, over much conversation with him and Attwater and an assorted cast of characters specializing in stings, we agreed upon a remote location, chosen for its isolation, darkness, and privacy. A place where Will and I wouldn't be overheard, or so Will would think.

Before the appointed time on Saturday evening, October 29, I drove past the village shops and turned off just before the High dwindled to a few cottages. I headed south until I reached the turnoff for Riverside Park, about a mile from Weycombe proper. As far as I could tell, I wasn't followed. These guys were good.

I parked and sat watching as a heron chased away first one, then two egrets from his territory. They put up no resistance; egrets pick their fights carefully. A mother egret will attack her young, and egret chicks will peck a sibling to death. The world of nature is always before us, setting an example.

The park officially closed at sundown so as to thwart lovers and drug dealers, but the rule is unenforceable since there are no gates, only signs with polite suggestions that people obey the posted hours. I mean, it's a forest and if anyone wants in, there's no stopping them. I suppose the police patrol here and there, and I would think it a plum assignment for any outdoors type such as Milo. He could get out of the car and stretch his legs, lift fallen trees for exercise, stand with hands on hips breathing in the fresh air. Yodel if he felt like it. He told me at some point as we discussed the sting operation that he'd been raised on a farm and how he couldn't wait to leave it. He had always wanted to be a cop. He had been happy; he and his wife had been happy, until his son fell ill.

That evening the park was crawling with law enforcement, and any teenage lovers or dealers would have been well advised to obey the closing signs. By the time I arrived the cops had already swept the area, and a patrol car sat by the entrance to bar any newcomers. That car would be hidden at a signal that my special date was arriving.

I'd dressed for the occasion in a heavy jacket over a bulky sweater. Despite the cold weather, I was rethinking this ensemble. I was nervous but I wanted to look pulled together and unflappable, at least up to a point. After that, it didn't matter if I looked bedraggled and disheveled, because surely I would be. I might be in for the fight of my life.

Tucked into my bra was a microphone. Not a pushup, following instructions from Attwater, who looked as if she could hide a marmot in hers, but a plain sports bra. The mic was attached to a wireless device that could transmit to the backup van the police had tucked deep in the forest. As Milo had explained to me, a system whereby I'd have to remember to punch the record button was too complicated. He didn't say it, but I gathered that an amateur, undone by nerves, could not be trusted not to fumble for the record button or forget entirely that they had to use one to make the thing work. Good thinking, there. Even though I was used to working with recording equipment, I was anxious: rehearsing what I'd say, and how I'd say it, and praying I could arrange words in the right order and in the right places before they had to charge in, guns blazing, and rescue me.

It was all being done in accordance with the Regulation of Investigatory Powers Act — RIPA — as Milo had also explained to me. There was no way, he added, that they'd send a civilian out without some way to signal that something had gone wrong with the interview.

I pointed to a button on the device.

"What's this for?" I asked, although it was clearly labeled.

"That's the mute button. And if you don't know what anything is, for God's sake don't play around with it."

"Okay, okay. But listen, what if I can't get him to talk?"

"I think it's a given that he will. Why else is he agreeing to a meeting like this? The whole point with these guys is that they *want* to talk; they want to explain themselves. Especially someone like Will, who was hardly raised to a life of crime."

"Right. Of course, you're right."

"Just get him talking. Open him up and . . ."

He didn't have to finish the sentence. Once they heard Will's confession, he was done.

The wait for Will to return my call had been one of the longest I can remember. If he didn't call, if he refused to meet with me, I was stuffed. I'd literally paced the house, front to back and up and down the stairs. Finally, my mobile rang.

"Is this Jill?"

"Yes, it's me. I lost my phone and had to get a new one. Where are you?"

I sounded pissed off, which allayed his suspicions. I sounded like myself. I wandered into the bedroom as we talked. On my return to the kitchen I nodded to Milo and managed a strained smile.

Game on.

■ ■ ■ ■

I should tell you right now that the murders of Anna Monroe and Frannie Pope were never solved to everyone's satisfaction.

As so often happens, the person blamed for the crimes was all that mattered. I'm not sure anyone would believe an alternate version, even now. Especially now that it's all settled in everyone's mind.

In life, there is no rewind button.

The relief when it was all over was like a thunderstorm on a humid summer day. The tension, the plotting, the nerves, the trying to remember if I'd forgotten anything, the making sure I'd left nothing undone. No loophole left open, and no way for him to wriggle loose. In the end the clouds burst open, the rain fell, and everyone could breathe a sigh of relief. Everyone but Will, of course.

40

The business with Anna dredged up some old memories about my brother I thought I had put to rest. I found that hard to forgive, too, for once I'd moved to England I was nearly able to forget him. It was all so far away in distance and in time. Surely it's healthy to have forgotten. How long are you supposed to punish yourself — how many years are you to waste in pointless regret?

Sometimes, though, I thought I could feel him standing at my shoulder. I'd imagine I could feel his breath on my skin, hear that gasping sound he made as he lay dying. Or feel him leap at my back and shriek in my ear as he used to do, horsing around, scaring the bejesus out of me. And while what happened to Anna was fated to happen and was in no way the same thing, her death started up the memories again. It was like taking the dust sheets off old furniture in a haunted house, flinging all the dust motes into the sunlight.

My brother's allergies kicked in on that final camping trip with the parents, one of their erratic stabs at normal family life. He was allergic to peanuts and bee venom. You would be surprised to know the many products that have peanuts lurking in them. But the bees were what finished him. Unlike with peanut allergies, bee sting reactions can begin in a matter of minutes. I'm a bit of an expert on this.

He knew right away what had hit him — in fact, it was in swatting the bee and making it angry he got stung by it. Self-defense works in the insect world, too.

He began showing all the symptoms I'd seen often enough — his hands, face, eyes, and lips instantly swelling; he was wheezing like a bagpipe and would soon turn a grayish blue. The parents, hovering over him, yelled at me to go get the injector out of his backpack. But it wasn't there. I shouted this news back at them. My father ran over and grabbed the backpack from me, turned it upside down, dumped out all the contents.

My brother had been fourteen, at the classic age of rebellion, flags unfurled. He thought our mother worried too much and he hated having to carry the injector around like some invalid. He would forget it on purpose. And that was apparently what he'd done, again.

Meanwhile, the sounds of his gasping grew harsher. And then fainter. He would lapse into a coma before long, as his blood pressure dropped to nothing. He would die without help.

"There's a spare epi in the car," my father said. That look on his face I'll never forget. He was senseless with fear, his eyes frozen wide, the whites showing all the way around. His own breath came in harsh gasps. I had never seen him afraid. Drunk, yes, with all the arrogant confidence of the drunk. He was only a little drunk now. "Go get it. *Now!*" he shrieked at me, right in my face. I turned to do what he said and I heard, from under his breath, "Stupid girl." I think that is what did it. That's what finally broke me open.

There was no question of his going to fetch it, drunk or no; he started to run but he was pulled back to his son's side, his precious only son, and I was more than old enough for the task, I was sixteen, and I could run like the wind, I was fit, my lungs strong. My mother couldn't tear herself away either. I looked back and saw she'd scooped my brother in her arms like a child. I saw his face and it was blue. I swear it was already too late.

I ran through the woods to the car, where we always kept a spare injector in the glove box, but the thing wasn't there, the epinephrine injector that might save him; I rifled through the glove box where it should have been, strewing maps and packets of tissue and gum and registration papers everywhere. I tore through the contents, scattering them over the seats and the floor of the car. The pen just wasn't to be found, as I told my parents later, as I told the authorities. Not at first. He had had an episode recently, so his two-pack of injectors was just a one-pack. I knew it was there, but in my panic it took forever to find, I told them.

And at last there it was, under the driver's seat, and I sat looking at it for the longest time, breathing hard. Not too long. Long enough. Screwing my courage to the sticking point.

Running back, I knew it was too late. Of course it was already too late.

There was an autopsy, completely unnecessarily given his long history of allergies. But the state got involved somehow. The ME found antibodies to the bee venom in his blood, making it conclusive he'd died of anaphylactic reaction. We all knew that, and personally I never forgave them for putting us through that ordeal. It needed to be over, and quickly. My parent's marriage went into a death spiral from which it never recovered.

They didn't blame me, not even my father, who was quick to blame, always. Somehow that made it worse.

The thing about having a sibling who died young is that you get a free pass for years to come. That's the upside. Teachers don't ask why you haven't done your homework. They think they know; they imagine you spend half your time seized up with grief, crying over your math equations, unable to think or focus. Nobody, in other words, expects anything of you, and for a high-flyer, a straight-A student like me, it came as a relief. They never stop to think you might be glad he's gone.

Then losing your mother practically on top of that? Bonus points in the sympathy department. Plus, my mother was barely in the ground when my father brought Tralee "Trailer Trash" Ashton out of the wings where she'd been waiting. No one knows what to say to a kid who has survived so many losses, who has won this booby prize of a stepmother in the bargain. So they leave you alone.

I think Tralee was a little bit afraid of me,

to tell you the truth, and I liked that. It gave me a power over her I didn't otherwise have.

Life is about evolving. Getting past the religious mania of the Middle Ages, past the invented morality, past the point of people telling you, for their own benefit, how to live your life. It doesn't matter, nothing matters, the rules don't matter except the ones you make for yourself. Choose your own path. Live free or die.

A cold winter was creeping in on Weycombe. The roof soon would creak with the weight of snow and ice, making sounds like a glacier rubbing against the hull of a frozen ship. I had to get out. Sell up and go.

I had once thought Will and I would be snug forever against the cold, wrapped in a fleecy white comforter, safe and warm as we read the papers cover to cover, drinking our morning coffee. Sundays in winter, we'd put on boots and sweaters and jeans and venture to the pub for our midday meal, and that meal would stretch until dinner time. We had all day to do nothing much but eat and make love, and knowing we both had to be at work the next day made us cherish those hours, stretch them out, hoard them, make them last as long as we could. When Monday came, already I couldn't wait until the next weekend. I know Will felt the same. Used to feel the same.

Once I didn't have a job to go to, Sunday was no different from any other day, and I frequently forgot altogether what day it was. Simple things like a dental appointment would have slipped right past me if they hadn't rung with reminders. This, I remember thinking, must be what retirement looks like. It's not that you're losing your mind to dementia, it's that one day looks exactly like the last. There are no buoys, no markers.

Of course the miscarriage didn't help. After all that trying, the worst had happened, right around my birthday. Even worse was Will's reaction. He barely pretended to be sympathetic. The biggest emotion he seemed to feel was relief, and he was bloody awful at hiding it. And somehow, the guilt or whatever it was he was feeling about Anna made him behave like even more of a shit. I fell into a depression and he grew tired of that too, poor thing. He kept telling me to snap out of it. So helpful.

One day he told me he was no longer in love with me. I ignored this. Children often say things they don't mean when they're frustrated, and to me Will was little more than a child.

While I'm in confessing mode: I got pregnant because I went off the pill and didn't tell him. That was the worst, certainly from his point of view: foisting a pregnancy on him he didn't want. Well, he *had* wanted at one time and wanted no more.

I guess that was wrong of me. I would say something like, "I'm going to get my prescription filled" and dash out the door. But I never said what type of prescription and he never asked; he just assumed. It might have been for depression, might it not? But he never asked, so to hell with him.

LONDON: 2037

The Thames rises, creating marshland of London's millionaires' rows. I had the foresight not to buy right next to the water.

I have lived not far from Holland Park for nearly twenty years. A woman who reminded me of Anna — bossy, ambitious, hard as nails — brokered the sale.

Most of the neighbors involved in the events of long ago have moved from Weycombe. I think only Macy remains in her mansion. Divorced from Barry now and driving a new, younger model.

God knows where the rest of them got to. Some, like Rashima, have died, in her case tragically young. An accident. Unavoidable. Some believe she knew or guessed too much about what really happened with Will. That is wild speculation you can safely ignore.

Jason is dead: overdose. Heather: no idea. I did hear Lulu turned out to be some kind of prodigy. Go figure.

Once I came into Will's money, not without a certain amount of horrified, genteel fuss from his mother, the Dragon Lady, I chose the anonymity of London over life in the fishbowl that was Weycombe. I've recently renovated my lovely flat, using money from the sale of production rights to my book based on Will and Anna, their betrayal, and all the rest. I titled it *Indigo,* for that was the code word I used to alert the cops that Will had gone berserk on that long-ago night in the park. Meta, I know, but the publisher and the folks in Hollywood thought it was a catchy title.

Write what you know, they say. So I did. And now, finally, it's really paying off.

I live here alone. I like it alone.

Milo came to call the other day.

His kid didn't make it, despite the gene therapy for which Milo would gladly have sold his soul. It was too new, too experimental. Nowadays, it undoubtedly would have worked, and his son would still be alive. Now we have vaccines for nearly every cancer going, and cures for the various plagues out of Africa, even though new viruses continue to evolve. Space travel is the norm for civilians. To the moon and back, easy, no big deal. To New York in half an hour, jet lag a thing of the past, with more time spent going through security than in the air.

So much has changed. Tehran reduced to rubble; chunks of California and Oregon lost to the Big One; the London Eye, gone. Spare body parts being cloned at birth and kept in special repositories, just in case. DNA collected at birth and stored permanently, heightening crime solves around the globe.

Milo has gone somewhat to seed, is rounded where before he'd been all muscle and sharp edges. My guess? He drinks a bit. More than a bit. He has that same woozy alkie look about the eyes that my father had before he ended his life, still sobbing about my brother.

It seems to me I've spent half my life surrounded by weak, whiny men. And the other half getting rid of them.

Milo phones early one sunny Sunday, asking if he can stop by. He is . . . curious, at a guess. He wants to see how I turned out.

He exclaims for a while at the view from my balcony, over the Thames and across the city. It really is breathtaking, worth every pound I paid for it. I keep a little herb garden out there that catches what is left of the sun.

The sky this particular day is a dusky blue.

The blue of my brother's face the day he died. I took just a little too long coming back with that injector, that's all. It really wasn't my fault. I was distraught at my brother's death, and not much more than a child myself; I'd done my best.

People are so credulous, but mostly they are lazy. Questioning preconceived notions, especially where children are concerned, is hard work. They don't want to think too much, and so they think in stereotypes. Dame Agatha knew this, to her advantage. It was how she fooled the idle reader every time.

This is why I studied her.

"Why are you here?" I ask Milo. "Not that it isn't good to see you."

He turns and comes back in from the balcony. I think about giving him a little shove, but . . . too obvious, and too many prying eyes across the way. Every town and village has a Frannie Pope.

"Don't worry," he says. "I just wanted to say hello. And goodbye. That's all. See how you were faring, after all these years." He looks around. "It seems crime does pay. For some."

I'll not be led. "Why goodbye? Are you moving?"

"In a manner of speaking. The doctors tell

me I'm dying, that I have only a few months. It seems I didn't give up the cigarettes in time. Or it's hereditary. Or it's in my stars or something. Apparently nothing can save me. Not even all the new treatments can touch this."

"I'm sorry." The only thing to say. Never, "I know how you must feel," because most people don't and all of us hope we never get to find out.

"Sure. Thanks."

I nod in solemn understanding, willing him to leave.

"Your place is beautiful — I've seen the photos in your interviews," he says. "Still, I'm surprised you never moved away. Back to the US."

"What for? This is my home now. England is my home."

At first I had wanted to run away, but in the end, what I tell Milo is the simple truth: this is home. All the moving around when I was growing up — those days are over. I used to like all the fresh starts but now I'm getting older, weary of it. Plus, I've a beachhead established here. I'm known and respected as a writer in ways I never would be in the States. I don't write potboilers for cash. Thanks to Will, I don't have to.

"I'm sorry it didn't work out. Your son

and all. By rights it should have."

He throws his jacket over the arm of a chair and settles in like he plans to stay awhile.

"When Anna Monroe was murdered," he says, "I saw the case as a chance to exonerate myself, to prove myself to the force, you know? I still cared about that, even after they tried to kick me to the curb over nothing, really. It was a big case for those parts, the Monroe case, the biggest I was ever likely to see."

I don't care. Why are you telling me this?

"The thing is, Attwater wasn't as dumb as she seemed. She just couldn't prove her hunches." He says this with a meaningful look. I can't be bothered to ask him what he means. "She sent me in, thinking you would let your guard down with me."

Thought so. Didn't work, did it? I smile, a soft, puzzled smile, like you'd use with someone in an asylum. I wait.

"She's gone now. Died last year."

Fine. Why tell me?

"That bruise under your eye," he said. "The day I came to talk to you about Colin Livingstone. You did that to yourself, didn't you?"

Of course I did. I needed Milo to see for himself what a brute Will was.

"It wasn't even a full-on bruise when I saw you. It hadn't had time to darken into that. But I didn't question it at the time. All I could think was what a shit your husband was. That made it easier to . . . you know."

"Okay, yeah. I saw you arrive and I knocked myself a good one with a hammer. I knew you'd assume Will had done it."

"Yes." He sits, elbows on his knees, looking at me, taking me in for the person he's finally realized I am.

Which is: brave and determined, if you ask me. I had stayed the course, having set a path for private justice. I had observed Will quietly for weeks, months, assessing the lies, my mind uncluttered by emotion. Once I was through lying to myself, I was strangely, eerily calm, able to think and plan my next move.

And I had followed through to the end.

I felt I knew Milo well, given that people don't really change over the years, they just become more so. More set in their ways. Solving the murder of Anna was his way to prove himself, to win his way back into the fold, sure. But he also saw himself as a fearless rescuer of damsels. It's a toxic mix.

There had been a lot of fun moments along the way. First I had to give Will a motive for killing his lover. And that motive was that Anna had wanted more; Anna, as was her way, wanted too much. I used the burner I'd found in the garage to text her the morning she died: *Sorry but I can't leave Jill. Let's talk, usual time and place. W.* Will clearly had lured her to that fatal meeting — at least it was clear as far as the police were concerned.

I made sure to hand her burner phone over to Milo, who reached his own conclusions: She'd not taken "no" for an answer. They'd fought.

I told Milo on the day of the threatening letter all my darkest suspicions about Will, that Will had as good as confessed to me. I knew for sure he was guilty, I said, but . . . Somewhat to my surprise, that was all Milo needed to hear. From that moment on, he acted accordingly. Never questioning. My hero.

They would need more evidence. I gave them more.

Of course I made a slip or two.

"The pool guy," he says, reading me. "You said you could see the pool house from your first floor window at the Weycombe house."

"And?"

"I assumed you meant you could see from what we Brits would call the first floor — the floor above the ground floor. But from what an American would call a first floor, you couldn't see who went in or out. I should have asked you to clarify."

I'm not going to enlighten him now. It was a very minor invention, intended to reinforce Anna's credentials as a woman who slept around. So maybe I misspoke a bit. So what. "You're right. You should have asked."

He smiles. It's one of those sad, accepting smiles of someone too weary to fight over trivial lies. I used to use that smile with Will.

"Then there was that woman at the lingerie shop. She told us your husband had been a customer, and she recognized you when you came into her shop. Checking up on why he'd be buying items that were much too large for you."

"You're calling that some sort of clue?"

"The only real clue we had," he counters, "was that dress. The dress missing from Frannie's shop. It was the only blue one in its size, and it was not in the inventory she'd taken just the day before, so the lack was noticeable. We guessed it had been shoplifted, for want of a better word — chances were good, by her killer."

Yes, yes, yes, fine. In a fit of spite and madness, I'd stolen a dress from Frannie's shop, stuffed it in my shopping bag as I was leaving. For once she had something in stock that wouldn't make me look like a refugee from the Woodstock festival. And, well, it's not like stealing, is it? Frannie would never miss it.

"She could have made a mistake, don't you think?" I say. "In the inventory? This sounds like a very minor connection. Tenuous at best."

I soon realized I was playing with fire with that dress, and the next time I went to Walton-on-Thames I put it in a bin outside the Sainsbury's.

"We looked everywhere in the village for it," he says. "Attwater put me on it — the sort of demeaning floater task she liked to hand me in those days. It never turned up. But there was nothing to link it *directly* to Frannie's murderer. It was tenuous, as you say."

"Another dead end," I say. "Too bad."

"But do you know, from Fannie's inventory description, it may have been the blue dress you were wearing the day you called me over — the day you got the poison pen letter? Long sleeved with 'ruching' — I had to look it up: 'ruching.' "

What foolishness on my part. And what luck he never made the connection. But if he'd asked me about that dress, I would have said I'd ruined it with bleach and thrown it away.

The real mistake I'd made in the beginning was going to Miss Kitty's, but what did that prove? The visit was a giving in to impulse before I realized I had a balancing act ahead of me that would require complete control: of myself, of the investigation. If I ever became a suspect, I needed to be sure there was a lineup of others a good solicitor could quickly pin things on to defuse any case that might be made against me: Jason, Colin, Macy, to name a few. Alfie, in a pinch. But in the end, I needed to make sure they had one suspect only, and provide them with the evidence to back it up: Will.

"But it wasn't the same dress," I say. "So another blind alley?"

He nods, his eyes never leaving my face. "Like that threatening letter you received."

I say nothing. Of course I sent it to myself, making sure only Will's prints were on the paper and envelope. It was necessary that the police know me as his terrorized victim.

"Killing Frannie is what I never understood. She was harmless. A bit of a scatterbrain. Why did you have to kill her?"

"You're taping this, are you?"

He pats his shirt in a "search me" fashion; shakes out his jacket, empties his pockets. "I'm retired, remember? No warrant. No authority. Off the force."

I give him a puh-*leeze* look but I see he's got nothing on him.

"Shoes?" Just in case. "Watch?"

He takes them off, turns them over. There's no hidden mic slotted into the heel or bug built into the watch in true MI6 fashion. But one cannot be too careful.

"Okay," I say. "I can tell you what *might* have happened. You ask, why Frannie? I thought you knew. She was a blabbermouth who knew too much." Frannie started piecing a few things together and realized who it was she'd seen that day on the river. She saw my two jackets, the red and the blue, hanging side by side in the hall closet the evening she came over to bend Will's ear.

The day she died — all right, fine, the day I killed her — she'd been fussing in the corner with that scarecrow display, her back to me. Just thinking aloud, not editing her thoughts. Babbling. She was putting some jeweled bracelets on the scarecrow's wrists when suddenly she stopped, turning as she spoke, brain not fully engaged with mouth.

"Do you know, Jill, I just remembered. As Anna argued with that person that day, the sun broke through and a flash of sunlight gleamed off something — something shiny on the other person's wrist. Just as Anna turned away — in fear or to try to end the argument, I don't know, but I saw it. The person was wearing short gloves, and I could see . . . diamonds, it had to be — bright and glittery. A jeweled watch. They were waving their hands around in this sort of wild, threatening way."

"Really."

"Which means it had to be a woman, don't you see? Only a woman would wear a dainty watch like that. A little diamond thing, diamonds all round the face and band."

She looked at me, at my wrist. At me sliding one hand over my wedding gift from Will.

"Like yours."

A sort of expectant look came over her face, as if she hoped I might be able to clarify what was puzzling her. Fortunately, I was.

"And those jackets. Last night. Please tell me I'm wrong. Jill?"

I couldn't choke her the way I had Anna. I'd lost that element of surprise Milo had talked about, and besides, Frannie was a big woman, tall, arms like a stevedore. Despite her age, she could leverage her weight against me in a struggle. I'd brought no weapon; it was supposed to be a friendly chat to find out if she'd realized the significance of the two jackets. To convince her those jackets were Will's, if so. But it was too late for all that.

I suppose a good lawyer could have demolished her account of what she thought she'd seen, that day by the river, a dotty old woman like Frannie, but I was not taking the chance. Live free or die.

There was a letter opener on the shop's desk. Make do and mend, as my grandmother used to say.

Milo's eyes on me now, as if he can read the memories on my face. "We realized, of course, that we only had your word that you'd seen Jason at Frannie's shop that morning. No one else claimed to have seen him. Or Will, for that matter."

Yes, it may have been unnecessary to toss them both in like that. I always did have a tendency to embellish.

Killing Anna was easy compared with Frannie. But up until the last second, I wasn't sure I'd go through with killing Anna. I always carried a knife in my fanny pack for protection. The habit was a holdover from my time in London, coming home late most nights. I liked the idea of surprising an attacker by fighting back; sometimes I almost hoped someone would try it on. This particular knife, a Swiss Army knife, belonged to Will. Afterward, I threw it in the river. They spent days diving and dredging for the weapon I kept hoping they would find, as it had his initials engraved on it. It turned up weeks later, washed ashore. By then it was just a bonus, the final nail in Will's already sealed coffin.

I wore gloves against the cold so only Will's prints were on the knife. I knew from *BM: London* that they can lift prints off an object even if it's been soaking in water. It was fairly risk-free to attack her that time of year: there were fewer people about because of the weather, except for old Frannie, of course. Bad luck, that. Of course I wanted to be the one to "find" the body to explain my footprints on the steep embankment. In the struggle Anna and I had ended up partway down the slope, the overhead foliage concealing what was happening.

As she fell, already dying, there was another stroke of bad luck: she made a grab for my scarf and took it down with her. I couldn't scramble after her without chancing my own neck, and I'd never be able to crawl back up. So I ran home and changed into my red jacket, threw the blue fleece jacket and gloves in the washer and turned the machine on in case they held any trace of Anna's blood. Then I launched the kayak from the back garden and, muffled to the eyes with a different scarf and hat, paddled to retrieve that damned scarf from her body. There was no explaining it if it were found on her. Then I paddled home, put away the kayak, ran back to where I could see her body from the path, and called it in. The whole thing took less than half an hour from the moment she died.

When Frannie noticed the two different-colored jackets hanging in my hall closet, the scarf and hat I'd been wearing were in there, too. There was never really much question: she had to go. Even if I convinced her the jackets belonged to Will, which would be handy for setting him up, there was no way — not once her mind flashed on that diamond watch.

"What about Jason?" Milo asks. "You didn't . . . ?" He leaves the question hanging with a delicate pause.

What an insulting suggestion. "Jason was an addict, you know that. Addicts die."

Jason overdosed shortly after Anna died. Collateral damage, it came as a surprise to no one. While Jason did remind me of my brother, I had nothing to do with his death. Not directly. What he did in the privacy of his own bedroom was his business.

But what a karmic way to deal with someone who rummages through your stuff looking for drugs on the pretext of stopping by to return a casserole dish. You could say, and I do, that Jason did it to himself. I had no idea he'd root around in my bathroom cabinet — how could I possibly know any respectful, law-abiding citizen would do such a thing when left alone in my house for five minutes?

Still, there was a possibility Jason had started to suspect. There was something in the looks he gave me during his intermittent flashes of sobriety, when his face wasn't glazed in addict sweat and a devil wasn't peering out of his yellowing eyes.

That last time I saw him at his father's house . . . Whatever he knew, or thought he knew, his head was so messed up I couldn't take the chance. Even people running their mouths in some brainless way can trip over the truth, like Frannie did, and get the police looking at things from a different angle.

So I invited him over a couple of times on whatever pretext — a condolence meatloaf or something like that to take back to his father. And I deliberately left him alone — a sudden errand calling me away — with an array of my prescription pills in the medicine cabinet. Pain pills from when I'd wrecked my ankle, and a few more from a visit to the dentist. The leftover script from my shrink. I never throw any of that stuff away — Yankee thrift. I also left a nice assortment in my purse, which I left open on the table, knowing he couldn't resist. The guest bathroom had another stash for him to pilfer, which he did. The little shit also took a twenty-pound note out of my wallet. Because that's what addicts do, and they think people don't know.

I didn't care when or even if he managed to top himself. I just wanted to give him every opportunity. Worse case, he'd destroy the last shred of his mind and credibility even further if he did start putting two and two together about Anna.

But I wasn't interested in talking about all this now with Milo. Leave the past in the past, I say.

He answers the question I haven't asked. "No one knows I'm here. Even if they knew, would they believe it after all these years? Would they care? Almost everyone who cared about Anna is gone."

That included, of course, my dearly departed Will.

A lie creates its own atmosphere. A shift in the air around the liar's voice that makes the listener say *Wait.* Wait a minute. That's not right. Something's not right here. With Will, that feeling went on too long, happened too often.

That night, Will's last night, I sent a message from my own new burner phone telling him to meet me in Riverside Park, at our favorite picnic table.

It had been a perfect night for a sting. Cool and clear, with the weather cooperating, and a new moon to provide sheltering darkness under the trees for Milo, Attwater, and Co.

Will drove up to the park to find me waiting. I'd wrapped myself in a blanket and was sitting on top of our favorite table — a sight that used to drive him wild with desire, by the way. Now he just looked wild.

"What's all this about?" he demanded to know. He stomped his feet against the cold. His words emerged in puffs of white cloud. "What are you talking about?"

It was just about his last live comment. I pushed the play button.

Here is what Milo and his people heard on their receivers that night:

Me: You killed her, didn't you?

Will: Of course I did. The faithless bitch.

Me: Anna and Frannie both.

Will: Of course, both. What are you, stupid?

Me: But why Frannie?

Will: Do you really have to ask? She knew too much.

And moments later, I stopped the feed that was going directly into the mic. "Did you bring it?" I asked. A judicious pause before I screamed and began hammering against his chest with my fists. "So it *was* you? You admit it?"

A confused burst of expletives from Will, who had grabbed my arms to pull me off him. I said, again live for the mic, "I promise I won't tell anyone. Let me go!"

"Jill, what the — ?"

"That *hurts*!"

I dropped the agreed-upon word, "Indigo," that told the cops I was in danger. I broke away as they rushed in, shouting, screaming at Will to put his hands up. I heard one shot, and another. And I ran for cover into the woods.

I had recordings of his voice, lines I'd spliced together from the detective play he'd acted in at the local theater. I'd saved the recordings of those endless rehearsals when I would run lines with him at home after dinner. Seamless splicing was another skill

I'd picked up at the BBC. They claimed, by the way, when they fired me, that I'd fictionalized some parts of the *BM: London* shows, editing and splicing and making up dialogue. Dialogue that could have occurred and should have occurred, in my opinion, but probably had not occurred. Whatever.

It's easy with a judicious edit or two to make someone sound as though they're threatening you, confessing to a killing, confessing to the Kennedy assassination or whatever you want them to confess to. My own lines the cops heard that night as they listened in were much simpler than Will's: "No! Don't! Stop! Will, that *hurts*!" And so on. This was followed by Will's rather maniacal laughter. He always overplayed that bit. I added some choking sounds of my own. It was really very good, quite convincing, if I do say so. Then there was a lot of "So it was you?" followed by "Don't worry, Will, I swear I won't tell anyone! I swear! Just let me go. *Let me go!*"

And so on. Some of it recorded — overall, a nice mix tape of woman-in-jeopardy dialogue — some of it live as needed. Then I simply screamed in time-honored, wom-jep fashion, the scream of a woman frightened out of her wits. I am seriously good at that. I used to love playing in thrillers.

■ ■ ■ ■

I cut it a bit close, escaping from Will at the last minute, making sure he remained the slow-moving target that he was, frozen in place by confusion, wrong-footed, stunned by these unexpected developments. The cops were already charging in as I ran, giving them a clear shot.

Will had the Browning with him, the gun I'd told him to bring along. We were there to set a trap for Anna's killer, I'd said, and he'd need it for self-defense. The last thing the cops expected was for him to show up with a gun. When he reached for it, actually to hand it to me, they completely freaked out.

I hadn't enjoyed anything so much in a long time.

I hadn't told Milo about the gun, of course. He'd have cancelled the sting. I knew the cops would go wild when Will pulled out this honking great Browning. There were half a dozen of them, hyped up, all young and macho and dying to play the hero, to rescue the fair maiden. They saw the gleam of metal, they heard my frantic screams about the gun, and well . . . they're trained in these situations to shoot to kill when they have no other choice. They told him to drop it and he just froze.

If Will had shown up without the gun for some reason? Or if he'd done as he was told and dropped the gun? I'd improv it — grab the gun from his hands and have it "accidently" go off. In case he survived — well, I'd brought a knife to make sure he didn't. Because his survival was the biggest risk to me. I could always tell the police I was so terrified I'd brought along a little something for self-defense. Just in case.

"Do your best, prepare for the worst," as my grandmother used to say. I think she got that one from the Bible.

Of course Will had to die. As mad as his story would sound, there would always be some conspiracy nut to believe him. What I really wanted was for Will to rot in prison, but I had to settle for less. I couldn't let him live to tell his story.

From where Milo stood, what was going down was clear: I had screwed up my end of things; I had set Will off. I'd warned them already about his hair-trigger temper. From a distance what they saw was a woman struggling to break free of Will's arms, fighting for her life. Milo, listening to the transmission, gave the signal to go in.

In the end, of course, the knife wasn't

necessary. The police did the job they were trained to do.

I also had transferred some photos from my phone to Will's before destroying my old phone. I'd taken random photos of women in Weycombe Court in various stages of undress, women who seldom bothered to draw their bedroom curtains. Photos of Anna were a particular highlight of the parade of lovelies, taken from a spot hidden by trees in her back garden. These password-protected photos were on Will's phone when he was taken down. It took their IT guys no time at all to break in. It was the descriptions of the photos by the kinkier news outlets that finally made Will's mother leave the country. Oscar was a big help in getting that insider tip published.

I'd thought it through dozens of times, rehearsing step by step how Will must have gone about killing Anna, so I could present my theory to the police, tied up with a ribbon when the time was right: Anna was killed early enough in the morning that Will still had time to get to the station and catch a train. He had arranged to meet her upriver, where he killed her, first stashing the kayak several yards downriver where the ground sloped to the shore, making the kayak easy to retrieve. He then paddled his way home, where he changed out of his gear into a suit. He figured if he was seen on the river — for example, by those Japanese tourists — well, his face was partially obscured by a scarf and hat. He was just another health fanatic out on the cold river.

I happened to mention to Milo that I saw Will come home that morning to change. And that this was a complete departure from his usual morning routine. I'd never known him to kayak that time of day, especially not in October, in the cold. How very odd.

I also left a pair of Will's glasses in Anna's car — she never bothered to lock her car any more than she worried about drawing the shades. No one in the Court bothered; it was gated, after all. The glasses were not conclusive evidence, but just one more matchstick on the pile I was set to ignite.

None of this, the theories and the glasses and so on, *needed* to work. Certainly it didn't need to hold up in court — I would make sure it never got that far. This was only to get the cops so certain they were in the right they'd be more likely to take him down.

Of course Will's mother cried bloody murder, but too late. She had a second stroke

— the first minor one, when Will had left Weycombe to fly to her side, had weakened her. By the time she recovered enough to take in what had happened to him, the whole thing was history as far as anyone was concerned. Still, she hired solicitors to harass the police. When they got nowhere, she got on the horn to Whitehall. She petitioned her old schoolmates in the House of Lords and on Fleet Street, demanding an inquiry. But as the facts emerged even her oldest friends began to back off, saying that time would lessen the hurt, useful things like that.

Her son, she claimed, was incapable of killing anyone: he barely knew the Anna Monroe creature. His so-called confession? It must have been staged, altered somehow. Or it wasn't him at all!

"You did this." She had her chauffeur drive her all the way over to Weycombe one day to accuse me. "I don't know how but you're behind this. You needn't think you'll get away with it." Politely, shaking my head in pity, I showed her the door. Poor old fruit.

She didn't shut up until all the evidence of Will's affair with Anna started rolling in. Honestly, I think she could stand for him to be known as a murderer rather than as the faithless and conniving creep that he was.

Eventually she disappeared into the south of France, where she waited for the scandal to die down. It never quite did. Will had made the famous White name infamous.

Rossalind did force a standoff through her solicitors over where Will should be buried. She insisted it be not in Weycombe but on the grounds of his estate, where he would be "among his own kind." She actually *said* this, looking straight at me. "His own kind."

She's long gone now, a heart attack following yet another stroke. I got to keep the fucking pearls.

But I'd let her have her way over a few things. I was like, whatever. I wasn't going to win the burial scrimmage, which I didn't care about, anyway.

I won everything else.

Had you been thinking Milo and I had a thing going on? No way. Attractive he may have been, but — no way.

You know that saying that two can keep a secret if one of them is dead? He may have needed cash for his kid, for that expensive, experimental treatment he couldn't afford, so I did consider bribery — I was going to be a wealthy woman once all this was over. But I figured Milo would need to be there for his son even more. That's the upstanding kind of guy he was.

Milo was solid. Although I'd had some reason to doubt that.

That day of the *BACK OFF* note, I finally asked him: "You were in uniform the day I first met you. You never did say why. And now you're back in civvies."

"Minor infraction of the rules. They wanted to remind me who was boss." Remembering his demeanor around Attwater, his barely disguised contempt, his obvious chafing at the bit, I could see this.

"You weren't undercover, something like that?"

He laughed. "Wearing a uniform? You are joking, right?"

"I know. But I thought in some John le Carré spy story way, you were in clever disguise."

"This is Weycombe, for God's sake."

It turned out he'd been suspected and cleared of getting someone an early release — checking the wrong box on the paperwork or something. The suspicion, never proven, was that he did it for money — I got all this from the ever-useful Oscar. Of course Milo claimed he was innocent. Oscar believed him. I had my doubts, and that's when I considered trying to bribe him. Honestly? I didn't think he was crooked enough to go for the big time.

I'm sure I made the right choice. All I needed from Milo was to point his investigation in the direction I wanted it to go. He was distracted enough by his own problems to let it happen.

Now, twenty years later, here he is in my flat. Somehow I don't believe it's just a friendly visit.

"When did you start to doubt?" I ask. "Or did you doubt?"

He doesn't pretend, he knows exactly what I mean. "I suppose it bothered me later that you tried to put the finger on that vagrant. He was in jail, and there's no way you could have seen him. Or anyone like him. As you yourself said, in Weycombe, we've got one token poor guy, and Roger was it."

I shrug. "A mistake. Mistaken identity. That happens all the time, right?"

"Maybe. Could have been. That's what I told myself."

"You had doubts but you didn't report them."

He shakes his head. "Then of course there was the kayak. More than one person besides Will had access. More than one person was physically capable."

Home, change jackets, quickly back. The

only way to make up the time was to use the kayak.

"But that amounted to nothing. And Attwater's opinions were worthless."

"What opinions?"

Milo smiles, a flash of that same white smile that had so impressed me when first we met. "I think she just didn't like you."

Someone in the *New Yorker* wrote of Robert Durst, "What the villain always knows, ultimately, is not why but why not." That's it, exactly. If there's no heaven or hell, why not, indeed? Why not go for the life you want?

Is there a God? I actually believe there is, although I haven't allowed it to get in my way unnecessarily. If worst comes to worst, I'll call for a priest and confess — hedge my bets. But heaven is not a question that makes me hunger for answers. Only the here-and-now is guaranteed.

At Oxford I went along one day to hear a talk by a famous atheist — a scientist known mostly for his disputes with the university's theologians. I can still hear him say, this handsome guy with the jutting brow and the shock of silver hair: "Look into the face of a child as it is slowly destroyed by disease, poverty, and ignorance and tell me there is a living God."

And there you have it.

But there are miracles along the way, wherever they come from, some invisible helping hand. And that day in my flat, Milo told me of one.

"The recording of your conversation with Will, of his 'confession' before he died — someone misplaced it," he told me. "Lost it, actually, because it never turned up. One of those bureaucratic snafus that can happen when the protocol on an evidence locker gets ignored once too often."

"I didn't know there was a recording." I should have known it wasn't just a live feed.

"Standard procedure, sure. Of course there was."

"I see," I said. "Go on."

"But the thing is, there were one or two odd gaps. Nothing glaring. Nothing you'd notice if you weren't looking for it. Some odd phrasing. And Will — he sounded genuinely surprised in places, puzzled. At least, I thought so. He started to ask something like, 'Why are you playing that?' — words to that effect. It could have been, 'What are you playing at?' and probably it was. It was a bit garbled. But we had some new kid on the team, a young woman, who started poking around and wanting the recording authenticated. There was talk of having an expert examine it. Attwater thought it was a waste of time. 'Why would we waste budget on that?' she asked. 'We were all there and heard what he said. And we can testify to what we heard.' They got into a bit of a contest over it but of course Attwater won. And then, it went missing."

I'm miffed. I'm a self-taught whiz in the recording studio and I don't like having my expertise questioned. The recording I played that night for the waiting team of police was seamless, I'd swear it was.

I couldn't have overlooked any detail. What gaps? There were no gaps. So even if they recorded the whole conversation, did it matter?

Milo sees the wheels turning. I look out the window, at my million-dollar view.

Counting up the bodies.

When I first met Will, he'd had a girlfriend. I think I told you about her. The one his mother thought was so great: Penelope or Clarice or Cordelia, one of those posh names. The one who up and left Will one day, breaking his mother's heart.

The poison I got from Rossalind's stable took care of her. I even thought if I got the chance, I might try to pin it on old Roz, but I never could figure out a clear motive for her. I kept some poison in reserve, though. Because you just never know when something like that might come in handy.

I'm sorry about Milo. I really am. After twenty years, he should just have left it alone. Curiosity/cat.

But you can trust no one, not even a slightly bent cop with a short time to live. He might be in a come-to-Jesus mode, especially with his diagnosis, and I can't have that. Some cases are not meant to be solved. Some secrets are meant to be taken to the grave.

I stretch out my neck, like an animal seeking the sun. I'm tired. It no longer matters, I think. It's too hard to prove at this long distance.

But I won't be found out. I'm young — fifty-five is young these days, when the life expectancy for women is 120 years.

Live free or die.

"It's all right," he says. "It had to be done."

Something tugs at a corner of his mouth, some sad smile of bitter remembrance, and I know. I know even before he says, "I loved Anna. And I'd have done anything to get the man who did that to her. I had Will in my sights early on. I just needed you to help me bring him down. This I did for me, and for no one else."

I nod. Weighing, judging. Live or die?

Had *Milo* disappeared the recording?

"She was on her way to meet me that morning. In the park. We always met in Riverside Park. Whenever we could. As often as we could."

What a touching story. Has he known all along? Suspected?

He sees me wince, one glancing giveaway, and thinks it has something to do with the park, or with the fact he used me to get what he most wanted. "I'm sorry. I . . ."

What in fuck *was* it about Anna anyway? She wasn't all that great. Was she? And yet all these men. And she cheated on them, every one.

He more than suspects me now — he knows. Why else wait so long before looking me up? This is a wrinkle that needs to be ironed out.

"May I offer you some tea?" I ask.

"Ah. Do you have something a little stronger?"

"I sure do."

And with that can-do Yankee spirit I go into the kitchen and rummage out the old Rossalind remedy I used to such good effect, so many years ago.

If that doesn't work, I have the dried herbs from my little garden on the balcony, and my Chinese lanterns growing in a pot. They say poison is a woman's weapon. What narrow-minded sexist claptrap. We use what we've got.

I have to figure out how to get rid of the body. In pieces, I suppose. I'm quite strong but Milo's a big guy. I smile, remembering that woman who put her husband in the curry. But no, I can't do that to Milo. He's a good man, as men go. But still. The thought of him in love with Anna makes it easier to do what must be done.

I jump at the sound of the kitchen phone ringing. I start to let it go to voicemail, but I'm expecting a call from Oscar about our plans for the evening, so I pick up.

A woman introduces herself as Lily Higgenbotham. She tells me she's a member of the committee to select the Rasmussen Prize for best screenplay. *Indigo* is on the longlist. The story I began writing so long ago. My true crime novel. My Capote book, my nonfiction novel, with names changed to protect not the innocent — who cares about the innocent? — but to protect me. The only names I didn't change were Weycombe's, and Anna's.

Indigo. I still keep my notes and research in an encrypted file folder, with the same password: IKilled@nn@.

"How wonderful!" I say, so flooded with happiness I'm practically dancing across my new Italian tiles. It was the call I've dreamed of, since . . . since all my life, really. Shot through with a lightning bolt of pure joy, for a second I think I might spare Milo after all, the way an emperor in a good mood might spare a gladiator's life. But as quickly, I think again. I have even more to lose now.

"I never dreamed of this!" I say to the woman. "*Thank* you! *Such* an honor." I'm gushing, unabashedly thrilled. She says she's delighted to be the bearer of good news and wishes me luck.

And she asks me to keep it to myself until the entire list has been notified and they officially release the news.

That will not be a problem, I assure her.

I am good at keeping secrets.

ABOUT THE AUTHOR

G. M. Malliet worked as a journalist and copywriter for national and international news publications and public broadcasters. Winner of the Malice Domestic Grant (*Death of a Cozy Writer*), Malliet attended Oxford University and holds a graduate degree from the University of Cambridge.

Malliet's first novel *Death of a Cozy Writer* was chosen by Kirkus Reviews as a Best Book of 2008, nominated for a Left Coast Crime award (the Hawaii Five-O for best police procedural), short-listed for the Macavity Award for Best First Mystery, nominated for the Anthony Award for Best First Novel and was a finalist for the David G. Sasher, Sr. Award for Best Mystery Novel.

The employees of Thorndike Press hope you have enjoyed this Large Print book. All our Thorndike, Wheeler, and Kennebec Large Print titles are designed for easy reading, and all our books are made to last. Other Thorndike Press Large Print books are available at your library, through selected bookstores, or directly from us.

For information about titles, please call:
(800) 223-1244

or visit our website at:
gale.com/thorndike

To share your comments, please write:

Publisher
Thorndike Press
10 Water St., Suite 310
Waterville, ME 04901